The Pecking Order

An Inspirational Story of Desperation, Hope and Redemption

STEVE JOSSE

Published by Steve Josse
Estacada, Oregon

PO Box 480
Eagle Creek, OR 97022

Edited by Jennifer Hager, Consuelo Collier, and Victoria Clevenger.

Special thanks to Victoria Clevenger for her editing, insights and unflinching support.

ISBN: 9781790182121

Second edition paperback: October 2018

Recycled paper and eco-friendly practices were used to manifest this product.

CONTENTS

1	Desperation	7
2	Right Action	10
3	Real Heroes	12
4	Aftermath	15
5	The Rest of My Life	27
6	Reflection	37
7	Nightmare	48
8	Ethics	54
9	Winning Is Everything	59
10	Circle the Wagons	67
11	The Good, the Bad, and the Mafia	74
12	Stating Your Beliefs	79
13	Families	94
14	Reactions	105
15	Perspectives	119
16	What to Believe	130
17	Butch, Sam, and the Flagpole	137
18	Seeds of Reconciliation	152
19	Right From Wrong	162
20	Diverging Paths	167
21	My Subscription Rate is Up	170

22	Here We Go—Let's Not Screw Up	174
23	Ramona	178
24	Honesty, and Council of Elders	182
25	Shifts Toward Bliss	195
26	Apology and Hope	203
27	Everyone Dances	208
28	Being Heard and Getting Options	212
29	A "Win-Win" Team	223
30	Transforming the Pecking Order	225
31	Newsworthy—"A Well-Earned B+"	235
32	Coached for Success	239
33	To Seek Revenge … Or Hope	246
34	Joy For all	249

PART ONE:

REVENGE

An eye for an eye will only make the whole world blind.

-Mahatma Gandhi

CHAPTER ONE
DESPERATION

A sheet of low, gray clouds covered Martin Luther King High School, preventing even a renegade sunbeam from sneaking through. One large drop of rain fell from the clouds, landing on Zack Diamond's thick crop of unkempt, oily-brown hair. A second, larger drop fell on his wide nose, rested there for a moment, then dribbled down his fleshy chin, disappearing into his black T-shirt. His light-blue eyes, hidden behind thick, brown-rimmed glasses, stared straight ahead. Except for a brigade of goose bumps parading across his bare, pale arms, he never flinched or moved a muscle.

Zack sat completely alone near the top of the concrete stairway. Fifteen identical steps dropped like a waterfall below him; three steps above and behind him stood the red-brick administration building. The words "Martin Luther King Bulldogs" were freshly painted in large white letters above the door.

He had situated himself in the middle of the stairway. The stream of students coming back from lunch had to fork either to the left or right to bypass him to the steel double doors, the school's main entrance. Zack's large black cello case was positioned across his lap. One at a time, his fingers began fidgeting with the silver snaps holding it shut.

The school's lone security officer, Rod Chavez, opened the newly installed steel security doors. Rod was a twenty-six-year-old Latino male in a dark-green uniform with a large gold badge. He walked outside and stood on the top step above Zack, with his hands on his hips and his rifle slung over his shoulder. As his eyes slowly scanned the school parking lot, he thought to himself, *Everything looks in order—just the usual students straggling back after lunch.*

Rod's eyes dropped to the steps below, where he saw Zack sitting with his cello case. Zack appeared preoccupied and didn't look up. Rod checked his watch and noted there were almost seventeen more minutes until the final lunch bell. Plenty of time to get to class, he thought, but his job was to keep things moving.

"Hey Diamond!" he yelled in a voice still struggling for manhood but trying to sound gruff. "Get your butt moving to class! You're going to be late, plus you're blocking the stairs!" Rod didn't wait for a response but turned away without another word. He walked back inside with a slightly exaggerated strut, sucking in his stomach, wondering if the girls coming up the stairs had noticed him in his dark-green uniform, accessorized by his semi-automatic rifle and gold-colored badge.

But Zack never heard Rod's voice; the words didn't register in his brain, as his eyes remained fixed on the stairwell below. Three long-haired girls wearing skin-tight, hip-hugging jeans with matching pierced belly buttons paraded past Zack. They chatted busily about an upcoming party at the local college fraternity—who was going to be there and who wasn't even invited.

Claire, the brunette, glanced down at Zack and almost said hi. She sat next to Zack in biology class and felt she knew him in a vague sort of way. But she was afraid her friends would think she was a dork for speaking to the school's biggest loser, so she quickly looked away, continuing to banter with her girlfriends about the party the following night.

Zack moved his head slightly to the side when the taller blonde girl on the left walked directly in front of him, momentarily blocking his view. On any other day his body would have felt a quick, uncontrollable rush of hopeless desire: normally he would have turned, as nonchalantly as possible, to take a good, long look as the girls passed by—but not today. This time his eyes didn't wander from the walkway below. He noticed his heart was racing but, to his surprise, his mind felt amazingly calm.

Kyle was nearly a hundred feet down the sidewalk when Zack saw him coming. His lean, nearly six-foot frame put him at least three inches above his stockier companion. He'd turned his black Raiders baseball cap backward and his large, perpetually lopsided grin made him impossible to miss. He was walking with a kid Zack recognized as Josh Smith, a popular, snobby, preppie senior with shaggy blonde hair that hung to the top of his shoulders, reminding Zack of some jerk celebrity. They wore identical blue and gold letterman jackets, each with a big "MLK" embroidered across the front.

As the two boys approached, Zack slowly unfastened the last snap on his cello case, opened the lid, and put his right hand inside. Touching the cold metal of the barrel, he felt the pain that had overwhelmed him for so long starting to lift and, in its place, a deep-seated numbness filled his head.

Kyle stopped abruptly on the fourth step from the bottom. His eyes widened? and his mouth opened ever so slightly. A small hissing sound slid out from below his tongue. Kyle stared at Zack as Zack stood up, the empty cello case clattering down the steps below. Kyle's mouth slowly opened wider and wider. The hissing changed to a gurgling sound that rose from deep in his throat as he tried to speak. His mind and voice had gone into momentary hibernation and he could not seem to reboot them.

Josh stopped about two feet ahead of Kyle, his right foot resting on the edge of the next step. He was looking back and talking to Kyle, but when Kyle stopped abruptly and stared straight ahead with a wild look of terror on his face, Josh turned to see Zack. "Shit!" was all he could mutter as his trembling left hand seized the metal handrail. He started backing down one step at a time, his mind chaotic with panic, while his blue eyes stayed glued on the object in Zack's hands.

The raw power was intoxicating to Zack. His whole body felt like that of a giant, alive and powerful, like he could do anything he wanted; no one could stop him. For once, he wasn't afraid of Kyle—or anyone else for that matter, as the eerie calm now controlled his mind. He could feel his hands sweating ever so slightly as his right trigger finger wrapped itself around the steel hook. He wanted to jump up and down and scream, *FOR THE FIRST TIME IN MY LIFE I AM IN CHARGE!* But instead, he stared into Kyle's bulging brown eyes and, without saying a word, pulled the trigger twice. Then he moved the barrel slightly to his left and pulled the trigger once more.

CHAPTER TWO
RIGHT ACTION

Popping of what sounded like three fireworks reverberated down the hallways. The students near the front entrance momentarily stopped in their tracks. Instant panic ran through minds and hearts for several seconds as they looked at each for confirmation and assurance. Within minutes the siren went off and most students anxiously headed to safe rooms provided on each floor, just like they had practiced in so many of the drills before.

Rod had punched the hand alarm while running down the hall toward the sound of the shots. He held his assault rifle in his left hand and used his right hand to push open the double doors leading to the front steps. Suddenly he found himself standing motionless on the concrete platform outside, his rifle hanging uselessly by his side, his heart pounding wildly, his eyes glued on Zack Diamond. Rod knew that if he moved his rifle up to shooting position he was a dead man -- he should have responded to the shots more cautiously.

Zack knew Rod would come running at the sound of the shots. He had turned to point his M16 at where he thought Rod would be as he came out of the steel double doors.

"Sorry, Mr. Chavez," Zack said calmly without a stutter, "but you're a dead man walking! You're such an asshole! Remember when you acted like I was a retard a couple months ago when you yelled at me to get my butt off the bench in the cafeteria? Because I was sitting at a table reserved for the popular kids? Only regular people can sit there, not freaks like me, right!? You said I was causing a problem, but whatever. Now *you* are the problem and I'm solving the problem my way and you are going to die for your stupidity."

Stunned and immobilized, Rod's eyes opened wide as he swallowed his voice deep inside him. He was shaking slightly. His mind wanted to beg for mercy, but his pride argued no, never. He could not make a sound—not even a squeak.

Behind Rod, the front door to his left swung open and an unarmed, dark-skinned young man with slick, jet-black hair quickly stepped out. Glancing momentarily at the carnage on the steps below and then at Zack—but without breaking stride, as if running by instinct, the slender boy took four quick steps to his right and placed himself directly in the line of sight between Rod and Zack. He stood perfectly still, his eyes riveted to Zack's eyes, as he said in a firm but compassionate voice, "Compadre, put the gun down on the ground. You did what you needed to do. You got your revenge. But Rod is just a rent-a-cop and he has two little bambinos at home. You don't need to shoot him. It wouldn't be right."

CHAPTER THREE
REAL HEROES

Paramedic Amy Schmidt turned on the sirens and flashing lights in the ambulance, as another paramedic jumped in the back and slammed the doors shut, flipping the handles up to lock them tight. A second ambulance, -- a Number Twelve, almost identical and from Station 26 too, the largest fire station in Arcadia, California—pulled out in front of them with its lights also flashing. Together they raced across the school parking lot and headed north up Tenth Street toward the local hospital, with Number Twelve taking the lead.

"Valentine, hurry up and get the other IV in him," barked team leader Phil Duncan. "Let's go Schmidt, *let's go!* We don't have a second to lose. Go up Fourteenth and maybe we can get ahead of Number Twelve—this kid needs to get there first. He needs more fluid, at least one more unit. We've got to hurry . . . his pulse is still dropping!"

"Jesus, I don't know if we can save this kid. He's a mess!" cried Valentine, the extra EMT from Station 26. "He has lost at least two pints of blood. Hand me that fresh syringe and give me more pressure. Shit, *shit!* I can't keep plugging this hole with my sponge; it won't stop the bleeding. Somebody give me a larger tourniquet!"

"Crank this jalopy up and do your magic, Schmidt. We need to get there in seven minutes—that's all the time we have back here!" yelled Duncan.

"I am moving this fricking machine as fast as it will go!" hollered

Schmidt, as she plowed through the red light on Bellingham and headed north on Second Street with sirens blaring and lights flashing.

As if by magic, every car and truck pulled over or stopped completely. The red and white ambulance swerved and bounced to the left and then to the right as it maneuvered its way through the intersection.

Judy Jamison, a nutritionist on her way to work at Good Samaritan Hospital, heard the sirens and stopped her Subaru wagon in the middle of the intersection. She watched in disbelief as the ambulance roared past, not four feet from her front end. Her fingers fumbled nervously with the radio buttons to turn up the volume, as the news reporter repeated the breaking story of a shooting at MLK High just minutes before.

"Oh, my God," she said out loud. "Oh, my God!" she repeated, as her thoughts raced to her sixteen-year-old daughter, Tess, a sophomore at MLK.

She immediately pulled into a crowded Costco parking lot and, without waiting for an oncoming produce truck, made a quick U-turn and chased after the ambulance.

God, she thought as she drove, *why have school shootings become a parent's worst nightmare?* Judy had a son in the army in Afghanistan, but it seemed she feared for her other two children—one in high school and the other in college—almost as much. She had just been telling her husband the week prior that it's like all this violent insanity from Iraq and Afghanistan has come home to America, and now all these crazy people are running around with automatic weapons trying to act macho just like in the Middle East.

"Give him more fluids, double the dosage!" yelled Duncan, as he ripped open the box and put another bag on the pole. "He's still losing too much blood."

"I'm hurrying, I'm hurrying!" said Valentine. "I don't want to lose this kid, either! We've never lost anyone this young in this buggy before, and it ain't going to happen now!"

"Yeah, well, we never had somebody with a hole in his gut like this one before," replied Duncan. "This kid has lost enough blood that he should be dead by now. Hand me that new blue tourniquet and turn up his oxygen. And Valentine—in case I forget to tell you later . . . good job. If you hadn't plugged up that hole with your fist when we got there, this kid would already be done for," continued

Duncan, as he fidgeted with Kyle's oxygen bottle.

Kyle's eyes stared straight up at the roof of the ambulance and never blinked once during the ride to the hospital. His mind was awake, though. Things were very blurry, but he understood exactly what was going on, and he tried to listen to what the paramedics were saying amongst themselves.

I've been shot, thought Kyle. *That bastard shot me with a real gun!* His mind reeled with the assumption that he was probably going to die. This wasn't like the movies Kyle had seen—he wasn't Arnold Schwarzenegger or any of those other fake heroes. *I'm really going to die*, he thought again. *Hell—my stomach has been blown out of my body. God it hurts, it hurts so bad.* The medics shot a needle of fluid into Kyle's IV, and he began to feel a numbing sensation spread throughout his body. He begged in his mind, *Please God, I'm not afraid to die, but just let me get it over with. I can't stand this fricking pain.*

For a brief moment, he remembered a gray squirrel he had shot while hunting with his father last summer. The animal just lay there, its stomach blown away, looking at him with its black beady eyes while its mouth hung open and its body shook wildly. Ironically, that's how Kyle now felt, and he, too, was starting to shake—he was the squirrel and he was dying, and he wanted to scream but he couldn't. The thought of the squirrel made his stomach turn and a mixture of blood and vomit started to leak out from his lips and nose, running down his face as fast as the medic could wipe it away.

It took seven minutes and twenty-seven seconds to go the twenty-two blocks to Arcadia's Good Samaritan Hospital. There were already four news reporters and three photographers waiting at the emergency entrance of the hospital. A small crowd of parents had gathered as well, like Judy Jamison, who had rushed to the hospital after hearing the news on their radio. A number of off-duty hospital employees looked on as the medics rushed Kyle Ritter down the hallways of Good Sam.

If Kyle had been able to notice, it might have felt like running out of the tunnel before each football game with everybody lined up on each side to cheer the players. But this time no one was cheering—and instead of cheerleaders there was just a young-looking ER doctor shouting out orders to several nurses. Even if there had been a stadium full of yelling fans, it's doubtful Kyle would have heard them at that moment.

CHAPTER FOUR
AFTERMATH

On the front sidewalk two stories below, Alan could see a half-dozen policemen in navy-blue uniforms with gray flak jackets, winding up spools of yellow tape. They were loading them into a white van with the words "Arcadian Tactical Squad" printed in bold, black letters across the side. A loud diesel motor started up and the large gray tank-like machine, which had arrived within fifteen minutes of the shooting, made its way across the parking lot. It had been full of combat police in camouflage uniforms who had jumped out with assault rifles pointed in every direction and, for a moment, Alan had felt like he was in Mosul, Iraq, not at a Southern California high school.

Alan looked at his watch; three hours and ten minutes had passed. A tall patrolman wearing camouflage fatigues with a rifle slung over his shoulder had started pacing back and forth in front of the school's main entrance. He kept looking around nervously, as if he expected something else unfortunate to happen. Several local news vans, equipped with large satellite dishes rotating slowly on their roofs, had been parked patiently outside the closed gate for several hours now, ready if there was some new tragedy to broadcast around the world.

"Alan, the phone. Line three. It's school board president, Bob Lancaster." Ruth's low, strained voice seemed to come from nowhere. Alan's body twitched as he realized his mind had wandered for far too long, which it seemed to do more often these days. Bob

Lancaster had agreed to step in when needed while the district superintendent, Mike Thomas, who normally would interface between principals and the school board, was out on extended medical leave.

"Hello, Bob. Yes, it is a tragedy, a terrible tragedy. You can imagine how we feel around here." Alan listened for a moment as Bob lamented on.

"Well," Alan interrupted, "I can give you a quick summary of what has happened up until now. The shooting was at 12:45, right at the end of the lunch period. When the building was deemed safe, the students were taken out of each secure classroom through the side doors, where they were escorted across the street to the Saint Jude's church parking lot. They all should be home by now; we let them out around 1:35, but only if they had a ride with their parents or were willing to board one of our buses. If they had their own car they were escorted by police to their vehicles; no one was allowed to walk home alone.

"Our most recent update tells us that there were two boys shot: one is Josh Smith, who is in stable condition; the other is Kyle Ritter, who is in critical condition and is touch and go. We are not sure if he is going to make it and best case it looks like he may be partially or more likely totally paralyzed. Both boys are at Good Sam's on Fifth Street."

"Paralyzed! I guess that's better than being dead, but not by much!" exclaimed Bob. "But thank God it's only two shot and no dead; that's a miracle in itself. Usually the shooter in these types of cases wants to take out as many students as he can." Bob was silent for a moment.

"Yes, you're right, but in this case the shooter seemed to have a very particular target in mind," answered Alan. "There were at least 13 students on or near the steps he could have shot with the M16 he had in his possession, not to mention our security officer. But, when confronted by another student, he chose not to shoot the resource officer. It was a rather odd scenario that we're still investigating.

"The shooter is a student named Zack Diamond," Alan continued. "He is a fifteen-year-old sophomore of Jewish descent. According to his home-room teacher, Zack acts like he has an undiagnosed case of Asperger's syndrome, which is a milder form of autism. He is smart enough, but Zack has had a difficult time fitting into the social setting of high school since he's been here, and he has a long history of being bullied by other students. A phone complaint was made by Zack's mother regarding an unconfirmed incident about three weeks ago having to do with a serious attack on Zack by one of the victims, Kyle Ritter, and two other boys. Josh Smith, the second boy who was shot, was not reported as one of those three boys who had accosted him."

"Alan, was there an investigation or interview of the accused boys?" asked Bob.

"Yes sir, the same day after receiving the call I did talk to all three boys together and separately. They all denied having been in the bathroom during the suspected timeframe, though none of them remembered where they were at lunch on that particular day. I kept Kyle—who it became obvious was the leader of their group—in my office until school ended. He denied everything and said he didn't even know who Zack was, though five minutes later in the conversation he inadvertently referred to Zack as 'that retarded Jew kid who everyone knows is gay.' Kyle has had a reputation as a bully and as having a racist attitude, but until now he has always skated by without major repercussions. So, after an hour of interrogation, I gave up in disgust and sent him on to football practice. I then called in Butch Cassidy, the head football coach, and within thirty minutes he was here. He claimed Kyle and the other two boys could not have been involved in the bathroom incident, because they had attended a defensive team meeting during that particular lunch period."

"Kyle is the team's middle linebacker, right?" asked Bob. "I remember him. He made All-League last year as a junior and played a major role in getting the team to the playoffs. It's going to be tough replacing him. And Cassidy is a topnotch coach, considered by many as a pillar of the community; I believe he has the most wins of any coach in the Southwest conference."

"That's correct, Bob . . . though I'm not so sure Butch has been active in the community outside of football." Alan paused, then continued, "Anyway, Lieutenant Baker from our local police department and I talked with Zack and his mother three days after she initially complained about the alleged bathroom incident. I could see that Zack was visibly upset and did not want to talk about being assaulted. He seemed quite embarrassed, sullen, and very angry. As you may remember, all our counseling services other than career guidance have been cut from the budget, so we had nowhere else to send him within the school system. We strongly recommended to Zack's mother that he go see a counselor in the county Social Services Department, and we even called them for her. But they, too, have had major budget cuts and the first appointment we could make for Zack was about six weeks out . . . let's see, that would make it in three weeks from now."

"Just so you understand, Alan," replied Bob, "there was simply no money in the budget for counseling! This was not a choice I or the rest of the board wanted to make. It was strictly about a lack of money."

"I understand, sir. But I believe counselors may be more important—especially in this day and age—than a brand-new second gym, sixty-two new computers replacing ones that were barely a year old, not to mention the new ROTC program."

"Priorities, Alan, priorities!" Bob interjected. "That's what our parents and business leaders seem to want right now—it's all about sports, the best high-tech education we can offer, and of course the military. Plus, the new gym was a bond issue. And the computers were partially funded via a matching grant from Facebook. The NRA is funding much of the ROTC program."

"Right," Alan replied, shaking his head in vexation. "Anyway, the other boy who was shot is Josh Smith. I talked to several of his teachers who substantiated what little I know about him: He is relatively new to the school but seems to be one of the more popular boys, at least with the girls. He is a fair student, also on the football team, kind of a happy-go-lucky chap, with a bit of an arrogant air about him. He and Kyle have been seen recently hanging with a small group of White Nationalist students. Up until the last several months they had kept a very low profile and we did not even know they existed until after the last presidential election. As I'm sure you are aware, we are the second largest school in the state of California, so we have a little of everything when it comes to diversity."

"You are not suggesting Kyle and Josh are white supremacists, are you Alan?"

"Not yet, sir. It's just a possibility at this point."

"Well, let's keep a lid on that one for now, Alan."

"Yes sir, we will do our best," Alan submitted, referring to himself as well as his two vice principals. He continued, "We believe Zack brought the weapon—an older M16 semi-automatic assault rifle—in his cello case. We don't know yet where he bought it. I have been told you can buy semi-automatic weapons most anywhere nowadays. He may have bought it at Walmart for all we know! I've also heard that semi-automatics now come in an array of assorted colors. You can even get one in camouflage to match your outfit!"

"Alan, that is a judgment; that's not really your department."

"Sorry, sir, I guess that was a bit out of line. But from my perspective as a high school principal, the ease and access of purchasing assault weapons is way out of control—and being able to buy at a local family department or sporting goods store a weapon of war designed for the sole purpose of killing large numbers of human beings seems totally ludicrous to me."

"Alan, these are not our decisions to make; that's why we have elected officials," responded Bob, his voice rising.

"Yes, sir . . . I guess we should leave this up to the politicians and of course the NRA as well as the gun lobby. I'm sure they are on top of it. But truthfully, sir, I think this whole gun thing is like a cancer in our schools. There are always going to be sick, angry kids with mental health issues . . . I mean, that's a given. But giving them easy access to guns of mass destruction—along with bomb-making instructions you can download from the Internet, only to then remove our mental health counselors and many families' mental health insurance—I believe is actually insane and literally a potential time bomb waiting to go off, and in each of our schools, no less."

"I can understand you're upset, Alan, and I don't blame you. You are probably right about the whole gun thing and the counselors, too—*this is very discouraging to many of us.* But it's not our job to make the laws, Alan. We just do what we can with the laws and money that's out there, and that's the way it is. I am sorry, but I do have an advertising meeting in five minutes with our local Pepsi distributor. Is there anything else?"

Alan sighed, "Yes, sorry—I realize I'm a bit testy. But I should add that our school secretary, Ruth Waterman, received a call from a youthful-sounding female just a few minutes before I got on the line with you. The caller said that this is only the beginning and that she or 'they' are going to use a suicide bomber to blow up a large portion of the school, though she didn't give an exact timeframe. I imagine the call was too quick to trace, but the police just walked back into

Ruth's office and are already investigating this. We have received these types of calls periodically over the years, but after what happened today we're taking no chances. Ruth did say she thought the caller had a foreign accent, but she couldn't place what part of the world it came from. It's possible the young woman had a speech impediment, or maybe was covering her voice with her hand or a handkerchief. She's just not sure, because it happened so fast and unexpectedly."

"Wow! Well, that opens up a whole new set of problems to deal with, doesn't it, Alan? Wow - let's see, we have a possible jihad's bomber threatening to blow up the school, along with a retarded boy who is an attempted murderer, two student athletes who are quite possibly white supremacists, both who have been shot, leaving one critical and possibly paralyzed for life. Will there be anything else, Alan?"

"That's a little bit of a simplified version, but basically that's correct, sir. Oh, and the politically correct word for Zack's condition is 'special needs,' but yes, that's all for now, sir."

"That's more than enough, Alan, *much* more than enough. Please call me right away with any more news. I hate finding out news about my schools on my iPhone, especially bad news."

"I will, sir. We don't plan to reopen school until Monday; that will give us tomorrow and the weekend to thoroughly search the school. I will contact you immediately if I hear anything else. Thank you for calling."

Alan, still holding the phone, took in a deep, long breath and slowly exhaled. His first inclination was to slam the phone down, but instead he took another deep breath and calmly set the phone back in its cradle. As he was talking, he had been looking out his office window facing the main hallway. A female silhouette paced back and forth, waiting for him to finish his phone call.

"Come in, Anne," said Alan. He walked over and opened the door. Anne Briggs, the girls' vice principal, blew through the doorway and into his office like a welcome gust of warm wind.

After a moment's hesitation, they put their arms around one another and held each other close. To Alan, this seemed like a moment of calmness in the middle of a hurricane. When they pulled away, Alan could feel the dampness on his shirt from Anne's tears.

Anne was a forty-six-year-old, spry, high-energy, single mom of two teenage girls—one a freshman and the other a sophomore at the local public university. To Alan's amazement, Anne always seemed to be upbeat and dressed in impeccable attire nearly every day. But on this afternoon her mascara was smeared below her sparkling green eyes and her face was pinched and drawn.

"Alan," said Anne, as she ran her hand through her short, jet-black hair, straightening her navy-blue blazer, "Brad and I, plus two-dozen police officers and two enforcement K-9s, walked the entire school, through every corridor, bathroom, and classroom. The school is clean as far as we can tell. We heard about the bomb scare. Lieutenant Baker said there would be twenty police officers and a bomb team from the FBI searching this place over the next three days. Baker said that he and several other officers would remain this afternoon, to canvas the area for another two or three hours; they'll be back at seven o'clock tomorrow morning. I told him the custodians could let him out when they were done tonight and one of us would be here tomorrow morning by seven to let him in. They're leaving two armed officers posted inside the front door of the foyer all night."

Alan nodded in response, "Thanks for the great job you and Brad have done today. I don't know what I would do without you both as my vice principals," he said, leaning back against his desk. "That was Bob Lancaster, the head of the school board, on the phone. He was very concerned about the shooting and the bomb threat but, as usual, didn't really have any help or advice to offer. I told him about the possible situation with Butch, hinting that he may have covered for Kyle, but he didn't seem to give the idea much credibility. He said Coach Cassidy was a legend, a pillar of the community, and reminded me that he has won more football games than any coach in the history of the county."

"And, of course, what could be more important than winning football games?" Anne interrupted sarcastically, pacing across the office, waving her hands like a conductor leading an orchestra. "We both know Kyle doesn't even live within the district boundaries. He got a waiver to come here as a school athlete. It's automatic nowadays."

When Alan did not comment, Anne continued, "I know I'm angry and starting to ramble a bit, and I know you're a sports fan, but Kyle was approved for this district so he could play football under the legendary coach, Butch Cassidy, and maybe win a state championship. And as you may also know, even before the incident with Zack, Kyle was well-known as a bully . . . though neither Brad nor I could ever pin anything directly on him. Apparently the sports community has its own set of rules and they protect their own." Anne shook her head while searching Alan's eyes for his thoughts. "We both know he's not a stupid kid, Alan; he covers his tracks. We have spent so much time and energy recently trying to curtail the cyber-bullying epidemic that we haven't had as much time to deal with the *in-school* bullying. It's a vicious circle. Unfortunately, we know Zack has been mired at the bottom of the food chain for a long time and has been an easy target for anyone with their own self-esteem issues. Up until now he has acquired such a poor-me, victim mentality that he has been hard to help, especially in a school this size and without any available counselors. Okay," Anne loosened her stance and tried to crack a grin, "so now I have said my piece—at least for the moment. Though as you well know, it's always a woman's prerogative to change her mind."

A smile forced its way onto Alan's face, as it often did when Anne got riled up. He had always thought there was something special about Anne, something disarming about her personality, especially when she got worked up, as she was known to do when discussing something she felt passionate about.

After a moment's pause, Alan answered, "It's true I am a sports fan. I love basketball, and I still like to play down at the 'Y' in the old men's league on Thursday nights. But I think too many of us so-called grownups are bored or disappointed with our own lives, and often we project our misplaced expectations on our kids and their coaches. So yes, you're right. Unfortunately, many sports activities have become very political and psychologically unhealthy, in my humble opinion, and I wish I had the power to change things. But right now, I don't.

"However, the immediate question is: Did Butch cover up this whole mess about Kyle to keep him on the team? I'm not sure what I believe at this point, Anne. I just can't imagine he lied to protect his star linebacker, so that he might win a few more games. He is rather rough around the edges, but I think he's a decent guy at heart, or at least I hope he is. He wouldn't go that far—would he?"

"I won't touch that one, but with all due respect, Alan, I think you're rather naive about some things," Anne answered. "Many coaches these days would do anything to win—and I mean *anything.* Plus, most coaches are now under more pressure to win, if they want to keep their jobs, and this kind of pressure is even registering in middle school. And now I'm really going to shut up because I don't think you want me to say anything else under the circumstances." Anne drifted toward the window, folding her arms across her chest, staring at the white chalk marks on the steps below.

Alan joined Anne at the window and both were quiet for several minutes. Then Alan broke the silence, "Obviously, Zack was very angry at Kyle and was specifically looking for him. Maybe Josh just happened to be with him at the wrong moment. Zack was at the bottom of the food chain and Josh was at the top, and Zack just figured he was handy. He decided this was a good time to even the score."

"I think you're right," replied Anne, "but then the million-dollar question becomes whether this was just one of the kids on the lower end of the pecking order fighting back in his own perverse way. Or do we have some type of organized supremacy group that's planning more insanity? And who is this crazy girl who called?" Anne inquired. "Where is she from and how does she fit in? Unfortunately, my intuition tells me she is for real. And now Kyle is hanging around those wanna-be supremacists . . . is he one of them? Who knows, but I don't think he'll be answering these questions anytime soon."

"My intuition has never been very good, so I don't have a good answer, Anne, or *any* answer for that matter—but God, what a mess! How did everything get so complicated?" Alan shook his head and stared hopelessly out the window.

Anne looked over at him with a sympathetic smile, "Tomorrow is another day, Alan. Things will look better in the morning," was all she could think to say.

"I'm not so sure the situation *will* look that much better tomorrow, Anne . . . I really am not. Those chalk lines we're looking at are a testimonial to my failure as a principal. And I won't be a principal in a school that can't take care of its students. We have proposed numerous changes around here, numerous times, but the school board doesn't want anybody rocking the boat. What kind of society do we live in where half our students can't complete a sentence without using the word 'fuck' three times and they spend the majority of their spare time violently killing people in their video games. Good God, they spend more time texting on their iPhones than they spend in the classroom. And now school shootings are almost a weekly occurrence. It's pure insanity! How can our society keep letting this happen and still survive?! Maybe this is the beginning of the end of our culture as we have known it."

"It's not your fault, Alan—you have done your best." Anne interrupted, putting her hand on Alan's elbow. "I know it seems like our society is disintegrating right before our eyes; this is the fifty-seventh school shooting in the country this year, and hardly anyone seems to care, especially in government. But you as one school principal can only do so much. Don't beat yourself up."

"But what I'm doing is not nearly enough, and now we've got the fricking NRA to deal with! Fred Smithers, the California chapter president, just announced yesterday that they are going to provide free side arms and training for any teacher in the state who wants to carry in the classroom. Can you imagine Butch—all three hundred pounds of him—running around the football field yelling at the kids with a .45 flopping around below his 45-inch beer gut, and then firing off some shots when somebody screws up? This is nuts!"

Alan sighed deeply and continued grimly, "Now I am the one on a tangent, but I believe the NRA has become more dangerous to this country than Al Qaeda or ISIS. The NRA are arming themselves and others, including the mentally disabled, with what are essentially personal weapons of mass destruction, designed to kill large numbers of people.

And what happens if our current President is impeached? Because his people are the ones with all the guns. Will he go peacefully? I am not so sure," Alan continued, his voice sounding strained. "Maybe that's why the NRA is courting the ROTC kids. If push comes to shove, it's probably to get the military on their side. Shit, if these people love their guns so much, why doesn't the NRA form their own battalion and go fight in Afghanistan or Syria where they could ride around in pickup trucks acting like lunatics while waving their assault rifles around? Instead they use patriotic rhetoric and flag waving to stir up young people right out of high school to go over there to do their dirty work. Damn! Let them put their guns where their mouths are, instead of just hiding like cowards behind the Second Amendment while the rest of the country goes to hell!"

"Wow, Alan, I've never seen you get this fired up before. Now you're starting to sound like a real progressive instead of some wishy-washy moderate who can't figure out what he stands for."

They chuckled together quietly for a few seconds and then fell silent for several moments. Alan stood with his hands in his pockets and Anne leaned against the windowsill returning his gaze. As he started to speak, she interrupted, "It's been a really long day. I'm bushed and need to go home and assure my girls that this is not the end of the world as we know it." She stepped in front of him and their eyes briefly met as she told him goodnight, and then he received the second-longest hug he'd had in recent memory.

After Anne left, Alan leaned back in his chair and rested his aching back as he often did when he got a free moment. He again contemplated the day's events, trying to make some sense of the whole thing. He figured if he was going to be honest with himself, he needed to either resign his position as principal and go back to just teaching, or somehow figure out how to change the social and political dynamics at Martin Luther King High School. But how was he going to do that?

When Alan looked up at the clock again it was 6:30 p.m. Ruth had left half an hour before. He rose from his desk, ran his fingers through the remaining stray hairs on top of his head, and plucked his tan windbreaker off the hook on the door. He put his hand in his pocket to make sure the half-empty bottle of Tums was still there. Turning the brass knob to open the door of his office, he avoided looking back out the window as he entered the deserted hallway.

Alan's feet made a clicking sound as he walked alone through the empty cavern of hundreds of gray lockers lining both sides of the chipped and bruised gray marble floor. He said goodnight to Joyce, one of the evening custodians, while she pushed her long-handled dust mop down the hall. "Goodnight Mr. Carter," she replied. "You have as good an evening as you can, under the circumstances. Try and get some sleep."

Sleep sounds wonderful, he thought to himself. He reached the back emergency door and without hesitation, knowing the alarm was off and no reporters would be in the back, he pushed it open. A rush of cool, wet air greeted him. He was free again for fourteen hours. He had made it through another day of high school.

That night it rained heavily, with sheets of moisture pounding the asphalt grounds. MLK High was awash in water and darkness, making the school buildings barely visible from each other at only a hundred feet apart. It has often been said that in California, when it finally does rain, it pours.

CHAPTER FIVE
THE REST OF MY LIFE

Zack Diamond lay curled up in a fetal position, his small body taking up only a quarter of his three-foot by seven-foot bunk. He wore the white-pocket T-shirt and blue cotton pants the guards had given him when they checked him into his cell at 5:36 that afternoon. His unruly brown hair had not had a comb in it since early that morning and his face felt oily and bloated.

He was not wearing his thick brown glasses. He had lost track of them when the cops tackled him as he was trying to enter the administration building. As Juan told him to do, he had left the black assault rifle with another twenty-seven rounds still in its clip on the steps. He trusted Juan—in fact, Juan was the only person in the world he did trust. He did not feel anything toward the school's security guard other than a cold, hard disdain, but not the deep, dark, gut-wrenching hatred he had toward Kyle. He felt ready to give himself up after shooting the two assholes; it was euphoria the first thirty seconds, then he felt exhausted, drained, like all the air had gone out of his lungs. He just wanted to go take a nap someplace quiet and think about how cool it felt to finally pull the trigger and rid the world of the monster animal named Kyle Ritter.

He had originally figured he would walk over to Kyle's body and reach down and run his hands through his blood and then put some in his mouth and taste it and howl like a lone wolf. Then he would put the rifle to his own head and pull the trigger—he had even practiced in his room with the gun unloaded. But in a moment of what he guessed was pride, right after the act, for once in his life he wasn't ready to die, and it felt good to put the weapon down . . . as it had always felt foreign, odd, dark, and cold to him. It was like the monster he had tried to kill; he had tried to kill it with yet another monster.

He moved over and lay on his left side, reenacting the scene in his mind, wondering why the cops had thrown him to the ground and held him down when he tried quietly to tell them he was surrendering. He had just stood there, unarmed, waiting for them to put handcuffs on him. But to have six men in camouflage with life-ending assault rifles pointed directly at his head, when he was laying on the ground, unarmed, and had given up, seemed like overkill to him. However, this was modern America and he had just shot two people and was now, he thought, considered a domestic terrorist. Maybe they would also arrest Joe, the asshole who lived next door to him, from whom for twenty OxyContin and 150 bucks, Zack had bought the used M16 and the hundred rounds of ammunition he needed at a local gun show the August prior.

He sat upright and squinted through the pale light at the black-rimmed clock on the white, concrete wall. It was 11:38 p.m. A sharp chill like a frozen knife blade ran lightly down his spine, causing him to hug his knees tighter to his chest, as he pulled the lone, gray blanket he had over both his shoulders. He was sweating, then shaking, and getting sicker to his stomach every minute. He wished he had another chance to turn the gun on himself or force the cops to do the job for him. Zack knew he was going through opioid withdrawal. He had forgotten about this part. In his planning he had figured he would be dead after the shooting, so it wouldn't matter. He had been stealing his mom's painkillers for over a year now, and every time he ran out he went into withdrawal and got sicker than shit. It had been about twelve hours since his last pills; he had taken a small handful before school started, about triple what he usually took. Maybe that's why he was so relaxed and had no fear when he pulled the trigger. Zack figured when fear is gone, you can do almost anything—and when one mixes Oxy-Contin with deep hatred, and plenty of self-loathing, you have a deadly mix. But there was no way he was going to get any pills in here, and his body was sweaty, aching, and cramping. This part was going to be tough, very tough, and now there was no way to get rid of the fear or the nausea.

I'll turn sixteen in jail in three days, he thought to himself. Three years ago on the coming Saturday had been his bar mitzvah, the only party he had ever had and the only party he had ever been to. Both his parents were shy and introverted, and they kept to themselves. Zack was also extremely shy, small-framed, overweight for his size, awkward. He had never made any close friends in or out of school, and of course he never played any sports. The young Rabbi, a friend of his uncle (his uncle being the only living relative he had ever met), had talked with Zack about his future, saying that maybe he would become a computer programmer for Microsoft, move to Seattle, have a nice little Jewish wife, a few kids, and earn tons of money. But what a joke that was—who would marry him? Even if he found someone to marry, he was sure he would never have kids. He felt that he was so screwed up he would probably end up impotent, unable to make any babies.

And now it didn't matter anyway; now there was no future. *My life is over*, he thought as he slowly rocked back and forth, sweating profusely, his head throbbing. A long, bleak, dull life in prison is what he had to look forward to, if he didn't die young—which was still certainly a possibility. But who gave a rip, because now Kyle Ritter and Josh Smith were toast. Maybe not dead yet, but Kyle was close. Besides, the tall, bald, potbellied deputy sheriff who'd brought him the crap that passed for his dinner had told him so.

He also told Zach they were going to try him as an adult and fry his fat little butt. Zack doubted that. They didn't fry kids in California—maybe in Texas or Alabama, but not here. But who gave a crap anyway? All he knew was that he was now an infamous school shooter, and no one would trip him in the halls, laugh at him behind his back, pee on him, or call him a "fag dwarf" ever again.

He was now as cool as his hero, Tee, the rapper he'd seen on TV and in video games. Tee was truly bad; he had a huge, mean scowl, wore camouflage pants, black T-shirts, not to mention plenty of bling. He also carried an automatic rifle and a grenade launcher in most of his videos so he could kill hundreds of bad guys, plus some other people who happened to be at the wrong place at the wrong time and were considered collateral damage. Now Zack was just as bad and as cool as Tee, and Josh was his collateral damage.

The only benefit, to Zack's way of thinking, was that now other students might forget about his occasional stutter, and that he was an overweight loser who stood only five-foot, four-inches tall. He knew some of the kids at school thought he must have Down syndrome, or was a dwarf, and of course he had no real friends except for Ramona, and also Juan. But now they would never forget what he had done, never in their whole life! Zack Diamond had become the highlight of his classmates' high school experience, and they would talk about what he had done until they got old and died. The more he thought about it, the more he wished he had killed a dozen more of them, just like in his favorite video game, *Call of Duty,* where massive killing inspires the soul. Nowadays you had to kill dozens of people to make the national news but, just the same, the kids in his school would never *ever* forget him. Or, if he had stayed with Ramona, things might have turned out much differently, and they both would be famous and dead.

"Ramona . . ." Zack muttered again and again. He stopped rocking and spread his legs out across the cot and laid his hand over his groin. For a minute a warm feeling engulfed his stomach and ran down through his loins. For a moment he could see her short, black hair and chubby olive-skinned face. He wondered if she hated him now for not waiting. Did she think he was a coward? A traitor who abandoned her? She had remained silent when he said he needed to shoot Kyle, but later said she wasn't going to give up the idea of blowing up the school and every white slut in it, shooting or no shooting. Besides, Zack had built most of the bomb himself; he was smart enough to do it, the instructions were all over the Internet, and it was already two-thirds complete. But he didn't want to kill Juan, just Kyle, along with his bastard white Nazi buddies. Whereas Ramona seemed to hate every white person in America, except maybe him, but now she probably hated him, too.

Zack thought about the years he had spent in his room all by himself playing video games; it seemed like his whole life. It was his only safe place, the only place where he didn't have to be in his fat, ugly little body. But when he entered the world of gaming, there he was, a brutal warrior, killing his enemies, and raping the wives and girlfriends of those who had hurt and abused him.

He closed his eyes. He was finally getting sleepy. He felt anxious and was still sweaty and sick and scared. Tomorrow would come early, the big, gruff deputy had said. Zack's last thought was that he wished upon all wishes that tomorrow would never come.

A soft groan passed through Kyle's lips, as his eyes attempted to blink themselves into focus. A large pillow propped up his head so that his face looked toward the door. He inhaled and exhaled several times, feeling his chest rise and then fall. For the first time since he had arrived at the hospital sixteen hours ago, he could breathe deeply without the help of an oxygen mask.

But he couldn't move his head or his legs. He couldn't move anything for that matter, not even his toes. Wild panic had set in two hours ago, when he first woke up. He had wanted to scream at the top of his lungs, but yellow saliva just leaked from his mouth and ran down his chin. Try as he might, he couldn't move his swollen lips, or make a sound—not even a grunt. He kept thinking that this must be a terrible nightmare and he would soon wake up and be okay, but reality set in and an unbelievable dark fear—darker than death itself—settled over him: the fear that he was now completely paralyzed for the rest of his life.

At this particular moment, though, he was very relaxed, and the world seemed like a great place. He couldn't even remember why everything had seemed so bad several hours ago. Finally, he figured it must be the medication, the morphine that was seeping into his body drop by glorious drop. He overheard one nurse tell another that he was getting the maximum dosage allowed. It also occurred to him that he had never felt truly relaxed before—not in his whole life! He had only felt relaxed when he was drunk or on something, but even then he was still angry. Was this possible?

He could not see his mother, but he'd heard her arguing with his old man a few minutes before. He knew she wouldn't be far away. She kept telling his dad to leave, and it sounded like she had finally pushed him out the door. He hadn't seen or heard the bastard come in the room, but the fresh smell of whiskey had alerted him to his father's presence. Then he had heard the deep, familiar voice ranting in a loud whisper that a Jew had shot his only son. He couldn't believe Kyle would let a Jew get the drop on him, and he kept saying it louder, and over and over—adding that, if Kyle had been allowed to take his gun to school, this wouldn't have happened. In a lower voice he muttered that he would get even with those damn Jews; he would show them a thing or two about guns. Kyle's father was the one who told him about the Neo Nazis and if there weren't any in his school, well then Kyle should start his own chapter, just like he had.

Kyle just lay there and thought this old bastard didn't seem to care that he'd been shot and might possibly die or might be a vegetable for the rest of his life. Instead, he was just angry at everything, like always; he was always pissed off at somebody or something. The world had been mean to Don Ritter and Don Ritter had been twice as mean back. To his father, anger was a way of life.

But, hell, Kyle didn't care anymore. He was not sure why, but for the first time in his life it didn't matter what his father said or did. The world had suddenly become a wonderful place. Intuitively, he knew his dad could never bully, poke, or hit him again. He was safe now and he was calm. The extra morphine the nurse had given him when she lowered his head into a more comfortable position was wonderful—better than the pain pills his buddy Dustin bought from the drug pimps who hung around Prichard's Market. Maybe that little kike, Zack, had done him a favor. And would they give him morphine for the rest of his life? The world, for the first time in his life, now seemed like a nice, safe place to be. The room was very quiet, and he dreamed of closing his eyes. But that was only a dream. While he slept, his wide-open black pupils stared, fixated at the large fly resting motionless on the ceiling light fixture. His last thought before drifting off to sleep was how had a fly gotten into his hospital room?

Josh, on the other hand, was still not sure what had happened. One minute he was coming back from lunch and walking up the front steps of MLK, and then bam! He remembered being with Kyle Ritter, another football player, a really cool dude, and a true believer. Then suddenly, some little nerdy Jew stood before them, opening fire with some type of huge, badass weapon.

He couldn't believe it had all really happened. At the memory of being hit, the dull pain in his stomach suddenly turned sharp. He remembered just standing there and looking down at the blood oozing from his T shirt. Then he felt himself falling and rolling down the concrete steps, until he hit the bottom. He was still coherent and shaking like a can of paint on a paint-stirring machine, as he curled up in a ball and proceeded to puke his brains out.

He must have passed out then, because the next thing he knew, he was here in this bed and some foxy redheaded nurse who didn't look much older than him was playing with his toes. His main doc had told him he was going to be okay. He had taken a bullet in the abdominal area, but no major organs had been hit. He was lucky, though, they said. If those teachers hadn't stopped the bleeding and if the paramedics hadn't shown up so quickly, he might have bled to death. Then he'd be smelling roses on a full-time basis.

Man, he could not figure the whole thing out. He just wanted to be cool, play a little ball, and party hearty. He didn't want any part of this shooting crap; he had seen enough of it in his life. And who was this Zack butthead anyway? He didn't ever remember seeing him before. He looked like some miniature geek with a big gun. Why did they even let these freaks into school? Josh had gone to boarding school at Mountain View Academy for Boys in Virginia the two years prior. But then one afternoon one of his closest friends, Billy Holt, had borrowed an M14 they were using for target practice and accidently shot and killed himself, right there in front of everyone and in the middle of the day, no less. Things had never been the same after that and Josh decided he needed a change. His father, a colonel in the Air Force, wanted him to stay at Mountain View, though. His father had warned him that going to public school would take some getting used to because they allowed anyone to attend, even retards, black people, and those damn Jews. Yeah, getting used to a new school was one thing . . . but getting zapped by a dwarf was a whole other ballgame. For some strange reason, shootings seemed to be following him wherever he went. Thank God his father had a cabinet full of liquor and never locked the door.

But being shot did have some advantages, Josh decided. The drugs were good, the nurses were cute, and all the cool chicks from school would definitely give him lots of love and sympathy when he returned. He could go a long way with this one, he contemplated, as he pushed the nurse's call button for more morphine. A large grin spread slowly across his face as he closed his eyes, thinking about the extra attention he was getting.

Karen Lynn lay sprawled on her back, next to an unopened algebra book. Her size eleven feet, tattooed with an orange basketball on each ankle, hung off the end of her double bed. Her head rested on the other edge of the bed frame, and her long arms drooped over the sides of the mattress.

Wow, she thought with a shiver. *Right now, Kyle Ritter is lying in a hospital bed with a bullet through his stomach, fighting for his life.* He had been sitting right next to her in English class an hour-and-a-half before lunch, and now he was almost, like, dead!

On the day of the shooting, like most days, Kyle had wandered into class a couple of minutes late and slouched down in his chair. He'd propped up his chin on the desk with his right arm and closed his eyes as if sleeping or meditating for most of the next sixty minutes of class. She remembered his only acknowledgement of her existence on that day, like most days, to be a cursory glance from his sullen face and a, "Hey, black mama," when he first sat down beside her.

An hour later when the two shots rang out, she was still eating lunch in the cafeteria while bantering with her girlfriends, Michele and Lindsey. Without a moment's hesitation, and forgetting her large size, she dove under the table and stayed there, frozen, not saying a word to the other three other girls hiding underneath the table with her. It wasn't until the cops came an hour later and told them it was safe to come out that she felt like she could finally take a breath. The first twelve years of her life had been spent inside the community of Watts just outside of Los Angeles, and she knew all too well what the sound of gunshots meant.

Karen Lynn didn't know Zack Diamond personally. She just saw him occasionally sitting by himself around school, but she'd heard from Michele that he was an outsider—literally on the very bottom of the pecking order. Michele said some people liked to make fun of him because he was about the size of a large dwarf. The rumor around school was that Kyle and some of his friends had molested Zack in one of the bathrooms several months back. Everyone seemed to think Zack was out looking for revenge and some, especially her other black friends, figured Kyle—who was a popular jock but had a reputation as a white nationalist and a bully—had gotten what he deserved.

Life could be tough in a big school with lots of kids coming and going. Some, including a few of her friends, were cruel even to each other. Karen Lynn felt like she always had to be vigilant to stay safe; otherwise she might be her best friend's next victim. Some of the other girls could be so sweet, but then could suddenly turn into black widows and prey on each other. She hated the stress, but shit—you had no choice if you wanted to stay cool. It was dog-eat-dog, but better than being an outcast and a loser, like Zack. He literally had no friends! And no one had befriended Zack, at least as far as she knew, except she had seen Juan Pacheco sitting with him a couple weeks back. *That's weird*, she remembered. *What was a tough, cool guy like Juan doing with Zack and why had he risked his life to save that guard? What was that all about?*

Anyway . . . she guessed Zack Diamond had fought back the only way he knew how. She hated that school nowadays; it was as dangerous as living in Watts, so she didn't blame Zack for what he had done.

After all, guns were easy to get. Her fourteen-year-old-brother had a Glock or some weird-named gun that he hid underneath his mattress in his bedroom next to hers. He was so proud of that damn thing, but the thought of that gun made Karen Lynn sick. She knew just having a gun in an unlocked place in their home put the whole family at a greater risk. What was wrong with insecure people that they thought it was cool to have some weapon that would kill lots of people, people who were other people's sons and daughters, mothers and fathers?

Now Kyle was facing death and Zack was in jail, probably for the rest of his life. A shiver went through her body and she looked up at the clock; it was 1:30 a.m. She didn't consider herself religious or anything like that, but she said a quick prayer anyway for both boys and another for herself and then one for her brother, hoping that she would finally fall asleep.

Claire sat cross-legged on her bed; it was well past midnight. Earlier that evening she had spent two hours on the phone with the person she considered her best friend talking about how they had seen Zack sitting on the steps just moments before the shooting. Her friend said that made them "witnesses," like they were almost famous or something. Her friend didn't seem to get the fact that two boys were near death, and another would be up for murder. It was just another drama to her friend, though a bigger one than usual. They had finally hung up around 10:00 p.m., and Claire's brain was fried.

But now she kept ruminating to herself, wondering why she didn't stop to talk to Zack, even for a minute. *Maybe that would have been enough? Why couldn't I at least have said hi? Why am I so afraid of what my friends think? I spend four hours a week volunteering at the local humane society; I love all the animals, especially the cats. I try to be a good person, but I am not!*

Sometimes I am just a little stuck-up bitch and I hate myself for it. My hormones and the peer pressure from my friends run my life. I can't even seem to think for myself. I am so fricking shallow and am so afraid of being left out and becoming an outsider. Why does school have to be so stressful?

Claire felt totally exhausted from the frenzy in her mind, and she cried herself to sleep.

CHAPTER SIX
REFLECTION

Alan tossed and turned. It was another tough night. He guessed it was close to four o'clock, his usual waking hour for the last several mornings. He was too tired to turn over and look at the clock on the opposite nightstand. His monkey mind kept asking him why he was doing this—something in his life had to change, or he couldn't go on. He closed his eyes and tried to get back to sleep, but his mind was turned on and his thoughts went back to being a kid again, back on the same day forty years earlier: October 27, 1978.

Alan remembered walking down the hall of his old school, Roosevelt High. As he walked, he saw Brian Meese, the tall, slim, student-council president with his petite girlfriend, Becky Blade. As if they were a gander and a goose, moving one right after the other, they each gave Alan a quick nod of acknowledgment—but their eyes were blank and cool, and their mouths stayed nailed shut as they walked on.

Several sturdy-looking boys, with shaved heads and identical gold and blue jackets embroidered with "Roosevelt Outlaws" on the back, gave Alan a quick look. Almost in unison they uttered, "Hey, man—good try," before turning their backs without another word, and resuming their conversation with Meg Wilson, a blonde girl who Alan recognized.

Meg had gone to grade school with Alan five years ago. He remembered her as a tiny, ponytailed brunette with one of those big grins that made you want to tell her funny stories. Now she was a blonde with a glossy painted smile. She wore a red cheerleader's skirt that didn't look half as long as the plaid boxer shorts Alan had put on that morning. He thought to himself, *Hmmm . . . her legs have certainly gotten long, like an advertisement for her sexy bod. Why,* he wondered, *did some girls advertise their bodies like that? It was hard enough being a horny guy; why did these girls want to make it worse?* He inhaled and exhaled a small breath of air. He knew she would pretend not to recognize him. He was not in her league anymore, and he put his eyes on the white sneakers in front of him and kept trudging down the long corridor of lockers.

Next, he walked past paper-thin Jeremy Robbins, whose long, shaggy, brown hair along with his bellbottom pants made it clear that he, too, was an outsider. In junior high, Jeremy had been his best friend; they had been almost inseparable. Now Jeremy seemed a complete stranger and Alan hadn't spoken to him in over a year. Jeremy seemed so intent on picking his way through the crowd that he didn't even look over as Alan glanced up to give him a quick smile, which Jeremy didn't return. Alan's eyes dropped back to the coffee-colored tiled floor littered with notebook paper and plastic cups. As he pressed on down the hall, he wondered whether he'd done something wrong to make Jeremy think he was a jerk.

Only fifty feet to neutral ground, Alan reflected, and the knot in his stomach eased up a notch. With his free hand, he passed his fingers over his recently shaved head. It still felt strange to his touch, almost foreign, like the bristles on his mother's spiked hairbrush. *Why did I ever let them do this,* he thought, slapping his forehead with the palm of his left hand? *I didn't want to play football anyway.*

His dad had been the one who pushed him to play and to become a right tackle, the same position his dad and his older brother, George, had played. But Alan would rather have played basketball or wrestled—or, truthfully, he would have rather played chess. He hadn't made the varsity team as a senior; they said he was not big or tough enough. In his heart, he just wasn't a football player, and he should have gone out for wrestling—but you couldn't do both at Roosevelt High. Now he was a disgrace to his family, or at least to his dad and older brother. No letterman jacket meant he probably wouldn't have a girlfriend this year, or maybe *ever* for that matter. Life sucked, sometimes.

"Hey freak! What happened to your head? Did ya get

chemotherapy or somethin'?" an unknown male voice bellowed from behind. Alan quickened his steps, but his stomach went back to feeling like he had just gotten off the Twister at Magic Mountain.

Suddenly, Mary Martin pranced by, her head held high and her books tucked tightly against her ample chest. Her pretty blue eyes darted toward Alan and he could have sworn a minuscule smile ran across her face. A quick dash of hope flickered through his heart, but she never slowed down, opened her mouth, or looked back.

We're like poor cows in the feedlot waiting to go to slaughter, Alan thought to himself, as he pushed his way toward the door. Only twenty steps to go, so Alan quickened his pace, almost tasting the freedom.

"Hey!" he cried, as his books were knocked out of his hands and sprawled across the floor. "Geez, man! Can't you watch where you're going?" Alan muttered under his breath, kneeling to pick them up.

"What did you say? Are you talking to *me*?" shouted one of the three boys who had stopped about ten paces ahead of him. Alan looked up from his knees. It was Shawn Nix, with a half-grin plastered across his freckled face. His two smirking sidekicks, Paul and Jason, just stood watching with arms crossed, chewing on toothpicks. Shawn was big and mean, and he had rolled the sleeves of his white T-shirt to his shoulders, showing his bulging muscular arms. He'd shaved his red hair to the scalp and held his wide lips in a continuous sneer. He told anyone who would listen that he wanted to be a pro wrestler. Some considered him cool, but Alan had never been one of his fans. He was usually looking for a fight. Alan didn't utter another word; he kept his head down, picked up the last of his math papers, got up without looking back, and walked the last ten feet to safety.

The brass door handle felt cool to his touch, and as he pushed the door open a rush of fresh air tried to push him back inside. He stepped out onto the sidewalk and felt the waning sunshine of a clear October afternoon. He had made it through another day of high school and was free again for fourteen hours.

Alan walked home through the new subdivision just east of the school. By going this way, he avoided the gangs who hung out in Alta-Berry Park. *All the homes look the same,* thought Alan, with garages bigger than the houses poking out at the rare pedestrian. He walked the last six blocks home at a quick pace. He was tired and hungry and hoped his mom had baked a batch of fresh chocolate-chip cookies before she went to work. He turned right onto Washington Drive; his was the yellow house with a big dying elm tree, the third one on the left about a hundred yards from the corner.

Alan knew immediately that something was wrong. A black and white patrol car sat parked in front of his house, and his Uncle Ben and Aunt Jean's white Ford pickup filled the driveway next to his mom's VW Bug. A sick feeling ran through his stomach and he ran as fast as he could the rest of the way home.

From that day forward, he would learn what it was like to live without his father. Much to his chagrin, in many ways his life would become better for it, but the sense of loss never left him.

Three days ago, Alan turned fifty-six years old, but he could remember exactly what it felt like to be sixteen. Some kids had had it better; some had it worse—much worse. Growing up, as he remembered, was a mixed bag. Sometimes it just wasn't much fun, especially at school, which never felt right. *Why*, he asked himself, *did life have to be so tough and complicated sometimes? But here I am, fifty-six years old and life is still tough at times, and even more complicated since the shooting. I need a win! I haven't had one in a long while and I hate to whine, even to myself, but I am well overdue. I have got to get my mind back in line and get more positive. Otherwise I'll go crazy!*

As he rolled out of bed and started doing his morning jumping jacks, he suddenly knew what he must do. For five years he had been coming up with changes he thought would make Martin Luther King High a better school, and for five years every one of his proposed changes had been rejected by the school board. *Not any more*, he decided. *Not ever again, not even if it costs me my job and my career. Hell, what was a career anyway? Just a decent- paying job with good benefits and a livable pension at the end.*

Six hours later, Alan walked onto the MLK High auditorium stage. The wooden floor creaked and groaned, just as it had every time he had walked across it over the last seven years. He set his reading glasses and notes on the well-used oak podium and adjusted the height of the chrome microphone stand.

His vice principals, Brad Smith and Anne Briggs, walked out after him and sat down in the padded, taupe, folding chairs directly behind him. Many of the teachers and staff stood around the perimeter of the auditorium, as did Rod, the school's security officer. Alan gave him an especially warm smile as if to say, *I am really glad you are alive and well.*

Alan took in a deep breath and stood looking out at the audience for several moments. The old auditorium was packed tight; Alan couldn't spot an empty seat anywhere. This would be the first of two assemblies on two separate days needed to convene the entire student body of almost 3,500 students.

The consensus in the audience was that the assembly had something to do with the shooting the Thursday prior. But no one, teachers or students, knew exactly why Alan had called them together on such short notice. Many of the students were chattering to each other frenetically. Some of them would glance up at Alan and then turn back to their neighbors, persisting in whispered speculation about why they were there. Some had heard rumors that armed guards would be put in each classroom, or that all students would have to wear identification bracelets, or maybe even be required to pack their own heat like it had been rumored in some Texas schools. At least a third of the students had recently seen the movie, *The Hungry Life*, the fourth sequel to *The Hunger Games,* which takes teenage violence to a new level. It had left some of the students with an unsettling feeling of dread. There was the violence in the other district high schools, and then there was the Mississippi shooting that had also happened recently, leaving twenty-one kids dead . . . just too much to think about.

Alan's eyes quickly scanned the audience. *Some things never change*, he thought to himself. He noticed that the pecking order, or the "food chain," as many of the teachers called it, dominated the crowd. The students in the auditorium were divided into numerous social hierarchies and cliques, into the social haves and the have-nots.

Alan glanced down at his notes, then decided to put them back in his pocket. He quickly wiped his forehead with his maroon-colored handkerchief and slightly loosened his traditional silk, Jerry Garcia tie. Briefly he closed his eyes and said a silent prayer, asking for help, trusting that somewhere in the universe a benevolent entity was listening and would give him the guidance to say the right thing.

He began with the usual welcome: "Ladies and gentlemen, could I have your attention now." The auditorium quieted down quickly as the students and teachers focused their attention on Alan. Twenty minutes later, you could have heard a pin drop, and ten minutes after *that,* it was bedlam. At the after-school faculty meeting that followed the assembly, Anne Briggs took the podium.

"Brad Smith, the boys' vice principal, and I have called this emergency faculty meeting with only two hours' notice because of the urgency surrounding Alan's announcements at today's assembly," explained Anne. "Nevertheless, it looks as though everyone is here, with the exception of Butch. I understand Butch believes there has been a robbery and he's trying to gather a hanging posse over at the school administration building." A light chuckle rippled through the staff, but the mood remained serious. It was the end of the day, everyone was tired, and it looked like it might be a long evening.

"Anyway," continued Anne, "we really appreciate this great turnout and we thought it would be important and beneficial to get some staff feedback on Alan's talk today. We know the speech was very controversial and disconcerting to some, while exciting and heartening to others. We feel it needs to be discussed by the entire faculty before it becomes public. Then we can have Alan comment on the feedback . . . so unless there is anything he wants to say first, we can get started."

Alan, who was sitting by himself in the left-front corner of the school cafeteria, had his hands clasped behind his head, leaning dangerously far back on a metal folding chair, a bad habit he'd had since childhood, especially whenever he was tired or stressed.

"No," he answered, "I don't think so. Everyone seems to have heard what I had to say at the assembly and I don't think I am any more delusional than normal, so let's proceed."

"Alan, I know you mean well, and I have great empathy for what you said, but I don't think you can get away with this—it's just not allowed," Bruce Robbins immediately declared. Bruce was MLK's thirty-eight-year-old, bald biology teacher and a twelve-year vet of the school. "You've attacked the largest sacred cow in the school system and I don't think you have that kind of authority. They will either fire you immediately or the athletic Booster Club and the Young Republicans will hang you in effigy on every light post in town within the week. Plus, Alan, if we're not careful, some of us could be hanging next to you. I have great respect for you and for what you're trying to do, but I think you need to back off and do that quickly."

"Well, I think it's wonderful," exclaimed Penny Briton, almost jumping out of her seat. Penny, a prim, gray-haired English teacher, had been a part of the district for over thirty years. "Alan, it's about time somebody had the courage to stand up and tell the truth. I agree with Bruce that you could possibly be fired by the end of the week, but maybe not . . . and if not, we all have a rare opportunity to do the right thing and wouldn't that be unique?!I think it's about time we fess up and admit that high school often is not a very nice or healthy place for many students. I think that most of us know in our hearts that many of our students are being left by the wayside and hate being here. We are trying to teach our kids how to pass tests instead of giving them the education they want and are interested in. We all know that most students could care less about all these test scores. And few of our students possess the interpersonal skills to function in a halfway-mature manner with their peers or with adults. I would hazard to say that not even half of our students know how to write properly or communicate verbally for their age group. The public school system is designed for a certain group of students, maybe fifty percent, and it's simply not working for many others. I support you one hundred percent, Alan. It's time for a change."

Before Penny could sit back down, Vern Duncan, the sixty-one-year-old, energetic athletic director, quickly stood up and ran a hand over his gray crew cut. Vern was like a tall oak tree, never bending or wavering. He could talk very fast and often gestured with his hands as he spoke.

"Alan, I am not going to mince words here. To take half of our athletic budget and put it into hiring seven new counselors, reestablishing the art department, building a new self-esteem program, and introducing after-school intramural athletics—that would bankrupt the sports program within a month. To me, this new jigsaw teaching device to connect the students and find out what they are interested in sounds like we're going back in time and creating some kind of socialist mumbo-jumbo nonsense all over again."

He continued, "You forget that's the reason the school board got rid of our gym programs and axed the art department in the first place. We don't need any willy-nilly social programs to fix kids. We just need to get rid of the bad apples—clean this place up! We—or should I say the school board—decided to build up our athletic teams and make them into powerful winners, to give us all something to be proud of. Our football team will be in the state finals in two weeks, and that's the single most important event that will happen the whole school year. If they win, that will do more to help our students' self-esteem levels than all these new programs combined! The entire student body needs to be taught to have respect and admiration for our student athletes. After all, they are our future leaders!

"Also, Alan," Vern continued, after a brief clearing of his throat, "the varsity football team alone has six paid assistant coaches you would be putting out of a job, and the varsity basketball team has three. There is zero chance you can get away with this move; it will only destroy your career. It's time to stop this talk right now, before it gets back to the school board and you are out on the street! We all know what you have personally been through over the last several years, and that has undoubtedly taken a toll. We also like and genuinely admire you, and we don't want anything unfortunate to happen to you. I implore you to back off immediately."

"We've gone on for three hours," interjected Brad Smith, when he was able to interrupt the parade of teachers still wanting to give their opinion. "The only consensus we've come to, as far as I can see, is that Alan may well be fired by the end of the week over these progressive and needed changes. Many of us on the faculty seem to agree with Alan philosophically, but that doesn't change a thing. What he wants to *do,* most of us seem to think, is probably impossible and will cost him his job."

Anne stood up and quickly looked around the audience. "I will try to keep this brief, but as many of you know, brevity is not always my specialty. I've been the girls' VP here for seven years and before that I was at Marshal Middle School for nine years. I can tell you much of what I have seen has been heartbreaking. Granted, I don't usually see kids when their lives are going well; those kids usually don't end up in my office. But I can tell you, with all my heart, the system is broken for many of our students.

"It's not just about grades, sports, social status, or tests scores anymore—it's about self-esteem, or if you like, you can call it self-respect. Many of these kids don't have any self-respect and many more don't have much, and I can tell you that without it they are not going to get far. They may be able to get married, make enough money to get by, or even become rich, if they are persistent enough. But happiness and personal satisfaction will elude many of them. And is that what we want for these kids?

"The ones at the very bottom of the pecking order—like Zack—

may shoot someone they perceive at the top and call our attention to the problem temporarily, but that's just a tiny sliver of the real issue. It's a huge problem that negatively affects many of our students and our society at large. We need to concentrate fully on all our students and not just a privileged few. We have to teach civility, respect, and compassion for all, as well as teaching our students how to read and write for their age level. Let's stop worrying about the test scores so much. And let's instead encourage these kids to find their passions and support them in whatever endeavor they choose. And until we have a perfect world with no mental illness, let's get rid of these damn assault weapons. I congratulate Alan for what he is trying to do, and I go on the record in offering my full support."

"Thank you, Anne, and as the boys' VP, I agree with much of what you have said," responded Brad. "Alan, you have been totally silent up until now; I think we need to hear from you."

Alan stood up slowly, slipping his hands in his pockets, and looked around the room. He put his hand over his mouth to cover up a yawn. "Sorry," he said, smiling sheepishly. "I am very tired; sleep has not come easily this week. I appreciate everyone's concern that I may be fired and have my career destroyed. But understand that I have given much deliberation to what I am doing, and I think I fully understand the possible consequences. I don't want to sound overly melodramatic, but there comes a time in a person's life—or at least in my life—when I feel I must do what I must do, because I have no other options . . . at least if I am to live with myself, that is. This is my time. Unless I am relieved of my duties before the morning, tomorrow we will start to implement the plan I outlined in the assembly. I am reassigning Jed Shaffer from his spot as assistant varsity football coach to the head of our intramural program. We've already talked, and he is ready to move ahead."

There was momentary shift of eyes from Alan to Jed. Jed, all six-foot four-inches of him, sat motionless. His rock-like jaw stayed shut, but his head nodded up and down as he continued to stare at Alan. One by one the staff returned their attention to Alan.

"Tomorrow, Vern, I will meet with you before school, and I will give you the amount of dollars your sports programs will have for the rest of the year. No one will lose a job, but your coaches need to be flexible and take on some new tasks, and give up some old ones. Vern, you're going to be in the counseling office half-days starting next week. If I remember correctly, that was the area of your master's degree. We'll meet with the rest of your coaching staff and get busy reorganizing later tomorrow afternoon. Understand, Vern—this is not about being anti-sports. As you know I am a sports fan, and they certainly have their place in this world. This is more about leveling the playing field for the whole student body."

Alan looked around the room. "Betty, you now are the lead counselor and we'll meet whenever you have an opening tomorrow. You're going to be a very busy woman as we build your team. Anne, Brad, and I will be working on the honest communication classes and will offer them as an elective this semester and as a prerequisite the following year. The jigsaw idea of teaching is not a totally new concept around here, but we're going to do a lot more of it. We will be holding a workshop on that topic two weeks from now, at our next teachers' in-service day. Every student in our school will have the opportunity to take assessments to find out where their real interests lie and then we are going to do our damnedest to help them fulfill their dreams, instead of shoving our curriculum down their throats. The last Friday of every quarter—if I am still here—we will have a full school assembly and get feedback from our students on how we are doing. I welcome and need your feedback and suggestions, too. If these changes are going to work, we need everyone's best ideas and participation.

"So tomorrow," Alan continued as he looked around the room, "will be a big day. I hope we all can look at this as a positive change. The responsibility is all mine, not Anne's, Brad's, Jed's, or anyone else's. You folks are just following my orders, so if any heads roll it will only be mine. Now, we are all exhausted, and if there are no more questions about what will happen tomorrow, let's go home."

"One minute, Alan," said Jed in a deep voice as he stood up and stretched his long legs. Jed was speaking for the first time that evening, and some of the staff later swore it was the first time they had ever heard the young coach speak publicly at all. "About you taking sole responsibility . . . I don't buy that. I don't have to do what you tell me. I could wait for the school board to act and we all know they surely will in some manner, and very soon. Regardless, I am putting my butt on the line with you, because I believe in most of what you say. It's about time we did some things differently and I support what you're doing.

"Kyle and Josh wouldn't be in the hospital right now, and Zack Diamond wouldn't be in jail, if we'd had better counseling and if these kids didn't have such a damn social hierarchy in this school. I love sports; they have been a big part of my life, but around here it often seems we've built an old feudal system from the dark ages around sports and social status. I think it's gotten way out of control and if you are like Zack, with no athletic ability, no friends, and at the bottom of the pecking order, life can be literally hell, and I don't believe it has to be like that, not at all. So anyway, if they hang you, they hang me, too. I am single and not too old to start another career." Without another word Jed sat back down, crossed his legs, cupped his hands around his knee, and stared straight at Alan.

"That goes for me, too," said Anne, standing up momentarily. "I may not be as young, but I am totally with you. You hang, and they can hang me right by your side."

"Count me in," Penny declared. "I stand with you one hundred percent. I am about to retire anyway," she smiled.

Alan looked like a deer caught in headlights as he glanced over at Anne and then back over at Jed. A low murmur rose from the teachers around the room, as all the eyes went from Anne back to Alan. He started to open his mouth, but then shut it again. Another few seconds passed as he tried to gain his composure. At last he said, very quietly and deliberately, "Thanks, Jed and Anne and Penny. I really appreciate your support, more than I can possibly say."

Anne could have sworn there were tears in Alan's eyes, as he quickly turned away to gather his coat and notebook. She stood there, wanting to follow him and tell him that what he was doing was right, and everything would turn out okay. But she knew that would be a lie because, truthfully, she didn't have a clue about what would happen. Well, honestly, maybe she did have a clue . . . but that was not something she wanted to think about.

CHAPTER SEVEN
NIGHTMARE

Kyle woke in the late afternoon on the third day after the shooting. He had been drifting in and out of consciousness for several minutes. When he finally came to, gaining some control of his thoughts, he was too afraid to open his eyes. He didn't really want to know where he was. There was a strong, vaguely familiar smell, though he had not recognized it at first. He finally gathered the courage to open his eyes, first his left and then the right. He spent several minutes trying to focus on the objects in the room until the realization began to sink in that, as he had feared, he was not home in his own bed. He glanced straight up and could only see the whiteness of the ceiling; the brightness of the recessed lights made him blink in rapid succession to regain his focus. There was a familiar-looking fly directly above him, taking some steps across one of the lights. Then the fly stopped and became motionless, as if stuck to the plastic of the bulb. *What is a fly doing in a hospital room?* was Kyle's first thought, and his second was, *Maybe it had become paralyzed?*

Paralyzed? Suddenly he remembered where he was and why he was there.

His stomach didn't feel so good and his forehead felt wet and chalky. There was a dull ache in his gut like something that was supposed to be there was missing. Tightness across his chest made him feel like he was bound up in ropes, or maybe he was having a heart attack? *The drugs must be wearing off*, he thought. He had an itch and needed to scratch his head, but his right arm would not move.

He tried his fingers, but he couldn't even tell if they were there—it was as if they were completely immobile, glued to the sheets of his hospital bed. He tried his left arm and fingers, but he could not budge them, either, or even feel a thing. The tightness across his chest grew stronger and his heart started racing. His head was stuck in place, too. He could not move it from side to side or look down or tell if it was still attached to the rest of his body. His legs and feet might as well have been made of stone.

Abruptly, the panic button went off inside his head—*he knew what was going on!* Now he remembered where he was and why he was there. *That little bastard shot my balls off and they tied me up so I can't see down there! Oh shit! Oh, my God!* He tried to yell for help, but his mouth would not form the words. He couldn't move his lips or even his tongue.

His mind raced but his body wouldn't move at all. This had to be a nightmare. No, it was too terrible to be a nightmare—had he died and gone to hell? This must be hell!? God, he *had* gone to hell! *Nurse! Nurse!* His mind kept yelling, but except for the pure utter panic in his eyes, his face remained totally expressionless. *God,* he kept praying, *this couldn't possibly be true. Please, God, please make this be only a nightmare and let me wake up!*

Mary Beth, the day nurse, washed Kyle's face and shampooed his hair. It felt very soft as she brushed it over to one side. She adjusted Kyle's pillows higher so that he could see down to the end of the room; at least he looked more comfortable this way, despite his distorted face. His pale blue eyes when open had held a dark, terrified look that reminded her of a cornered feral kitten she had once found behind the water heater in her garage.

Kyle kept his eyes closed the whole time Mary Beth was cleaning him up, though she knew he was not asleep. It seemed to her that opening and closing his eyes was the only control he still had over his body, maybe over his whole life. When she had first walked in, his eyes had been open, and he had looked wild and crazed. But after she had upped his morphine, they started to glaze over until he closed them tight. He would not open them now, though she knew he could; she expected Kyle would not reopen them until the morphine had completely kicked in and his panic began to recede. She decided to suggest to the doctor that they up his regular dose, to help control these difficult mood swings. Neither she nor the doctor knew what else to do for right now.

Mary Beth had been one of the nurses on duty when Kyle and Josh first arrived in the ambulance the day of the shooting. She had worked on Kyle with Dr. Hyde and several other physicians, along with a team of five other nurses, for over eight hours. At first, it was touch and go as to whether he would make it. The bullet had gone through his stomach lining into his spine. It now looked like he would live, but he was completely paralyzed, probably for life, Dr. Hyde had confirmed. She looked at Kyle lying there pretending to sleep, hooked up to all the life-support, and wondered what high school had turned into, with all the shootings going on.

She was now twenty-six and had a busy life. She'd gotten married three months ago and hoped to start a family soon. But she remembered what high school was like. She had not been very popular in high school; she was tall but not particularly pretty, shapely, or coordinated. She'd been rather shy, wore glasses, and as a strong "B" student she was not good enough to be in honors classes or student government. She went to school almost every day, but she had to admit she couldn't wait to get home. High school was just a big blah for her, except for science, the only class she had really liked.

The more she thought about it, the more she remembered how she resented the popular kids. How the girls on the volleyball team were always getting out of school and going somewhere exciting, and how they thought they were so cool. They didn't even know that she existed; to them she was just a nobody who lived in a different world. Martha, the captain of the team, had been her best friend in junior high, but once she made the high school varsity team, she barely gave Mary Beth the time of day. The other girls all seemed to have so much more fun than her.

But a couple of days ago, a bunch of the nurses had gotten together after work for pizza down the street at Regina's. The topic of conversation had turned to high school after she told them about her patient, Kyle Ritter. The nurses all shared similar experiences and none of them had felt like they had fit in during high school. They all had thought everyone else was having more fun than them, and almost all the women shared painful experiences of feeling ostracized and alone. It had been good to talk to the other nurses; it was validating and made Mary Beth feel better about herself. Yet she still didn't understand how so many adults felt like they had not fit in during high school. Where did all those kids go—the ones who seemed to be having such a great time and felt like they *did* fit in?

At first, she thought the shooter, Zack, must be some kind of psychopath, but then she could understand some of the resentment and rage he must have felt. She had seen his picture in the newspaper; he was rather small and odd-looking, and according to the article, had a mild case of Asperger's, so she could only imagine what school must have been like for *him*!

Life is funny, she thought. She remembered Kay Dunaway, a blonde gal who worked as one of her nursing assistants. Kay had been one of the cutest and most popular girls in her high school, and she was voted homecoming queen during their senior year – she was definitely a "somebody"! Kay never said boo to Mary Beth in school, even though they had been classmates since grammar school. She had hung out with the cool kids, and Mary Beth had been a "nobody."

Right after school, Kay had gotten pregnant by her longtime boyfriend and they had three kids in five years. She had lost her girlish figure and was now a little overweight but still pretty, even though she didn't believe it. Kay thought she should still look like she had in high school. She had never gotten the chance to go to college or nursing school because she was working and taking care of her kids. She had more problems than Mary Beth ever dreamed of, and Mary Beth often found herself giving Kay advice during their lunch breaks in the cafeteria. *What a strange, strange world . . . the way things turn out,* she mused as she walked out of Kyle's room. She was thankful she had gone to nursing school, gotten married to a great guy, who was now a plumber, who she absolutely adored (and who also had been a nobody during high school). She decided maybe she was lucky after all, though it had taken her a long time to figure that one out.

Zack lay across his bunk in what seemed to be his new, but more permanent living quarters. The room was an eight-by-ten concrete rectangle that would normally be shared with a cellmate, but because of his celebrity status, he was alone.

He was watching professional wrestling on a small television that sat on a platform built into the wall. It was the only luxury the cell provided. He looked forward to pro-wrestling, where the wrestlers pulled each other's hair, pulverized one another, and the winner often spit on the loser—this was exciting in a kind of painful way! At home, he would have jumped up yelling and screaming during the match, letting out just a little of his anger, much like a fissure in lava rocks letting off steam before it erupted. But here he remained quiet on his bunk, not wanting to attract any unwanted attention to himself.

However, Zach missed his video games most of all. He loved the graphic violence of killing hundreds of bad guys. He could even kill thousands without ever getting off his butt. Zack thought about how many times he had wanted to smash in Kyle Ritter's face. Kyle was so cool and thought he was so tough. The day he and his friends held him down in the boys' bathroom while they took turns peeing all over him—that had been the worst day of his life and there had already been a lifetime of terrible days. He had wanted to die so many times and spent hours upon hours trying to cry it out, but now it was Kyle who was crying, and would be for the rest of his life, every single hour of every day. He remembered how Kyle's face had turned crimson and his eyes bulged to the size of pool balls, like he couldn't believe what was happening when Zack pointed the M16 at his stomach and pulled the trigger. Every once in a while, life could be ever so cool.

The deputy had told Zach that Kyle was going to live. Yes, he was going to live but he was totally paralyzed from head to toe. The bullet had gone through his gut and fractured Kyle's spinal cord, and he would never walk again. But this really didn't register to Zack, because in Zack's mind Kyle was not a human being. He was just another monster like the ones in his video games.

Yet this monster had been alive and had attacked Zack. Never again—Zack had taken care of that. He was glad Kyle was going to live, so Kyle could learn what it felt like to live in a deformed body and have everyone think he was a freak. Maybe there was some kind of justice in this world after all.

The fat deputy also told Zach that he probably wouldn't be fried, now that Kyle was going to live. But that he would likely spend the rest of his life in a men's correctional facility. Zack was mildly disappointed, even though that's what he had expected. Somehow the idea of being electrocuted had seemed rather heroic; it would have made front-page news. He could see it now: *High School Dwarf Electrocuted!* The problem, though, was that he wouldn't have been around to read about it.

The last time his mother visited, she had cried the whole time, while rambling on about the injustices being done to Zack. Zack had done his best not to listen to a word she said or to feel a thing. *At least crying was better than yelling,* he thought. *She didn't yell at me once during the whole two-hour visit, and that must be a record.* After his old man had left, back when Zack was five, his mother started yelling and putting guilt trips on him, just as he could remember her doing to his father, and she had never stopped since.

Zack met with his lawyer, Jerry Cutter, a guy who thought he was a cool-looking dude with his black cowboy boots and red tie. He made Zack want to puke. Cutter told him he might spend much of his life in jail if he was tried as an adult. He said it was very important that they try him as a juvenile. He explained that, as an adult, he could get life in prison, whereas if he was tried as a juvenile he would most likely be out in five years or less, at least if Kyle lived, that is.

"It doesn't matter to me," Zack lied to Cutter. "Hell, I don't care what they do to me!" But deep inside, he did worry. He wondered what prison food would be like, and whether they would let him bring his computer. But most of all he worried that he would be raped and beaten and become one of those in-prison sex slaves he had read about, passed around like a used joint. For a few moments, his mind focused on the thought of being raped by some huge, ugly biker, until he started shaking uncontrollably and felt like he might throw up. He was covered from head to toe in sweat and knew he was still going through withdrawal; he wished to hell that he had never tried those painkillers of his mom's. He pulled his single cover over his head, curled up in a ball, and began to shake and sob uncontrollably. When he finally did stop shaking, something miraculous happened: he started praying—more like pleading for help than praying, yet he had no idea who or what he was pleading to. He didn't even know what he was asking for, just something to make the pain go away. This was the first time in the almost ten years since his father had left that he'd asked an unspecified God for help.

CHAPTER EIGHT
ETHICS

Jerry Cutter pulled his eleven-year-old black Porsche convertible into his private parking spot at his law office, Tyson, Smithers, Cutter & Carlson. He put his cell phone back into his breast pocket, threw his black baseball cap on the passenger's seat, and flipped off his 200-dollar Ray-Ban sunglasses, letting them hang by the cord around his neck. He stepped out of the convertible and stretched his hands into the air, as if thanking the gray smoggy skies for today's good fortune. He reached down onto the black leather seat and picked up the manila folder marked "Zack Diamond," and then loped up the two flights of stairs outside of what, before the recent remodel, used to be a '70s-era two-story motel.

He smiled and winked at Jan, the partners' long-legged, redheaded secretary. Jerry often thought she was the brains and the glue that, like in many law firms, kept the company organized and solvent. She looked up and smiled back and said, "Hey Jerry, Bernie's door is open . . . he's on pins and needles waiting to hear the news on this Zack kid."

"The news, I think, is very good," he announced, as he walked straight into Bernie's office. "The judge has officially given me the case, but this is one screwed-up kid," said Jerry, sliding into a brown imitation-leather chair before a large imitation-oak veneer desk across from Bernie. "He doesn't seem to give a damn about anything. The kid is like a zombie with no feelings at all—no conscience—and I can't get a thing out of him. All his mother does is cry and tell me to get her kid off, so she can have him home with her. I can't relate to either of them, but then, hell, I guess I don't have to—my job is to represent the kid to the best of my abilities, not understand or fix him and his mother, right?"

Bernie leaned his sagging jowls toward Jerry and said, "There is nothing to figure out or fix, Jerry. We are not doctors or shrinks. The kid's a psycho and a loser; let it alone. We can't lose this one. We will get lots of press and national exposure by defending this monster—that already started a few hours ago, as soon it came across the wire services that you're the attorney of record."

Bernie pushed away the last fries of his double-meal-deal and rested his greasy hands on his ample stomach. "This shooting is the biggest thing that's happened in this town all year. Shit, all the rest of the towns around here have had their own school shooting, sometimes a dozen kids are killed, but we haven't even had a mall shooting. And the good news is we are right in the middle of this one and we got a dwarf as a client—a dwarf, mind you, is great PR. This could be our trip to the big leagues! The really good news is nobody besides his mother wants or expects us to get him off and, truthfully, I can't figure out why she would want him back. But the big money question, Jerry, is do we let him get tried as a juvenile, or do we throw him to the sharks and let him be tried as an adult? I mean, he has just turned sixteen years old, but he used a gun and paralyzed another kid. In California that gives the prosecution the opportunity to try him as an adult, if they can convince the judge that he is a menace to society. You can be sure the prosecutor will want to try him as an adult. They all want the glory and every prosecutor is a wanna-be politician looking to be mayor. Hell," he laughed, "sometimes they're actually slimier than we are."

Bernie leaned back in his chair with a pen hanging out of his lower lip and his feet propped up on his desk. "We will get a lot more exposure and a lot more money, probably three times as much, if he gets tried as an adult. The courts will have to pay us more than triple—I said *triple*—if he is tried in adult court. It's a lot of money, Jerry. If we handle this right, we can get half a dozen extensions and drag this case on for years, and the state of California will just keep on paying us the dough, plus we'll get free TV exposure."

"Yeah, but is that ethical?" asked Jerry.

"*Ethical?* Shit, what's that mean?" Bernie snorted. "We're trial lawyers! And excuse the term, but the kid is a freak—a nutcase—and this case could become a giant freak-show worth over a cool million to us. But if they try him as a juvenile the case could disappear into oblivion, because nobody cares about juvenile cases. Then it's back to the minor leagues for us. It would be unethical of us, as attorneys, to *not* milk this, because that's what we do in America! We milk, milk, milk, and when the cream comes to the top . . . if we're smart, we get rich. In reality, Jerry, most trial lawyers, if they are successful, are just rich milkmen—and I for one am honest enough to admit it. I already checked and it's just a shame his mom doesn't own her home, or we could get that right up front."

Jerry laughed nervously, "Well, he doesn't seem to care whether he gets tried as a juvenile or not, or whether he lives or dies. Hell, if he doesn't care, I guess why should we?"

"Right, Jerry, you got it," nodded Bernie, moving his large head slowly up and down. "But bottom line—it's going to be up to Doug Smithers, since he is our senior partner. I know he can be a pain in the butt sometimes, but he makes the final decisions in a case this big. So we'll just have to wait and see what he wants to do, but I don't think he'll go ethical on us. He knows there could be a small fortune hanging on this one if we handle it right. Doug isn't the smartest cookie in the pan but when it comes to making money he has his head screwed on tight. He is a pro and a firm believer in making sure a case doesn't get to court until every cent possible has been sucked out of it."

"You know, Bernie," Jerry stood up, his voice grew deeper and quieter, "the part I just don't get is why these kids are doing this crap to each other. Hell, in high school I graduated with honors; in my senior year I was voted most likely to succeed. I worked my butt off and did not have much fun, but high school was a piece of cake. I don't get this stuff at all—something is radically wrong out there when kids are shooting each other. I just don't get any of this."

"It doesn't matter, Jerry. Trust me!" Bernie repeated several times as he stood up, waving around his extra-large chocolate milkshake. "You *don't have to* understand them. Besides, what would we do if this kind of shit didn't happen? The NRA is our best friend right now—and of course they're full of shit. I mean, the more guns floating around, the more bad shit happens, we all know that . . . it's the way the world works. This office has handled three cases where a family member has shot another family member with a gun they kept in their house supposedly for protection, but we have never tried a case where a family member has had to use a personal firearm to shoot a 'bad guy.' Now they want to give guns to the teachers, that's great news, too! Can you imagine the first time a teacher loses it and pulls out his .38 to kill some little punk? Litigation heaven, I tell you, Jerry! Personally, I think the NRA'ers are idiots and they scare me sometimes—they really do. But let's be honest . . . they help keep us in business. We don't tithe to a church, we give to them. We need them, they need us.

"Yeah," laughed Jerry lightly. "I have this friend from high school, Danny Pyle, an NRA advocate who shot the end of his dick off with his concealed handgun. Stuck it in the holster and forgot to put the safety on, then bent over to tie his shoe. Now his wife has left him because he can't even start, let alone finish, the job.

"Yeah, ain't that bad luck," chuckled Bernie.

"But remember, it's the law of the jungle, Jerry. So don't waste your time worrying about this kid. He is toast any way you look at it, and I'm sure he's too stupid to know it. We lucked out when the judge gave you this case. We finally got a real break and hit the judicial lottery! We've represented a hundred of these court-appointed jerks over the past ten years, and what have we got to show for it—nothing! The State barely gives us enough to pay the rent. But this is an attempted *murder* case by a screwed-up Jew against a possible neo Nazi, and it's the biggest case we've ever had. If we just milk it, soft and easy, we'll all add another zero to our bottom lines next year and get the fame we so richly deserve."

"Yeah . . . I suppose you're right," Jerry sighed. "Like I said, if he doesn't care, why should we? It would be nice having a new Porsche instead of that piece of crap I have now. But it's kind of weird. This isn't what I thought practicing law was going to be when I started law school. I thought I would be truly helping people, and getting rich doing it."

Bernie eased his feet back up on his desk as he sat back in his chair. "It never is what we think it's going to be, Jerry. Believe me, I was idealistic once—lasted about six hours before I saw how the system really works. What a fool I was, but hell, that's life. Just listen to me and next year you will have a brand-new Porsche, not some ancient junker like you have now. Just listen to me and you will do fine, Jerry. And you're going to have to buy yourself a couple of AK-47s to protect the loot you are going to be making. Trust me, just trust me . . .." He looked down and checked his watch.

"Now run along, kid. I have got to finish this Beverly Jones divorce settlement. Shit, she doesn't want her two kids, but she does want child support and alimony from her stupid high school janitor husband, who actually *wants* the kids. Greed, greed, greed. I don't understand why we get all the slime balls, but I have a very good relationship with Judge Perkins and think I can get him to give it all to her. That's what I love about this business: the challenge of making the system work. So, Jerry . . . Smithers and I will meet you down at the Pastime Tavern around four for a couple cocktails, and then we'll talk more about this Diamond case."

CHAPTER NINE
WINNING IS EVERYTHING

This was the sixth night in a row that Alan had spent tossing and turning in his double bed. His legs felt like they were tied in knots and he realized the sheets had become wrapped around his ankles. He pulled his legs up to his chest and spent the next minute untying himself. By that time his mind had snapped on, and he couldn't turn it off, no matter how hard he tried. He looked over at the clock on his dresser: it was 4:35 a.m. *The bewitching hour,* he thought. Those two hours before daylight when your mind can go crazy, if you let it.

He had been dreaming and thinking about his own family all night. He wondered about the luck of the draw people have in ending up with certain parents. He had grown up in a post-World War II bungalow in Spartan, Illinois. His mother, Paula, had been a nurse—a nurturing woman who adored her kids, and her kids had adored her as well. But along with her big heart, she sometimes could disappear, especially when Alan's father was on a rampage . . . and that kept the house pretty chaotic at times. Paula had died four years ago, and Alan missed his mother tremendously, though he'd never told anyone besides her that . . . not even his boys.

His father, though, had been a horse of a different color. He was a big, burly, ruddy-faced beer salesman, with bushy, brown hair just like Alan used to have. Like many salesmen, he could be funny and lighthearted, but when he drank too much—which was usually about twice a week—the Carter world changed dramatically. And he was a mean drunk. Many nights, their mother would send the boys next door to the neighbors until he passed out in his recliner in front of the TV. Then the three boys would be allowed to sneak back into the house.

Alan's dad died from a heart attack forty years ago, at 2:25 pm on the same day, Oct. 27th, that Alan told his staff about the changes he was going to make at MLK High. *What an amazing coincidence*, thought Alan, *amazing!* The most unfortunate part was that his father's drunken episodes were what Alan remembered most about him. He knew his father had loved him, and he had often taken him camping and fishing when he was a boy. But as the years went by, the alcohol eventually stole his father away.

Alan began to wonder why he had so wanted to be the principal of a high school. At 4:30 in the morning, everything seemed gloomy, rather hopeless. He thought of his younger brother, Mike, who had followed in their father's footsteps. Mike was the vice president of Millers, a local Coors beer and soft drink distributor located on South Street, only three blocks away. Growing up, Alan and Mike had always been very close. Alan's older brother, George, had been the apple of their dad's eye. He was large, like their dad—six-feet, two-inches, 240 pounds. Big enough to play high school football as a tackle, like their father. But Mike and Alan, though both stocky, were only average in height, so they weren't exactly football material, and that had given them a common bond growing up. Mike had been the one to go into the beer business and, for almost five years now, he had been bugging Alan to come to work for him. "Twice the money, twice the perks, and half the stress," he would always say.

"Selling beer? I don't think so," had been Alan's reply. Alan had given up drinking anything, besides an occasional glass of wine, three years and twenty-seven days before, on the day he attended his second memorial service of that year for a student killed in an alcohol-related accident. This time, one of his students was killed and two were seriously hurt when their minivan rolled over a freeway embankment and plunged a hundred feet below. The sixteen-year-old driver had been at a local college fraternity-house party; she had a blood alcohol level three times the legal limit.

From then on, Alan had decided that alcohol, for some people, could be a truly evil drink, especially if alcoholism ran in their family. That said, Alan thought those who control the alcohol corporations are playing a part in destroying some people's lives and sometimes he thought they should rot in hell for what they are doing—even though one of them is his brother, whom he loves dearly. And so, once again, life was complicated. But since that fateful day three years ago, Alan had nothing more than an occasional glass of wine or beer, even though he considered himself to be one of the lucky ones, because alcohol had never had much of an effect on him. Yes, being a principal could often be very stressful and complex, but the things he witnessed happening amongst his students had, in many ways, helped him to shape his own life.

Alan rolled over onto his stomach and pulled his extra down pillow snug to his chest. It took several seconds for his mind to catch up with what his arm already had discovered: he was alone.

Well, there is a bright side to being alone, thought Alan. Now that Martha was gone and the boys off on their own, he had no one to worry about except himself. *But then again,* he thought, *there are 3,000 students I'm responsible for.* He had lost the mid-size, old-colonial-style house in the quiet neighborhood where they had raised the boys. After his divorce, Alan had bought himself a small, boxy, two-bedroom condo on the east side, five minutes from the school. But at least he had a spare bedroom for when the boys came home from college to visit, which wasn't nearly often enough.

He had often wondered what it would be like to resign from MLK, buy a yellow, pop-up Volkswagen camper-van, and drive around the country doing odd jobs. Alan missed the simplicity of the '60s and '70s. He did a three-year stint in the army, the year he spent in Iraq being the longest of his life. He spent the next five years pumping gas at Mike's Texaco while studying at UCLA. To have no responsibility, no house or car payments, nothing but free time . . . that sounded wonderful. A smile crept across his face and he started to quietly sing John Denver's "Country Roads" to himself. What a great fantasy.

But his tranquility was suddenly shattered by three short, loud beeps from the desk phone near his bed. "Oh, God," Alan muttered, "it's already starting." He reached for the phone.

"Alan, it's Ruth. I hope I didn't wake you?"

"Unfortunately, I have been awake for two hours already, but a call from you at 6:00 a.m. is not a good sign. What's up?"

"It's the newspaper people, Alan. Ben Langston from *The Sun*, and Karen Kendrick from *The Globe* were standing outside the front door of the school when I pulled up. You remember I always come in early on Thursdays to do the attendance reports for the previous week. The news is out, Alan, and this is just a little bit disconcerting. Ben is the chief sportswriter at *The Sun* and he has already asked me a hundred questions that I have not even attempted to answer. And that Karen Kendrick—oh, you have heard of her, right? She is quite sophisticated, and a tough nut for a woman. They both are sitting over in the attendance office right now waiting for you. What should I tell them?"

"Just relax and sit tight, Ruth. Tell them I'll be there in twenty minutes . . .half an hour at the most. *Twenty minutes leaves no time for breakfast, which is just as well,* he thought, patting his slightly protruding belly before rolling over to put his feet on the floor.

When Alan arrived, both journalists were waiting for him. With a handshake and a smile Alan acknowledged Ben, whom he had met briefly at a sports banquet last winter. He then introduced himself to Karen Kendrick, whom he had never met but had heard about through the local grapevine; he occasionally read her articles. He invited them both into his office and, as soon as they were seated, Alan launched into an explanation of his plan. Thirty minutes later, Ben and Karen put down their pens and notebooks, and Karen turned off her small silver recorder. They sat looking at each other in complete silence for what, to Alan, seemed an eternity.

Finally, Ben shifted his large feet on the carpet and leaned forward, resting his hands in his lap. His eyes peered out of his round, bearded face as he said, "Alan, this is off the record, and I don't know you very well, but I think what you're saying has some merit to it. Maybe more merit than most people, including myself, might want to admit. I am just an old jock, but I know there is something very wrong out there. The whole competitive sports thing has gone crazy and it's often become just about winning, money, and power. I never could put my finger on what could be done about it, but I think maybe you just did."

Ben continued, "That being said, I also think you're overly idealistic and you're going to get your butt kicked, big time. Every sportswriter, ex-jock, and wanna-be ex-jock in town—except maybe me—is going to be all over you. It will be like the Romans throwing the Christians to the lions—and as I am sure you have already guessed, you're not going to be part of the audience. Actually, some of the more conservative Christians may be the ones doing the throwing! You are going to get mauled, beaten up, and eaten alive, with whatever is left of you nailed to a goal post.

"I just don't think your plan will work, however well-intentioned it is. If you handed every student a semi-automatic rifle when they walked in the door and told them to defend themselves against other students, that would probably be less controversial to some of these parents.

"Alan, this country has gone nuts over sports, winning, money, and guns. To many people sports is their religion, their God. It's why they get out of bed every morning; they all just want to watch their favorite teams beat the crap out of the ones they despise. So to take money from hardcore sports programs and put it into social education, arts, and intramural athletics, that is not going to happen in Arcadia, California. I can almost guarantee you that."

After a brief pause, both men looked at Karen, whose green eyes were fixed on Alan's face. She sat straight in her chair with her long legs draped one over the other, dressed in an immaculate, tan, wool suit that looked like it had been designed just for her. Her flawless complexion perfectly matched her pink lipstick.

She started to open her mouth but closed it again quickly, and instead ran her fingers through her long brown hair. Karen, at forty-four, was the managing editor for *The Globe.* She had a reputation for being moderately conservative, like her newspaper, but very much her own person. Her family was the majority stockholder in a chain of conservative newspapers scattered across the state of California. About a dozen years ago, Karen had almost made it as a professional equestrian riding English jumpers, but Alan had heard she'd never quite made it over the hump. *Or jump*, he chuckled to himself. Regardless, he did not expect any allies from *The Globe.*

Picking her words with precision, Karen finally started to speak. "Mr. Carter, I, too, admire what you're trying to do here—I really do. Actually, I think you're right on target, but the world is a tough place and it's often dog-eat-dog. These kids have learned from us adults that there are winners and there are losers. It's the way the world works, no matter what we teach them in grade school.

"Have you noticed how many people detest a tie game, even when both sides have played well? Most sporting events have eliminated a tie as a possibility; forty years ago, it was the norm. Even in video games, it is kill -- or be killed. Kill as many of the other side as you can, that's the culture we're building in this country. Winning has become everything. It's scary to think about what may happen as we arm our population with all these weapons designed with one purpose in mind, and that is to kill as many people as possible. I think we may end up just like Afghanistan or Syria, and I think all these weapons could lead to the undoing of the American dream. I don't think any of this is necessarily right, good, or healthy, but it's the way it is, and I don't know how to stop it and, being a good Republican, I'm not at liberty to admit that in public.

"Now, Mr. Carter, you can try to build an artificial world here at MLK, but these kids are going to have to face the real world eventually. Like Ben said, you're going to get yourself crucified. Being a martyr does not pay well nowadays and, remember, there is no health insurance or any other positive benefits that I know of. I also doubt whether you will sleep any better at night, because you will be worrying about *where* you will be sleeping and where your next paycheck will be coming from. Why do you think so many politicians don't do anything? They are afraid they will end up getting voted out of office and since many are not the best and the brightest, they may well end up homeless and on the streets!

"So," Karen continued, "the bottom line is this: I would strongly advise you, Mr. Carter, to quit this idea right now. If you do, my newspaper won't print a thing about your statements to your students and faculty; we will pretend this all never happened. I understand the pressure you must be under with the shootings, two boys in the hospital and another in jail. There is a time for newspapers to do the right thing, and ignore some unsubstantiated local stories, and this could be one of them. So, let's not be rash. If you walk away now you may well keep your job and your outstanding reputation in the community as an educator. Let's pretend it was all a misunderstanding, and we're now setting the record straight. Right, Ben?"

"Yeah. Alan, I play dumb real easy—hell, I have been practicing at it my whole life. I can act like it was some wild rumor, blown way out of proportion. I am with you guys."

Alan listened carefully while his stomach cried out for a dose of Maalox.

Karen was still looking him straight in the eyes. Alan thought for a quick moment, then simply asked, "If I don't back off, will your paper lead the call for my crucifixion, Miss Kendrick?"

Karen stood up and a smile mysteriously appeared just above the cleft in her chin. "No, Mr. Carter, we won't lead the crucifixion. Obviously, we won't have to. However, as you may well know, crucifixions make great news stories; our readers love them, especially stories about do-gooder, liberal educators being the crucified.

"But," she continued, "if you stick to your original plan, my newspaper is going to take another tack. We're going to support your position editorially, albeit with some reservations. I will personally write the editorial for Thursday's paper. I, like Ben, more or less agree with what you have said, and I love a good fight. It sells lots of papers, and God knows we could use that. So, if you are crazy enough to stick with your plan, at least for now and unless you get fired, we're going along with you. However, we may end up changing our minds, if it gets so hot that we, too, start getting crucified.

"Off the record—you're going for broke, and I don't for a moment think you have a snowball's chance in hell of winning or even keeping your job. But that's alright with me; you're a big boy and it's your head, not mine. Like I said, controversy sells newspapers, and this is a very interesting, debatable subject that needs to be talked about. Also, my uncle owns the paper, so I doubt anyone will fire me either way."

Karen stood and moved toward the door, her smile now completely gone. "I will call you in two hours, Mr. Carter, to see if you've come to your senses. If not, let the games begin."

Alan was somewhat stunned, and more than a little disconcerted. Was this a joke, or maybe a trap? He gathered his thoughts quickly, and before she could leave he managed to quietly say, "Thank you for your concern, but you won't have to call back, Miss Kendrick. I don't think I will be changing my mind anytime soon."

Karen stood at the door, her notebook held against her flat stomach with both hands. She looked at Ben with a frown, then over at Alan, a look of pity crossing her face. "Okay," she said, "it's your life. Good day, gentleman." She turned, and both men couldn't help but watch as she walked out of the office.

Ben's big frame stood up and he shook Alan's hand. "Wow, who would have expected that *The Globe* would support you? Alan, things are certainly beginning to look very interesting." Then, with a look of hopefulness, he told Alan, "Call me with any new developments and I will treat you as fairly and impartially as I can. I can't guarantee my paper will support you, but I promise I will do my best to make sure you are treated right." Ben shook Alan's hand a second time, then turned and lumbered out the door—hoping to get on his cell phone first and beat Karen to the printing press.

Alan closed his door and sat quietly in his chair, enjoying a few minutes of solitude, but his stomach felt like a lead balloon. He didn't know what to think of the whole meeting, but he agreed with Ben: things were beginning to look very interesting, maybe even a little crazy and scary. Alan knew his life would never be the same as it had been before this interview.

CHAPTER TEN
CIRCLE THE WAGONS

Lieutenant Baker and Alan walked casually through the halls of MLK High School. Baker explained the new security precautions that the district, with the help of the police department, had put into place at all area high schools.

Alan thought the lieutenant's face resembled a detailed road map of Los Angeles that reminded him of the singer, Willy Nelson. He stood five-foot, seven, at most, with a sturdy build and a grizzly, gruff exterior that Alan guessed was more of a bluff than reality. He was dressed in civilian khaki pants, brown Dexter shoes, and a starched, white, Arrow shirt. He still had a nice patch of light-brown hair atop his balding head, which he kept slicked back, and he walked with a slight catch in his right leg. He had a very good reputation in the community as a crime solver and an honest cop.

Within the first five minutes of their meeting, Baker told Alan that he was a twenty-eight-year City Police veteran with only two more years until he retired. Then, he explained, he would start to enjoy life and live in Yachats—a quaint little town of about 1,000 people on the Central Oregon Coast, where no one was ever shot, and a person could still catch his limit of cutthroat trout every morning before breakfast, as well as a couple of thirty-pound Chinook salmon every fall.

"It is not going to help you, coddling these kids, Mr. Carter, I can guarantee that. You got a real mess here. I know you don't like fingerprinting all your students, but we've got to do it. Frisking all the kids before they come through the new gate every morning, that's gonna take time, and they aren't going to like it—especially the boys. But it will be well worth it. We have got to do it until we get all their prints, and then we will only have to do it sporadically, just to keep them in check. You can bet two months of paycheck there won't be any students walking onto these school grounds with assault rifles now."

Alan responded, "Well, Lieutenant, we had an armed security guard here at the time, and it did little good; he almost got himself killed."

"You're right, Mr. Carter. A lone security guard who is not properly trained is almost worthless; he or she doesn't have much of a chance against an intelligent armed intruder who has the advantage of surprise. That's why we are going to have a three-person SWAT team down here at the entrance, and nobody will go in or out of this school without us knowing about it." Of course, you will have to have a closed campus, and every student will need to have an ID badge that they wear around their neck when they're on school grounds."

"How long can the school district afford that?" asked Alan.

"Don't know, Mr. Carter—that's not up to me to decide. There is some federal money out there for the moment and, until that dries up, this is the only way we can attempt to guarantee that your school will remain safe. If we took the money Congress keeps talking about for building that wall along the Mexican border and instead build a concrete wall with barbed wire on top, with one way in and one way out around every school in America, that might help keep the guns out, but hell that's no way to live. Until we keep automatic weapons out of the hands of the mentally ill, we're going to have mass shootings. But off the record some people think some of our congressmen and our president are mentally ill, so how is that ever going to happen?

"Honestly, the other thing that really worries me," Baker continued, "is that we still can't discount this mysterious female who keeps threatening your school. She has called three times, but we've only been able to trace the most recent communication to a phone booth on the corner of Miller and J Streets, in front of that old 7-Eleven. None of the employees recall seeing a young woman using the phone booth. But my gut tells me she is for real."

"Great," said Alan somberly, as they stopped at a water fountain. "I initially dismissed her as a hoax, but she certainly has been persistent, calling three times and all. This school is so over-crowded that a bomb set off during school hours would be unbelievably horrific. Is there something else I should be doing?"

"We will figure it out, Mr. Carter . . . we'll catch her—that's our job. But you never know, maybe she will just disappear, that happens sometimes. You just keep teaching these kids, and keep passing on any helpful information, anything at all. Then let us decide if it's pertinent. You know, locking down this school is not going to fix the problems. It's just a Band-Aid until we get the will to address the hatred and the mental illness epidemic we've got going on in this country. In the meantime, we're going to watch this school like a hawk, 24-7, for as long as it takes, or as long as the money lasts. By the way, keep practicing those lockdown and fire drills . . . just in case," he said, bending down to take a drink from the fountain.

What if she is real and doesn't disappear or get caught? wondered Alan, as they walked the last fifty feet to the attendance office, both in deep thought. A bomb going off in his school was well beyond Alan's biggest fear. "Well," Alan remarked, "at least you are not asking me to arm my staff—that would put many of us over the top."

"No, Mr. Carter, arming the teachers would be a disaster waiting to happen. The more people running around here with guns, the more likely someone will get hurt or killed. I don't even like having my men armed to the teeth here on your campus, but for right now that's the way it's going to have to be. But the last thing we need is a bunch of armed vigilantes running around."

"One last question, Lieutenant Baker: I know you think I shouldn't coddle these kids, but Zack is still one of my students. How he is holding up in jail?"

A look of compassion washed across Baker's face as he shook his head, "I didn't mean you shouldn't care about your kids, Mr. Carter. We all care; we just show it in different ways. That kid is hurting, I can tell you that much. But at the same time, he's like a walking zombie who doesn't seem to feel a thing. And I'll tell you another piece to the puzzle," he said, rubbing his grizzled chin. "When we took him down to the station to book him, he said he needed to take a whiz. When Detective Maloney told Zach he had to be escorted, that he couldn't be left alone to use the bathroom, his eyes got bigger than a pan-size pizza, and he told us in no uncertain terms that he didn't need to go after all. When we tried to coax him to go, because he wouldn't get a chance once he was in the interrogation room, he became very agitated and told us to stick it where the sun doesn't shine and that we were a bunch of perverts. That's the only time I've seen him be assertive or show any emotion and it came out of nowhere."

Baker thought for a moment before continuing, "The more I think about it, the more I feel we may be on to something. Maybe you and I need to talk to Kyle's two friends again, because something still doesn't smell right here. Now that Kyle has been shot and Zack is in jail, those two might be a little more congenial. Let's talk in the morning to set up a time to meet with the two of them. I think it might prove more interesting than the last time."

"Good idea," replied Alan. "I have felt all along there is more going on here than anyone has been willing to admit. And maybe more information will give us a lead to this mystery woman. I will call first thing in the morning; for me it's a top priority." They shook hands and Alan headed down the hall to his next appointment, his mind whirling a mile a minute. *What a way to have to run a high school! Might as well be in Afghanistan,* he thought to himself.

Alan closed the door only part way behind Karen Lynn. He offered her a seat across from his ancient oak desk and she sat down on the edge of one of the chairs. She sat so close to the edge of her chair that Alan was afraid she would slip off and end up on the floor. Karen Lynn was the star center on the girls' basketball team; she had led them to a third-place finish in the state tournament last year. She was lean and six-foot, four, black as coal, a sharp, intense gal with integrity dripping out of her pores, and one of Alan's favorite students.

Karen Lynn took a deep breath and started with, "Mr. Carter, I hate to bother you, because I know you're really busy after the shooting and all that. I guess most of the students are still scared, or they're still in shock. But after your speech, all the kids are talking like we're going to have a whole new school. Everyone is either excited or pissed off, I guess, depending upon whether they're in the haves or the have-nots. Last night, some of the boys on the basketball team were even talking about spray painting your house. But Mick Epstein, the team captain, talked them out of it. He said you are a fair guy and would make everything okay."

Alan listened quietly, and Karen Lynn continued, "But Mr. Carter, I am worried! I have seventeen colleges all over the country looking at me this season, deciding whether to offer me scholarships to play basketball for them next season. If we don't have a team this year, I could lose out big time. Life as I know it would be over! My parents would kill me first, and then my dad would kill you. He is already saying people ought to tar and feather you, whatever that means. Basketball is my life; it's my identity. I am not like the rich girls on the team who have all those clothes and their own car. I depend on this for my future. There's no way for me to go to a four-year college without some kind of scholarship money.

"So anyway, Mr. Carter, I thought I'd ask you directly." Karen Lynn sat back on her chair, her hands clasped tight together. "What is going on? Are we going to lose the team?"

Alan ran his fingers through the thin patch of hair left on top of his head. His soft, wide smile—once his trademark—briefly made an appearance, but he just as quickly swallowed it.

"Karen Lynn, you aren't going to lose your team. I promise. Now, you won't have four coaches this year—just your head coach and one assistant. And you won't have all the perks, like going to Las Vegas for a pre-season game, but you will have a good competitive team. At the same time, all the other kids who want to play less-competitive intramural basketball at lunch or after school will have the opportunity to do so. The idea is to get more kids involved. Karen Lynn, you're going to play, but you may not feel quite so special because more attention will be placed on intramural sports where everybody does, and can, participate. Some of the money from the athletic department will be spread into other programs as well, but you'll have your team, your uniforms, a very good coach, and transportation to your away games. Plus, you've got four seniors coming back and your fans love you girls. I think you will have a very good team this year."

Karen Lynn sat quietly, digesting what he had said. She replied, "That sounds fair to me, Mr. Carter; I'm okay as long as I get to play. My dad won't like this, because he already thinks I'll be a pro, but that's his problem. This might even take some of the pressure off me. Maybe now people won't expect so much of me all the time. The pressure gets intense in high school. It was more fun in middle school when we all played because we truly enjoyed the sport. Sometimes the night before a game, I can't sleep, and my stomach gets upset from all the pressure to perform perfectly and then win. Yesterday, a couple of the girls on the team said they wanted to transfer to another school because of your new policies, but I guess it's too late in the year to transfer, so we're okay."

"Listen, you can't take the games so seriously," responded Alan earnestly. "I know how important this is to you, but remember the old cliché: it's not whether you win or lose, it's how you play the game that counts, and you should be having fun, that's what matters."

"Yeah, right, that sounds good, Mr. Carter, but that's not reality, at least not nowadays. My dad only cares about winning and the same with a lot of other folks. I know my dad loves me, but he is so intense, I can hardly stand it. When we lose, we pay the price.

"But the good news is that some of my girlfriends who aren't on the basketball team are already talking about playing intramural basketball. Actually, it sounds like fun. It would be nice to just play ball without all the pressure. You know, it will be good for my friend, Michele—she is not real coordinated, but she needs to do something constructive with herself, "cause all she does for exercise now is hang out with the boys, if you know what I mean."

"I hope we can help to change that," Alan replied, feeling slightly embarrassed.

"Thanks, Mr. Carter, now I can sleep tonight," said Karen Lynn, as she jumped up and momentarily towered over Alan. She gave him a large grin that spread from dimple to dimple, and without another word she was gone like a bolt of lightning, out the door and down the hall to spread the word: "Right from the horse's mouth," as she would tell all her friends.

Lack of self-value, thought Alan after Karen left. *It's what makes the world go around, or not go around. All these kids just like us adults fighting to prove they're okay, and it's still survival of the fittest. Some folks give up and shut down, others create constant dramas, and some need to over-achieve to prove that they're good enough. We're all a part of the game and it's so simple, yet so hard to change.*

Alan got up from his chair and grabbed his tan windbreaker from the hook on the door. "Thank God for the Karen Lynn's of the school world," he said out loud. "If she only knew the power she had inside her, she wouldn't need basketball for her only identity." Yet he wondered, *Would the world be willing to accept a six-foot, four, black girl as anything but a basketball player or maybe some type of supermodel?*

Alan felt in his jacket pocket for his Tums and took three of them out of the round paper wrapping. I guess this is lunch, he groaned inwardly. Tonight was the emergency school board meeting that had been called in his honor, and he could not miss it because of an upset stomach.

CHAPTER ELEVEN
THE GOOD, THE BAD, AND THE MAFIA

Zack walked down a long, dim, quiet hallway with his wrists handcuffed together. The guard opened the steel door at the very end and motioned Zack into a twenty-five by forty-foot room with white-washed walls, completely devoid of pictures or any type of paraphernalia. Only a large, older, color TV sitting on a pedestal in a corner brought any life to the room.

Five young men were sprawled around on a couch and three chairs in the room. Two beefy, older boys sat in another corner on straight chairs playing some type of board game; Zack couldn't see which game over the broad shoulders of one of the boys.

"Hey, man—look who's here!" cackled a tall white boy from the couch. "It's the geek man of the hour. Ya know, boy, they're already calling you geek man. Geek man, geek man, that's your new name. We've been watching you on the tube and waiting for you to show up, so we can have some fun getting to know you."

The guard—a thin, older, gray-haired man—undid the lock on the chain and removed the cuffs from Zack's wrists. "This is your social time, son. You got two hours in here to socialize with these boys—your peers. You can watch TV or play a board game. You have an emergency, or those boys get too rough, you hit that red buzzer up there on the wall." He pointed to the right of the television, then looked at the other boys with a frown. "I'll be back for you at 3:30," he said as he closed the door and walked back down the hall.

Zack looked down at the floor as he walked over to the only empty seat, which was in the middle of a worn and uncomfortable-looking brown couch. On one side sat the tall white boy and on the other a friendly-looking black kid with a slight build, a shaved head, and a small goatee.

"Hey. I am Monte," he said, tilting his head toward Zack for an instant, before turning back to some game show Zack did not recognize that they had been watching on TV.

"My name is Bad Ass," said the tall boy on his left who had cackled at him a moment ago. "I'll bet you can guess where I got my name. You got any dope on ya, geek man? Any kind will do, even some pills. I can't be too fussy right now . . . I just gotta have a hit real bad."

"Sorry. I don't have anything," Zack replied, looking up at the red buzzer next to the TV.

"Look man, you're a celebrity—we all saw you on TV over the last couple of nights—so you must get some special privileges. How about a hit? Hell, I can get you most anything you want, including a piece of ass—though in here it'll have to be a dude's ass, 'cause the chicks are in another cell block across the street. Now empty out your pockets, geek man! Let's see what you got! Better yet, drop your drawers and we'll go through your pants ourselves."

Zack felt totally numb as he looked up at the tall boy with his head shaved who had a broken set of teeth outlining the grin across his face. Zack figured he must be insane.

"I said I don't have anything!" Zack almost yelled.

"Calm down, geek man! Not so loud!" Bad Ass looked around the room. "Now wake up—off with the pants or we will do it for you, right boys?" None of the other boys said a word or even looked over.

"I am not taking off my pants and I don't have any drugs," Zack replied in desperation. "I don't even know what you're talking about. I have never had the opportunity to even try a drug, except my mom's pain meds. I've never had a friend to help me get anything else, so I just do alcohol and the OxyContin I steal from my mom. I couldn't sneak that in here, so I have been sicker than a dog. So, cackling man, just leave me alone." Zack looked at the floor and mumbled, "I don't want any trouble."

"Don't want no trouble but you called me *cackling man*? Look, little brother, you already got more trouble than you can even dream about. You might as well get used to being a slave, 'cause that's what you're going to be when you get to the real joint. You ain't big enough to defend yourself, or smart enough to figure out how to work the system. So, child, just start doing what we tell you and life will be easier."

Zack looked back up at the emergency button but then looked straight at Bad Ass and said, "Fuck you. My head hurts and I am tired of being bullied. I got a knife back in my cell and I'll cut off your dick and stick it in your mouth where it belongs. You forgot, man, that I shot people a lot badder than you."

Monte turned his attention back on Zack. "Woo-wee, man! Now you're talking jive! You keep talking like that, boy, and you just might stay alive and still be a virgin at the end of the day. You get yourself a box cutter and learn how to use it and you'll do just fine."

"Where do I get a box cutter?" asked Zack, leaning over and whispering in Monte's ear.

"Oh, man, they're easy if you got cash. I was in Farrell's School for Boys last year and I bought one for twenty bucks," Monte replied loudly. "You just stick the money up your butt before you get there, but don't forget to wrap it in cellophane first or it will only be worth half as much. Shitty money is fifty cents on the dollar."

Everyone chuckled around the room; even Bad Ass snorted, and the two chess players, acting like they weren't paying attention, laughed for a brief second.

But Bad Ass immediately got up and sauntered over behind Zack, grabbing the back of his shirt collar. "Listen, geek man, you ain't got no knife, box cutter, or gun right now, and I need a hit, or I am going to die. I am tired of fooling around, ante-up or I am gonna bite your balls off," he whispered in Zack's ear as he twisted the collar tighter. "You've seen my teeth close up, boy. They could cut those tiny gonads off you in one snap. Come on, boy! Ante up or you are dog food."

Zack started to panic, and his heart felt like it was going to explode. He couldn't breathe, and his asthma started to kick in. Bad Ass's breath was so bad it made him want to throw up. He knew he wasn't strong enough to fight him off, or to break away and hit the red buzzer.

"Leave him alone!" a low, deep voice barked from across the room.

There was a moment of silence while the three boys stared over at the dark-skinned, husky, bearded, older boy with the slicked-back, dark hair. He was playing chess with a ponytailed blond-haired boy, who was otherwise almost a near duplicate. Neither chess player seemed to be paying the slightest attention to Zack -- or the altercation with Bad Ass -- and kept their eyes on the game.

"I was just kidding," said Bad Ass hurriedly, "just putting the geek man on—no harm intended," he said to the room in general as he let go of Zack's shirt, set the collar straight, and threw himself back down on the couch. "No harm, no foul," he repeated twice, before closing his eyes and seeming to fall instantly asleep.

For several minutes, the TV blared, and nobody said another word. They all stared at the television. Zack just sat there shaking, his eyes closed.

"Mafia sons," whispered Monte, as he leaned toward Zack's ear. "No one screws with them boys, no one. They got a funny code of honor, but I guarantee he who fucks with them ends up dead, or hurt very bad, and real fast. They wouldn't let a slime ball like Bad Ass shine their shoes with his tongue. They got the guards bribed, I am sure. Just ignore everybody here and don't say a word. Just watch TV. This rerun of *The Jefferson's* ain't half bad! Don't say nothing and you may make it through the rest of the day in one piece and maybe still be a virgin."

"Yeah, thanks," said Zack, moving ever so slightly toward Monte. He pretended to watch TV while glancing over at the chess players through the corner of his left eye. He could feel himself start to shake so badly that he thought he would break into little pieces and find himself scattered across the floor. He felt a panic attack coming on and told himself to stay calm and breathe deeply. *What the hell kind of place is this?* he thought to himself. *This must be a lunatic asylum! Maybe I have already died, and this is hell.*

Three hours later, Zack was back in his cell sitting on his bunk, wondering what kind of hell he had got himself into. Life in prison was going to be very long and hard, and the reality of it all finally started to sink in. There was nowhere to hide; every day for the rest of his life would be like this. He wasn't an Internet hero, he was just a punching bag for a bunch of crazy people. *Hell, that is all I've ever been good for anyway. Everyone thinks I am just a worthless sack of horseshit and I guess they're right.* But this was going to be worse than before, maybe much worse. His stomach felt so terrible he wanted to vomit, but he could only dry heave twice. Maybe if he told them about his withdrawal they could give him something to help, but then he would have to tell them about stealing from his mom—and then he would just be in more trouble.

Zack felt tears come to his eyes and he quickly wiped them away with his sleeve, but more followed closely behind. He grabbed his knees and started to rock back and forth. A numbing pain spread across his chest and he kept asking himself, *What the hell have I gotten myself into?*

Was there any way out except suicide? If that was the only way out, how would he do it? Hang himself, but he was way too short. The questions kept repeating in his mind as he rocked back and forth and thought about what a screwed-up life he had. How could he get off this planet, while he was locked in jail?

CHAPTER TWELVE
STATING YOUR BELIEFS

Since the school board's conference room was not nearly big enough, Bob Lancaster suggested the proceedings be moved down the street to the old Hollingswood gym, where the wooden bleachers could seat nearly 500 people. The rest of the board agreed.

As the meeting commenced, every seat was filled, with dozens of people standing in the outside hallway and in the aisles separating the four seating sections on the main gymnasium floor. The proceedings were running forty-five minutes behind schedule and the crowd was growing restless.

Alan sat in the first row, where several folding chairs had been saved for him and "anyone foolish or brave enough to want to be associated with him," as he had heard someone mutter. Anne flanked Alan on the right side and Jed and Brad sat on the left. The four of them looked up in awe from the main floor to see the old wooden bleachers overflowing with more attendees than any of them had ever seen at a school board meeting.

Alan felt embarrassed for causing all the uproar, but he also felt surprisingly calm—the calmest he had felt in several days. He had talked to the parents of all three boys earlier that day. Talking with Zack's mother had been toughest. She was a single mother and her son was the center of her life. Now she felt her life was over. The devastating conversations had reinforced Alan's decision.: he wasn't going to back down. It almost seemed a luxury to feel like he had been boxed in a corner and no longer had any other choice but to take action.

"You made the headlines on the front page of both papers today," quipped Anne with a tight smile. "Cute picture in *The Globe*, the photographer even caught your right dimple."

"That Karen gal, the editor—she must like you," added Jed, "because that was some editorial. It's going to back the school board into a bit of a corner. But this is probably the best thing that could have happened for our position. I mean, it's one of the most conservative papers in the State, yet they're coming out in support of many of our positions. You should have been a politician, Alan."

"I don't think so . . ." was all Alan could modestly mutter, but he noticed and appreciated how Jed and Anne kept saying *our* position. It made him feel much less alone.

"I would like to bring this special school board meeting to order," announced board president, Bob Lancaster. Bob stood on an elevated platform with the five other board members along with the schoolboard stenographer sitting behind him. Alan had met Chris Rodmaker, the newest board member, several times over the last year. Chris was an accountant for Payne Wilkins and he had approached Alan after Alan's previous proposal to the board. Chris had always seemed interested in Alan's proposals and they'd had some good talks, but those talks hadn't really gone anywhere.

Besides Chris, Bob Lancaster was the only other member Alan really knew. Bob was a local builder and had been on the board for eight years. Alan basically liked Bob and felt he meant well, even though he figured they might as well be on opposite sides of the planet, politically speaking, that is. Bob had always been courteous and seemed interested in what Alan had to say, though as with Chris, nothing ever seemed to come of their conversations regarding Alan's proposals. But this time Alan had not made proposals. He had gone around the board and changed much of his school's curriculum without waiting around for permission. It was unlikely that Bob Lancaster or the rest of the board would be so congenial this time.

"Could I please have everyone's attention?" Bob repeated, as he stood behind the makeshift, wooden podium.

"This emergency meeting has been called to discuss and make decisions regarding changes Mr. Carter has made, without school board authorization, to the MLK High School curriculum. I hope everyone was handed a copy of those changes as they walked through the door. The board has decided it would be in everyone's best interest to first hear public input before we take any direct action."

Bob glanced at his notes before continuing. "We will allow a limited amount of input from interested parents and teachers. We have had 111 requests to speak, but due to time constraints we must limit these requests. So, we put all the requests in a hat and randomly chose out twelve names. It's not the State Lottery, but it's the best we can do considering the circumstances."

"First, we thought it would be fair—and hopefully enlightening—to give Mr. Carter thirty minutes to explain his actions to the board, parents, and teachers. We're running late so, without further ado, let's get going . . . Mr. Carter?"

Alan rose from his seat, walked behind the podium, and looked out at the audience with a welcoming smile and the hope he could allay their concerns -- and even inspire their support. Taking in a deep breath, he sent his quick, silent prayer to an unnamed God of the Universe, asking for guidance and perseverance.

"I want to begin by thanking the school board for this opportunity to speak to all of you here tonight. I realize I have put the board in a bit of a tenuous position by my decisions at Martin Luther King High School in the last week, so I appreciate this time to more fully explain how and why I decided to take these actions now and not delay any longer.

"As you know, the last several weeks have been terrible for our district - the shooting at our school followed the gang shooting and wounding of three students at Truman High one week earlier, the killing of a math teacher at Grant High two weeks before that, and the incident at Kennedy High when acid was thrown in a cheerleader's face by a girl who was cut from the team the week before.

"This is a horrific series of events. Unfortunately, it seems to be getting more common across our nation. These tragedies reinforced the questions I've been asking myself – and perhaps you are asking yourselves, as well:

- "Were there changes the school leadership could have made that would have helped avert these violent acts?
- "What could have been different about the school experience that Zack had, that Kyle and Josh had,

that the other students had, that might have kept everyone safe?

- "Going forward, what more can we do to try to prevent troubled students from taking actions that harm *everyone*, including themselves?
- "And, thinking *beyond* the goal of preventing harm to how to optimize their learning and wellbeing, is our continuing to do things the way we've been doing helping our youth make the best use of their time with us, or of their many talents and abilities?
- "What do we want our students to feel – and say -- at the end of each day here – and when they look back on their time in high school?"

He paused briefly, noticing some in the audience nodding their heads and others looking down.

Alan continued, "Declaring a state of emergency, as you did for this shooting, and the other incidents, was definitely necessary and called for. California Statute 8611, Section H, of the State Charter for Public Schools states that when the local school board or the State School Superintendent designate a state of emergency, it is then the *duty* of any principal in a public school to take whatever legal action is necessary to ensure the safety and wellbeing of his or her students in time of crisis.

"So, to sum up why I am making changes, I am legally compelled by this state of emergency, as declared by the board, to institute changes to the Martin Luther King High culture and curriculum, as prescribed by State law, to protect the safety and wellbeing of the students in my charge – and in your charge. And I also feel compelled personally to do something to avoid future tragedies.

"Are the changes I'm making guaranteed to succeed? I think and hope so, but of course I don't know. I'm very aware that the actions I have taken might not be the same as some of you might have taken.

"I do know there is no simple, quick-fix solution. If there was, we wouldn't be meeting right now.

"Now I hope you have a better understanding of the intent for these changes. Additionally, I want to provide a more complete description of the reality I see that prompted me to take the actions I have.

"Martin Luther King High is a very large school with a population that is bigger and more diverse than many small towns. We educate – or at least try to educate -- 3,426 students, spanning five different races, at least eight different religions, and eleven varied nationalities. The school is like a microcosm of our country at large—a melting pot, if you will—which includes a continuum of 'have's' and the 'have not's,' both socially and economically. Another way to describe this is that, as in our country and the world, we have students who are seen and treated in some situations as 'somebodies' – with respect, status, privilege, and in other situations, as 'nobodies,' as *not* worthy of respect, dignity, understanding, consideration, being listened to, being included.

"The 'haves' tend to do well or at least okay. The 'have not's generally may have a harder time feeling safe, respected and successful.

"I want to acknowledge that there are a lot of things we do well here. Many students – maybe the sons and daughters of those parents present tonight -- have a good experience the way things are, though I don't know if any student consistently has a great experience, even those who are among the have's, the somebodies, and at the top of the social hierarchy. They still have lives that aren't always full of wellbeing. Though they may be a 'somebody' at school, they may bring the experience of being treated as a 'nobody' at home, yelled at, not listened to or respected.

"Being seen and treated without dignity and respect is stressful for *all* human beings, no matter how young or old they are. Their ability to learn, to feel safe and to make healthy connections with others is impaired.

"I'll be very blunt: The staff, when talking among themselves, often calls this whole scenario 'the pecking order' or 'the food chain.' We occasionally laugh when we talk about this, but in reality, it's a very serious matter—one that can turn deadly, as we have seen on more than one occasion. In turn, this issue allows few of our students to escape high school psychologically unscathed. I wrote a paper on the subject last year called *The Pecking Order,* and I have copies available for anyone who is interested.

"I am going to be bold enough to say that I believe the vast majority of us adults here tonight carry what I call 'life-altering baggage' from our school days—especially high school—as this is a very formative, important time of life for most people.

"We don't have enough time to go deeply into the social order and the numerous cliques. But they range from what I refer to as the 'socially astute' – the 'somebodies' -- on the top of the order, to the 'socially inept,' – the 'nobodies' -- these being the kids at the bottom who are struggling to make it both personally - and academically - as well. Kids -- or adults -- who feel like they are at the bottom may feel loneliness, rage, hopelessness, numbness, or even suicidal despair. Their self-esteem and self-respect are damaged, sometimes for life. Without sufficient guidance and support, they may lash out with violence, as we have seen.

"Being on top often is no picnic either. It can be very stressful and can bring about anxiety attacks, depression, or a false sense of superiority. One of our star athletes spoke with me the other day about the pressure to do well and how that has reduced the fun of playing sports and increased the daily anxiety they experience. Sometimes these students have not learned how to have empathy or compassion for others who may not have the material or social resources that their families have—"

Suddenly, a large man with a red baseball cap stood up in the third row.

"Hey, let's cut the social crap and get to the meat and potatoes!" he yelled. "We want to know what's going to happen to the football and basketball teams. That's the only reason most of us, or at least most of the men, came here tonight! We don't care about all this other feel-good stuff."

"And we're missing Thursday night football for this!" another male voice shouted from several rows back. "Let's get with the program!" Several other angry voices, both male and female, shouted from around the room in support of the interlopers.

"Well, that's not why this meeting was called," interjected Bob Lancaster, quickly standing while grabbing a second microphone from the lower stand. "And if everyone can please calm down and come to order . . .."

A hush fell over the crowd as Alan stood back, allowing Bob to speak. "This is a fact-finding meeting to deal with Mr. Carter's proposal to change the curriculum at Martin Luther King High School, nothing else. It's not about football or any particular sports issue. I firmly request that any more questions be tabled until the time allotted for Q and A at the end of this meeting. Please continue, Alan," he reaffirmed and then sat back down.

Several men and one woman got up and walked out from different parts of the room, but the room quickly quieted and Alan, glad for the support, continued.

"Thank you, Mr. Lancaster. I will try to make this very complex issue as brief as possible. To assure we have time for questions, I'll highlight a few facts about the reality of our students that I considered when I made the changes, and you can get more information from the written text of my speech.

- Many students have poor communication skills and their self-esteem is seldom what we would like it to be.
- About twenty-five percent of our students have what are often referred to as disorders, like bipolar disorder, autism spectrum disorder, attention-deficit disorder, that present an enormous challenge to their everyday social and academic lifestyle.
- Additionally, it seems like an epidemic of mental illness is striking students of all ages and genders, with the teenage suicide rate on the rise by twenty-six percent in recent years.
- We believe that at least 20% have high ACEs scores. ACEs stands for "adverse childhood experiences," which can result in trauma, difficulty in controlling their emotions – think of PTSD -- and other mental, emotional and learning difficulties. Adverse childhood experiences include having a parent with drug problems, mental illness, or in prison, having witnessed or experienced domestic violence, and having been abused or neglected, physically, emotionally, mentally or sexually. Students with these experiences may come to school traumatized, definitely *not* ready or able to learn, and easily triggered to be disruptive and to lash out. Suspending or expelling them does not help them succeed or get the help they sorely need. And it doesn't teach them or the rest of the students how to maturely and compassionately deal with problems, be accountable, make amends and repair connections to others.
- The environment in which we all live presents its own daunting challenges: the media is full of violence, social media is a constant distraction, and our country has the most

available semi-automatic weapons tenfold, the highest student-shooting rates, the highest teen-suicide rates, and the highest teen obesity rates.

- Yet the safety net of social services in and out of school, especially counseling amenities, has been cut drastically and there are fewer places that these kids can go for help in our more complex world. This becomes a real problem when we have students in crisis. *All* of our kids need our support, and don't need our indifference or condemnation.

"So how do these kids learn the communication skills needed to get along with one another, have empathy for others different than themselves, deal with their own self-esteem issues and personal demons, while facing a world that often feels out of control with no rudder?

"These skills are challenging to develop for both youth and adults. I have wanted to try and change this, but thus far we educators simply have not had the resources or the permission to do much in the way of social-emotional education. In fact, we have gone in the opposite direction, as the importance of test scores and grades has become the predominant focus of schools, instead of the ultimate success of the student both academically and personally.

"We know structure is important for youth. For some parents the answer to implementing structure has become sports. But let me tell you, folks, for many kids, sports does not work the way we would like it to work. First of all, let me be very clear: I think sports can be great for the right kids. I enjoy many sports and I consider myself a sports fan; I even coached my own kids in soccer for six years. But by the time high school rolls around, only about twenty percent of students participate in sports on a regular basis. So what about the other eighty percent? Yes, some get involved with band or other activities, but many do very little—or absolutely nothing—and these are often the students who need extracurricular activities the most.

"Ironically, the average teenager is ten pounds heavier today than just twenty years ago, from consuming processed, fast food diets along with a lack of exercise or becoming 'couch jocks,' as the kids like to call it. My point here is that cutting out gym and intramural programs in favor of putting more of our school budget into competitive sports for a privileged few, has only exacerbated the problem.

"And the type of pressure we're putting on these young athletes to win is also taking its toll. High anxiety is becoming an epidemic. Some are training like professional athletes at ten years old. Sports are supposed to be about staying fit, having fun, learning to work together, while building self-esteem. But now, for many, sports is primarily about winning at all costs and status, and the emotional cost can be just as high for the parent or coach as for the student. A win-at-all-costs attitude can create stress, anxiety, and increase drug and alcohol addiction—and for the ones who don't succeed or don't participate, it actually can reduce self-esteem instead of *building* self-esteem. In school nowadays, the attention given to the youth participating in more competitive sports often separates them apart from the rest of the student body—especially from those at the bottom of the pecking order. I don't believe this is healthy for anyone.

"So, what is the answer? That's the billion-dollar question.

"Though there is no easy, fast solution, I think we can do a lot more with what we currently have and that is what we're planning to do at MLK.

"What about the money?" a woman's shrill voice from the third row bellowed. "Are you going to raise our taxes to pay for your new and enlightened curriculum?"

"No, we're not," answered Alan. "But what I *can* do here at Martin Luther King High School is to take the power that the legislature has given me and use it to protect our kids and help them learn not only academic information, but also gain the ability to respect and connect with each other through improved listening and honest speaking, and to increase their respect for and connection with themselves.

"So, what specifically are the changes we've made and want to make to help students experience more ability to learn, more positive relationships, and more self-value? You can refer to the handout you received when you entered. I'll touch briefly on those changes now, as well.

"1. Intramural sports – Competitive athletes will continue to play their sports and compete on the level that they desire, with the coaching support that they need. Some of the time of the seven varsity coaches will be redirected to work in intramural sports with the less-competitive athletes so more students can learn how to work and play together, get some much-needed exercise and have fun, without stressing about how good at sports they are. This means that more students will benefit from the myriad talents of our coaching staff *and* that more than twice as many kids will be participating in sports, and there will be less social distinction between the highly competitive athletes and those who are less interested in physical competition.

"2. More support - We will now have twice as many counselors. This way, when a student is in trouble, he will have a place to go . . . someone available who she can talk to. With more counselors, each will have more time to spend with each student, as well as more overall availability. This, in turn, will allow all students to receive better vocational guidance as well as more life skills. Every counselor will be trained in spotting mental health issues, and alcohol, drug, or depression problems, which have become an epidemic in some of our schools. We obviously don't have the skills or the staff to treat all these kids on campus, but I promise you we'll develop the most comprehensive referral base that we possibly can.

"3. Service - We also want to put more emphasis on our students' service to the community, to each other, as well as to the elderly, and the less fortunate. We would like to see our students admired for being good people and good friends, for working hard, and for showing integrity and ingenuity, as well as being excellent students or athletes, if they so choose.

"4. Unique value - We want to bring out the creativity and motivation to learn in every student, whether he or she aspires to be an athlete, a bus driver, or a mechanic. Whether he or she is technologically gifted, plays chess, plays the tuba, or is an artist, or an actor. Whether he or she is interested in becoming a farmer, or a doctor, a historian, or a stay-at-home parent. Because what could be more important than learning how to become a good mother or father?" Alan continued, his voice rising slightly. "It doesn't matter what they're doing so much as whether it feels intriguing and satisfying to them. Whether or not a child is an honor student or a super athlete should have little to do with how they are treated and his or her self-worth or value to society – or to their classmates or themselves. And if a student isn't aware of talents or interests at this point in their young life, let's encourage them to find whatever it is that works for them right now, because everyone does have their own unique talents.

"We are researching assessment tools that students can take to help them gain more awareness of themselves and potential directions for them to think about investigating.

"5. Connecting - Fifth, and maybe most importantly, we are going to teach these young people to honestly speak and listen to each other. There is no way -- other than genuine connection -- to help them value each other as human beings no matter their social status, racial background, athletic ability, appearance, gender, sexual orientation, or emotional state. We will provide opportunities for them to practice these skills -- which most of us could improve as well -- in safe environments and get to know each other more. We would like them to learn to have respect, tolerance, and even admiration for the differences we all have. That is why we are implementing our self-respect program and our jigsaw program. Our jigsaw program is where students work as small teams to solve problems together. By working closely together with other students who have varied backgrounds, they can break down some of the social barriers that often separate them.

"6. Less focus on tests - Finally, we will not be taking the usual six weeks out of the year to practice for standardized testing. We believe that reducing stress in their learning environment will help students learn better and thereby do better on the tests. We will certainly abide by the laws requiring the tests and aim to fulfill the intent of the tests, which is to ensure everyone is learning. They might improve their scores if there's not such a big to-do or focus on these standardized exams and how well they're supposed to do on them. This said, if they don't end up doing well because of this change, then I am the only one to be held responsible.

"You can be assured that we will be closely monitoring the results of these changes and making ongoing adjustments as needed.

"Down the line, with school board approval, we'd like to institute restorative practices that will help students be accountable when they have behaved inappropriately. *Restorative* practices – rather than *punitive* practices. Suspending or expelling students when they are disruptive or do something that harms another is punitive and doesn't teach any positive life skills or create the connection and support we all need. Those who are suspended or expelled feel even more excluded and disconnected and get farther behind in their work. Restorative practices enable the person causing the harm to hear the bad impacts others experienced and to find out what he or she can do to make it right and be accountable.

"We also want to be trained in what are called "trauma-informed practices," which simply refers to how to avoid retriggering the distraught person and instead help them feel safe and able to calm down. Yelling at a student for not having his homework done is unlikely to have any positive effect, especially if they are traumatized because they saw their dad beat their mom the night before or were kicked out of the house for leaving their coat on the floor or didn't have light because the electricity bill wasn't paid. Instead of saying with anger and impatience, 'what's wrong with you?!', we want to shift toward asking with concern, 'what's happening for you?' When students are experiencing stress or distress that is interfering with their ability to learn and to relate to others, we will make it easier for them to seek help and get the compassionate support we all want when we're troubled.

"I truly believe the only way we are going to change things is through education, but we must do this through role modeling as well as lecturing, walking our talk, valuing all students and helping them value themselves as well as each other, which in turn will assist them to be in the state of mind which promotes their taking in the academic information.

"So, if we truly want all our children to prosper psychologically as well as financially in this ever-changing world, then I believe this is the direction we must take. But let me be very clear: our academic standards will *not* be lowered. In fact, I believe our students' progress will rise, as they become more involved in choosing their own area of interests and their enthusiasm for school increases.

"That's it in a nutshell, folks; it's fairly simple on the surface, though obviously it's much more complex in the details. We have put our plan into a thirty-six-page document that we have given the school board, and it will be ready for public viewing after we work out the final details.

"I believe that's all I have for right now. I thank you all for your patience, and you know where to reach me with questions and suggestions."

The auditorium was silent. One could have heard a pin drop for the first few moments. Then sound erupted in many different locations as most everyone began to voice their varying reactions.

Alan was physically and emotionally exhausted after two more hours of questions from the audience and the school board following his speech. He knew he needed to go home as quickly as he could.

He walked out the back door with Lieutenant Baker at his side, as Jed and Brad ran interference to clear a path for him through the crowd. Most people just stared but a few had something complimentary to say. He received a couple not-so-friendly remarks and looks as well.

"Just thought I'd show up here tonight and check things out," said Baker, as they walked toward Alan's car. "Thought you might even need a little police protection leaving the building, plus I stationed a couple of my men around in some key locations. You sure got folks stirred up in there. I like what you had to say, though. You actually made sense out of something that I never could make sense out of. You did good, Alan . . . I'm impressed."

But be aware he continued, "We're going to have to start keeping a closer eye on you, though, because some people didn't like what you said in there, and there could be some trouble. You may be seeing more of us in the near future."

"Great. That's all we need," said Alan, as he opened his car door and stepped inside. "Guys, thank you very much, all of you. It means a lot to me that I have your support."

Alan drove home, rubbing his eyes at every stoplight, trying to stay awake. *What have I gotten myself into?* he asked himself. *And where will it all end, or will it ever end? Is this the end of my career? Life looks quite different now at 11:30 p.m. compared to how it looked at 11:30 a.m. Of course*, he laughed, *the whole week hadn't looked so good, no matter what time it was.*

He came to the last stoplight, just two blocks from his condo. The flashing lights from a black-and-white squad car seemed like a blur at the 7-Eleven parking lot on the far-right corner. An older, gray Honda Civic with an array of scratches covering it from top to bottom was being searched. As Alan slowly cruised by, he could see an officer giving a breathalyzer to a young man who he recognized as one of his sophomore students.

Alan shook his head as he sped away and thought, *You know, it never really ends.* That boy could have been any one of hundreds of students who had gone through his school since he had become principal. And this boy was exhibiting the same behavior as thousands of other kids who had gone before, and that tens of thousands were showing at that very moment across the country. The whole picture started to come together, and, for a moment, Alan felt that boys of this age had probably been behaving this way since the beginning of time, and the only things that had changed were the faces and habits and customs. Every day, he decided, is just a new page of the same story and all we can do is try to make every step forward just a little bit better than the one before. He shook his head, knowing he desperately needed some sleep.

PART TWO:

REVELATION AND RECONCILIATION

Whatever course you decide upon,
there is always someone to tell you that you are wrong.

There are always difficulties arising.

To map out a course of action
and follow it to an end
requires courage.

-Ralph Waldo Emerson

CHAPTER THIRTEEN
FAMILIES

As if in slow motion, Kyle's mother sat down and leaned back in a padded hospital chair, adjacent to her son's bed. It took Kate several turns and squirms to make her large body comfortable. Against the brightly colored chair, her brown sweatshirt, gray polyester slacks, and the smoking-induced wrinkles on her face made her look much older than her actual 36 years.

She figured she was good for maybe two hours before she would have to get up and go outside for a smoke. But alcohol was a bigger problem—she had not gone a day without a drink in almost twenty years. Her husband, Don, carried his flask with him wherever he went, but he didn't often share. The first several days of Kyle's stay in the hospital had been an exception, but she did not expect him to show up today. She had already found the Laredo Inn, a bar just a block down the street, but a double scotch was seven bucks; almost the price of a whole bottle at Costco. She hoped they would let her take Kyle home soon.

Though her chair was lower than his bed, Kate had a clear view of Kyle and all the strange plastic hoses sticking out of him. Her once-strapping, muscular boy now looked so small and frail. She wondered how much weight he had lost in the days he had been in the hospital. Was he only half as big?

Kyle was her only child, and she had adored him since the first moment she held him in her arms. It had been an easy birth—only half an hour of labor—and he had been an easy child to raise. He had never been in trouble; her husband, Don, had made sure of that. Don had never let up on Kyle, and he had kept him too busy to get into trouble.

Sometimes, though, Kate thought Don was too rough on the boy, the way he slapped him and poked him with that fireplace poker when he lost his temper. Or when he got too drunk . . . which usually started about dinnertime every evening nowadays. No, Kate did not like any of these behaviors and, in fact, they scared her—but then again, this had kept Kyle in line, made him tough, and he had never talked back. She also knew, deep down, that if Don wasn't beating on Kyle, then he would be beating on her. And Kyle was younger and a boy, so he could take it better, at least until now.

But now Kyle might never walk again. That was sad for Kyle, but Kate thought about what the minister on TV had said—that everything happens for a reason. *I can take care of him and this way he will never get into trouble,* thought Kate. *In the grand scheme of things, this is okay. This will give meaning to my life and Kyle will be safe.*

That morning at breakfast Kate thought, *Hell, I am almost forty years old; I am five-four and 210 pounds, with a bottom the size of a couch. Don has long since lost interest in me. But with Kyle's injury, at least I'll have something meaningful to do now besides work part-time at Walmart.* She had served a traditional breakfast of hotcakes, sausage, hash browns, and eggs, even though neither Don nor Kyle were there to partake. Eating helped make her feel not so alone. She had prepared breakfast this way almost every morning for the last eighteen years, at Don's insistence. He said a big breakfast would help Kyle grow big and strong and it was the one meal they all shared together. After that it was usually fast food for the rest of the day, with plenty of beer and scotch in between.

Before the shooting, Kyle had been Don's son, always hunting, working on cars, or playing football. She often did not see him all day long, and for only an hour or so in the evening. He had planned to go into the Marines the following year after graduation, just like his father had tried to do after his two years of college.

Many people who didn't know them well thought Don was a good father. They didn't know that Don believed that he was not Kyle's real father. He thought that Chester McBride, their insurance agent, had fathered Kyle during his brief affair with Kate—because this was happening about the time Kyle was conceived. Kate didn't know which man was Kyle's father, though Kyle was a lot like Don (especially his temper, so she figured Kyle was his). She remembered doing both of them one Sunday—Chester in his office that late afternoon after the church picnic, and then Don later that night before they fell asleep.

Kate had always liked boys, at least since she was thirteen. Boys paid attention to her, even though she had never been what people called "pretty." If a boy would tell her nice things, she would crawl in the back seat with him and do most anything he wanted. Both her mother and father had always been too drunk to pay attention to what Kate or her three sisters did.

But looking back, she realized how lucky she had been with her pregnancy. After Kyle was born, her doctor told her that she had an extremely tipped uterus and that she was very lucky to have gotten pregnant at all. She had never even known what a condom was back then, yet she hadn't stopped to wonder why she had not become pregnant sooner. Kate realized that if it wasn't for her tipped uterus she might have had a half-dozen kids before she was twenty-five.

She figured that her affair with Chester was where a lot of the rage came from when Don drank. He, too, had come from a home with alcoholic parents, and once in a fit of rage and drunkenness he confessed that an uncle on his father's side had sexually abused him. But the bottom line was that Don had never trusted Kate. She had been one of the town sluts when they met; she did not deny that. She hated high school; it was boring, and she never fit in because she didn't have the right clothes, was already overweight, wasn't cute enough, nor was she considered particularly smart. Though oddly enough, she had really enjoyed math class, at least until her father poured beer all over her report card when she showed him her "A" in arithmetic. She and Don were in most of the same classes in school, and they were both addicted to sex and beer and wanted to get out of their homes . . . so that seemed like a good enough reason to get married. And so, Kate dropped out of school at age sixteen.

But staying faithful didn't work well for Kate back then; she didn't last six months after the nuptials. Don had beaten her up badly after he caught her with Chester in the Shady Grove Motel on the outskirts of Wilsonville. She assumed that one of the county cops, and an old friend of Don's, had spotted her and Chester when he drove past them just before they turned into the motel. He must have called Don. After Don kicked down the door, he beat up Kate and broke her right arm and wrist. Chester was tall and slightly built, not a fighter but surprisingly agile. He had jumped out the back window, clothes in hand, as soon as he heard Don hammering on the door.

Don started beating her regularly after that, even when they found out that she was pregnant. Her face often looked like a prizefighter's after a bad night in the ring. The only saving grace had been a social worker who lived next door in their trailer park. She had Don arrested once a week for about six months. Finally, he got so tired of going to jail every weekend and missing Saturday and Sunday football that he stopped beating her up. She always figured if it wasn't for her neighbor, she and Kyle would both be dead, and Don would probably be in prison for the rest of his life.

Don began taking his anger out on Kyle after he was born. Their relationship was always the love-hate variety. They were often inseparable but, underneath their comradeship, Kate could taste the rage they each had toward one another. Don was never sure, even though they looked similar, if Kyle was his son. But now, because he was crippled, he would be her son, too, and not all Don's. Now they would have to share him because Don would not want to look after a cripple. She remembered when Don shot their pit bull, Avenger, after it broke its leg while fighting with a neighbor's dog. Don didn't want to pay for a vet to set the leg. But maybe Kyle's injury would finally give them all something in common, a real purpose in life and as a family.

Kate's favorite television preacher had said that there was a purpose behind everything. He also said he would pray for his congregation and all those tuning in at home to ensure everything in their life turned out okay. All the audience had to do was just keep sending in those checks to keep his show, *Love of Abundance*, on the air. Kate herself was no good at praying, as she usually forgot—so instead she sent in every dime they could spare and some they couldn't. She figured this might buy her some extra credit with God, and she knew Kyle's injury happened for a reason. It was going to be good for their whole family, and the problem with the scars that the doctor talked about, would be okay, too. If she could just get a drink, everything would be okay.

Kyle sensed his mother's presence, but he couldn't move or see her. He could smell her perfume, the one that smelled like apple vinegar. He just wanted to be alone, but he couldn't open his mouth to tell her to leave. He had heard the doctor—the same one who told his mother and father he would never walk again—ask them about the deep, permanent scars he found on Kyle's butt. He said they looked like they had been done with a hot fire iron of some type, via multiple incidents over a number of years. He was required by law to report his finding to the police, he explained. Neither his mother nor father had replied, at least that he had heard.

Kyle's eyes were still on the fly glued to the ceiling light directly above him. It had not moved at all as long as he had been awake. The fly sat there motionless, just like him. Would he ever walk again, play football, go hunting, or dirt bike riding? Or would he be like the fly?

Kyle's thoughts went back to his father. He guessed maybe his dad loved him, whatever love is. Heck, his father had been good enough to take him hunting up in the San Gabriel Mountains, about fifty miles east of where they lived. His father was an avid gun collector, and he had shown him how to shoot and skin out a mule deer to provide fresh meat for the table. They often went hunting out of season, of course, so they didn't have a license. His father used a semi-automatic M1Garand rifle, which was illegal for deer hunting, but his father said that just made it more exciting and screw the government.

So . . . was *that* love? Kyle was sure he knew all about hate, and he knew he hated his dad. He hated his dad for lots of reasons but mostly for getting drunk and poking him with that hot poker from the barbeque. It hurt so bad and he screamed so loud he thought he would die. Both times, his useless mother had stood by crying while watching in silent horror. He sometimes hated her as much as his dad because she was so putridly passive.

The first time this happened was back in Oklahoma, when he was about five or six. Kyle couldn't remember all the details of how it happened. He just remembered his mother had put ice on the wound for hours afterwards, and cream and bandages for a week after that. The second time it happened after they moved to California, into the crummy little suburban house where they still lived. He was about eleven or twelve years old. His dad was drinking more bourbon than usual and trying to barbeque hamburgers. Kyle had been playing freeze-tag with a boy his age who lived next store. He had been chasing him across the lawn when he got too close to the barbeque and accidentally knocked over the tray with the raw hamburgers on it. His dad went ballistic! He grabbed Kyle by the arm, threw him on the ground, and held him there with his foot, just like he was a calf getting branded. Then he grabbed the red-hot poker from the coals. Kyle had been too late in figuring out what was going on and he hadn't been able to get away. Kyle had refused to scream as his father pressed harder and harder, until the poker burned right through his jeans to his skin beneath.

Kyle hid in the garage all night after that. He could still remember the pain. Two days later the wound became badly infected, and yellow pus began running down his leg. His mother would not let him go to school. Finally, she took him to a fat, old, gray-bearded man who smelled like smoke and beer. The man lived in a little, old, brown house not far from them. Kyle remembered asking if the man was a doctor and his mom told him to shut up and not say a word; she could not stop crying the whole time. The old man cleaned the wound with alcohol, then put some heavy ointment on the burn that made it hurt like hell. Then he put a large piece of gauze over the burn and gave his mother some huge white pills for Kyle to take five times daily. After that, the pus dried up, the wound healed, and Kyle went back to school. But Kyle never forgot, nor did he ever forgive. *Someday,* he thought, *when I am older, I'm gonna kill my father.*

The world was a tough place all right, and the little faggots like Zack running around made it even worse. It always made him feel kind of good about himself to beat up on one of those little dope heads. It released some of the pressure and anger that always seemed to build up in his head. Shit, his dad beat him up and so he just passed it on, just like in that do-good movie, *Pass It On.*

Roger Speiglman had been a child psychologist for fourteen years, and he'd worked with countless kids who had so-called "disorders." He had to use that term when dealing with his colleagues in the medical profession, but he didn't like it because it meant little, except to cause the recipients to think there was something wrong with them because they had different characteristics than the person making the assessment. In reality, Roger believed these "disorders" were just traits that many people share to some degree or another. It's when these traits spike in a specific direction that they then morph into out-of-control problems. For that reason, to his patients, Roger often referred to their disorders—such as ADD or autism—as their *gifts*, not their malady, an approach many others in his field didn't share.

He was considered an expert in his field and possessed all the right credentials. He had been a great student—as many excessively compulsive people are—so Roger knew all about so-called "disorders" because he had several himself. He had learned we all have one or more—they just aren't something most people like to talk about; it isn't politically correct. And so, over time, Roger realized that many of his patients were just like him and his other doctor friends. Doctors often are obsessive-compulsive, the complete opposite of people with ADD or ADHD. In some cases, the doctors he knew had a lower level of autism called Asperger's syndrome mixed into the equation, which usually put that person on the far end of compulsivity. These were usually the doctors who had the most difficulty in relating to their patients. And as their characteristics become more extreme, they become more of a problem to both themselves and their patients.

During graduate school, Roger had participated in a two-year study that showed if you had a bell graph with hyperactivity at one end and obsessive compulsivity at the other, everyone fell somewhere along that curve. And the more you fell toward one end or the other, the more pronounced effect it had on your life, with ADHD on one end and OCD on the other. The effects of this could be staggering and could certainly make life more challenging, but also interesting! Roger believed that where a person's brain chemistry ended up along the bell curve was maybe the most important characteristic in a person's life. And he believed this was passed down by genetics and the "luck of the draw," as far as what genes an individual had inherited from their ancestry. Add in a case of bipolar disorder or alcoholism to the mix, and this made life all too interesting sometimes!

Deep down, most of us think there is something wrong with us, he decided some years ago. Many of his patients became his patients because they registered as more extreme on the bell curve—in one direction or the other—and for one reason or another had finally broken down from the pressures of trying to fit a square peg into a round hole. There were answers and hope for his patients, but there first had to be recognition of the problem, as well as a willingness to find balance through a practice of awareness, and medications, when necessary.

After reviewing Zack Diamond's file, Roger felt empathy for him. He remembered his own adolescent secrets being very left brain, that he also had been a "nerd" who didn't fit in. And he, too, had been an outsider in high school. He never could get the hang of dressing like the cool kids, and usually his outdated clothes hung awkwardly on his tall, heavy body. He recalled what it was like his freshman and sophomore year at his new high school. His parents had moved his family from Baltimore to Los Angeles when he was fifteen. It was tough enough being a nerd, but an East Coast nerd made school even more difficult. Not knowing a soul and sitting all by himself at lunch for the first two school years was very hard. The humiliation and pain of that experience was still with Roger, just underneath the surface. Just thinking about it made him feel nauseous all over again.

These days, life was much safer. He was a PhD—a doctor—and doctors commanded respect. He liked what he was doing and, surprisingly, he really liked most of his patients. He had a solid marriage to a good wife, though she, too, had her challenges with ADHD and a borderline case of bipolar disorder. They both had to learn to live with her excitability and her need to paint the inside of their house a different color every nine months. Daily meditation, a healthy diet, the occasional right medication, and focusing on what she loved had helped her to slow down, and she had become a very successful dance and yoga instructor.

But Roger was compassionate toward his wife, because she had to live with much of his compulsiveness as well. For instance, Roger often could not sleep at night, wondering if he had locked all the doors and windows, and then worried whether the neighbors had locked *their* doors and windows. Depression could also sneak in if he had too much time on his hands, which did not happen often anymore. They had both learned it was all about accepting each other's differences.

Roger had been asked by the court to do an extensive evaluation on Zack, and they spent four hours on two different occasions together. He had been rather surprised by Zack, he had to admit. The first three hours, Zack had stonewalled him, which was not at all unusual. He had done his typical one-line answers "zombie" routine, sharing little. But for the final hour, when Roger had pressed him about his father, Zack finally lost his composure and started screaming to be left alone. Then Zack started sobbing uncontrollably on the concrete floor of his cell in a fetal position, and this went on for almost half an hour. He was still crying when Roger left. He hadn't expected Zack to break so easily. This meant there was hope that Zack could still feel, because where there are feelings there is hope, Roger wrote in his summary of Zack's condition.

This perspective gave Roger another angle to pursue with the judge at Zack's upcoming hearing. His job was to psychologically evaluate Zack, and he had done that. But he was also supposed to give an opinion as to whether Zack should be tried as an adult, and Roger did not think Zack should be tried as an adult. He just hoped the judge would be the open-minded type instead of a strict, by-the-book jurist. The judge at Zack's hearing was a black woman with whom Roger was familiar. He hoped she would be more compassionate and understanding toward Zack the underdog and his very interesting predicament.

Zack lay on the damp, rumpled sheets of his bunk. He had been crying and shaking in fits since the night before, and it was now 11:30 the next morning. He'd had these shaking and crying fits since the day that doctor—*that asshole doctor!*—would not leave him alone. He kept hammering at him about his father and how Zack felt about him . . . until all of a sudden it was like a light bulb went on, and Zack remembered.

He had been in his room on his bed, listening to his father and mother arguing, like they often did. Usually, his mom did most of the yelling while his father listened passively. But this time he heard his dad tell his mom to calm down, that he could not deal with her anger anymore. This was followed by a loud crack that sounded like one of his mother's slaps. Then it got very quiet and he heard his mother go out the back door. For several minutes there was absolute silence, then Zack could hear the sound of drawers opening and closing in his parents' bedroom. A few minutes later, his father came into his room with a large army surplus duffle bag in one hand, and a worn, brown suitcase in the other. Tears rolled down his father's red swollen cheeks as he set his bags down on the floor. Zack noticed his left cheek had a paper-thin cut below the eye. Zack's father was not a big man but, when he grabbed Zack, he wrapped his arms around him and squeezed so hard it had hurt his chest.

"It's going to be okay," he told Zack. "I have to go away for a while, but we will be together again, I promise." Zack thought his father was going to break down and cry but instead he grabbed his bags and was gone out the front door without another word. Zack felt stunned and helplessly alone, and that feeling had never gone away.

One day, many months after his father left, he had been looking for a piece of scrap paper in the kitchen trash and found an envelope addressed to him from his father. His mother had thrown it away without showing it to him. After several days he summoned the nerve to ask his mother about the letter, but she just screamed at him to shut up, and Zack had never asked again. About a year later, out of the blue, she blurted out that his father had become a wino on the streets of LA, and that he was a worthless bum. Zack tried for several days to ask her for news about him, but she would never talk about him again, *never*. She said all men were worthless. Her own father had left when she was only three years old. Men always left.

Zack's mom always said he was lucky to have her there to take care of him, and when he was younger he'd guessed she was right—she was the only adult in his life. He had no brothers or cousins to compare himself to, just an uncle on his mother's side whom he rarely saw. And since his mother never dated, that ruled out any other adult males from entering his life. As far as school was concerned, most of the nicer boys had ignored him and the ones who were not so nice used him for their punching bag, or in Kyle's case, a pissing post.

Several male teachers over the years had tried to be friendly toward him. His third-grade teacher tried to get him to join the Cub Scouts, and another encouraged him to join the chess club when he entered the eighth grade. Both times Zack had wanted to respond, but he was deathly afraid that his mother would give him an outright, emotional "*no*" if he dared asked. He'd read in the paper about Boy Scout leaders, just like the priests who abused young, innocent boys, and his mother had confirmed what he read. "Why else would a grown man be nice to a poor Jewish boy like yourself?" she would say. She made it sound horrible what these men did to these boys—even more disgusting than normal sex. He'd get sick to his stomach when she talked about it, and would run outside to throw up, which made his headaches much worse. He believed what his mom said: that even if he met an adult man who wasn't a pedophile, he would soon tire of Zack and leave, just like his father had done when he left the both of them.

His only attempt at joining anything since that time had been Beginning Band, four weeks ago, and that was only an excuse to get his hands on a cello case. He needed to bring it to school to hide the gun.

Zack propped his pillow sideways, laid his head back down, curled into a fetal position, and wrapped himself tight in his blanket. But he continued to shake, his headache intensified, and he felt like he was going to throw up.

CHAPTER FOURTEEN
REACTIONS

On Friday night, MLK hosted the first girls' home basketball game of the season. As State football playoffs stretched into late fall, the games associated with the two sports now overlapped. The game would be played in the school's second gym, built primarily for the girls' basketball and volleyball teams. It was just two years old, cost four million dollars, and could seat 600 adults. Funding for the gym came from a levy the school district had passed five years prior, which raised 120 million dollars to build new athletic facilities throughout the district.

Alan had mixed feelings about the gym. It was certainly nice for the girls to have their own facility, and it was a beauty. Borrowing money by using bonds for capital improvements had seemed easy enough—but at the same time, the district had increased class sizes by fifteen percent and made cuts to the arts, drama, and counseling departments due to a lack of operating funds. Against Alan's adamant protests, they had also done away with gym classes some years back, to save athletic funding for competitive team sports. None of this made much sense to Alan, but at the time he felt he had no choice but to go along with their decisions.

By the middle of the second quarter of the girls' home game, the gym was almost full except for a few empty holes near the top of the visitor's side. The girls were playing against Truman High, their arch rival, and the two teams were tied at twenty-five points each, according to the new digitized Pepsi scoreboard. The crowd was noisy, and Alan wished he had thought to bring his earplugs.

He usually walked through the crowds on the home side, while Brad Smith surveyed the crowds on the opponent's side. The idea was to keep their presence known to discourage any problems before they started. For this game, and since the shootings, two uniformed police officers kept a low-profile watching the parking lot and walking behind the bleachers, where they could be called upon if needed.

Alan's Tums did not seem to be working that night; his stomach had felt uneasy and slightly off-balance all day. He thought about splurging on a Pepsi—maybe the carbonation might help—but he remembered he was boycotting them. He still felt riled up about the local Pepsi distributor's highhandedness when they donated $100,000 for the new gym, in return for exclusive rights to sell their products in the school. The school board had allowed them to put their vending machines all around the campus, despite Alan's disapproval. *Standing up for what you believe in has its downsides*, thought Alan, *especially when you need a quick fix of sugar and caffeine.*

Karen Lynn saw Alan from the floor during a timeout and gave him a big smile and wave. That was always enough to make Alan feel a little better and helped him remember why he loved his job as principal.

"Hello, Alan," called out Tom Kelly, a local electrician. As they shook hands, Tom put his left hand on Alan's shoulder and said, "Keep up the good work. I liked what you had to say the other night. It made some sense, and not much does these days. And it looks like Bryan is going to graduate! I can hardly believe it." Alan couldn't help but grin—Tom's son, Bryan, had gotten himself into quite a few minor scrapes over the years. So much so that Tom and Alan had spent enough time together to become more than just acquaintances, while helping Bryan to walk the straight and narrow at the same time.

Alan said goodbye, thanking Tom for his support, and then moved on down the front aisle. On his way he said hello to Sandra Champ and Marge Fisher, as they walked back from the refreshment stand with popcorn and sodas in their hands. Sandra was married to Stan Champ, the president and largest stockholder of America's Best, a mortgage company with offices scattered across Southern

California. Marge's husband, Les, was a stockbroker with Dean Whittaker—also wealthy, but not in Stan's league. Both were parents to senior basketball girls who had hoped to transfer to other schools after Alan's cuts to the athletic teams, but to their chagrin, it was too late in the year to change schools and still play basketball.

Like many large California schools, MLK had some of the wealthiest parents and some of the poorest. That was one of the things Alan loved about sports: kids from both socio-economic extremes were out there playing together on the same team and becoming friends, at least as long as the parents left them alone.

Marge said a crisp hello to Alan, with a hint of a smile, but did not slow down while moving past him into the crowd. Sandra's brown eyes did not even waver from some distant object and her mouth remained glued tight as she followed close behind Marge.

Alan began humming to himself, "You can't please everyone, so you got to please yourself . . . " as he moved on past the two women. But then he heard Sandra's angry voice right behind him.

"Mr. Carter!" she said sternly, trying to whisper but too angry to control the volume. "I wasn't going to embarrass either of us, but I have to get this off my chest. I must tell you in a very blunt way: you're just another chicken-livered liberal, just like that peanut farmer, President Carter! You don't seem to understand that you are just an employee of the school district and you don't make the rules. You aren't going to get away with cutting money from the athletic teams. My husband already has his lawyers working on a private suit, and if my daughter loses out on a financial scholarship because of your stupid decision to cut our basketball program, we're going to hold you and any teachers who follow you personally liable. My husband says if we go to court we can attack your retirement funds and get some of our hard-earned tax money back, from at least some of you so-called 'public employees.' Remember, we have both the money and the power to bury you, and you'll end up penniless after you're fired, Mr. Carter, so think about what you're doing." After a final glare, she turned and walked off without looking back.

A few of the fans in the front row overheard Sandra's anger, and they looked a little confused and embarrassed by her outburst. But the game was at a crucial moment and everyone's attention quickly returned to the floor. Alan used the increase in action to move back into the crowd.

Wow, Alan thought as he kept walking, *where did that come from? I feel like I just got blindsided by a runaway bus. Sandra always has seemed intense, but at least sometimes friendly, until now. She must be boiling mad inside and right now it's all directed toward me.*

He decided he would duck into the boy's bathroom at the north end of the gym, rationalizing that he was checking for smokers. He wanted a moment to regroup—and he had forgotten his medication again, as he often did when he got too busy. Now that he was past age fifty, forgetting his medication meant more frequent and unwanted trips to the bathroom.

As he stood against the urinal, he thought about what Zack Diamond must have felt, alone and accosted in a similar bathroom by three bullies with no way out. It had been a total nightmare, he was sure, and the thought gave him some reassurance that he was doing the right thing.

"Carter, you're a horse's ass. Who in the hell do you think you are?" a harsh voice growled. Alan's right shoulder was shoved hard and he fell against the urinal. Urine ran down his pant leg and on to his shoes. By the time he could get zippered up and turned around, the assailant was gone out the door. One middle-aged man and two teenage boys stood nervously looking around, not sure what had just happened.

Alan went into a stall and dried himself off the best he could with paper towels. From the sound of the deep voice, Alan guessed his assailant had been a man in his thirties or forties, definitely not a teenager. There was no point going after him, as Alan didn't know what he looked like. Even if he found him, he'd say he had just bumped into Alan by accident. Walking out the bathroom door with the front side of his pants soaked was not very dignified for a high school principal, but heck—he didn't see many other options. *So much for my moment of regrouping*, Alan thought as he walked back to the gymnasium.

When Alan opened the door and stepped back inside, the gym was in a deathly silence. The players on the floor were standing still, looking at the announcers' table on the far side of the court. A voice that sounded like Lieutenant Baker came over the PA system, asking everyone to stand up and calmly walk, single file, out of the gymnasium doors to the parking lot.

"It's another bomb threat," whispered Brad, out of breath from running across the gym floor to meet Alan. "This one bypassed us and went right into police headquarters, about ten minutes ago. It was a female, and she said a bomb would be detonated in one hour in the girls' gymnasium."

"Wonderful. Was that all she said?" asked Alan.

"Yes, that was it," replied Brad.

"Well, come on! Let's get everyone out of here!" Alan exclaimed, trotting toward the visitors' bleachers.

She hung up the phone and took a deep breath. She glanced at her watch; the call had taken less than seven seconds. She made sure the hood of her black parka covered her hair and obscured her face; only her dark-black eyes under her heavy-brown eyebrows were visible. She passed her fingers over the scars on her left cheekbone, a habit she had developed a long time before.

She opened the phone booth door and looked around in all directions, then started walking quickly toward home. *No sense taking a chance*, she thought, in case they did get a trace on the number. She had called the general number at the police station instead of the school so they wouldn't be prepared to trace the call. If only she could use a cell phone, calling would be so much simpler, but too dangerous and too easy to trace back to the owner or her location.

Home, she thought, as she walked down the caverns between the large dilapidated office buildings. *I haven't had a home since I was fifteen.* Home was a word, not a place to her. It was a word for other people—normal people—but not for her. Revenge was her home, she guessed, and killing dozens or maybe hundreds of white, American, spoiled brats would give her the right, as a martyr, to live for eternity in a perfect afterlife home. Revenge was her mantra, and the pain that hung in her heart drove the hate, which was the energy that kept her going.

Ramona touched her scars again with her fingertips as she walked. Her cheekbones felt lopsided, distorted, and wet with tears. She reminded herself there would be no more crazy men in her life ever and if that meant never seeing her mother again, so be it. She figured she didn't have long to live on this planet anyway. . .

That bastard had raped and beaten her while her mother lay passed out from booze in her bedroom. She was only fourteen and had hung out late that night with some of the neighborhood boys. When she got in at midnight her mother's boyfriend—all six-foot, two of him—was extremely drunk and had lost it, lost it bad. He told her no boy would want her again after he was through with her, and she guessed he was right. They had lost their health insurance again when the politicians cut her mom's low-income supplement, and her mom had been afraid to take her to the emergency room the next day when she sobered up. Maybe she was lucky; maybe they had done her a favor. Her face had kept men away from her ever since, all except young Zack.

Becoming a Muslim was a saving grace for a lot of reasons. Keeping her face covered when she wanted could be especially helpful in that people didn't think much of it. Also watching other Muslims attack America had helped her gain courage. America, she believed, was a land of bigots, and the current President had proven that. All the Muslims she knew personally were against jihad as a way of solving grievances, but thanks to the Internet and newspapers, she knew there were others out there just like her. She saw it all the time in the papers she pulled out of the dumpsters and on her only luxury, an older HP laptop . . . and thank Allah for free Internet.

Ramona had attended the Temple of Prophets for a while, but the Imam kept preaching about brotherhood among all the races and religions. He said that is what being a Muslim is all about, but she did not believe it. She held so much hatred, especially against whites, and also against both Jews and Christians. Therefore, she stopped attending services and paid the piper, losing the last of her Muslim friends. She now had no one, no one at all.

Blowing up a school in America wasn't as good as blowing one up in Israel, she decided, but it was much more personal, especially after what had happened to her in school in the United States. She had come to America with her mother to live with her sister after her father had been killed in Gaza by Israeli security forces during one of the many uprisings. How strange the workings of the world, that she was working with a Jewish boy now. But he had been kind, the only time she could remember a boy ever showing her respect, and they both figured they could get their revenge and die together as martyrs in the process.

Zack had become her only friend. He had been good to her and he had loved her, even though he was just fourteen. She met him four years ago when she still lived in the Old Mill neighborhood with her mother, and Zack lived just a block away on Sullivan Street. Zack's mother had hired Ramona as a babysitter, not knowing she was a Muslim girl; his mother assumed she was Latino, like most of the other neighborhood teenagers. Of course, Zack thought he was much too old for a babysitter, but his mother treated him like a baby . . . or a retard. The first couple of times that Ramona was there, Zack totally ignored her, and she just hung out watching TV.

She babysat a third time, and Zack raised the courage to ask her what had happened to her face. After she told him in very angry, explicit terms what her mother's boyfriend had done, Zack and Ramona found a new bond. Zack was a victim, too, but with Ramona he became her knight in shining armor. He swore that he would never let anyone hurt her again, though she knew he would be as defenseless in protecting her as she had been. She swore the same for him in return. They shared secrets and shared kisses, and she had him touch her in places that gave her much pleasure—it almost felt like a sacred pleasure born out of innocence. He would not let her return the favor, though, and she knew he thought his penis was too small and inadequate. She felt bad for him, but he would not relent, nor even talk about it.

But that all changed after he was molested by Kyle Ritter. Then Zack became darker. After that, all he could think about was revenge. They had been working on the bomb for several months, but after the bathroom incident Zack started focusing on Kyle Ritter—shooting him—and their progress on the bomb slowed down.

Ramona's body quivered, but it wasn't from the cold. She thought again that she would like to get away, get on a bus and go to Oregon, but she owed it to her family in Palestine—and to Zack—to stay and do her duty. Besides, she wanted one more chance to get even with those MLK bitches. She should have never enrolled in school there—she should have known better than to choose such an uptown school. They had thrown her out twice for fighting, but the vice principals always let her come back and try again. She thought of the way the prettier girls had bullied and ostracized her because of her poor English and because she wore a hijab over her head. The strength of hate welled up inside her head as her mind became more frantic.

She slowed down as she turned into her alley. She felt safer now and couldn't help but stop at the large green dumpster behind the House of Pancakes. The dumpster was like her supermarket—she never knew what she might find on a warm Friday evening.

"We have got to stop meeting like this," said Alan to Lieutenant Baker, as they ushered the last of the crowd out of the gym's side double doors.

"It does seem like it's becoming a habit," replied Baker, closing one door and pushing the steel rod into the hole in the concrete.

Alan locked the other side and took a moment to watch more than a dozen bomb-control officers and their dogs scatter around the gym. With his hands on his hips and a tired frown on his face, he said, "It's going to be a very long night."

"Yes, it sure is," was Baker's only reply. He shook his head and briefly put his hand on Alan's shoulder, then turned and walked toward the center of the gym where several of his men were in conference with Brad.

By the time they locked the doors of the gym for the night, it was 3:36 a.m. No trace of any bomb of any kind had been found.

On Monday morning, a small group gathered in the school conference room next to the attendance office. Alan, Lieutenant Baker, and Brad Smith sat facing and Jeffery, the two boys accused of helping Kyle accost Zack. Both boys had been asked pointblank by Baker what they had done to Zack in the bathroom three weeks before the shooting.

"I don't have anything else to say," said Jeff with a scowl, tapping his fingers on the table in front of him. Jeff was a solidly built boy at sixteen, six-foot and 210 pounds, with a crew cut on top of his large head. He was left guard on the football team and a shot-putter on the track team in the spring. He looked straight ahead, then crossed his arms round his huge chest and continued, "I don't know what you guys are talking about; I don't know a thing about Zack Diamond being attacked. Like I said before, I was at a lunch meeting with the coach and some other football players. I am exercising my Second and Fifth Amendment rights and that's all I have to say."

"This is not a court of law, Jeff," said Alan. "You can't plead the Fifth, but you can choose to lie, or to tell the truth, or to say nothing at all."

Alan, Brad, and Baker all looked over at Dustin. "How about you, Dustin? You must realize how serious this situation is," said Alan. "You boys are right in the middle of an attempted murder charge. There is a friend of yours in the hospital who may never walk again, and another boy who could be in jail for a long time on the account of what happened in that bathroom. You two boys seem to be the only ones who know the truth. Do you have anything you want to say?"

Dustin sat with his lean body hunched over in distress, his hands between his knees, staring at the floor. Now he raised his head and looked over at Jeff, his thin, pale face contorted as if in great pain. Jeff started to open his mouth as if to say something to Dustin, then grimaced and shrugged his shoulders. Dustin turned his head and stared off into space for several seconds, before looking back at the three adults. His eyes gave a quick look back at Jeff, and then he opened his mouth and started to speak.

"Yes sir, Mr. Carter, I have something to say. We lied. We did mess with Zack and, well, I guess we did hold him down and pee on him. It was Kyle's idea; he was in charge, he is always in charge. We were all tweaked out—we had been doing pills and whiskey for over an hour that morning. We skipped math and then it was fifth period. We had been hanging out in the bathroom for almost half an hour when Zack walked in. He tried to walk out as soon he saw us, but Kyle grabbed him by the collar before he got to the door and stopped him. Kyle said that the little kike—that's what he called him, anyway—was watching us pee and that he was a homo. He said we needed to teach him a lesson. Before anyone could say a word, Kyle just picked up Zack and threw him to the floor, then unzipped his pants and started peeing on him, as he held him down with his foot. He just lay on the floor and cried when Kyle told us to pee on him, too. I knew it was wrong when we did it, but I guess I was afraid of Kyle, so we all did it. Kyle kept ranting on about how we needed to keep this deformed Jew in his place. He sounded like the drunk Nazis we learned about in our history class. Then he told us to see if we could hit Zack's open mouth with our pee and make him drink it. It was a terrible thing to do, I purposely missed. I am really sorry—I think about it every day, lots of times each day, and I still have nightmares about it."

"Then what happened?" asked Baker.

"That's when Juan Pacheco and one of his gang members walked in . . . I don't know the other guy's name. Pacheco figured out what was going on right away. He looked at us like we were crazy and then called us a bunch of stupid monsters. He told us to help Zack up and apologize, then he told us to get out. Jeff and I just wanted to get out of there anyway. We knew how bad Juan is and we didn't want to mess with him. At that point I was beginning to wake up and realize what we had done was wrong, but Kyle wouldn't back down. He said no low-life Mexican was going to tell him what to do. Well, they got in a really bad fight—or I guess you could call it a massacre. Juan was so quick and, man, was he pissed . . . he became like a wild man! Kyle got his butt kicked real bad. I'm sorry—I can't remember all the details, it happened so fast. The whole thing didn't last more than thirty seconds, and Kyle was a bloody mess, just lying there on the floor crying, or I guess 'whimpering' would be a better word. Juan didn't do or say anything to us, like we were nothing to him. He just looked at us like we were less than human, like dog shit.

"Then Juan and his friend started trying to clean Zack up with paper towels. He was still crying and was curled up in a ball on the floor. They helped him up and took him to a sink and both of them took off their T-shirts, wet them in the sink, and started to clean him up. They kept telling him everything was going to be okay. Juan then turned around and told us to get out of the bathroom and to take Kyle with us. We picked Kyle up off the tile by his arms and helped him down the stairs to one of the other johns on the second floor. We tried to help him the best we could, but he was in bad pain. It was during class time and we were supposed to be at afternoon football practice. He was still bleeding pretty bad and all we had was toilet paper to try and stop the blood. I finally ended up taking off my undershirt and held it against his eye until it stopped bleeding. He was pretty much out of it and could barely talk.

"Then we went downstairs, before class ended, hoping no one would see us. We took him to practice but he was still a mess and kind of groggy, like he had a concussion; we had to almost carry him part of the way. His nose was already the size of an orange, and he had a big gash above his left eye, and a lump above his ear from hitting his head against the sink.

"We got to the gym unseen, at least by any teachers. Coach Cassidy was walking out of his office door to the field as we came up. He saw us and came over and we told him that Kyle had got in a fight with some Mexican and had lost, that was all we said. We didn't tell him about Zack or give him Juan's name and he didn't ask. He told us to go get our uniforms on and that he and the trainer, Woody, would take care of Kyle.

"The next day we heard Kyle and Coach Cassidy telling everyone that he got hurt in a fight off-campus after football practice, and we all backed him up when anyone asked. We figured if Coach Cassidy said it was okay, then it was okay.

"When you called us in we just outright lied to you, but man, we didn't know all this was going to happen. I am really sorry—sorry for everything!" Dustin began to sob, his head between his hands. "This is so bad, just bad all around. It's screwed up my whole life! I can't even sleep at night. I feel like a completely worthless asshole. Kyle, poor Kyle—and Zack, who can blame him for what he did? God, how I just wish he would of shot me, too."

There was a long silence as Alan, Baker, and Brad glanced at each other. Then Brad leaned forward in his chair, "Dustin, where did you get the pills and the whisky while in school?"

"We brought the whisky in our backpacks and got the pills here at school, I don't know who from. You can get them from almost anybody nowadays. OxyContin is easy to get—kids just steal them from their parents. They give you a buzz at first, but if you take too many or mix them with whiskey you can get kind of crazy.

"But I just want to say—well, Kyle is an angry guy, or was . . . but he really isn't that mean. He has got a crazy old man who beats him. He wouldn't have gone that far without the whisky and pills. He just goes crazy when he drinks," Dustin continued, pleading Kyle's case.

"Well, we have got quite a situation here, Mr. Carter," sighed Lieutenant Baker, as he sat on the edge of a straight-backed wooden chair. The three men remained in the school conference room after Jeff and Dustin were sent back to class. "I don't know if this evidence will help Zack Diamond much, but depending on the judge, it might help him get a lighter sentence. It's also bound to get some sympathy from a jury, that is if he gets tried as an adult. Hell, it gives me a lot more empathy for the kid. I see a lot of bad stuff go on in my business, but this was nasty, very nasty. There is something about humiliating a person that can destroy their soul, and it sounds like this is what happened to Kyle at some point, and he is just passing it forward.

"Anyway, I will file a report and give this information to Zack's lawyer and Dr. Speiglman. But you know," he continued, "it sounds to me like you've got a very popular football coach who lied to you to protect one of his boys. Hell, I guess they do it all the time. As I am sure you know, Mr. Carter, high school sports has become all about winning and winning at any cost; it's often very tough to be any kind of a coach nowadays. But now we have unforeseen complications. There is an attempted-murder charge stuck right here in the middle of this mess. This whole shooting might never have happened if you had known the truth about what happened to Zack and had been able to take disciplinary action against those boys."

Baker thought for a moment as he used his fingers to momentarily massage his face. "Very interesting situation, indeed," he continued, "but as I think upon it I don't think your coach has broken any state or Federal laws. He only lied to you—but not in a court of law or to a police officer—and we don't really know whether he knew about the attack on Zack. I have no legal options that I know of right now that would allow me to take him into custody, but I am going to keep looking. I don't envy you, gentlemen. You have some tough decisions to make," concluded Baker, as he stood up and walked toward the door. "I'll be in touch. Call me right away if anything else comes up. I will do the same."

"Very interesting, indeed," Alan repeated to Anne, Brad, and Jed. The four of them were in Alan's office for an administrative briefing, an hour after Baker left. "We have a very complex situation that just got much more complex," said Alan, as he characteristically leaned back in his chair with his hands clasped behind his neck.

"Shit! Excuse my French," said Anne, standing quickly and walking across the room, "but I think 'complex' is a bit of an understatement. I can't believe those boys did that to Zack! It's like they're a bunch of animals. What kind of kids do we have here? Hell, we can't even protect them from each other. Are we doing our job?" Anne shook her head in disbelief.

"On top of that," added Brad, "we have a popular football coach who the town loves because he wins games and is quite the character. But he lied to you, Alan—and because of that, two boys got shot, and the boy who was accosted is up for attempted murder. This whole situation seems very out of control."

"Yes, and if I suspend him like I should and will," said Alan, "and replace him with you, Jed—the one coach who has defended my cuts—a week before the team goes into the State finals . . . that's going to look *real* good. We might just all get hung after all, but this time it won't be in effigy."

Anne continued to pace back and forth across the room, "All that, plus three bomb threats from the same person, while we're trying to implement major curriculum and social changes in the middle of the school year. No wonder we're tired!" She laid her head back and closed her eyes while leaning up against the wall.

"Yes," Jed interjected. "Plus, let's not forget there are some people out there who are very angry at us, not only for cutting sports, but now they seem to equate us with the whole gun-control issue. Those folks would like to see us go away—far away—maybe even be buried underground.

"Alan," continued Jed, "the school board did not know what to do when you threw that California Statute in their face. But I think several of them actually support us, especially Chris Rodmaker. And seven of the twelve speakers at the meeting also supported us. So now we've got the week that the school board gave us, while they try to figure things out with their lawyers."

Brad added, "And on top of all that, we've got coaches, parents, alumni, and a few kids who are pretty pissed off about the athletic cuts and are threatening to sue us. But on the other hand, the Teachers Association is taking a hard look at endorsing our curriculum changes. The PTA has remained fairly neutral, but they seem to be leaning our way. And segments of the news media, especially *The Globe* piece, seem to be behind us one hundred percent. More parents are getting on our bandwagon every day. In fact, I received eleven emails today, all favoring your—I mean *our*—plan, although five of them were from other states."

Alan leaned back in his chair and silence filled the room for a moment, as Anne frowned. "On top of all *that* stuff," she said, "Alan is going to fall all the way back in that chair and break his head open one of these days, leaving the rest of us to figure this out on our own!"

A bell went off as they all chuckled. A grin crept over Alan's face and he leaned a little farther back in his chair. "One good thing," he said, "At least we're not bored!" and the first smiles of the day brightened each face in the room.

CHAPTER FIFTEEN
PERSPECTIVES

Karen Kendrick sat at her large oak desk in her redwood-paneled office. Papers were scattered in a dozen somewhat organized piles, covering most of her desk. Her administrative assistant—a young woman just out of journalism school—had brought in the latest, local police reports, as she did every morning. She handed them directly to Karen with a smile—or maybe it was a flirtatious grin, Karen was never sure. *Ah, to be young again,* she thought to herself, as she watched her young, long-haired, blond assistant sashay out.

First on her to-do list were the two police reports dealing with the MLK shootings. One was about the bathroom incident involving Kyle and his friends. She flushed with anger, first at Kyle and then at Coach Cassidy. What kind of beings could do these things? How could anybody hold down a helpless boy and urinate all over him, only for a grown man to then lie to protect the bastards so he would have a better sports team? She had been a journalist for nine years, but she'd never gotten used to this type of story and this was one of the most disgusting.

Karen leaned back in her office recliner to read the second report, the one about the permanent scars on Kyle's buttocks. She thought of the anger and resentment Kyle must carry around with him, and what a tyrant his father must be—he made her own parents seem like angels. Kyle's father must be the villain, she thought; the ultimate culprit. She would make sure the bastard hung, she would use the power of her paper to destroy him. But then she sighed. Intuitively, she knew better—she knew that he was just part of a vicious family cycle and that, more than likely, he, too, had been victimized as a child. Was there any end to it all, or is the world just too crazy? Was there any way to break a cycle of violence and insanity within a family?

She heard knocking on her door.

"You called for me, Karen?" asked Ned Bannister, *The Globe's* feature writer. He poked his bearded-face and bald head in to look at her. in

"Come and sit down, Ned. You're one of the few wise people I know, and you're going to be a very busy man for the next couple of weeks proving it. So, you had better sit down and rest your legs and mind, while you have the chance."

"This sounds rather ominous," he replied. Ned leaned against the door, facing her but making no move to come all the way in.

"Well, to be brief, we are going to do an eight-week series on what it's like growing up in modern-day America," she continued, "and we're going to try and syndicate it across the country through the wire services, as well as in our own papers. And I'm placing you as the lucky man in charge—so it better be not just good, but *very* good.

"Ned, I want to show the good, the bad, and the ugly of this story. I want to focus on teenagers and the struggles they go through, trying to find their identity – and their dignity -- in this crazy world that seems to have lost its rudder, if it ever really had one. I want to talk about why so many of them have lost their moral compasses, and why they have so few good role models. I want to know why girls giving blowjobs has become almost as common as French kissing was twenty years ago, and what the girls get – or don't get – in return. Why do parents let all this happen on their watch? They stand around and do nothing! Then, of course, the larger question is: Why have our schools become as dangerous as schools in Afghanistan, Syria, Pakistan, or many other war-torn countries in the world? I mean, is this the end? The downfall of America with us adults refusing to protect our own children while they're in school because we, as Republicans, are afraid? And afraid of what? That's the real question. What are we so afraid of?

"Wow," interjected Ned. "We're getting very deep and broad here. You're asking for the meaning of life, and then some! But we have to be careful, Karen—we don't want to imply there could be anything deeply wrong in this Christian nation we live in. You know that is strictly taboo in a conservative newspaper like ours, which believes we are the most moral, superior country in the world. Plus, we represent the people who think they're the tough, gun-toting, wanna-be cowboys . . . so I don't know if there's room for any of that touchy-feely stuff in *The Globe*."

"Ned, I understand. I know I am asking a lot, but times are changing, even in this old, conservative newspaper. The conservative movement as we know it is disappearing—or maybe it has already died—so let's be at the front of rewriting the new script. Let's see if we can help it become more compassionate and practical. You write it and, if it's good, I'll print it, no matter what you say—at least until I'm fired."

"I'll take your word," said Ned. "I'll write it, and it will be good, but it may not please your uncle. I don't think that old fart is going to change anytime soon. This could well be the end of my career at *The Globe,* maybe both of our careers. Also, this is a very big task. Can I have Katie, Michel, and Bryn for a month? That's about what it will take just to scratch the service."

"You can have all three and this is going to be good, *really* good! Isn't this fun, Ned?"

Don Ritter, Kyle's father, had been asked to be the primary speaker at the "Save Our Sports" rally held at the Arcadia Elks Club the night before. He was very nervous about speaking in front of a large group; he had never done so before. Fortunately, the Elks bar was open for the occasion, and Don had arrived an hour early. By the time it was his turn to speak, his fear had evaporated into several pints of Coors Light and a gin and tonic kicker.

About 200 people, mostly men, arrived and packed the room. Don began to tell the group about his experiences in sports, especially being a linebacker in football, and how sports had saved him and made him what he is today. He explained how the team had helped him get through high school—the first person in his family history to do so—and how football had helped him to become a married man with a partial scholarship to the University of Alabama, the number-one team in the USA that year. Now he was a successful businessman and owned his own mechanic shop, right on the corner of Tenth and Elm Street.

Of course he didn't tell them about the money he received from the school's alumni group, or the new, blue Ford Mustang convertible he received from a local car dealer, or the redheaded hooker with the gigantic tits he got for two nights after signing with Alabama. That stuff was all part of the recruitment deal—but even in his slightly snookered state, Don knew that was the kind of information you saved for the boys at the local bar, not here in a public place where there was sure to be a damned community reporter hanging around. Nor did he mention how when he tore the cartilage in his left knee in his sophomore year, they pulled his scholarship and he never actually became the first college graduate in his family.

He also didn't tell anyone that night that he would do anything to feel okay about himself. That he had nightmares every night and carried self-loathing with him every day. What would they say if he had told them his wife was a good-for-nothing whore, and he only kept her around so he wouldn't have to do the laundry or cook, and so he could have a very occasional blowjob. And he had never told anyone about his own father, who would get drunk and beat the snot out of him and his mother almost every night. Nor did he mention his uncle, Shane, the so-called "nice brother" who really wasn't so nice; but only Don and his little brother Mark knew why.

And what if everyone found out about the doctor's report? The one showing that during drunken rages he had branded Kyle, his only son, on his butt with a fireplace poker. He'd done that twice since the boy was three years old. Or what if they knew that he was a full-blown alcoholic, just like his dad and his granddad? Even though he usually just drank beer, it had him totally hooked. Secretly he wished they would take the beer commercials that ran during his sports shows and shove them up their butts, so he wouldn't always be thinking about beer, even when he was trying not to drink. He knew that the Coors family was getting richer than rich off his beer-drinking, but they had him and millions of others hooked as well. He hated being a drunk like his old man, but it ran in the family and helped the Ritters cover up their pain. Pain was something Don knew all too well. Hell, if he could write better, he would write a book about it, and he would call it *Beer and Pain*. Kyle had started drinking beer two years ago, with his permission more or less. Getting crippled might save rather than doom Kyle. Who knew these things?

If the cops came to arrest him for what he had done to Kyle, he had already decided he'd shoot it out with them before they would ever take him alive. He was not going to jail. He packed a .38 Police Special wherever he went. In California, he could not get a permit for this type of gun, but that didn't stop him. Hell, maybe he should leave the country first. He was sorry for what he had done to Kyle, but shit! Kyle was a vegetable now, and there was nothing he could do about it anymore. His fat old lady could take care of Kyle for all he cared. She would be as happy as a clam to have him all to herself now.

Don put down his wrench on the mat beneath an old Pontiac Le Mans and pulled himself out from underneath. Another hour and he was off work. He was going to go home, get rip-snorting drunk, and plan his escape to Mexico. And that two-timing old lady better keep out of his way.

Karen Lynn sat in the locker room, her left ankle swollen to twice its normal size. Lindsey brought her another bag of ice from the cafeteria.

"You know, Lindsey, you're okay for a white girl," said Karen Lynn, laying back on the bench while Lindsey tied the plastic bag on with an old t-shirt.

"Babe, you have been training too hard all year, you know that. You played twenty-six games straight with the club team before the high school season even started. You haven't taken a week off this entire year. You have pushed your beautiful, black body beyond its capacity," Lindsey confirmed as she massaged Karen Lynn's thigh.

"I know, hun, but everybody—my coaches and my dad—keep pushing me. Basketball is my way out of the ghetto, they keep saying, even though we live in the suburbs now. My teachers keep telling me how bright I am, but I know I am only a fair student. To be a professional basketball player is my only goal right now. Damn . . .*damn*," she muttered as the tears streamed down her face. "Shit, Lindsey. I don't want to end up like my other best friend, Michele, whose only hobby is men. Men have told me many times what they would like to do to my long, hard body," she giggled. "I even let Slide Gordon try once and it felt okay, but not right. I knew I was not ready yet and he was one disappointed homeboy when I made him stop."

"I can relate totally," said Lindsey, "trust me."

"I guess you can, sweetie," said Karen Lynn with another giggle, "but just because I let you kiss me that one day and feel me up doesn't mean I am a lesbian or even bi."

"But you told me you thought I have a really cool body and you liked it," answered Lindsey, rubbing the back of her thigh with more pressure. "You said you found it really exciting."

"I did. I admit it felt good and I am keeping all my options open till I am ready. Trust me, you will be one of the first to know when I decide which way I am going, but right now I think I still like boys, too."

"I'll wait," smiled Lindsey. She helped Karen Lynn to her feet and put her arm over her shoulder as they hobbled out to Lindsey's car.

Right now, she just needed to get home and get her foot propped up on ice. There was another game against Lewiston in two days and she had to be ready. She knew the college scouts would be there.

Juan Pacheco was tough; no one questioned that. His parents had come over the border before he was born. They lived in the same house, in the same barrio, alongside the other Mexican immigrants with whom they had found a way over the border. His parents spoke very little English and were not legal citizens even though they paid their withholding taxes and property taxes; only Juan and his sister—who had just joined the Navy—were legal because they were born in the USA. His mom and dad had always been afraid to register for their citizenship, and now, twenty years later, it seemed too late. They were always worrying about being deported, especially now with the Republicans owning Congress and the White House. His mother was a maid at the Best Western Inn, and his father was a twelve-year cook at El Burrito, a local eatery in the east part of town.

Juan grew up in a Hispanic gang called "The Roosters." They hung together for protection against what they considered the white and black hordes who surrounded their part of the city. Now, at age seventeen, he was their leader. He was just five-foot, seven, and lean—but his friends and enemies knew he was very strong and quicker than a tongue on a Gila monster. He was also quick in the mind, a street-wise smart. His high school history teacher had told him he could do anything he wanted with his brain, but what he wanted was to be The Roosters' gang leader, and that's just what he'd become.

Lieutenant Baker walked into the school conference office. He said hello to the young girl behind the counter and told her he was to meet a student by the name of Juan Pacheco.

"Hi, Mr. Baker," said Melinda, the student helper. "You're beginning to be a regular around here. Are you going to become one of our teachers or another vice principal?"

"I don't think they could pay me enough either way," responded Baker with a smile, "And I don't think you and the rest of the students would want me here."

"Actually, Juan is already here waiting for you, in Room C. Second door on the left," she instructed, still smiling. "Just between you and me, Mr. Baker, Juan sure is cute," she said with a giggle and a blush.

"Thanks," said the lieutenant with a smile. "I won't tell him. I am starting to feel like one of the faculty—heck, maybe I should sign on and then I'll get this summer off and go fishing for a couple months!" Baker turned and entered Room C.

"Hello, Juan," said Baker, as he walked in the room and put out his hand. Juan hesitated for a moment and then reciprocated. "I appreciate you coming down here to see me on such short notice. Have a seat. This will take only a few minutes."

"I didn't know I had a choice about coming," replied Juan.

"You always have a choice," said the lieutenant, "but you may just like some of the choices better than others.

"Anyway, Juan, I haven't come here to waste your time or mine, so I'll get right to the point—or I guess to the *two* points. First, I want to personally thank you for talking Zack down on the day of the shooting. You undoubtedly saved one person's life and maybe more. I think I understand now why Zack trusts you and decided to put down his weapon. But I would like to hear your version of what happened when you and your friend entered the bathroom on the second story of the Science Building, and found an altercation going on between Zack Diamond and Kyle Ritter several weeks back. Understand this is not about you being a snitch, nor is this being entered into the record as any type of confession on your part; you are not in any trouble. From what I have heard, if there is a hero in this situation, it would be you. I am just here to find out exactly what happened between Zack and Kyle so everybody involved gets a fair hearing."

Juan leaned back in his chair and said, "Okay, it's no skin off my nose. It's like this: I wouldn't exactly call it an altercation; I'd call it a ruthless attack. We walked in the door to take a pee and found Kyle holding Zack down on the floor by twisting his hair in a knot and his foot was on his butt. The two other white boys—I don't even know their names—had their cocks out and were peeing all over him. They were laughing and acting totally crazy like they were drunk and probably had some drugs, too. Yeah, then I kind of lost it. I told him to stop and to let go of Zack and get out of the bathroom, but Kyle refused and told me to "F" off. I went ballistic. I was worried that I might kill him; and for several moments I truly wanted to. To me, Kyle was an animal gone completely mad. Humans do not do that type of thing to other humans, especially ones that can't stand up for themselves. Understand I ain't no do-gooder, but Kyle deserved the beating that I gave him. Fortunately, I was still in control enough to know that if I killed him I would spend most of my life in prison—otherwise, I may have done it at that very moment and Zack would never have had the chance.

"Afterwards, me and my friend cleaned Zack up the best we could. He was crying the whole time. We had a car at school and we cut the next class and drove him home. Shit, he couldn't go to his next class like that . . . he still smelled like pee and was sopping wet.

"There was something I felt—something inside me that I hardly ever feel—like a sad ache for Zack. Maybe it was pity. Hell, I don't know. We told him we would put the word out that anybody who screwed with him again would answer to The Roosters. But Zack didn't seem to be listening. When he stopped crying he told us he would take care of Kyle Ritter himself. He would kill him, and he asked if we could get him a gun. We told him no way, we couldn't do that, and that he could leave any retribution to us—but Zack didn't want to listen. I guess he was in too much pain, he had been shamed. But he did what he had to do and there are a lot of us around school who understand why he did it.

"So out there in front of the school -- what was that about?" asked Baker.

"I didn't want him killing Rod. I have gotten to know Rod a little this past year, and he is kind of a dork, but he is okay . . . he is just trying to make a decent living. He didn't need to die, and I knew Zack wouldn't shoot me, no way. So, like I said, Zack did what he needed to do, and I did what I needed to do, but I am no hero. That's all there is to it."

Baker let Juan's statement sink in for a moment, "So Juan, hypothetically speaking and for my own curiosity, what would you have done if it had been an active shooter who you did not know, who came into the school to kill as many students as possible?"

Juan thought for a moment and then replied, "It's like this, Mr. Baker: This school is what I'd refer to as a 'hybrid' school—a mixture of wealthier, pretty, white honkies and a bunch of us Latino and black dudes who ain't so rich. And some of us not-so-rich kids are from the hoods and the gangs; we know what guns and knives are. That's why if some crazy-ass dude walks in this school with an AR-15, some of us are going to try and take him out, gun or no gun, or we'll die trying. This is our territory—our turf he is on—and we ain't gonna let him shoot our people, it's just that simple." Juan continued, "You don't see this stuff happening at project schools. There may be gangs shooting at gangs, or somebody knifing somebody, but it's not people shooting other people at random. That kind of thing just happens mostly at white schools where there is no other recourse if you're a loser. So nowadays they go down to Walmart and, for a couple hundred bucks, get a gun that can kill lots of people in a minute's time . . . end of story."

Juan abruptly stopped speaking; he was obviously finished. The two of them sat looking at each other for several moments. Then Baker just said, "Damn." He didn't ask any more questions; he knew what the answers would be.

Baker looked Juan in the eye for several seconds then reached into his front shirt pocket and took out a card and gave it to him. "If you ever get in a jam, you call me," he said. "That's my cell phone, and it doesn't matter what time or what day it is, you just call that number."

Juan knew the card was an offer of grace and he stuck it in his wallet after he walked out of the room. The way his life was going, some day in the not too distant future, he might need it.

Lieutenant Baker used his key and walked through the steel backdoor of the precinct house. Without a word to anyone he went into his office, then shut and locked the door. He put his feet up on his desk and leaned back in his chair. Thirty-three years on the force and he had seen it all—murders of all kinds, beatings, rapes—but he could not get used to the idea of school kids attacking and abusing one another. Something about it was not natural, like things had gone haywire. *Something is dreadfully wrong out there,* he thought. Maybe he was just getting soft in his old age, but the world of the '60s and '70s, with all its promises of peace and love, had gone to hell in the twenty-first century, and the world seemed to be rapidly heading in a very wrong direction.

Ever since Mabel had passed away from throat cancer three years earlier, his attitude seemed to have changed. Watching her suffer for nearly two years had taken something out of him. They had both quit smoking three years before she had been diagnosed, but for her it was too late.

When he got too lonely, he would babysit for his daughter and her husband, to give them a night off. He loved playing with his two grandchildren: nine-year-old Coy and seven-year-old Daisy. They made life seem so much simpler and he felt true moments of joy when with them.

But life at work was never simple or joyous. He had just gotten word that there were two more calls from the female mystery terrorist; she said a bomb would go off in the school if they didn't release Zack from jail. They hadn't been able to get a trace on any of the calls except to an empty phone booth. The person making them knew exactly what she was doing, and she had been very quick and to the point. Were the calls related to the shooting? Was Zack a member of some type of cult, gang, or extremist group that they hadn't been able to track down or identify? He would not talk about it. There were so many unanswered questions, and he felt very tired.

Butch Cassidy was alone in the living room of his ranch-style home in the Los Gatos suburbs. Dark brown mahogany paneling covered every wall in the room and the thick, green drapes were closed tight. He sat on his brown-tweed couch with a Coors Light in his right hand and the TV remote in his left, watching the Rams against the Steelers on his big-screen television.

His usual group of coaches and friends were not here today. Coach Cassidy had decided he needed some space. He had no real interest in the game he was watching and wondered if he was depressed. He had been this way since the day of the shooting. At football practice after school on Friday, he had been terribly preoccupied, even though State playoffs were only a week away. Indeed, the whole team seemed preoccupied. If this lethargic attitude kept up, and without Kyle, Josh, Jeff, and Dustin, they were going to get creamed. But in truth, he really couldn't have cared less.

Was the shooting my fault? he wondered. He had agonized over it a hundred times. Three times divorced, he now lived alone. There was no one he could talk to about an issue like this—he couldn't approach any of the other coaches and tell them what he had done, or that he was scared. They didn't talk about personal stuff. They just talked football or women. He stumbled to the fridge and took out another beer. He could hardly open it. He had been trying to drink himself into oblivion for the last thirty-six hours, but he'd been practicing drinking for so many years that it no longer dulled the pain.

Why? he kept asking. *Why did I continue to protect Kyle once I learned what he was accused of? I never even asked him what had happened. Was it just because he is a football player? Did I want to win that bad? Or is it because I believe athletes are superior and more special than the other kids? Or was I afraid to admit that I had been wrong? What the hell is wrong with me!? Maybe it was all the above. Have I gone nuts?* he wondered as he paced across the kitchen.

He took his beer and walked out the sliding glass door onto his covered deck. The clouds had thickened, and the sky was getting dark and gray. It was starting to rain lightly. He sat on the edge of his old, green lounge chair and put his head in his hands. He felt heartsick with a deeper sadness than he ever imagined possible. *What the hell is wrong with me?* he inquired again. *Aren't I known as one of the toughest coaches in the State? Real men aren't supposed to feel this way . . .what a joke!* Slowly, one tear after another started running down his cheeks, and soon there was a small puddle on the red brick beneath his chair.

CHAPTER SIXTEEN
WHAT TO BELIEVE

"Sit down, Vern. You're making me nervous towering over me like that," said Alan. Vern, who was slender and six-foot, three, often reminded Alan of an oak tree. Bending or being flexible like bamboo was not part of his nature.

Vern immediately sat down in a chair facing Alan and started in. "I have five sheets of paper filled from top to bottom with issues related to the downsizing of the athletic department, plus a list of over 400 signatures from parents who have students in this school. We need to start re-evaluating—"

"Hold on, Vern. We have a more immediate problem to deal with," said Alan, his voice slow and deliberate. "We need to talk about the shooting."

"The shooting is old hat, Alan. Most of us have moved on, and the kid is in jail—and hopefully won't be getting out for a long time," interrupted Vern impatiently. "We're just lucky that no one died from that wacko kid going on a rampage. It's just very sad about Kyle—he is a really good kid. Anyway, what's that have to do with my athletic cuts?" demanded Vern, rising from his chair and hovering over Alan like an angry genie.

"Vern, Butch Cassidy lied about what happened with Kyle after the attack on Zack. I believe, as do the police, that Butch knew all along about Kyle's attack on Zack, and he covered for him because he knew that Kyle would have been suspended from school . . . or more than likely expelled for the rest of the school year. The team would have lost its key defensive player, not to mention Jeff Myers and Dustin Biggs, two other important players. That would have made it much more difficult—if not nearly impossible—for the team to get very far in the playoffs.

"Jeff and Dustin have admitted they lied about accosting Zack. They have said that after Kyle knocked Zack down and kicked him into submission, they participated in holding Zack down in the boys' bathroom and taking turns peeing all over him, while under the influence of dope and alcohol. If Kyle was not in the hospital right now he most likely would be in jail and would not be returning to this school or any school in this district, ever. Jeff and Dustin have both been suspended from school and they will miss the final playoff games."

When Alan finished talking it was like winter had snuck up on Vern. Known for looking young and spry, he now looked much older than his sixty-two years. He sat down in a very slow, methodical way, and after several minutes of silence he responded.

"I don't understand this, Alan. I can't believe those boys would do something like that. They're athletes, not gangsters running around with tattoos all over their bodies. This is just very hard to accept. I guess logically, when you put the pieces together, it does make some sense; though why did Zack go after Kyle and not the other boys?"

"Kyle was the leader, Vern. He was the instigator, and the other boys followed him; he goaded them on. Plus, it would have been hard for Zack to find all three boys together at the same time. From what I understand, the three did not hang out together that often after the incident. Also, Vern, it was the 'gangsters,' as you call them, who came into the bathroom during the attack and *stopped* the assault on Zack. One of them had to beat Kyle into submission to get him to stop. That was Juan, the same boy who talked Zack out of shooting Rod."

"The Mexican?"

"Yes, Vern, the Hispanic boy."

The men sat in silence for several moments, both contemplating where to go from there.

"I believe I should be the one to speak to Butch," Vern continued after the long pause. "He loves those boys, in his own way. I don't think he ever asked what happened when Kyle was first brought to him. I guess he just figured he got in a fight and lost. Then Butch got caught up in the whole mess when Zack's mother reported what had happened, and one thing led to another. Butch has never been the most mature guy on the block; he probably didn't know how to fess up and tell the truth. He should probably be the first one enrolled in that Honest Communication class you guys are starting—maybe it is really a good idea after all. Shoot, I guess maybe I should sign up, too.

"But, shit, now look what has happened. I feel very responsible," Vern continued as he stood up quickly and held on to the desk, shivering momentarily, as if a cold drop of rain had run down his spine. "I will talk to Butch today about what he needs to do, and get back to you by tomorrow morning, if that is okay."

"That would be fine," Alan replied.

Without another word Vern turned away, slightly stooped, and took careful, smaller-than-usual steps out of the office. He quietly closed the door behind him.

Alan took in a deep breath, but before he had a chance to exhale, Ruth called out, "Alan, it's your ex-wife, Katherine, on the phone!"

Wonderful! thought Alan. *Just what I need now.*

"Thanks, Ruth. And please remember I have only one ex-wife," he answered much too quickly.

"Gee, aren't we touchy," replied Ruth.

Alan's mind froze for an instant, or maybe it was just his body that froze. He put his hand on the telephone and held it there taking several deep breaths.

"Yes. Hi, Katherine, it's been a while. How are you? Hmmm . . . sorry to hear you have a cold. Oh, you had to miss your bridge game this afternoon? Yes, you must have a doozy.

"So you have been following our drama in the newspaper?

"Yes, things have been very crazy around here. You can't imagine. No, we still haven't figured out who has been making the bomb threats, but things are starting to settle down a bit.

"Yes, both of our boys are doing well, isn't that amazing? It does help my peace of mind tremendously. Actually, it's the only thing that keeps me sane right now.

"So how is Rick? Good, it looks like you picked a good one; I am glad you're happy. It's great you are traveling so much, dentists often make lots of money. No, I didn't mean it that way, Katherine, now please don't take it personally.

"Well, anyway, I am sorry. So—what can I do for you?

"A private investigator called to see if you had anything to pin on me? You must be kidding. Like, what kind of stuff? Child molesting? Spousal abuse? You've got to be putting me on.

"Oh my, God, these people are crazy," said Alan, as he stood up with his portable phone and started pacing back and forth. "No, I can't believe they would stoop so low, but I guess this is a political issue now, and I am fair game. That's the way the system works but I wonder who these people are and who is paying for the private investigator?

"No—I wouldn't imagine he would tell you, but I do appreciate you telling me. Thanks, Katherine, I appreciate the support. It's good to have you on my side. Yes, I know we're still family and we have to stick together. Say hello to Rick for me. I love you, too, and if you hear anything else let me know. Goodbye."

A private investigator? Who would have believed it? Alan wondered if this was courtesy of Mr. and Mrs. Champ. *Well, I fear they are going to find my private life rather boring: no arrests, one speeding ticket, and one divorce—though I did think about killing Rick one time for a couple of hours, but that would have set a bad example for the kids. But that's about it. I really am kind of boring.*

He thought about his cousin Roy, the only famous person he knew. Roy had been the longest serving governor in Oregon's history. A very popular guy, he did a lot for the state and instigated probably the best state health care plan in the country. Everyday hundreds if not thousands of Oregonians received care that they could not have afforded otherwise. Then not long ago, politics reared its ugly head when a zealous reporter wrote an article with several damning innuendoes against Roy and his first lady/partner. Some of the new Democratic younger guard seemed to want him out, so they could get their turn. Roy and his girlfriend, a dedicated environmental activist, were crucified until Roy tired of the game and resigned. After all they had both done for the state, now they lived in what seemed like exile to Alan. Politics could be brutal and ugly especially when you stood up for what you believed in and now it seemed to be his turn.

"Wow," said Jed to no one in particular, as he sat in the teachers' lounge at noon. "Look at the headlines in *The Globe* and *The Sun*: 'Attempted Murder Suspect Had Been Attacked—Bomb Threats Terrorize School'. They have all the lurid details of the attack on Zack, plus Butch's cover up attempt. They know more about the bomb threat than I do."

"Poor Butch," said Penny Briton. "His career is ruined. I have had philosophical differences with the man, but I think he has a good heart. I wonder what he is going to do now."

"This could break him," replied Jed. "Football and his players are his life. I've always had a love-hate relationship with him because he is such an over-the-top football fanatic, but I like him, and I'd hate to see him destroyed. But he screwed up, big time."

"Look at this," said a history teacher who was reading the Community Section. "Starting tomorrow, *The Globe* will publish an eight-week series about "Growing Up in Modern America," featuring an inside look into what's not working in American high schools."

"That should be an eight-*year* series," said Bruce Robbins. "They won't even scratch the surface in eight weeks."

The history teacher continued, "Martin Luther King High School will be the primary educational facility used in the series. This article says they're going to interview staff and students about all the changes we have implemented here. I guess we are going to be famous whether we like it or not." A collective groan came from all nine teachers who had gathered that afternoon in the lounge.

Bruce Robbins went back into his classroom for C block. *Jigsaw teaching,* he thought. The idea was to get kids who would not normally socialize with each other to work together in pods, so they could get to know one another and reduce the tension between them.

He had been giving it a lot of thought over the last couple of days. He remembered his own high school days when he was somewhat of a bookworm and, for all practical purposes, a social outcast. It was not a terrible time in his life because he had his books, but he could not say that he was happy, either. He knew he still had some leftover resentment toward people in cliques and people of authority.

I guess I can give this a try, he'd decided. Alan's speech to the school board had moved Bruce. Alan had put his rectum on the line, so Bruce decided he could at least do his part. His physics class was already in their seats and had settled down nicely. Bruce had a reputation for being a strict disciplinarian. He loved order, but he loved his students, too. And much to his surprise, his students seemed to like him, even if they thought he was a nerdy teacher and a bit anal at times.

"Okay, students, starting today we're going to structure class and study times in a very different manner. I have assigned each of you into one of nine groups or pods. There will be four students in each pod. You will work in this group for two weeks and then switch to another pod for the next two weeks, and so on until the end of the semester.

"You will have no choice about who your partners will be. The idea is to get you to work together with people who you would not normally get to know. By doing this, we hope to break down some of the social structure that often separates students, thereby teaching you to work in harmony.

"Our class material will also be a little different this quarter," he continued while holding up a book on quantum physics. "We're going to talk some about string theory and parallel universes in addition to our regular curriculum. This is all part of quantum mechanics, which many of you may or may not have heard of. This may be a bit far out there for some of you, but there is some good science here that we all can learn from. The idea is fascinating—that each of us creates our own reality by the energy we put out, instead of just our physical or mental labor—although this concept may be a little hard to imagine at first blush.

"We will set up practice stations around the room and each of your pods will be assigned to a station. At each station we will pick a simple idea, such as everyone in the pod getting an 'A' in this class this semester. Then we will practice, as a group, creating our own energy around the idea, and then watch over the next several months to see if we have created what we intended to do. It should be very interesting.

"Maybe we will even create a new parallel universe where each of you in this class gets straight 'A's' in all your subjects! Wouldn't that surprise a few people? So if you're all ready, let's get started. Everyone please stand up."

The usual moaning and groaning came from many of the students as they moved around to the pod where Bruce assigned them by the luck of the draw. Several of the shy boys who ended up with three girls in their pods sat silently, looking a bit overwhelmed, not sure if they had won the jackpot or the booby prize.

"Oh man, what a pain!" said a five-foot, eight, white boy nervously, as he sat down in his new group next to Karen Lynn.

"It will be just fine," said Karen Lynn. "I won't bite you, I promise."

"Bummer," said the boy as his face turned peach color and a tiny smile crept out of his mouth.

"Hi. My name is Margaret," said a husky, raw-boned, blonde girl as she stuck out her hand.

"And my name is Tracy," said a petite brunette with unusually large brown eyebrows over her coal-black eyes.

"I guess I am one lucky dude," the boy managed to stammer, as he shook their hands one by one.

One of the two girls who ended up with three boys in her group looked smug and pleased, while the other seemed perplexed and quiet at first. But by the end of class they had all relaxed and opened up a bit.

After class, Bruce reflected on what had gone on with the new pod structure, and he was pleased. The students had seemed to enjoy working with others whom they had not known well, and working as a group seemed to heighten their awareness as individuals. He felt like their level of maturity had been ratcheted up a notch. Yes, he was very pleased, very pleased, indeed. He was also excited to begin teaching some of the philosophies associated with quantum mechanics, even though some considered these philosophies to be a little woo-woo. But there was some good, solid science in it, and he liked that it heightened the students' interest because they would be taught how it affected them in their everyday lives.

CHAPTER SEVENTEEN
BUTCH, SAM, AND THE FLAGPOLE

"Anne! Line three!" called out Ruth over the intercom into Anne's office. "A man named Sam Diamond is asking for someone in charge of the school. He says it is very important and Alan is in a teachers' meeting."

The name Sam Diamond rang a vague bell in Anne's mind. She picked up the phone with some apprehension, wondering whether this was some type of prankster or another threatening phone call.

"Anne Briggs here. Yes, Zack Diamond was a student of ours. Are you a relative? Oh, I see . . . you're his father. Yes, he is okay, but he is now in the County Juvenile Center downtown. Yes. Where do you live, Mr. Diamond? I see. What can I do for you?"

Alan slowed his eleven-year-old, light-blue Taurus station wagon as he turned off the San Diego Freeway and came down the 236-C off-ramp to Wilshire Boulevard. He looked over at Anne in the passenger seat and asked, "How are we going to find this guy? Do you even know what he looks like or what he is wearing?"

"No, not exactly," replied Anne, "but I trust my intuition. I'll know who he is when I see him. He said he would be on the corner of Wilshire and Madison, and we're just two blocks from there now, according to my phone. By the way, Alan, when are you going to come into the modern age and get a GPS or use your cell phone?"

"Probably never, it would take all the fun out of finding a destination, and it wouldn't help us find this guy anyway," replied

Alan, as he looked around at the old rundown buildings. “This is one crazy place. I am not sure what I am doing down here, especially on my first Saturday without a school function in three weeks!" Alan complained.

"You are chaperoning me," replied Anne. "You said you wouldn’t let me come down here by myself, even though you think I am crazy. You’re my knight in shining armor, Mr. Carter, and I duly appreciate this."

"Oh." was all Alan replied.

"Hey, Alan, watch out for that old Pontiac! He is turning left! Oh shit, that was way too close. You almost got him! Couldn’t you see he was going to turn left?"

"It’s okay, Anne, I have it under control. I saw him in plenty of time; we had lots of room."

"I don’t think so, Alan! Not unless you call three inches a lot of room. But be a man and have it your own way—at least we're still alive.

"This is sure a tough looking area of town. I guess he won’t be wearing a business suit," said Anne. She stared out the window at the dozens of people on every corner, while continuing to glance at the map. “Zack’s mom said this guy is a wino and a lot of these folks fit that description. Get in the right lane and pull over—there . . . in front of the Saint Vincent Shelter for Men, please. I think that’s it. That’s where he works.

"Let me ask that man in the gray, crumpled suit standing over there on the corner. He looks sweet and sober. Can you pull over there a little closer to the curb?”

"Sure—if I get out and pick up the car and set it over there," replied Alan. "Hold on, let see if I can make it."

"Wow, that was close again. You made it, but just barely. Good job, Alan!" Anne rolled down the window and spoke to the man. "Hi, I am Anne Briggs, a vice principal at MLK High School. I am looking for a Mr. Sam Diamond who lives in this shelter. Can you possibly help me?"

"Yes, I am Sam Diamond, and I believe you’re looking for me," said the man in a low voice, as he bent down in front of the open window. His soft brown eyes looked directly into Anne’s bright green eyes.

"Oh, great! I am glad to meet you, Mr. Diamond. Would you like to get in the back seat?" asked Anne as she leaned over her seat and unlocked the back door.

Sam was a slightly built man who looked to be in his fifties, with an almost clean-shaven head except for a small patch of dark hair on the far back of his head and another tuft of black scruff below the cleft of his chin. As he settled himself into the back seat, Alan reached over to shake hands.

They drove down the street in awkward silence for a while. To break the tension and satisfy her curiosity, Anne asked how long it had been since Sam had seen Zack.

"Six years, thirty-one days," replied Sam in a voice so quiet that Alan had to turn his head and strain to hear.

"That's a long time," replied Alan after another brief silence.

"Yes, it is," said Sam almost whispering. "I won't make excuses, Mr. Carter, except to say Zack has never been out of my mind or heart in all that time, not for one day."

There was another minute of quiet time and then Sam started again. "My ex-wife will tell you I have never missed a child support payment in all those years. I wrote Zack weekly, sometimes daily, for over a year, until I realized his mother would not let him receive my letters. Finally, I rented a taxi and went to see Zack, because I knew he was not getting my letters, or he would have responded. When I got there she told me she had a restraining order that prevented me from seeing Zack. I had never heard anything about this. She called the police while I waited outside the house I had bought for us five years before. The police officer said he was sorry, he said he could understand how I felt, but there was nothing he could do. I did not get to see my son.

"I know she meant well, but she has had a lot of pain throughout her entire life. The sadness of losing Zack was larger than my soul could bear at the time. I thought the fighting between the two of us would just make things worse, and so I gave up for the time being. I live by faith, so I trusted it would work out in the end, and I still believe that. Though I am not a strong man, my faith is strong."

For several more minutes, none of them spoke. They did not know what to say, and the only sound was the hum of the tires on the pavement of the freeway.

Anne felt the need to know more, and asked Sam, "Do you have a job? Where do you live?" She adjusted her body and her seat belt to be able to look back at Sam as she talked.

"Oh, yes," said Sam. "How else could I pay child support? I am the lay rabbi at Saint Vincent. I know that sounds like a misnomer, but the shelter has been nonsectarian for the full time I have been there. We have never gotten around to changing the name—I guess we have all been too busy. We often feed and house more than a hundred men a night. I was the janitor there for several years, when I was much too depressed to do anything else.

"Now I still do janitorial work, but I also do counseling and run our crisis line for people in emergency situations. I seem to be pretty good at it. I guess it's my penance for failing as a father. All my small pay I send to Zack's mom. I have no car or other worldly trappings. The center provides my food and shelter. In a lot of ways it's a very good life, maybe more than I deserve . . . " His voice trailed off again.

This is not what I expected at all, thought Alan as he listened to Anne and Sam talk. He was there on his day off because Sam had pleaded with Anne to intervene and help him see his son. He had not expected Sam to be so pious and articulate, or to have an air about him that felt almost out of this world. Anne glanced over at Alan and raised her eyebrows, but not a word passed between them until a buzzing sound came from the glove box.

"That's your cell phone, not mine. Alan, do you want me to answer it while you drive?"

"That's okay, Anne, I've got it. I only use it for school emergences," Alan said, reaching over to pull out his phone from the glove compartment.

"Men!" replied Anne, "What kind of example are you for our kids?"

"Hello? Yes, this is Alan Carter," he answered.

"This is Lieutenant Baker, Mr. Carter. I am on top of the third story of your school's new gymnasium. We have a serious problem here. Butch Cassidy, your football coach, is holding on to the flagpole that hangs from the ledge on the east side of the building. He says he is going to jump, but so far, he has held on. We have tried to approach him but then he lets go with one of his hands, and we back off. We've got a trained negotiator from the County Health Department out here trying to talk him down, but Cassidy seems to be in some type of wild suicidal depression, almost like he is in a trance. Mostly he is not responding to us at all, as if we're not even here. His only response has been telling us to go away and leave him alone; besides that, he just ignores us. We got your emergency number from our emergency database. I hate to bother you on your day off, but we could use your help. We don't know who else to call."

Butch Cassidy wanted to let go. God, he wanted to let go and get out of this mess. And suicide was the only way he knew out of this pain. But Butch was a fighter, and fighters don't give up easily. It was bred into his DNA and then pounded into him physically by his father. He was in a terrible dilemma and soaked to the bone by the on and off rain, torturing himself while trying to figure out what to do.

He had drunk way too much over the last three days and felt terribly weak, though his jumbled mind was racing a million miles per hour. All that kept going through his head was the same tape recording: *What have I done . . . what have I done? There's no way out of this one. I am totally screwed and so is Kyle. Let go, let go!* The pain wrenched through his body and he felt like he was going to throw up. For a moment he wondered whether he would even die—maybe a three-story building wasn't high enough to get the job done. It certainly looked like a long way down. Maybe he would end up a human vegetable like Kyle. Poor Kyle. Oh, God, what had he done?

Through the corner of his eye he saw a human figure approaching. He could see that it was a man, but he did not recognize who it was. He yelled at the top of his lungs for the man to go away. Where had this guy come from anyway? Was he a cop who had come to arrest him? He knew he would jump before he let them arrest him, but the man was not coming any closer. He was trying to talk to him, but Butch didn't care; he could hardly hear him over the wind and the rain. After several minutes, the man was gone, and he was alone again.

His mind kept asking God for the power to let go, but he couldn't seem to do it, no matter how much pain he felt inside. He just wasn't a quitter. All he could do was hang on and hope for a miracle, but he didn't know what a miracle might even look like. He had been hanging on for a long time already and he was getting very tired.

Alan, Anne, and Sam arrived at MLK and approached the top of the building all together on a small steel platform. None of them had ever been on a boom this high before, especially one that was attached to a giant red fire engine. In fact, Alan had never been on top of a building this high before. He'd never liked heights, especially on a wet and windy day. Sam and Anne seemed more relaxed as they stepped over, one at a time, until they all stood on the roof of the gymnasium.

"Over there," said Anne, pointing to a small group of men clustered behind a large heating unit about twenty feet away.

"Hello, Lieutenant. You know Anne, our vice principal, and this is Sam Diamond, the father of Zack," said Alan loudly, trying to talk above the twenty-plus-mile-per-hour gusts of wind blowing past them. He knew Baker couldn't possibly comprehend what he was telling him about Sam being there—he still didn't understand it himself, but bringing him up to the rooftop with them seemed the right thing to do. After all, Sam had said he was a crisis counselor, so he just introduced the two and waited.

Baker's face looked befuddled. His world seemed to be spinning out of control, and he was a man who prided himself on staying in control. What was he doing on the Martin Luther King High School gymnasium rooftop, with an alleged murderer's absentee father, trying to coax down the coach who had protected the boys who had accosted this man's son?

The world was a crazy place, but this seemed way too weird. He reminded himself that he was a cop and cops had to get used to doing their job, even if they don't always understand why.

"Mr. Diamond," he said with a nod of his head, not extending his hand. Then he quickly explained what little he knew about the situation to the threesome.

"We have been up here thirty minutes with our negotiator, Grier Jordan, trying to talk to Butch, but nothing has changed. Butch's arms have to be getting very tired and cold with this chilly wind and the rain starting up again."

Anne commented, "Butch is a big man and he is now forty-eight years of age. He has gained maybe forty pounds over the last ten years I have known him." She added, "I don't see how he can hold out much longer!"

"Time is running out," said Baker. "We all agree we don't know how long he can hold on, even if he wants to. Alan, I don't mean to push but, as his principal, we need you to try to talk him down, and we need you to do it as soon as possible."

Alan was dubious that Butch would listen to him, considering their relationship and Butch's state of mind, but he had no other ideas. Under the circumstances, he knew he had to give it a try.

Without saying another word, Alan turned and started walking out near the edge of the flat, wet, pebbled roof, trying to stay in clear view of Butch. He worried that he might be the one to slip and go over the edge instead of Butch. "Wouldn't that be ironic," he muttered. His stomach felt queasy and he didn't dare look over the side.

As he walked toward Butch, strong gusts of the coastal wind coming in from the west pushed against him. Alan was not sure what he should say, or not say. Butch was not a sixteen-year-old student. He was a grown man, at least in years and size.

Butch had been looking down toward the asphalt pavement below and didn't see Alan separate himself from the rest of the group and start walking towards him. Upon looking up and seeing him, Butch let go of the flagpole with one hand and yelled, "Go away! Go away, Alan—I can see it's you! I am going to jump, and you can't stop me!"

Alan's heart stopped beating for an instant and he immediately knelt down on one knee.

"Hey, Butch . . . yeah, it's me," Alan yelled loudly, trying to be heard over the wind. "I am not going to come any closer so don't worry. I am not here as your boss. I am just here as a friend, to talk, and tell you that there are lots of people who care about you and what happens to you. Please talk to me if you like. What is going on?"

Alan sat the rest of the way down onto his knees and waited quietly for a reaction from Butch.

"No, Alan—you know what the hell is going on. No one cares about me, everyone hates me now. I hate myself. It's completely hopeless, there is no way out." Then he let go with both hands, only his legs remaining on the pole, and Alan yelled in desperation, "Don't let go, Butch!"

Butch wavered for a few seconds before suddenly putting both hands back on the flagpole, and Alan's heart slowed back down.

Butch went back to staring at the pavement below with only an occasional glance over to see if Alan had moved any closer. But he didn't say another word.

Several minutes passed, and Alan started to feel desperate again. He tried to think of some carrot he could use to coax Butch off the roof.

"Butch, talk to me. Tell me what's going on in your mind. Maybe I can help," said Alan. "You are not responsible for what Kyle did to Zack. Are you upset about the newspaper article about Kyle's cover up? You know our newspapers exaggerate. Butch, I imagine you are depressed, but everything is going to be okay." Alan hesitated, knowing he didn't really believe his own words. "It's too windy and wet up here to think straight. Why don't we go downstairs and go somewhere by ourselves and talk, maybe a pub to have a beer and some chili where it's warm. We can figure this out."

Butch made no response whatsoever. He didn't even look over at Alan. But at least he still held on with both hands.

After sitting in the rain for five more minutes, Alan knew Butch was not going to listen to him. There was too much distrust right now and he knew Butch did not consider him a friend. They had to try something else. He thought about rushing Butch and trying to grab him, but the odds were worse than terrible. Even if he did not let go first, Butch was bigger and stronger, and rolling around on a rooftop until help arrived sounded like a losing proposition for both of them.

Slowly he got up, telling Butch he was leaving but not to give up. He started slowly walking back across the roof to where Baker and the others waited.

"Sorry, no response whatsoever," reported Alan. "I don't think he even cared that I was there. He wouldn't even look at me. I do know he recognized me because he called me by name but had no interest in talking to me. I am his boss but we're not close. In fact, right now we're just the opposite—he may consider me his antagonist. This whole thing is a real mess and he is in a bad situation in a lot of ways."

"We could be running out of time," said Grier, the negotiation specialist. "He is getting tired, cold, and more despondent, and he might just let go at any time."

"We have 200 feet of flat roof to cross to reach him. Except for the other air conditioning unit near the middle, there is absolutely no cover. I could try and make it that far without him seeing me," said Baker, "but then I still have a fifty-foot span of open space to reach him after that, and I don't run quite as fast as I used to. Plus, he is a very heavy and strong man. I don't think there is a ten-in-a-hundred chance that will work."

"Maybe we could distract him with some warm food while the two of you sneak up from behind the air conditioning unit." asked Anne.

"I don't think so," said Grier. "Any distraction might cause more anxiety, which could cause him to jump. Also, when we first got the report they said he was sitting on the edge of the building eating hamburgers, which we assume were several Big Macs. We found the wrappers and a fresh McDonald's bag on the ground below the gym."

"No wonder he has gained almost fifty pounds," quipped Anne, halfheartedly.

"We have another fire engine around back with nets and ladders," continued Grier, "but we're afraid of the same thing—that he will get nervous when they pull up with the net and that might put him over the edge, literally."

"Great," said Baker. "We're running out of options. I heard from your school secretary that his last ex-wife dislikes him immensely, but how about his kids? Does anyone know whether he has any around here?"

"No," replied Anne. "I believe he has a daughter, but I think she lives somewhere around Reno, Nevada, and as far as I know they don't communicate much, if at all. That's all I know and that's from what he told me over a glass of wine several years ago at a social gathering after a teachers' meeting. That's the most I think he has talked to any of us about his personal life. I don't think he has anybody else, except several ex-wives, and like you said, I don't think he's on great terms with any of them."

There was another period of desperate silence.

"I should try to talk to him," came Sam's voice out of the back of the group. "I think there is a reasonable chance he might actually listen to me."

Alan, Anne, Baker, and Grier turned in unison and stared at Sam as if he suddenly appeared from nowhere as a leprechaun. "Butch is very desperate right now, and I know all too well what that is like. I have an idea, and I think I can give him hope . . . something to live for. I don't know him personally, but we talked about him on the way over here and I believe it's possible he could be a help to both Kyle and Zack, and that might lead him to redemption. I believe redemption is his only hope here, and the only hope for the boys. I do suicidal-crisis intervention at the center. Let me talk to him and see if I can make him understand."

"No way," said Baker, after getting over the initial shock and regaining his thought process. "He would jump in a minute if he sees another stranger coming up to him. We have already pushed our luck. If he didn't jump then, he would when he found out you are the father of the boy he let all of this happen to. Hell, he will be over the side in a flash!"

"Excuse me, sir," said Grier, raising his hand tentatively. "Sam might just be right. Cassidy seems to believe he has no chance of finding any hope. He seems to blame himself for everything that has happened to both the boys. Hope is what makes the world go around. It keeps people going. If Mr. Diamond has something to say that might give Butch hope—any type of hope—he might back off from jumping. At this point, I don't think we have anything to lose. We may only have five or so minutes at the most."

Baker looked over at Sam and gave him a quick once-over; for the first time he actually seemed to acknowledge his presence. "What do you want to say to Cassidy that would change his mind about jumping? What could you possibly say, Mr. Diamond? I still don't understand your motive."

Sam was quiet for a moment. "I just want to tell him it's okay. We all screw up. He and I both have made mistakes. I want to tell him that Zack and Kyle's best hope is that we show up for them, right now, both of us. All we have is this moment, because we can't change the past—it is what it is. I want him to know it's just going to make things a lot worse for everyone if he jumps. I need to convince him that he would be bailing out on the boys if he jumps. Kyle is going to need a coach in rehab, and who would be better than the football coach he already knows and trusts. I need to convince him he is Kyle's best hope.

Baker looked around at each person to see if they had an objection or a question. No one said a word, and Anne and Grier were nodding their heads up and down.

"I may lose my job over this, but this idea makes some sense to me. I guess it's our only hope. We have another negotiator from the LAPD on the way, but he won't be here for at least another half-hour.

"Okay," said Baker, "I am open-minded. Give it a try, Diamond, but don't get too close. Try sitting on the cooler while you talk to him. The wind has died a bit, so he'll hear you. If he seems to get more nervous, get back over here ASAP."

Alan and Anne stood behind Baker, intensely interested observers of the unfolding drama. Anne reached for Alan's hand and was holding it tight.

Sam took a deep breath and walked methodically across the rooftop until he reached the cooling unit. He sat down on the edge of the steel box, facing Butch.

Butch noticed him immediately and stared straight at him, trying to place him—trying to figure out who he was and what he wanted. He didn't look like a cop, more like a preacher or a rabbi, or maybe a monk of some sort.

"Mr. Cassidy, I am Sam Diamond, the father of Zack Diamond, the boy who shot Kyle. I am here to desperately plead for your help. You are the boys' only hope. Both these boys are hurting badly. You and I together can maybe help them. We are their only hope. Please don't jump off this building. That would be the coward's way out and it would not help anyone and could cause Kyle to give up hope. Those boys need our help—they need *your* help."

Butch held Sam's gaze, taking several minutes to register who he was. Why was he here? What was he saying—how could they help the two boys? One was in jail for life and one was paralyzed for life and he had inadvertently caused all this. Everything was hopeless. Was this man insane or was Butch insane? Did this man know something he did not know? Was Kyle coming out of his coma, and was he not paralyzed after all? A small flicker of hope darted through his body. "What are you talking about?" he shouted at Sam. "There is nothing we can do now! It's too late—are you fricking crazy?"

Across the roof, Grier leaned over to Baker. "He got his attention; got him to respond and to think. That's good, very good."

"Butch, we are those boys' only hope," Sam continued. "You can be there in rehab for Kyle. He is going to need a coach, and his parents can't afford a private physical therapist, you know that. You can help him—remember you're already his coach. He will listen to you. You're his only chance at any kind of possible recovery. Without you he is lost. He loves you, man. And you can help Zack by explaining to the police what happened, by testifying for him in court. If we can get Zack help, he can get through this and come out the other side. Come on, man, don't give up now! We all make mistakes and we can't change the past, but we can be there for them right now. I am not going to run away any longer, either. I am going to be there for both those boys, but I need your help—come on man! Let's get down from this wet roof and get our butts to work. Do you realize what it would do to Kyle if you jumped? It would kill him. From what I understand, you're his only positive adult role model. Without you, he would give up and wither away and die a slow death. We can't let that happen."

Butch did not know what to think or do. His arms were very tired, but his brain was starting to slowly function again. Was there really hope? Could they help those boys, and was he a coward for wanting to jump? He looked at Sam, trying to focus his eyes clearly. There almost seemed to be a pink light surrounding him. Was he hallucinating—had he gone crazy? Maybe the booze was starting to wear off, or maybe it was just the sun casting its glow as it settled in the west . . . but as he looked around, dense black clouds covered the sky, with no sun in sight. The man had said "Let's get to work," and Butch could understand that. Butch knew how to work; that's what coaching was about.

Sam could feel Butch coming around, and he signaled with a slight wave of his left hand for the rest of them to get off the roof. Baker was leery, but Grier said he thought they should do what Sam wanted. One by one they slowly made their way down the fire escape on the east side of the building.

Butch began to sob as he slid down to a sitting position with his legs wrapped around the flag pole. "I'll never get another job. I'll starve to death. They will never let me coach again." His voice rose until he was yelling, "How can I be there for them? Kyle is paralyzed, and your son is going to prison! How can I help those boys?"

"Butch, come with me to Saint Vincent Shelter for Men. You can live and work there; we need all the help we can get. Aren't you a Catholic? It will be like doing penance," replied Sam in a soothing voice. "Come and work with me. We can help Kyle. You can be his personal coach, and we can get him walking again. Lots of people walk again after doctors don't believe they can. I believe he can do it with help from both of us. We can help my son get a more lenient sentence and get him a second chance."

A tiny, warm glow ran through Butch's body. Living like a monk, helping the poor and disabled . . . he could feel the hope swelling in his heart. He was tired of living alone, drinking, chasing woman on Match.com, and watching sports and porn movies all night. He didn't really want to die. Maybe they really could help the boys. Maybe there was hope, something to live for after all.

Tears ran down his cheeks as he sat quietly for several minutes, then slowly he got his large body up and stood straight while holding onto the flagpole for support. He looked around like huge grizzly bear sniffing the breeze to get his bearings after waking up from a long winter's slumber. Gradually and with a bit of a wobble, he started walking toward Sam.

The two of them awkwardly embraced on the top of the roof with the sun peeking through the clouds. Neither was sure who needed the other most but at that moment they didn't care. They held each other for almost a minute before they let go. Then they walked over to the ladder and started down the stairs to join the shocked group of rescuers on the ground. Little did anyone know—especially Butch and Sam—but at that moment a new chapter was opening in both their lives, and in the lives of Zack and Kyle as well.

"You're a great date, Alan. I've never had a Saturday quite so exciting," quipped Anne before taking a bite of her chow mein. "This real-life drama is interesting as hell, but it sure takes a lot out of a gal."

The two of them had never been alone in a purely social situation before. Butch and Sam had left the school with Baker in the back of his unmarked car. Alan asked Anne whether she wanted to go to Chan's for dinner, then found himself feeling a bit awkward. When Anne had held his hand earlier in the day, a strange uneasiness had come over him . . . a deep, sad longing that also felt so natural and right.

He had not dated since the day Katherine came home from work three years before and announced she wanted a divorce. He was caught off guard and had tried to talk her out of the idea and suggested marriage counseling, but she wasn't willing to give it a try . . . she said she was done. She told Alan that the boys were basically raised now, and she didn't want to be married to a high school principal any longer. She had decided that it was way too stressful, and she had set her sights higher for the second part of her life. Three months after the divorce she married Rick, her orthodontist and boss.

This isn't a real date, Alan reminded himself while reaching for the last eggroll. He thought of Anne as his closest female friend and a great vice principal. But as he sat with her at an intimate table for two with flickering candlelight, a warm feeling filtered through his body. He'd always appreciated her bubbly, fun personality and her large smile that lit up her whole face, but lately she sure seemed a lot more attractive to him. With fair skin and her hair as black as a moonless winter night she looked absolutely radiant. But then suddenly he wondered whether she had changed her hairstyle, or what was different about her now to make him feel this way. Was he dreaming?

"Alan," she said, bringing him out of his trance, "you still look a bit perplexed. I am not making you nervous, am I? The principal and vice principal having dinner together by candlelight—what a great scandal, don't you think? You know, you look very handsome, Mr. Carter. I don't know why we have not done this before."

"Thanks for the compliment, but maybe I am a wee bit perplexed," Alan replied, looking up sheepishly from his plate of garlic green beans. "With a glass of red wine, you become much bolder, Miss Briggs."

"It's a bad habit I have. Give me one glass of wine and I spill my guts," she replied. "I've never been able to tell you before how much I admire you. You remember when you stood up to those cheerleaders and their moms who wanted to change the girls' uniforms to be more revealing and sexy with those pink panties? You told them no way, and you did not allow them to start dirty dancing on the field. You became my hero right then and there. Our girls got a little perturbed at the time but several of them have recently told me they aren't feeling like sex objects like some of the girls at other schools, who look and act more like strippers than high school cheerleaders. Anyway . . . at that moment I kind of developed a crush on you, and it's slowly grown from there."

Anne's large, green eyes looked at Alan for a long moment. She put down her chopsticks while resting her hand under her chin for support. Alan was stunned but shyly replied, "Well, Anne, I guess this is 'true confessions' night. I really don't know what is going on, but I do know that over the past year I have become very fond of you. Maybe more than a principal should of his vice principal. But because we work together like we do, I have been clueless about how to act or not act. I guess some things are out of our hands, so maybe we should wait, observe, and see what happens.

A lazy smile crept out from behind Anne's tired face. "You know, Alan, you are absolutely right. Some things are out of our hands and we just have to wait and see what happens. But I like you a lot. I used to think you were kind of a stuffy old Capricorn, but that changed last June when we started talking after school. I find you fascinating, so the next few months should be very interesting."

They smiled and toasted to a better tomorrow. As they returned to eating their beans and chicken chow mein, both seemed to realize that their lives, too, had been forever changed.

CHAPTER EIGHTEEN
SEEDS OF RECONCILIATION

Zack was reading a *Harry Potter* novel in his cell when he heard voices coming down the hall. One of the night-shift female guards had given him the book. He was embarrassed about reading the story and didn't want anyone to think he was just a kid or a wimp, so he stuck it under his mattress. He sat up quickly and leaned back against the white-concrete wall, his feet barely dangling off the edge of the bed. Since he had broken down a couple of days prior, his treatment from the guards had improved. They were actually treating him as a human being that they knew and not just some freak shooter.

A dark-haired female night guard, who looked not much older than Zack, had tried to sit and talk with him earlier in the evening. Zack was feeling very lonely, which was not an unusual feeling for him, and he welcomed the attention. He tried to be polite and answer the questions she asked about his life. He didn't know how he felt about his new status, but he did know he feared it wouldn't last.

At about 6:30 p.m., Zack saw Lieutenant Baker's wrinkled face appear in the small window of his cell door. "Hello, Zack," said Baker, as he opened the steel door to Zack's cell. "I've got a couple of visitors here to see you."

Zack recognized his father immediately. He looked just like the picture Zack had carried in his mind of him for the past nine years. He also recognized Coach Cassidy from school, but he couldn't begin to fathom what the hell these two men were doing together, here in his cell. Zack did not say a word. He just pulled back against the wall like a rattler recoiled to strike.

"Zack, I am not going to stay," said Coach Cassidy, "but I need to tell you something. I want to truly apologize to you from the bottom of my heart for protecting Kyle Ritter. I did not originally know what he did to you, but I did not ask any questions, either. I just blindly protected him so he would not get into more trouble. I take full responsibility for causing great harm to you both. I wish I knew something else to say, but I don't, except I am going to do my damnedest to make it up to you. I promise that I will be here for you. I am going to get out of here now and leave you and your father alone for a while."

Zack watched Coach Cassidy leave, as Baker closed the door behind them. He wished Baker would stay—he did not want to be left alone with this man who said he was his father and who looked and acted like the father Zack remembered. But how could this man be his father? He looked like one of those monks he saw on TV. Zack had been told that his father was a wino, a bum . . . so this man must be an imposter.

As Sam looked at his son crouched on his mattress, his insides did a somersault and he felt his energy level drop dramatically. He sat down on the single, wooden chair facing Zack. Sam fidgeted on the lumpy, mustard-colored cushion, trying to get comfortable and figure out how to start what was going to be so difficult to say.

Sam took in a deep breath and said, "It's been a long time, Zack. I know you may hate me, and I can't blame you if you do. I suspect you don't want to listen to me, but you don't have much choice because they aren't letting you out and I am not leaving for a little while. I need to tell you, right up front, what happened when I left you nine years ago. Then, if you want me to leave, I will."

After his father left, ninety minutes later, Zack lay back down on his bunk. He still felt angry and his stomach felt sore and raw, but he also felt new things—feelings he never knew existed. Something warm pulsated through his body, penetrating the cold numbness that usually engulfed him. He knew it was some type of hope and hope was a rare experience, one that had always disappointed him. What was the purpose? He wanted to cry just thinking about it. But he couldn't deny it, he was feeling something . . . he felt alive again.

Kyle could see Coach Cassidy standing over him. He tried to move his head to the left to see his face more clearly, but his head would not budge. Through the corner of his eye he could tell there was a smaller man standing behind the coach, but he couldn't make out his features. Coach Cassidy introduced him as Zack's father, Sam. *This nightmare is just getting more bizarre*, Kyle thought in alarm.

What would Zack's father be doing here? Had this man come to beat him while Kyle could not defend himself? How did Zack even have a father, or a family? He always thought of Zack as just a freak who lived under a bridge or something, and he'd never thought about where freaks come from. But now *he* was the freak! And he knew where he came from--or did he?

Coach Cassidy leaned over Kyle with his hands on the bed so Kyle could look directly into his large, brown eyes. Coach looked different, especially his eyes. They were not bloodshot like before—maybe because Kyle had never seen him this close up. But it was more than that. He looked as persistent as usual, but kind of peaceful, not his usual rough, grouchy self. He kept talking about how sorry he was. He said that a lot of what happened was his fault, and that he was going to be here for him.

Kyle didn't understand what he was talking about. What did it mean that Coach was going to be there for him and that he had gotten sober? Nothing in Kyle's world made sense to him anymore. The world he lived in before the shooting no longer existed.

Zack's father said that Kyle would someday walk again, that everything was going to be okay. Kyle could barely see this man and he wondered what this man could want from him. Why would he be here after what Kyle had done to his son? If he was here to hurt him, he was way too late. Kyle couldn't hurt anymore. Zack had already taken care of that.

But Zack's father had a look about him that Kyle had never seen before—intense, yet peaceful and calm. He was like a monk, or like that mystic guy named "Tolle," or something like that. He'd seen Tolle on *Oprah* one day when he was home faking being sick and for some reason he remembered him. Coach Cassidy, the gruff, foulmouthed old guy, was starting to look that way, too. This was way too weird. How could this other guy be Zack's old man, and what could they be doing together? Were they gay? Were they a queer couple? *It must be the morphine*, Kyle decided. This had to be a dream, just another part of the ongoing nightmare.

The two men said they didn't want to wear him out, that they wouldn't stay very long, and Kyle was thankful of that—at least he thought he was, but maybe not.

After they left, the nurses gave him more morphine and Kyle felt tired but wonderful for several hours. Hopeful thoughts went through his mind and he thought about playing football again. He felt like he was going to make it, and everything might turn out all right after all. But an hour later Kyle could tell the morphine was starting to wear off just like it always did. The pain was coming back, and his legs were starting to ache even though he didn't know for sure if they were still there. He could tell his blood pressure was also starting to rise again and he felt his body tremble, but nothing seemed to move. He wanted to crawl out of his body but there was nowhere to go and no way to get out. The world looked suddenly hopeless again and he could feel the wetness from his tears running down his cheeks and onto his lips. If he could just go to sleep and die, all his prayers would be answered.

Monday

Roger Speiglman had always been a risk taker. It seemed to be part of his nature, though risk-taking, he understood, was a rather unusual trait for psychologists. When he went out with his wife on their first date, she told him up front that she didn't lie, and she didn't cheat, but she did sometimes break the rules. He pondered that for several minutes and realized he was the same way. Like her, he was willing to break the rules if he thought they needed breaking and if he could help someone by doing so. It had become a lifelong habit—sometimes it served him well, other times it made life more difficult. But having a wife who lived the same way made these choices easier. He had often thought it would be a good idea for every potential couple to ask that question of the other when getting to know one another. He was not sure what people should do if the answer was different, but he knew the question about rule-breaking was important nonetheless.

Occasionally in his business, he met up with a kid so badly damaged that he could not help him. He had spent over a dozen hours now with Zack, enough to know that, thankfully, Zack was not one of those.

The year prior, Roger treated another potential school shooter: a seventeen-year-old who had recently turned pro as a professional kickboxer. He was originally from Northern Idaho and had been boxing since he was eight, because there it was legal with parental guidance. Roger had spent eight months with the boy after he had made numerous violent threats to the alternative school he'd been attending. Going around fierce parental resistance, Roger had finally received permission to have a CAT scan performed on the boy. It was then discovered that his brain had been slightly dislodged and disfigured, and there was no hope that he could be rehabilitated without brain surgery, which the boy and his family refused. Consequently, the kid continued to be out in the world untreated, with these kinds of violent tendencies, like hundreds of somewhat similar cases. But what to do? Roger did not have an answer.

With Zack, however, it was different. Roger knew that they'd had a breakthrough when Zack broke down after Roger pressed him about his father—and then his father appeared, out of nowhere! After interviewing Sam, Roger believed he was sincere in wanting to help. From a psychological standpoint, Sam seemed as though he really had it together. Yet Roger didn't understand why Sam was broke and living in a shelter for homeless men . . . this did not make any sense.

One thing Roger did know was that Zack was very vulnerable right now. He had come out of a state of psychosis, at least temporarily, and Roger wanted to act while there was an opening. Therefore, he arranged a meeting with the key players: Lieutenant Baker; the presiding judge, Stephanie Jenkins; Zack's attorney, Jerry Cutter; and the district attorney, Wayne Ableman. As the group gathered in the judge's chambers, Roger spent at least twenty minutes outlining Zack's case.

"Therefore, to wrap this up," Roger asserted, "my theory—very simply stated in layman's terms—is that Kyle and Zack are both victims. They are both victims who turned into perpetrators, because of circumstances beyond the control of their rational minds and their conscious ability to understand their thoughts and actions. They both had similar issues going on, even though as young adults they despised each other. From a general point of view, I would diagnose both boys as having borderline personality disorder. We don't understand all the root causes of this mental illness—whether biological or psychological or a combination of the two. But what we do know is that in some cases these symptoms can be traced to kids before they even hit puberty . . . kids who have been consistently abused at a young and vulnerable age. The abuse can come in different forms and from different caregivers, including parents, relatives, friends, educators, and even the general public. I know Zack's history very well, but I don't know all of Kyle's history. However, I have pieced enough together to make this general diagnosis.

"My belief is if we can help the boys find common ground and open up to each other, this step forward might significantly help both of them to come out of their emotional trauma. I know this sounds a bit farfetched, but I believe it is possible and could be extremely beneficial to both boys and well worth trying. Thus I am recommending that the two boys meet under strict supervision and we work to see if we can't get some type of reconciliation.

"In conclusion, I want everyone to understand that I am here not at the request of the defense attorney, Mr. Cutter, nor by the insistence of Zack's family. I was hired by the State to conduct an independent examination of Zack, and to present that to the court. And that is what I have presented to you, along with my recommendations."

"Well, Dr. Speiglman, you presented your case very well. I am duly impressed," responded District Attorney Ableman. "I like to think of myself as open-minded, but never—and I repeat, *never!*—have I heard such a farfetched idea as bringing a victim and the accused perpetrator together in a hospital room, to try and have some type of reconciliation! I don't see it helping anybody, at least in the eyes of the law. I am sure I don't need to remind anyone that we still operate in this country under the principle of 'an eye for an eye' and 'a tooth for a tooth.' Zack Diamond is accused of attempted murder, and Kyle is his victim, no matter what the circumstances were before the attempted murder, or how you, Dr. Speiglman, have diagnosed him."

Cutter started to interrupt, but then thought the better of it when he looked over at Judge Jenkins. The stern expression on her face as she listened to Ableman and a little voice inside him told him this was a time to remain silent.

"I understand your hesitation, Mr. Ableman," responded Judge Jenkins. "District attorneys build their careers on convictions, and compassion is not usually part of their job description, nor even in their vocabulary, and sometimes that is for very good reasons. Yet both these boys are juveniles, and we won't be ruling on whether Zack should be tried as an adult until later next week. I have a little time here so let's see what we can do in the meanwhile. I am assuming you are willing to supervise this reconciliation meeting, Dr. Speiglman?"

"Yes, I am, your Honor," Roger replied.

"Sometimes, for the benefit of a victim—and truthfully, both boys do seem to have become victims—we need to try something a little unorthodox. I am proposing we encourage Zack to visit Kyle in the hospital one time. Dr. Speiglman, the Lieutenant, and Mr. Cutter will also attend to monitor the interaction—and if all goes well we might encourage more visits. Both these boys are in very sorry states, and their futures are looking rather dismal, so let's try something bold. Perhaps we can help Zack instead of locking him up and throwing away the key. And Kyle . . . well he needs anything we can do for him at this point."

This time it was Ableman jumping up to open his mouth, but one look from Judge Jenkins told him any further arguments would be futile, and so he sat back down and said nothing.

Roger took in a deep breath. He had hope for Zack, and he believed that if they could keep him in a state where he was in touch with his emotions, they might be able to reach him. Taking Zack to see Kyle might be the necessary jolt to keep him conscious and open him up to his feelings. But at the same time, Roger was a bit nervous about the whole process, and felt he needed all the support he could get. He appreciated how the judge included Lieutenant Baker and Cutter in on the first trip to take Zack to the hospital to see Kyle.

The next day when Zack learned that he'd be going to see Kyle, he did not want any part of the idea. He refused and screamed and yelled and called Roger every name he could think of. But two days later, when Roger arrived with Baker and Cutter, Zack lost his resolve. He felt powerless to resist in front of three adults. For a moment he grabbed hold of the bars of his cell, but once outside he went quietly, if sullenly.

Zack felt nauseous and he was sure that if he didn't sit down, he'd get sick. Zack couldn't ever remember being in a hospital before, except after his suicide attempt, and then only for a day or so. The hospital was large, with high ceilings. People in green gowns and funny green hats seemed to be going in every which way. Zack again realized that he actually felt something: this time he was terrified.

Kyle had been moved out of intensive care to the third floor. As the four walked down the halls, the doctors and nurses they passed couldn't help but stare. It seemed most everyone in the hospital knew Kyle's story and recognized Zack from the newspaper pictures. Speculation ran wild and rumors spread up and down the corridors of the hospital in a matter of minutes, as texts and tweets filled the airways.

"Room 309," said Baker, as they stopped outside the door to Kyle's room. Zack expected them to stop, talk, and make a plan, but instead Baker opened the door immediately. Roger put his arm around Zack's shoulder and led him into the room, while Baker and Cutter slid behind him and stationed themselves against the back wall.

Zack felt shaky and dizzy and wanted to bolt. He could see a bed directly in front of him but not who was in it. Large white pieces of equipment filled the room, and a terrible smell wafted in the air, along with a light buzzing sound coming from the equipment. Roger took Zack's elbow and slowly ushered him to the side of the bed. Zack couldn't recognize the body in the bed—it looked like a small boy, a complete stranger. They must have come in the wrong room by mistake. There were tubes everywhere, in the mouth and in the arms of this pale, scrawny stranger. This could not be the ferocious Kyle Ritter, the monster who had peed all over him—this must be the wrong bed. Zack scanned the rest of the small room, but this was all there was. There were no other patients in the room. He looked over at Roger who quietly said, "Yes, Zack. That's Kyle. He is very sick and has lost about thirty pounds."

Kyle had heard the door open and he felt someone walking towards him. His ears had become much more sensitive and alert over the last week. Not being able to move his head, he had to stretch his eyeballs to the side to see who was approaching. When he saw Zack's face, his body jolted in shock and he felt burning sensations through his heart right into his arms and legs. *Oh my God*, he thought. *First Zack's father and now Zack! Has he snuck in to finish the job?*

Kyle's body jerked again ever so slightly, his pupils became dilated and a deep redness came over his pale, white face—then suddenly his mouth opened and closed twice.

That was very strange, thought Zack. They had told him that Kyle couldn't move anything, even his mouth.

Kyle's heart raced a million beats per minute and he wanted to scream so badly that he could have sworn his mouth had indeed opened, but he must have been hallucinating. Zack was staring at him with his mouth closed tight. Kyle's heart slowed slightly as he now saw someone else in the room behind Zack. He looked like a doctor. *Maybe they had Zack in chains and brought him in to show him what a horrible crime he had committed.*

Suddenly Kyle's head jerked back and he went into convulsions. He could feel the vomit rise from the bottom of his stomach and go up into his mouth. He felt it running down his chin and he automatically moved his head slightly to the side so he would not swallow any of it.

Zack quickly grabbed a wet towel from the washbasin next to the bed and reached over to wipe Kyle's face. Kyle could hear Zack excitedly telling the nurse that Kyle had moved his head and mouth. Kyle's heart continued to race as he again gradually opened his mouth ever so slightly. It worked, it actually worked! He lay still for another thirty seconds as he tried to move his hand; nothing happened, so he tried moving just a finger. He swore he felt the slightest flinch.

"Kyle," the nurse kept repeating. "Kyle!" Slowly he moved his head ever so slightly, just enough to the left to see her excited, smiling face.

Zack stepped back as two nurses worked on cleaning Kyle up, talking to him all the while. Zack's mind felt overwhelmed and he could feel his heart beating so fast it hurt as he tried to comprehend what was happening. This was a *lot* more than he had bargained for. Roger had told him they were afraid Kyle might be totally paralyzed for life, but now he'd moved his head and mouth at the sight of him!

Roger was stunned and at a loss for words for what seemed like several minutes. He finally managed to gain some composure and put his hand on Zack's shoulder, and told him they better go and let the nurses finish their work. He tenderly squeezed Zack's neck and said that if Zack wanted to, they could come back tomorrow. Now Zack did not want to leave, and he looked up at Roger with bewildered but pleading eyes.

"Sorry," Lieutenant Baker mumbled, after finally finding his voice. "I think the Dr. is right. We need to give Kyle some space." Zack reluctantly succumbed to Roger and Baker's coaxing and, after another glance at Kyle, the four of them walked out into the hall.

Back in his cell that evening, Zack pondered the day's events. He'd felt elated when Kyle moved his head. He couldn't remember feeling that way since before his father had left. How could his hate for Kyle disappear in an instant when he saw him move? Was that what they called a miracle? He surprisingly felt some type of compassion for Kyle and, stranger yet, he felt connected to him. Was that because he had been the one to shoot him? He didn't understand any of this.

On the ride back from the hospital, Zack's feeling of joy seemed to be contagious. Even grouchy Lieutenant Baker and his attorney, Cutter, were happy and joking. They kidded around with Zack like he was one of them, instead of a dwarf kid prisoner. Since his father left he had never remembered being treated like an adult, never once.

At the same time, Zack felt shaken by the recent events. He thought about his father and the reasonable, logical explanation he'd given for his disappearance. His father had seemed so sincere and a big part of Zack wanted to believe in him. But could he really trust him? The pain of not having his father in his life for so long had taken its toll, and it almost overwhelmed him every time he thought about it. Maybe the spark of love was still there; maybe that ember was still burning. As scary as that felt to him, Zack knew that deep down he did not want to let go of that spark, even if he had to spend his life in prison.

Zack would be in court again tomorrow, and everything could change. Yet, if someone had asked him how he felt right now, at this moment, he would have answered, "Fine, just fine . . . on a scale of one to ten, maybe even an eight for the first time in my life.

CHAPTER NINETEEN
RIGHT FROM WRONG

When Jerry Cutter saw Kyle move his mouth, he felt like he was watching a miracle happen right in front of him. Jerry never remembered seeing a miracle before. He didn't even believe in them or know what they looked like. On the way home, they were all laughing—even that grouch Baker—but the unbelievable part was Zack. When Cutter looked in his rearview mirror, Zack had a big smile on his face and he actually giggled when Baker told one of his corny off-colored jokes. The kid had feelings after all. Even with all that anger, he was a real person.

Jerry didn't bother opening the door of his Porsche when he arrived at his office. He rose to sit on the back of the seat and, swinging his legs over the driver's side door, he landed with both feet on the ground. He walked whistling into the office, smiled at Jan, and asked where his partners were.

"They're in Bernie's office, and they have been waiting for you, Jerry. Go on in," she replied.

"Thanks, Jan. By the way, I like what you did with your hair. I have always liked ponytails."

"You just like women, period!" Jan replied.

"That may be true," said Jerry, opening the door to Bernie's office, "but I do like ponytails."

"Hi Jerry. Come on in and have a seat," said Bernie, who was sitting across his desk from the senior partner. Doug Smithers was impeccably dressed as always, his graying hair slicked back neatly with a bit of a shag around his neck. "We have been here for an hour-and-a-half discussing our—your—Zack Diamond case, so your timing is perfect."

"Great," replied Jerry, "because I just spent the morning with the kid, and with his victim, Kyle Ritter. It was a real eye-opener. I think there may be hope for that little turd. I saw him loosen up and show some real emotion this morning when Kyle unexpectedly moved his head as he puked all over himself. That means Kyle is not completely paralyzed. I am getting excited about this case. I think we can do something for this kid, maybe for both of them."

"Well, we're glad you're excited because we're excited too . . . *very* excited. In fact, that's what we've been talking about," said Doug in his baritone voice, rising from his chair to reach his full six-four height. "Trying the kid as an adult is going to be by far the biggest thing that ever happened to this firm. This will not only make us a ton of money down the road, but it will also instantly make us all celebrities. We've decided to defend this kid as a team, Jerry. As senior partner, I will become the lead attorney, naturally, but you are still the attorney of record. The two of you will become my co-attorneys and we will all share in the work and notoriety and, down the road, we'll share in the dough as our bylaws spell out."

"Slow down, Doug," said Jerry, interrupting Smithers. "I thought we called this meeting to discuss whether Zack *should* be tried as an adult or as a juvenile. I did not expect to walk in here and find out that you're now the attorney running the show, and that we are trying him as an adult, period. That's not what I call a partnership! Hell, you aren't even slightly interested in what happened this morning!"

"Calm down, Jerry. Of course, we are interested," stated Doug, "but I want to remind you that you are a junior partner, which is quite different from a full partner. Our corporate bylaws clearly spell out that the senior partner is the final decision maker. I have given this much serious deliberation and talked it over with Bernie. I have made a decision based on what I think is best for the entire firm and the client, not just what is best for you. Don't get selfish, Jerry. We're a team here. It's time to discuss how we're going to defend Zack as a team and not spend our time arguing a moot point. Believe me, Jerry—the decision has been made. It's a done deal, so let's move forward."

Bernie jumped in, "Now, listen to me, Jerry. We defend this kid as an adult and we'll draw a lot more attention to what happened to him in school. He may hang—figuratively speaking, of course—but so will this Kyle kid. We can make this case interesting to the media by showing what a shit Kyle is. We will get our PI to dig up any trash that's out there on Kyle and his whole family and I have a feeling there is a bunch. We'll make him look like a juvenile Jack the Ripper, and Zack will look like the victim—the poor dwarf who has been picked on his whole life finally gets revenge. We may get Zack off with ten years for attempted murder, which is quite darn good, considering it was premeditated. And hell, with good behavior he could be out in five."

"Attempted murder, as an adult?" asked Jerry.

"Of course. We've already decided that," replied Doug, his voice getting louder and deeper.

Jerry sat in Bernie's heavily padded, imitation-leather chair and closed his eyes. He put his hands to his face and ran his fingers down and around his nose. Then he leaned back in the chair and slid his hands behind his neck, thinking quietly for a moment as he took it all in. His partners stared at him in anticipation.

"Well, gentleman," Jerry said softly, "I guess you're right. We don't have anything to argue about, because you have already made up your collective mind. But I do want to remind you that Judge Jenkins appointed me, not the firm, as Zack's court-appointed attorney, and she is the only one who can change that appointment. And I have no intention of asking her to do that, so now we do have something else to talk about."

Jerry took in another deep breath before continuing, "I am resigning my partnership in the firm, as of today, right now this minute. I will be taking Zack's case with me, as I am entitled to do so by California State Law, and I am going to do my best to have him tried as a juvenile. I'll start cleaning out my files immediately and we can conference again tomorrow at noon, if you'd like, so we can tie up any other loose ends. Right now, I have a lot to do before tomorrow afternoon."

Before anyone else could say a word or move, Jerry quickly stood up and took two steps toward the door.

"Wait! Just a minute!" Bernie almost yelled as he also stood up. "Jerry, you can't just get up and leave—we're partners, all three of us. Sit back down and let's talk this over like grown men. I am sure we can work this out. This was just a starting point."

"I don't think so. Sorry, Bernie, and you, too, Doug, but I don't belong here. I guess I have known that for a long time, deep down, maybe since my first day. This case is just the catalyst I needed to make a shift. I'll see you guys tomorrow." Jerry turned and walked out the office and into the reception area, leaving the other two still sitting there speechless. "Jan, are you interested in a new position? How'd you like to be the office manager of my new firm, Cutter and Associates?" he asked, as he stood in front of her desk.

"I just might be, Jerry. I have already given Bernie and Doug my notice and told them I was tired of them making passes at me all day long, like they own me. It's amazing that we get anything at all done around here when all you guys seem to think about is drinking and sleeping with me. But you are single, not married like those two jerks—and cute! So I don't mind you flirting, Jerry, and you have never seriously propositioned me or grabbed my butt. You have treated me as if I am a valuable employee, so yeah. You get an office and I'll be there. By the way, though—who are the other attorneys?"

Jerry grinned, "Don't know. I guess it's just me for now, but the name sounds better that way. Don't you think?"

By the end of the day Jerry had signed a new lease on an office two blocks down on Hagen Avenue, and had hired Jan as his new legal secretary and office manager. Jerry was feeling no pain, only gain, and life was good. As he thought about it, he realized he hadn't felt this way since the day he'd graduated from law school almost four years before.

Judge Stephanie Jenkins was tall and thin, a gray-haired black woman with a serious demeanor and nineteen years of judicial experience under her belt. She called the hearing to order and asked the prosecuting district attorney, Ableman, and the defense lawyer, Cutter, to step forward.

"Our primary purpose today," she explained to them, "is to decide if Zack Diamond should be tried as an adult or as a juvenile." Judge Jenkins went through the formalities for five more minutes and then asked both counselors if they had come to a formal agreement on Zack's fate.

In unison they announced, "We have, your Honor. We have agreed that Zack should be tried as a juvenile."

"Good. That makes my job much easier. Now let's talk about the hospital visits," she replied

After the hearing, in the back of the courtroom, Jerry told Zack that he had cut a deal with the district attorney's office. Zack would be tried as a juvenile. "Once news of the attack by Kyle, Jeff, and Dustin—along with Dustin's confession—became public, the district attorney had no other choice . . . the case now was very messy for him," Jerry explained.

Jerry went on to say that, because Zack had been attacked by Kyle, and could plead that he believed Kyle might attack him again, the case became extremely dicey for the district attorney who did not like to lose. Jerry also told Zack that if he declined a trial, Ableman would recommend to the judge that Zack spend three years in a home for boys, and Roger would treat him during that time. If Zack kept his nose clean while he was there, he could be eligible for parole within a year.

As they walked down the courtroom aisle, Cutter told Zack that he had just been given a new lease on life. Then he remarked that maybe they had both gotten a new lease on life. Zack didn't understand but he felt happy because Jerry was happy. As they left the courthouse, Zack could not believe that life looked so different this week compared to last week—it almost seemed impossible, like it was a dream, or a miracle.

CHAPTER TWENTY
DIVERGING PATHS

Zack's mother sat alone in the back of the courtroom and wept with gratitude and relief when the judge announced that Zack would be tried as a juvenile. A trial, the judge said, was unnecessary since she and Jerry Cutter agreed to the district attorney's offer. Zack would now spend three years in a home for boys. If he did well, the time could be reduced to just one year. She shivered when Dr. Speiglman explained the necessity of having Zack's father involved in the treatment.

The day before, during a two-hour meeting in the Juvenile Center visiting room, Zack had told her that he loved her. This was the first time she heard those words since her ex-husband, Sam, had left nine years before, and her heart cried for joy. But Zack also told her about his new relationship with his father, and said that his attorney, Cutter, told him she could not keep his father out of his life any longer. On hearing this, she cried again—but these were not tears of joy.

As she drove home from the court that afternoon, Zack's mother reflected on the last several months. She had been thrown a major curve ball that had turned her life upside down. Her son was gone. He might never live at home again, and her contact with him would be limited for the next several years. *Thank God those two bullies did not die*, she thought to herself. *At least Zack may have a second chance.*

Don Ritter, Kyle's father, had passed the border station in San Diego four hours before. The narrow road was paved but the dirt shoulders dropped drastically, with no room to pull over in case of emergency. The countryside was barren and brown except for the green, spiky cactus plants that grew up to twenty feet tall. *It must be close to 110 degrees*, Don thought. He'd never been in such a bleak, dry land. With no air conditioning, it felt like he was driving through hell. *Well, if hell is like this, I guess I can handle it. I probably belong here anyway*, he remarked to himself.

The afternoon before, he had withdrawn all the family savings from the First National Bank: all 3,223 dollars of it. He left two dollars in to keep the account open, although he didn't know why. He wasn't planning to ever come back.

Driving alone had given him time to think and to make a plan. In Mexico, he had been told, you could camp right on the beach along the Sea of Cortez for five dollars a day. You could fish all day and if you didn't catch anything, you could buy fresh fish and fruit for a couple of bucks. The people were supposed to be friendly and easygoing. What else did he need? He planned to get there by morning, at which time he would start a new life.

When he crossed over the border he decided he would never go back to the States, and never face the possibility of jail time. Screw Kate and Kyle, too. Hell, his dad had beaten the shit out of him at least twice a week until he was eleven years old, and the bastard had never gone to jail for it. His old man had left when he was twelve, and he had turned out okay. So, he reasoned, Kyle would turn out okay, too, even if he spent the rest of his life in a wheelchair. Hells bells! Kyle's getting shot by a Jew was just plain stupid. The shooting wasn't his fault, and there was nothing he could do for Kyle now, he reminded himself for the tenth time that day. Besides, his old lady would be happy taking care of Kyle, and the two of them could live happily ever after—just like in a fairytale.

Don had not seen a town in two hours and it was quickly getting dark. He had heard not to be out on these roads at night. It wasn't like the old days before the turn of the century when the roads were relatively safe. The narrow shoulders made the road hard to drive, and there were rumors of banditos and drug runners running wild in Baja. He had already been stopped once at a checkpoint by four young kids wearing army uniforms; they'd looked no older than Kyle. One of the boys who wore a helmet with a braid across the top seemed to be in charge. He came out and spoke to Don in garbled English while the rest of his crew hid behind sand bags with machine guns pointed at him. After peeking into his front seat, the kid waved him on while talking excitedly in some foreign language that Don assumed was Spanish. It had made him nervous. Why couldn't these damn Mexicans learn English if they wanted his tourist dollars? He was looking forward to getting to a town with a campground.

Suddenly there was a jerk, and a bang, and a thump, thump, thump! His rig pulled hard to the right. With a sudden lurch and a loud scraping sound, his 1988 Chevy truck and overhead camper came to a screeching halt in the middle of the road.

Don turned on his flashers, got out of the truck, and walked around to the back-left side. Sure enough, the back-left tire was almost totally gone, and the truck sat on the bare rim. Pieces of the rubber were strewn for a hundred feet behind him. He also noticed his right blinker wasn't working. *More bad luck,* he muttered under his breath, *the story of my fricking life.*

"Shit," he muttered again, as he unlocked his camper door to get his jack and saw his belongings scattered everywhere. He stood in the road, already drenched in sweat, wondering when his luck would ever change, when he saw a light coming up behind him—the first vehicle he had seen in a half-hour. Maybe, he hoped, it was one of the government repair trucks that were supposed to be on the road day and night to help stranded tourists. But as it got closer he could see it only had one working headlight, which was not a good sign.

As the vehicle slowed, he saw it was an ancient one-ton Dodge truck with a large flatbed in back. On the bed were four dark-haired, hatless men, all carrying old rifles or shotguns. The truck pulled up abreast of Don, but the driver's tinted side window kept Don from seeing inside and the passenger did not roll it down. The three older men in back wore deep scowls on their faces, and stared at him silently, even when he waved his hand and said howdy. The fourth and the youngest one looked about fourteen and must have been drunk. He started laughing so hard he seemed uncontrollably crazy.

The smell of tequila was potent, and Don could see several empty bottles on the bed of the truck. This made him lick his lips and he wanted a drink desperately, but they all had their rifles pointed in his general direction, so he felt it wise not to ask. These were obviously not soldiers or highway repairmen, he realized, with a sick feeling spreading down into a cavern in the pit of his stomach. His luck, he decided, was not changing today, not even close.

CHAPTER TWENTY-ONE
MY SUBSCRIPTION RATE IS UP

Karen Kendrick was relaxing in her office chair with her bare feet up on the desk and her plaid skirt half way up her long, tan legs. She had been on the phone with her Uncle Marty—the managing partner of the largest chain of newspapers in California—for more than half an hour. After the first five minutes of meaningless pleasantries, the conversation quickly began slipping away from both of them.

"Look, Karen, I understand what you're saying, but that doesn't change a thing. The guy is a flaming liberal and he needs to turn to toast. It does not matter whether he is right or wrong. I mean, some of what he says makes sense to me, but it's simply against our company policy to support liberal educators. It doesn't matter whether we personally believe they're right or wrong—that's not the point. We have given you some slack here, but now you have gone too far. You need to be reined in like any good filly."

"Like any *good filly*? Is that what you said, Marty?"

"I didn't mean it like that, Karen. That's just a metaphor for a high-spirited woman. You know what I mean."

"Marty, I do know what you mean, and you're just digging yourself deeper. Let's get back to Carter before we split up the family even more and I disown you completely.

"Look," she continued, "our incoming responses have been in the range of sixty-five percent in support of our editorial position on this piece . . . and numbers don't lie."

"I understand that, but it's the other thirty-five percent that makes up our base that I'm concerned about . . . and they are adamantly against what this Carter fellow is doing. They don't like this self-esteem, touchy-feely stuff, and they don't like Democratic big spenders, and they don't like change, unless it means getting rid of a lefty politician. They simply want the kids to learn 'the three R's' and nothing more, unless it happens to come from the Old Testament of the Bible."

"Big spenders! Marty, you've got to be kidding! Your conservative Republican boy, George Bush, took over a country with a balanced budget, and when he left us we were very close to bankruptcy. He also had us in two wars that he didn't even count as expenses. And the new moron we've got now has put us so deep in debt with these tax cuts that we will probably never get out of it, and that was just to pay off his election promises. He has gone against everything the Republican Party has stood for since World War II and has made fools out of all of us. Remember, Marty, I am one of the few remaining dinosaurs who likes to be referred to as a 'moderate Republican,' and I think this new fella we've got in office is the worst president this country has ever had! And let me add that the thirty-five percent you're talking about are the *far*-right wackos who don't like anyone with an IQ above 90. And now they have voted in a president already in the first stages of dementia."

"Well, I agree Bush was not an Einstein," answered Marty. "Sometimes he was an embarrassment to the Republican Party and some of these extremists in the Tea Party aren't even that smart—and I totally agree that this new guy is a . . . But whatever, and by the way, I never said that. The point is these folks are an important part of our readership—of our base—and we've already had a number of them cancel their subscriptions, and a few advertisers have not renewed their contracts."

"Marty, my subscription rate was up eleven percent last month when I printed the initial articles surrounding this story. So again, numbers don't lie—you're the one who taught me that. Believe it or not, there are still real conservatives out there who don't want us wasting money and lives on unnecessary wars; or raising the debt limit and borrowing to pay supporters for votes; or using this money to support big oil companies and banks. They want tax money spent prudently and they want an educated society. I think Carter is doing exactly that. He hasn't asked for one additional dime to fund these new programs."

"Yes, Karen . . . I understand that. But he is taking money *away* from the sports teams and putting it into social programming. And you just don't do that in America, especially post-911 America."

"Oh . . . that's the real rub, isn't it? We can't touch our giant sacred cow: *sports!* Keeping our sports teams is even more important than owning a gun for some folks, so we can't do that—can we, Marty? Not even in high school."

"Oh, Karen."

"Come on, Marty. That's what this is all about. In reality, Carter is just making these teams more lean and efficient. Why would a high school varsity football team need *seven* paid coaches? And why would the boys' basketball team need four, while the gym, art, and music classes get cut to zero?

"Competitive sports are totally out of control, Uncle Marty. They are sacred cows and even your Tea Partiers are afraid to touch them. You remember my alma mater, where you and my dad sent me because of their great journalism department? Well, their football coach makes more than the entire journalism staff combined—more than the school's president, and eight times more than the President of the United States, and most importantly three times more than you do! And that is at a publicly funded university. I think it's insane."

"Karen, you're the most opinionated, hard-headed woman I have ever met . . . outside of your mother, aunt, and grandmother, of course."

"Why, that's the nicest compliment you have ever given me, Uncle Marty. Thank you very much."

"That's not exactly the way I meant it, Karen. Anyway—try to tone it down a little, for my sake. We both want to keep our jobs, right? As for your editorial support on gun-control, you may be right; things are getting out of control. Shit, look at Vegas and Parkland. And all these years later I still think of those little kids at Sandy Hook. It still makes me sick to my stomach. The country has got to soften on this issue. But remember you can lead slowly, just don't get too far out there ahead of the mainstream."

"Right, right . . . okay. For your sake I'll try to soften it a little. I am sure you are aware that Oprah is also doing a whole week of shows based on this same 'High School in America' theme. And some type of gun control is now being supported by sixty-seven percent of Americans. Therefore, I expect my subscription and advertising levels will be even higher next month."

"Oprah is a left-wing liberal and the last person I want to be associated with! Karen, just try to tone it down a bit, and I'll talk to the Board of Directors and try to keep them off both our backsides. Let's take a break and let my mind regroup, then we'll talk next week."

"Bye, Uncle Marty—I love you."

"Yeah, right. Well, anyway, I love you, too, kid. Say hi to your mom for me."

Karen put her feet back on the floor with a smile. She hadn't told Marty that she and Alan Carter were going to be Oprah's talk show guests during the weeklong series coming up in two weeks. It might have put him over the edge and she hadn't wanted to push her luck that far.

CHAPTER TWENTY-TWO
HERE WE GO—LET'S NOT SCREW UP

Alan walked from the dark of the parking lot into MLK at 6:36 a.m. He needed to at least try to catch up on some overdue paperwork. At this hour, he hoped he might have a few uninterrupted minutes to himself.

The halls were very quiet, and his shoes echoed on the linoleum. The floors had been swept clean and a fresh coat of wax glistened in the pale light. Last week had been both intense and exciting. Alan wondered what this week had in store, and a gush of fear and excitement rushed into his stomach. He took two deep breaths and slowly exhaled. *Just another day in another week of high school*, he thought to himself, and walked into his office.

Alan sat at his desk and started working on his new, revamped, athletic budget. It was hard to concentrate knowing that any moment he might get a call or a visit that would tell him it was all for naught.

Then his phone rang at 6:54. Alan let it ring three times; he was reluctant to pick it up and deal with another potential problem. Finally, he decided it might be an emergency and picked up the phone.

"Hello, Alan, this is Bob Lancaster. I had a feeling you might be in early today. I was hoping to catch you before you got too busy. How are you this morning?"

"I am doing okay, Bob. How are you?" Alan answered, with a lump in his throat and his mind racing through a half-dozen possible reasons for the call.

"Well, Alan, I could be better. It's been a tough couple of weeks, though I know it's probably been much tougher for you." His voice sounded tired and worn as he continued, "The school board has been embroiled for the past weeks in dealing with the changes you have proposed and implemented at Martin Luther King High.

"I am going to level with you, Alan. At first, even though what you said made some sense, I was not in favor of what you are doing. I don't much like change and I don't like rocking the boat unless it's really important, and I knew there would be a lot of fallout, which of course we've already seen.

"But I haven't slept all week. I've been dreaming a lot—more nightmares than dreams. Truth be told, I didn't really like high school myself. I have never told anyone that before. In fact, I don't think I was conscious of it myself, all these years, or at least I haven't let myself dwell on the subject. Instead of looking at personal issues, like many men, I just push myself harder. According to my last ex-wife, that habit has made me, at times, an asshole workaholic."

"I can sure relate to that," Alan responded.

"I am sure you can, and trust me—I think a principal's job is tough at any school. And dealing with thousands of kids, as in your case, seems overwhelming to me. But as you know all too well, being a kid can be tough as well, sometimes really tough. Alan, I am not a tall man—five-seven with my shoes on—and I got picked on a lot in junior high. I did not fit in and I guess I was kind of an outcast . . . this worried me a lot. I guess my parents often worried that I was on the edge of being, what they considered, a loser. I made it through by becoming a people pleaser or, I guess, a suck-ass, you could say. But I paid a price for this, maybe a bigger price than I realized."

Bob continued, "I have been rambling, so I'll get to the point. I think you're right, Alan. We must do things differently. And Chris Rodmaker feels just as strongly about this as I do. He does not share much but he is very passionate about what you're doing, so I figure he has had some bad experiences along the way as well. Anyway, last night, the school board held an open session, and we voted by a five-to-three margin to make MLK a pilot school. Three out of three women board members, plus Rodmaker, voted with us. Basically what I am saying is that we've approved all the changes you have introduced. You have a one-year mandate to implement your curriculum changes, and then we—the school board, the superintendent, and your administrative staff and teachers—will sit down together and see how we have done.

"We will all take a lot of flak over this, Alan, but that's okay. We'll deal with it for one year and go from there. I am excited about this! Let's go for it and see what we can get done. I doubt if I'll get reelected as president of the board again, or if I'll even be on the board again, but I am tired of the game the way it's played anyway. I think it's worth the gamble."

"Hopefully it won't come to that—" Alan started to say.

"Doesn't matter," continued Bob. "Alan, you're the one who is taking the big gamble. We're just volunteers, but this is your career. You may still lose your job over this, but obviously you have already given plenty of consideration to that possibility. So let's go for it. Alan—are you still there? I have been doing all the talking. Alan?"

"Yes, Bob, I am still here. But I needed to pinch myself to make sure I was hearing you right. I am still in shock. Thank you very much, Bob, thank you very much. This is amazing. The staff—at least most of them—will be excited and challenged. I hope you won't be sorry."

"I hope neither of us will be sorry, Alan. I will support you the best I can. There are a million more details to go over, and you will receive an official letter from the district, but I wanted to let you know this much over the phone. You've got my private cell phone number and don't ever hesitate to call. Even though I don't have as much to lose as you do, I will see this through with you until the end. I am not just blowing smoke. I mean it."

"Thank you, Bob, I appreciate this. I expected the women might go our way as this seems to be their time to stand up and be counted. But you and Chris, well . . . all I can say again is I really appreciate this opportunity."

"I hope he won't be sorry," Alan repeated to himself after he put the phone down and took out his handkerchief to wipe his eyes. "I hope neither one of us will be sorry." Then his positive mindset switched back on, and he felt truly amazed. *I can hardly believe this; it's like a dream come true.*

Alan immediately picked up the phone and called Anne's number.

"Hi Alan," she answered, out of breath. "I was just about to walk out the door. You must have been missing me so much that you could not wait another fifteen minutes until I got there, right?"

Alan chuckled, "Sure, there is some truth to that. Sit down for a minute . . . I just heard from Bob Lancaster, and the board has approved our changes for one year. We're starting a pilot program. We did it—we actually did it! We're being given this opportunity to show what we can do."

"Wow! I can't believe it!" yelled Anne. "This is a miracle—we ought to be on *60 Minutes* or at least the local news. This is great, Alan! We're going to get our chance." Anne was silent for a moment. "So . . . what do we do now?"

"Well" Alan smiled thoughtfully, "we have already started, and I think we just keep going. Some things will work, and some may not, and we just have to learn through trial and error, but I am sure it will all be worth the effort no matter how much we get done."

"Yes," said Anne, "I know it will be."

Soon the entire school was buzzing with the news.

"I think the majority of the faculty expected the school board to turn down most, if not all, of our changes," said Bruce to Penny Briton, as the two of them walked down the hall after A block.

"I don't think anyone, including Alan, expected them to approve the whole package," said Penny. "I thought they might give us some token changes to keep us from outright rebellion, but I didn't think they would give us the whole enchilada. To tell you the truth, I was worried that Alan would be fired, or put in jail, or beaten up by some of the mad dads. But instead we have the chance to do something very big and special."

"I still can't believe it," said Bruce. "Pinch me and tell me this is not a dream! This is just the beginning; it's not over yet by a long shot. Everyone in town is going to be watching us. If we screw up, we'll still get crucified."

Penny replied resolutely, "Everyone who steps out and does something worthwhile seems to get crucified eventually. It's part of the game so you just suck it up and keep moving. But let's not worry about that yet. We'd all better work hard and do it right the first time. Let's not screw this up."

CHAPTER TWENTY-THREE
RAMONA

On Wednesday afternoon, just as Alan finished talking on the phone with Karen Kendrick at *The Globe*, he heard Ruth scream. "Here we go again! Alan!" He jumped up from his chair and ran into the secretary's office, knocking over his metal wastebasket in the process and scattering the contents over the linoleum floor.

Ruth sat in her high-backed swivel chair with the black touchtone phone on her lap, looking surprisingly calm. "Alan, we've got another bomb threat. This time it's in the cafeteria. Sounded like the same girl with the accent who called before. She said a large bomb will go off in the cafeteria in twenty minutes, and then she hung up just like before."

Alan told Ruth to call 911 as he raced to the hall outside the office to hit the fire alarm. Then he remembered to make sure there was no active shooter before activating the alarm. Both vice principals were in Alan's office within three minutes after scanning the hallways and then hitting the alarm.

"Jesus," said Brad. "Here we go again, but if it's a real bomb threat this time we just lost five minutes. It's like she knew we just took off the monitoring device connecting us to the police station."

Alan nodded. "At least she keeps changing the buildings she is going to blow up, so we get to practice evacuating different areas of the school each time."

"That is definitely a glass-half-full attitude," Anne answered, rolling her eyes as she headed out the door. She shouted at the students milling around in the hallway to keep moving.

"Brad, make your way down to the cafeteria to ensure everyone is gone—and then get out yourself," ordered Alan. "Ruth, where did I put that loudspeaker?"

"We might as well send everyone home early," said Alan to Anne and Brad, once they met out in the parking lot waiting for the bomb team to check out the cafeteria. "It'll be five o'clock before they finish up in there."

"I'll let the rest of the teachers know," said Brad. He turned and headed towards Bruce Robbins, the closest teacher available, to pass the word down the line.

"Do you think it's the same girl who calls every time? Do you think she is a terrorist? Or is this some type of conspiracy brought on by parents who are angry about the athletic cuts who are trying to scare us?" Anne asked.

"I think this is the same gal, and I am beginning to think she is very serious," replied Alan, a dark gloom creeping over his face. "There are still some very unhappy people out there who may never appreciate what we're doing, but they would not threaten to blow up the school every week. This woman is not giving up, and she may keep trying if only to drive us nuts."

Ramona hung up the phone and took a deep breath, examining the hands on her watch. Again, this call had taken fewer than seven seconds. She touched her cheekbone and made sure her black hair was tucked under her green scarf. Then she put on the new ultra-dark sunglasses she'd just bought at the Dollar Store. She opened the phone booth door, looked around, and quickly walked out. She glanced into the 7-Eleven where she could see the bearded clerk who was busy helping customers. She was grateful that there were still four phone booths left in the northeast part of town, within walking distance of where she lived, and decided that was a good sign.

She ducked down the alley leading her toward the ten-by-fifteen-foot room that she called home. Her landlord, an older Latina woman, had divided her garage into two partially finished rooms, with a shared bathroom. A very old white man rented the other room, which was a pain because he seemed to be in the bathroom at all times of the day and night. But it was cheap, and that's what mattered most to a girl who was making a living reclaiming other people's trash.

As she walked, she thought of all the work she still had to do. She had found a calendar in the green dumpster next door and decided she would give herself two more months. But she wanted to make it happen before then. She was tired of waiting, but she wanted to keep the enemy off balance, to make them suffer just like her people did every day, and that's why she kept calling. It would be so much easier if she was not alone—and if she was more mechanical.

She passed dozens of homeless people as she walked, but she kept her head and shoulders hunched over and stared at the cracks in the sidewalk. She stopped to check out the large green dumpster, even though she was in a hurry. She opened the lid to look for food and recyclables, as usual, but she was also after an old piece of carpet to cover the concrete floor next to her mattress. She needed about four feet of electrical wiring, as well. The diagram on the Internet called for Class B wiring, but she wasn't sure what Class B meant. She needed fertilizer, too, but she wasn't sure what the fertilizer was supposed to do. At least she knew that she could choose from numerous kinds at the Home Depot around the corner, if she could just get enough money. That meant she had to dive deeper into the dumpster.

Without Zack, money was a problem for Ramona. The little money she made from recycling cans and bottles barely covered her meager living expenses. But still, she was getting closer—maybe only six more weeks—if she found the wire and if the fertilizer wasn't too expensive.

She missed Zack. Ramona knew it was odd that a Jewish boy had been her only friend since she had become a radical Jihad, and it was also odd that he had acquired the main components for the bomb. Her few other acquaintances were all Muslims who thought she was crazy. They were all Jordanians or Egyptians and didn't have the same anger toward the United States government that she did. Although they hadn't always liked school in America, and sometimes felt ostracized (especially since 9/11), they didn't hurt inside like she did. They had felt lucky to live in America—at least until the most recent President had entered office, who was hell-bent on deporting them all—but he was the Jihadist's best hope, as he was getting her people worked up and angry again.

Ramona was Palestinian, and she'd learned to hate all Westerners.

She felt frustrated with the millions of Muslims in this country: only a sacred few seemed to share her hatred of Americans, and they were hard for a girl on her own to find. She felt like a little shark in a very big sea. If only she was a white supremacist, then she would have lots of friends. She missed her family, her home in Palestine, and especially her father who had been murdered by the bastard Israeli infidels.

The newscasters referred to people like her as Internet radicals. Her prize possession was a nine-year-old HP laptop she had bought used on craigslist, back when she was still babysitting Zack. Now Zack was gone. He had betrayed her by shooting Kyle; that act was personal, not part of the jihad plan. By going to jail he had left her completely alone.

CHAPTER TWENTY-FOUR
HONESTY, AND COUNCIL OF ELDERS

Jed was now the varsity football coach, and Tess Carlson was the new art teacher. They both felt overwhelmed. Football season ended after the varsity lost their first playoff game, 28 to 17, and now it was time to concentrate on intramural sports. They had expected at least one hundred kids to show up, but 263 signed up—thirty more girls than boys. The kids were of all sizes, ages, and athletic abilities. Some were hyper, some were slow, some were heavy, and some were thin.

Jed started with a talk on the importance of good sportsmanship and emphasized that they were out there to have fun. Then he divided the kids up by sport: soccer, basketball, volleyball, and touch football. After that, Jed broke the students into teams, trying to make them as equal as possible while knowing little or nothing about most of the players' skills, or lack thereof. Jed, who was used to an orderly football practice, found the whole afternoon problematic and chaotic.

Tess was a petite, 120-pound brunette—a brand-new teacher right out of college with the energy of three regular teachers. She'd not played sports herself since being a junior in college, and at first she wasn't sure how they were going to handle all these teenagers, with just her and Jed running the show. She felt less overwhelmed by the chaos than did Jed, but was a little intimidated by Jed himself, both because of his size and age, and the fact that he had close ties to the principal, Mr. Carter. Ever since he took on the school board, Tess had come to revere Mr. Carter. In her book, he was right up there next to God. She had also gained respect for him when he stood up for what he believed in at the school board meeting, even though he received only lukewarm support from some of the other faculty.

Thirty minutes into organizing the kids, Tess realized that Jed was overwhelmed. He looked at her with a bewildered expression and asked, "Do you have any ideas about what to do now? There are too many kids! How can we make this work?"

Tess knew how to organize. She also liked the idea that Jed was not above asking her advice. That was a definite point in his favor.

"Of course we can do it, Jed," Tess responded enthusiastically. "Let's pick a senior for each sport—one who knows the rules -- and make them captain or coach. Then we split up and take ten minutes with each group of teams to get them started, and after that we let the captains take over. We can re-evaluate at that point."

"Sounds like it's worth a try," replied Jed hopefully.

One by one the games started, and by the end of the day some semblance of order prevailed. Jed felt somewhat better, and he was very impressed by Tess. Afterwards, the two agreed to go to Alvarado's to have a pizza and plan for the following afternoon's games.

The second day was much better, as the kids now had an idea what was expected of them and how to organize themselves. Several more teachers showed up as volunteers: one each from the biology and Spanish departments organized two soccer teams, and Brent Sandalwood, the tennis coach, jumped in on the tennis courts.

"It's good to see these kids out here laughing and getting exercise. They've spent too much of their lives behind computer or TV screens," said Jed to Tess as his eyes panned across the playing fields. Everywhere he looked kids were doing something active and seemed to be having a good time. *This might actually work*, Jed thought. He had put his butt on the line along with Alan to make this happen, and the program was taking shape.

He looked over at Tess and hopefully asked, "Pizza tonight?"

She laughed and said, "Sorry, no pizza . . . how about Mexican food for a change? I know a great restaurant run by real Latinos and the head cook has a son here. It's cheap and only a mile away."

"Great," he replied, "I love Mexican food."

The first *Honest Communication* class had twenty-four students and two instructors. Alan and Anne had decided that teachers would double up, so they could work out issues and train themselves at the same time. This class was made up of kids who were experiencing social challenges at school. That usually meant three or more office referrals during the school year. They were being pulled out of their afternoon C block classes.

Anne and Jim Williams, a guidance counselor, teamed up for this class. Jim was a forty-one-year-old black man with fifteen years of teaching and counseling experience. He was a laid-back type of guy with a good sense of humor and a go-for-it attitude. Anne had made him her choice because, whenever they got together at lunch or after school, Jim always seemed earnest and willing to talk about real issues. Like her, he had done a fair amount of personal-growth work and he, too, remembered some exercises that they could now use in the class.

Anne and Jim pushed the tables to the back of the room and arranged two dozen chairs in a circle. They ended up with fourteen boys and ten girls, all tenth and eleventh graders. The group was mixed by race, and social skills as well. Some of the students were shy, while others were outright brazen. Before class started, there was the usual giggling, laughing, and talking about why they were there. Jim and Anne sat on barstools in the center of the circle and called the class to order.

"What I really want to stress in this first hour," started Anne, "is the importance of honest, direct, kind communication. If you can get this one thing out of this class, I promise your life will be better. So few people truly open up about what's really on their mind or, more importantly, how they really feel about all kinds of things. And I am not talking about complaining, but about stating how you feel regarding any specific issue. The power of telling your truth can literally set you free. Many of us spend our time in endless drama and anger, because we aren't honest with ourselves or others."

"Remember," interjected Jim, "your best chance to get your needs met is to articulate your preferences and thoughts, not your complaints or judgments. I can't stress enough how important it is *not* to become a victim. Victims spend their lives in pain and sorrow. But by being proactive, you can take charge of your life, and that may mean asking for help when you need it."

Anne added, "And this can often be true for women. I know quite a few women who had long-term marriages, during which they kept their opinions to themselves. Their anger built up over the years, until the day they reached their limit. They exploded, and their marriages imploded. By that point, it was too late. The men were willing to work on making changes, but the women were done. Unfortunately, what might have been good marriages sometimes end this way, and all due to a lack of honest communication."

One of the boys spoke up, "I have never met any girls like that. Every girl I have ever known just spends their life bossing me around—especially my sisters." There was general laughter and agreement from the rest of the boys.

"Well, that's sometimes true," agreed Anne. "Women are learning to be more assertive and that can be good, as long as it's done with respect and not just trying to be bossy. No healthy person, man or woman, likes to be bossed around. Think about what you say before you say it and think about how the other person is going to feel when you have said your piece and don't be a blamer. If you screw up, own it.

"There is an art to communicating and that's what we are going to try to explore together. We will also talk about having healthy, honest boundaries that help us to feel safe.

"Remember the old adage: 'If you don't have anything nice to say, don't say anything at all.' That expression is only partially true—because it's very important to be honest. However, most things can be said nicely and respectfully, even when you're angry. Often we become angry when we haven't been communicating honestly, and it's caught up with us. This is a vital but complex subject, and it is something obviously many of us adults are still learning."

"I understand what you guys are saying about being honest," said seventeen-year-old Marcy. "I don't know if I can articulate this very well, but last year I lied to my best girlfriend of nine years and we haven't spoken since. It's been almost a year now, and I still feel guilty. I'd told her that I wouldn't date a boy we were both interested in. I did not want to hurt her feelings, but that boy had already told me that he was more interested in me than my friend. A couple weeks later, my girlfriend saw us together, holding hands and kissing in the mall. She was so angry and hurt that she never even gave me a chance to explain. She hasn't spoken to me since that day, and I really miss having that girl in my life.

"The boy—I won't say his name—is now long gone, and so is my best girlfriend. If I had told her the truth upfront, I think we still would be best buds; now she just thinks I am a rotten blankety-blank person."

"Marcy, you articulated that very well, except for your adjective at the end. That story is a perfect example," said Jim. "It's amazing how much pain we cause ourselves and others when we think we are protecting someone else's feelings.

"One thing you might think about, Marcy, is that it might not be too late. It would take courage to approach her after all this time, to explain and apologize, but it might just work."

"She won't have to look too far," said Melinda, a dark-haired girl who raised her hand on the other side of the circle. "I am the girl Marcy is talking about in her story, and I got her message loud and clear. Let's talk after class, Marcy."

During the second hour of class, they did an exercise where everyone wrote down the five worst fears that they'd ever had in their life. Each person, including Jim and Anne, then shared those fears with other individuals in the group. At first there was some awkwardness, then a little laughing and joking, but by the end of the exercise the whole group had settled down nicely.

Only one person, a sixteen-year-old black boy named Steven, who'd spent the class slouched low in his chair and looking bored, refused to participate.

"Man, I don't have any fears. Even if I did I'm not going to share them with a group of honkies and kiss-ass brothers. You people with this 'honest communication' crap don't mean shit in my part of town. A revolver or shotgun is real honest communication. Everybody gets the message real quick and there ain't no questioning about who's the boss man."

"Steven, you can just sit and observe this whole process if you choose. You don't have to participate, but you might be real surprised with what you see and hear," said Jim.

"I ain't gonna learn anything I don't already know," said Steven, "but everybody got to be somewhere, so I'll sit here anyway."

When the exercise was over, the group dynamics had changed dramatically. Jim asked the group if anyone had anything they wanted to share, but most of the group was now quiet and introspective.

"I am amazed," said one girl, breaking the silence. "Almost everyone in the group had pretty much the same fears, especially us girls. Everybody, boy or girl, mentioned being afraid to be alone, or broke. All of us girls mentioned we didn't want to be left out by the rest of the girls. It's like we're all afraid of each other. It's like really weird. Every time I get a message on my Facebook page I get this sick feeling in my stomach because I never know whether it's a friend or foe. Am I going to be attacked or hear news from a friend--one just never knows."

"I thought it was strange," said one of the boys, "that all of us guys worry about being alone, and that most of us worry that our parents might die. It was also weird that we live in the richest country in the world and yet everyone worries about having enough money in our lives. Those things blew me away. I thought I was the only one who thought about stuff like that. I guess at least us guys don't get attacked on Facebook as much as you girls."

At the end of class, after everyone had their chance to speak, Steven sat up straight in his chair and announced, "I gotta admit, you dudes did alright. You got balls for spilling your guts like that. I don't think I could do that. Yeah, that shit was alright. I will be back tomorrow. This is better than sittin' around in history or math class."

Anne knew that they had taken a major step in bonding. They had gone farther than she thought they would. She knew intuitively that the kids in this group would begin treating each other—and those outside the group as well—with more respect and dignity by the end of the semester, Steven included. *This is what teaching is all about,* she decided. She walked with Jim Williams down the hall, and they gave each other a high-five. *This,* she thought, *is the way a teacher is supposed to feel at the end of a class.*

Marshall Livingston's American History class met three times a week at 10:00 a.m. for ninety minutes. The original syllabus for the class covered the political system of the United States and its effect on the quality of life of the average American citizen. As the first month progressed, the topic began to turn inward, as his students examined the political and administrative system at MLK, and its impact on the average student.

Each student had been asked to join a three-person team to study and propose changes that could be made, at both the administrative and student level, to improve the quality of life at school.

Phillip Englewood, a senior boy, led his group to propose "The

Council of Elders." This group would be made up of senior students, teachers, and past alumni. Their mission would be to guide the student body through the process of making high school a more satisfying and productive place for all students.

Phillip and his team concluded that the student council elections were really nothing more than a popularity contest (much like the larger political system), and the council did little to affect the life of the average student. The Council of Elders, on the other hand, would be an advisory group only, and would focus more on the moral and ethical questions faced by students, the student council, and the school administration. They felt its influence on both the students and the faculty could be immense—a guiding light for the school as a whole.

They proposed that the council members be nominated by both students and teachers. A referendum would be held, and each student or teacher would get one vote. No campaigning or electioneering would be allowed. The elected students or alumni could then decide whether or not to serve. Also included in the vote was a referendum where students had a write-in area, so each voter could jot down the issues he or she thought the Council should address.

The entire class got behind the idea and created a proposal to give to the faculty. They debated the merits of the idea for about an hour, then approved the idea as presented. The faculty was so impressed with the concept that they decided to present it to the student body and set a referendum date for the vote.

By the final weeks of Phillip's history class, the students decided that the whole country needed a Council of Elders, and a referendum system to guide both the Council and the Congress of the United States. With Marshall's help, they spent many hours after school and during lunch writing a comprehensive national proposal. After securing a grant from the Ford Foundation, the students sent copies to every major newspaper, magazine, congressman, and senator across the country.

Marshall was more than pleased with the class's effort. In fact, he suspected that something quite significant was happening at MLK and he felt humbled to be part of it. The class came up with the following proposal:

*****

The Council of Elders

A Proposal for Change from the Students of Martin Luther King High School

We need consensus on what's important to us as a culture. We need a consensus-building apparatus, a structure that, starting with the so-called "grownups," is then implemented into our homes, businesses, and schools. Economically and technologically, we've come a long way since our country's conception, but sociologically speaking we are still in the Dark Ages. In many ways the world has changed more in the past one hundred years than in the previous 10,000 years, but sociologically we've done little to keep up.

It's time we get honest with ourselves, because we can do a lot better. If we don't, today may be the breaking point for the rise and the fall of the American experience. We can't buy our way out, or use our military and economic power to get us out of this one. Our culture and society are in steep moral decline, much like the Romans and other once-dominant cultures before us. We could just take another Prozac and hope the bad news goes away. But it won't. We can depend on that.

We, the students of Martin Luther King High School, think that new and bold leadership is required. We need visionaries with deeply honest, dynamic, and persistent leadership abilities, instead of just representatives of special interest groups. Integrity is a must. Sometimes those who strive to become our leaders are the angriest, most fearful, or damaged among us. Some are intelligent and well-intentioned, but too often they feel a need to prove to the world that they're okay. This drive can turn into a need to control, lie, and manipulate. They don't develop the qualities needed to become an enlightened leader.

So where do we find enlightened leadership? We can continue to wait, and hope that a messiah shows up, or we can become innovative and proactive. We must move beyond politics and seek the wisest among us—not necessarily the best orators, the most driven, or the most personable. We want people who know how to bring us together in honest dialogue and move us past the limitations of secular and spiritual dogmatism. We want people with inner strength and emotional substance, people who want to save our culture more than feed their own egos.

We, therefore, propose the formation of The Council of One Hundred Elders.

We'd include people from a variety of perspectives, like Jimmy Carter, Colin Powell, David Brooks, Deepak Chopra, Jack Kornfield, George H.W. Bush, Bill Clinton, Bishop Tutu, Michelle Obama, Rabbi Michael Lerner, Oprah Winfrey, Bill Moyers, Rossi Bernie Glassman, and Dr. Phil McGraw.

A group such as this could become our culture's moral and spiritual mentors. They could work on different issues facing our society. Could they not agree on ten principles that we could all try to follow? Principles we could teach our children and young people?

We would need to get past our own egos and give them this opportunity, even though some of the council members might have different philosophical and spiritual points of view from ours. But could they not help us transfer these principles into domestic and foreign policies that complement our ideals as a nation? Perhaps they could lead the way for a world Council of Elders? This concept is simple—we just need to get out of our own way.

Let's start the process. Here is how we do it:
Send a list of the ten people you most respect to CouncilofElders.com. Be sure to choose ten people whom you think are honest, who have emotional and intellectual intelligence, and integrity, and who can put aside their egos and personal agendas and do what is best for all of us.

It's your choice. The Elders you choose could be community leaders, respected media trailblazers, retired statesmen, community activists, national and international leaders, or your parents or partners. We'll collect the names for four months and then compile them, along with a list of the ten most important issues facing us as a people and a nation, as submitted by our readers. We'll then present the names and the issues to the news media, Congress, and the President of the United States. We will send out invitations and convene the first meeting.

We've got nothing to lose but everything to gain. Let's get started.

Howard Teague, MLK's veteran science teacher and assistant JV baseball coach, had given a lot of thought to Alan's overall plan, and decided that he supported most of the concepts. The fairness of high school sports—or the lack thereof—brought up old issues within him that he thought he'd forgotten over the years.

During his junior year of high school, Howard played on his high school baseball team. He was a reliable shortstop, batted 326 with fourteen home runs, and he cherished the experience. But he remembered the pressure the coaches put on him to be the next Babe Ruth and to play year-round ball in Arizona's warm climate. When he told the head coach that science was his passion and he didn't want to be the next Babe Ruth, the coach replied that he had better get his priorities straight. By the beginning of his senior year, he felt like he had been blackballed, and he quit baseball to make time for his senior science project. He'd loved working on the project, along with his two best friends. He was glad to say that those two people remained among his best friends after all these years, and one was now his wife.

The week before he and his wife took a long Sunday drive to the mountains, and he had her undivided attention for several hours. During their conversation, he realized he still carried some resentment about the high school baseball incident, and that it had irked him his entire adult life. He and his wife discussed Alan's ideas about taking some of the pressure off student athletes and coaches, and they agreed that would be good for everybody. As a result, he decided to bring the subject up with the head coach and the faculty advisory board and see if they couldn't make some changes.

He also was a fan of students working in pods to learn the value of cooperation and how to socialize with those outside their usual group. Climate change had become an important topic in science, and one that Howard felt strongly about, so he decided to use the pod approach. He divided his classes into pods and each small group picked a possible environmental solution to research. After presenting their findings, they'd try to reach consensus on an overall solution.

Howard was pleased by the interest the students showed in the subject. Most seemed to grasp the concept that humans are throwing the natural balance of the world's climate out of whack, with catastrophic repercussions that were going to drastically affect their lives and could be even more destructive for their own children's generation.

After much research, the class decided as a whole that there are six known solutions that could help reverse the trend of global warming, none of which could work individually. All the solutions needed to be implemented in unison. Howard was impressed by how much the students had achieved with only minimal guidance from him. He so wished that Congress and the nations of the world could do the same.

On Thursday Alan sat in the cafeteria with his students. It had been a long-standing practice of his administrative career to stand in line with the students at lunchtime and to eat the same food as they were eating. Every week he picked a different table so he could sit with a different group of students. Sometimes the students, especially the younger ones, would react in stunned silence and it would take several minutes to break the ice. But the juniors and seniors had gotten used to the drill over the years, and many of them were open and talkative right away.

On this day, he picked a table of juniors and seniors, most of them self-described nerds. After being in the system for several years, they usually had found a group of like-minded kids to hang out with.

"Hey, Mr. Carter, what's happening?" was the cry from a half-dozen boys, as he sat down with his tray.

"Sir," said Donny, "things are starting to change around here. Shannon Douglass and two of her socialite friends said hi to me this morning, and they actually called me by my first name, and not the usual 'hey, dink head.'"

"Yeah," said Rob. "Two of the football jocks came over when we first sat down and asked how we were doing, and then invited us to a party that they already had last Friday night."

The boys broke into a chorus of laughing and hooting.

"Well, actually, the party is *this* coming Friday," he said with a broad smile, "but you know they used to come over here and tell us we were sitting too close to them and that we sent off highly magnetic nerd waves that were hazardous to their health—especially their reproductive organs!"

He grinned, adding, "I think they heard Mrs. Tish tell her economics class that in five years we're more than likely gonna be their bosses, so they might as well start giving us the respect we deserve right now. It's just self-preservation. They're trying to butter us up now so they can get raises in the future."

There was another wave of laughing that went around the table.

"It was really interesting," noted Jacob, "for one of the most popular girls in school to write in our school rag sheet about how she felt obligated to give boys oral sex because she thought it was the only way they would like or accept her. Hell, what is the world coming to? Doesn't anyone have good self-esteem? I would have paid big bucks just to talk to her. I thought the whole blow-job thing was just for the girls who didn't think they were cute enough. I bet it will be interesting around her house if her mother reads that."

"It's a wild world out there," replied David. "We're stuck with our computers and the popular guys in school are getting head from the cheerleaders because the girls have poor self-esteem and the guys no self-respect."

Alan smiled a little sadly. "I know it sounds glamorous, in a sick way, but it isn't. The reason she wrote that article was because she was in serious pain. It wasn't because she was happy or feeling good about herself. A lot of the kids who seem popular are working at it so hard because they need acceptance, sometimes at any price. It took a tremendous amount of courage for her to write that, and I had a hard time approving it even if she did not give her name. It took more guts than I would have had. As she said, she had been with three members of the football team—one of them the captain. Now he is paralyzed in the hospital, because he abused a younger, defenseless boy. So, it's not like he was a real happy camper, either. From what I have learned, he has had one tough life. The moral of the story is that happy people don't go around making fun of people or beating up on others."

"On TV or YouTube they seem to be berating and making fun of people all the time!" Donny interjected. "They're all partying on and having a good old time. And every sporting event touts advertisements for drinking and partying and making fun of someone else. What's that all about? Because they seem happy enough."

"I don't know, Donny, but all I can tell you is that is a make-believe world. Those actors are being paid to read those scripts, and the people who write those scripts or advertisements are seriously lost. I personally don't believe that an individual making fun of someone else can really be happy, deep down inside. Love and sex are about intimacy," Alan continued, "and these people on TV aren't being intimate. They're just looking for quick fixes, trying to be cool, using too much alcohol to fit in, just like so many others. You guys wait until you get to college. Then you can find yourself a girlfriend who you really care about and it will all work out just fine."

"Hell, I don't think we have any choice in the matter," piped in David. "Most of the smarter girls are going to fool around with the jocks for now, then wait until after grad school and watch us become the robber-barons of Wall Street, the tech industry, and the banking industry, where we can legally steal from the poor and give to the rich and get paid the big bucks while doing it. Then they will flock to us and we will finally get laid! Whoops—I mean have girlfriends and wives."

Alan couldn't help but laugh with them as he shook his head.

"But you're right, Mr. Carter," said David, "I don't think most of us appreciate how lucky we are that we're not caught up in that popularity contest. From what I have seen, it looks rather deadly. Speaking for myself, I am pretty happy just being me and hanging with my friends."

Everyone at the table, including Alan, nodded in agreement.

"Thank you, gentlemen," said Alan as he stood up to go. "Like always, I have received much more wisdom than I have given during lunch with you young scholars."

CHAPTER TWENTY-FIVE
SHIFTS TOWARD BLISS

Kyle lay totally motionless in his hospital bed. He had tried and tried to move the big toe on his right foot the afternoon prior in physical therapy, but it wouldn't budge. Earlier that morning, he had moved his index finger on his left hand, but it took all his might to do so. In a little while, he was going to try to move his middle finger on his right hand, but he needed to rest first. This was exhausting work.

His mother had come alone last night. Kyle had not seen or heard anything about his father in quite a few days. She arrived several hours after they brought Zack over. She sounded totally confused and almost angry when the nurse told her that Kyle had moved his mouth and his finger while Zack was here. She kept telling Kyle not to worry, that she was going to take care of him for the rest of his life. She kept asking how they could have brought that boy—that Jew boy—to see Kyle after what he had done. She said she was going to 'call their lawyer,' as if she and Don had a personal attorney on retainer. But on second thought, maybe she *could* find one now that Kyle had been shot. There were bound to be legal vultures hanging around hoping to sue somebody.

A cold chill had come over Kyle while Kate was saying all this to the nurses. He realized for the first time that maybe she did not want him to get well. What if she told the doctors that she wanted to take him home with her and take care of him there? His mother would take him to their dinky, dark house in the East Valley and he knew he would never leave there alive.

His only hope was to get help from Butch, and he guessed Sam, too. Without them he was lost. But what if they never came back, what then? Then there was the shock of seeing Zack, which had scared the crap out of him, but also had caused him to move, if only ever so slightly. Afterwards, when Zack wiped his face, a strange and peaceful feeling had come over him and he had wanted to cry. What the hell was that all about? Was he going insane?

Lieutenant Baker told Butch and Sam about how Kyle moved his mouth the evening before. He had made a point of calling them at the shelter almost every day to keep them abreast of the latest news. This news sent Butch into a state of pure, natural exuberance like he had never experienced before. He wanted to go to the hospital that very minute, but Baker told him to relax. He would have to wait until morning visiting hours.

Sam also seemed to go into a state of bliss, and he walked around with a subtle smile on his face for the rest of the evening. Butch saw Sam put his hands together in a prayer of thanks after hearing the news about Kyle. In turn, Butch did what he knew how to do. He went to his bunk, looked around to make sure no one was watching, and knelt down on one knee. Then, for the first time that he could remember since he was a child, he said a small prayer and thanked God for Kyle's new ability to move his mouth. He also gave thanks for his friendship with Sam and for the fact that he had been sober for ten days now—the longest period since he was fifteen years old.

Butch stayed at the shelter frequently now, and he and Sam would talk into the wee hours of the morning. Butch almost felt like a kid back at summer camp. He could remember when he was ten years old and his parents sent him to Valley Lutheran summer camp at Waldo Lake. At night, when the counselors were sleeping, the kids would take out their flashlights and look at the pictures of naked women that his friend, Randy, had brought. When they got tired of that, they would have pillow fights, and then just lie around on their bunks and talk about their favorite foods, girls, rock 'n' roll singers, and everything else in between. That was the best summer of Butch's life. *Why*, he wondered, *don't adults still do that type of thing? It was so much fun.* Then he wondered what Sam would think if he hit him with a pillow.

Butch marveled at how he had gone from feeling total despair into a peacefulness that he'd experienced very rarely, if ever, in his lifetime. Sam kept reminding him to be present in the immediate moment and not to dwell on the past or worry about the future, to stay in what Sam called "the now." He said everything is possible when you are present in the now. Butch didn't completely get it, but he did know life was much better when he could stay more focused on the present moment.

Butch also noticed that Sam sat on his bed at night and read from a book as big as the Bible, but it was called *A Course in Miracles*. He thought Sam might be a Buddhist, but Sam said he studied several religions, including Buddhism and Christianity. *A Course in Miracles,* he said, was not a religion to him, but he enjoyed reading it like the Bible, because it gave him support and inspiration.

At times, all of this felt overwhelming to Butch. But at the same time, it was like a miracle and the guidance he was receiving seemed to be helping him—even though he still felt such guilt about Kyle and Zack, especially if he woke at three or four in the morning and started thinking about it. At those moments, he had to continually remind himself to shut down his mind, breathe deeply, let go, and trust that everything would turn out okay.

Butch did not mind doing cleanup work around the shelter, either. He mopped the floors, cleaned out the urinals, and made his own bunk every morning. He was used to being the boss, telling kids what to do all day long, but now it felt good to be just like everyone else. The rest of the men were a mixed group of all ages, races, and ethnic backgrounds. And they all had one thing in common: they were all down on their luck and Butch felt right at home with that. Funny how things worked: just a month ago Butch was a local hero and considered to be one of the best—if not the top—high school football coaches in the state of California. But now he was much, much happier with his simple and sober role at the shelter.

The hardest part was giving up the booze. Butch knew it had been destroying him, but he had been drinking beer since he was twelve and the hard stuff since he was twenty. He knew it had caused problems in each of his three marriages, but it always had been easier to blame the women for nagging him rather than admit he was a drunk.

Why did he start drinking that early on in his life? His parents were strict Catholics and they did not drink much at all, although he had heard from other relatives that his grandfather was an alcoholic. He figured genetics surely played a big role. Was it an inherited trait? Or was he just rebelling? Maybe it was because some of his friends were starting to drink by the age of eleven. He could always remember wanting to fit in and be one of the boys. Maybe it was because drinking made him more relaxed and social and not so shy. The one thing he knew for sure was that once he started, he couldn't stop—he was addicted.

Anyway, it didn't matter anymore. He was giving it up, and he was done with it. He knew it would be tough when every other commercial on the sports channel was about beer or hard liquor, but he knew he had to stop drinking. It was his only hope. He had gone to three AA meetings now and felt like he belonged. Everybody there had the same problem, and he liked the way they shared their stories and were vulnerable with their feelings. For the first time in his life, Butch didn't have to be drunk to be emotionally honest. He felt like this was his tribe. He finally belonged to something other than the gaggle of drunks who gathered every night down at the Pastime Bar and Grill. He had now been sober for ten days and had a new lease on life. What a blessing.

Butch and Sam went to the hospital to see Kyle the following day at 10:00 a.m. when visiting hours began. They thought that Sam's presence might upset Kyle's parents, if they were there, so they decided Butch would go up to Kyle's room on the sixth floor by himself, while Sam waited in the lobby.

A young-looking, dark-haired nurse with a soft, serious smile introduced herself as Mary Beth when meeting Butch in the hallway outside Kyle's room. She said Kyle's mother had not been in yet this morning, and that she thought Kyle was still asleep, though it was always hard to be sure. She said he was doing better, and that one of the night nurses had sworn Kyle smiled ever so slightly at one of his infamous, risqué jokes.

Butch quietly opened the door and slipped into Kyle's room. He could see his shapeless body covered by a white linen blanket, and he immediately noticed that Kyle no longer had a tube in his mouth, though there was still a tube bandaged to his arm. Butch thought Kyle looked much smaller and helpless in his blue and white dressing gown with his covers folded below his arms. The perpetual grimace Kyle usually wore—the one Butch had loved to see on the football field—was absent, and his mouth was slightly open as he slowly breathed in and out.

Butch stood at the foot of the bed watching Kyle for a full minute, his mind still on empty. Then it was like someone turned on the spigot in his mind, and he started to beat himself up about his guilt. *What have I done? Look what I have done! This is all my fault. If I just hadn't lied. Why did I feel like I had to win every damn football game?*

For a moment Butch held on to the railing on the side of Kyle's bed for support, but he began shaking so badly that he feared he would wake Kyle. He let go and walked over to a chair and sat down holding his head between his hands.

Why, why, why has winning been so important to me that I sold my soul to the devil? Look what I have done to this poor boy! Tears slowly made their way down his cheeks.

Butch was glad the nurse had left him alone with Kyle and hadn't seen him cry. After several minutes of sitting he remembered what Sam had told him, and the techniques he had been practicing. He put the palm of his hand to his forehead and let his fingers massage the front of his scalp while he took a series of deep breaths. As he sat there, his mind started quieting back down, and the only sound was the faint hum of warm air squeezing its way out of the heating vent below his feet.

Once he regained his composure, Butch stood back up and approached Kyle's bed. Slowly Kyle opened his eyes and blinked several times as if trying to re-focus. Then he stared blankly at Butch for a minute or so. Butch smiled and put his hand on Kyle's shoulder. Kyle gradually opened his mouth and tried to push out a word. Butch put his head down next to Kyle's ear and heard him whisper, "*Hey . . . Coach.*"

"Kyle, Kyle . . . you're going to be okay. Hey man, you're talking! That's great!" Butch exclaimed, trying to keep his voice low. "I can't believe it! You know, we'll have you up and talking and then walking in no time. I am going to be here for you, son. You know that, don't you? I promise I will be here for you, for the rest of my life, no matter what or how long it takes." Butch heard the door start to open and he stood up straight, turned, and saw Kyle's mother peek her head in. Kate broke out in a quick smile when she saw Butch. A short, thin, dark-complexioned man wearing a light-green gown followed her into the room.

"Oh, Mr. Cassidy, I am glad you're here," said Kate nervously, trying to keep her glued-on smile from leaving her face. "I am so glad to see you. I read those awful, nasty things they said about you and Kyle in the newspaper, and of course I knew none of it could be true. Kyle wouldn't do something like that. That's not the way we raised him, and I know you would not lie. After all, if we can't trust you—the famous coach, Butch Cassidy—who can we trust? I know people kid you about having the same name as a bandit, but a coach as successful as you has to be honest."

Butch stood quietly for a minute trying to gain his composure and find the courage to tell the truth. But then he figured he was back in control now, talking to an adoring parent, so why tell the complete truth? What in the hell is the truth anyway? In his line of work, being a bullshit artist was now an important skill, especially for coaches who recruited for college ball, and competition for talented athletes was fierce. High school was now becoming that way and fact and fiction sometimes became blurred. Coaches sometimes felt they had to tell people what they wanted to hear. For him, the bullshit had started in earnest when he was twenty-six and changed his name from Gary to Butch.

But deep down he knew that he was never going to coach college ball now, so he figured this was the perfect moment to start making the change.

"Well, Mrs. Ritter," replied Butch, after taking several deep breaths, "for my part, what was written in the newspaper was basically true. I did lie, and I take full responsibility for what happened. I was more worried about keeping Kyle and the other boys eligible, which equates to winning football games. I was more concerned with keeping my reputation as a football coach than I was about the students I was responsible for. I have had to admit that I am an alcoholic, but that's no excuse. I made a huge mistake in the way I handled the incident with Kyle and Zack. I guess I was so desperate for respect, and I so wanted these boys and the fans to love me, that I was willing to lie and ignore the truth to get it. I have no excuse and I am deeply sorry. Kyle did have a very unpleasant altercation with Zack, and I am not going to speak for him, but it was a very bad situation. I should have taken disciplinary action right then and there. If I had done that, this might not have happened. I have resigned both as coach and as a teacher at MLK, because I am not fit to call myself either one of those. I am not sure what else will happen to me, but I am willing to face any other consequences that might come of this whole mess."

"Oh, my God," said Kate. "I didn't know about any of this. I just can't believe all this about Kyle or you. He has always been such a good boy. I can't grasp it all right now. Let's change the subject, talk about something more optimistic, like Kyle's future. We can talk about this other stuff later, Butch, just the two of us.

"I am sorry . . . I don't know where my manners are. Dr. Hyde, I didn't get a chance to introduce you two. This is Butch Cassidy, Kyle's football coach," Kate continued. "I should have introduced the two of you right away; I don't know where my mind is! Dr. Hyde is Kyle's neurosurgeon. He was just telling me out in the hall, that after Kyle's dramatic improvements, and with proper rehabilitation, that Kyle may someday have use of his arms and upper body again, and possibly some of his speech."

"That sounds great," said Butch, shaking Dr. Hyde's hand, "but I also expect he is going to walk and maybe even run again. I believe he will become fully functional within the next two years."

"That may be a bit optimistic," said Dr. Hyde with a half-smile. "Kyle has had his spinal cord splintered and there has been considerable nerve damage. We just don't know how he will respond to treatment. It may take years of therapy just to move his arms."

"I am not being overly optimistic," replied Butch confidently. "I am going to be his personal coach, and I am going to work with him every single day that I can. Kyle has always been a very hard worker and he is tough. He will walk again, and he will do so within a year—you just watch." Butch looked down at Kyle lying in his bed and said, "I guarantee it."

Dr. Hyde frowned as he looked at Butch, but then his expression softened and turned quizzical. "You never know, Mr. Cassidy—you may be right. Miracles happen every day if you are open to them," he added in a quiet voice. "I will pray for both of you and of course I will do whatever I can to assist you from a professional perspective. I might add that I believe a personal trainer—especially one as experienced and dedicated as you are—can be a great help to a person with this type of injury. You may be the inspiration and motivator he needs. He is young and otherwise healthy, and that helps greatly in recovery."

Kyle listened to every word spoken by everyone in the room. Even though he couldn't see Butch, when he heard him make his promise, Kyle's heart jumped with joy. Then when he heard Dr. Hyde tentatively support Butch's beliefs, he was ready to get out of bed and start trying to walk right at that very moment.

CHAPTER TWENTY-SIX
APOLOGY AND HOPE

Roger Speiglman and Zack returned to see Kyle at the hospital four days later, accompanied by a judge-ordered deputy sheriff. Roger asked the deputy to wait outside in the hall. The deputy reluctantly agreed after Roger stated that he would take full responsibility if anything went wrong.

The young deputy wasn't sure what to make of the whole situation. A shrink dragging his incarcerated patient to the hospital to meet with a paralyzed boy that his patient had shot and almost killed? It didn't make any sense. Zack, the attempted murderer, looked petrified before they walked into Kyle's room. The whole thing seemed bizarre to the deputy. He liked things neat and orderly, not crazy like this. It made him feel uneasy and restless. He couldn't sit down in the chair outside the room but kept pacing back and forth in front of the door, occasionally stopping to glance through the small window to ensure the situation was under control.

Zack was both nervous and afraid, but this time he'd come along willingly. Something mysteriously drew him back to see Kyle. Intuitively, he knew seeing Kyle was his only hope and, however small that hope might be, it was what he needed to get out of the mess his life was in. This time he knew Kyle would be more conscious, and that he could unleash his verbal wrath on Zack, although he guessed Kyle couldn't talk well enough yet to verbally abuse him. But Kyle couldn't hurt him, and Zack could walk out or spit in his face if it got too crazy. He felt reassured by the deputy outside the door.

He also knew that Kyle was a freak now. And Zack, for the third time in a row, had the upper hand. He could walk, talk, and even fight if he had to, but Kyle could only lay there. Secretly he hoped that Kyle would not verbally attack him and that they would not fight. Part of him still hated Kyle for what he had done, but a part of him that he didn't understand yet hoped Kyle would get better and that he would someday walk again.

The afternoon nurse pulled them aside and explained that Kyle was doing much better, but still had very little upper-body control and no lower-body response at all. He had some broken speech and his words were very slurred, but he was understandable if one listened carefully. The nurse emphasized that he was improving steadily and that she had never seen anything so miraculous in the twenty-two years she had been in nursing. This had truly been a miracle, she said.

She also told them that Coach Cassidy and another man named Sam, who was a minister or something, had been there several hours ago. She said they had taken him to rehab on the lower floor where they massaged his arm and neck muscles for about half an hour, so Kyle might be very tired right now.

As Roger and Zack stepped toward Kyle's bed, they could see that he was sitting up. The nurses had turned his bed and propped him up with pillows so he could look outside through the windows and see the city below.

Zack braced himself as the nurse rolled Kyle's bed around to its original position, so that he faced them and the hospital room door. He walked up next to Kyle expecting the worst; after all, he had tried to kill this person and had ended up partially paralyzing him. Kyle stared at Zack without any facial response, as if he did not see him or recognize him and Zack did not know what to say.

"Hello, Kyle. My name is Roger Speiglman. I am Zack's psychologist," said Roger, as he stepped forward and stood to the right of Zack.

Kyle's eyes made no effort to turn toward him and did not leave Zack's face. The two boys' eyes locked and stared at each other, mesmerized. Roger was not sure what to do so he quietly stepped back against the wall and just observed.

Finally, Kyle broke the spell. Very slowly, and with great

concentration, he slurred, "*I am—sor—sorry*," and a lone tear ran down his cheek.

Zack's whole body felt shocked, and a sharp pain rushed up to his head. He started feeling light-headed and his heart began to pound, until he thought he must be having a heart attack. *Could this be really happening?* his mind screamed as he stared at Kyle. *Was this another wild dream? Did the vicious Kyle Ritter just tell him he was sorry? How could this be?* He put his hands on the bed railing for support, but he couldn't open his mouth.

A great sense of relief poured over him, like nothing he had ever felt before, and he wanted to weep. He stood motionless for several more moments, not sure how to respond, until he let go of the railing and found himself putting his left hand on Kyle's shoulder. He heard himself mutter, "I am the one who is truly sorry, Kyle. I really am. Man, I cannot believe I shot you; I really can't." Tears started streaming from Zack's eyes, and he wept as if he had been waiting fifteen years for the chance. He wanted to stop crying, but he just couldn't seem to do it, and he finally let himself go, sobbing but still trying to speak. "I was in so much pain, and so embarrassed. I wanted to die—to kill myself—but I just couldn't get myself to do it. Now look what I have done to you instead."

Kyle's eyes dilated as he strained to respond, and perspiration covered his face, but with great effort he muttered, "*No. It was me-ee . . . cruel to you . . . I'm an an-imal. So ash-amed.*"

Zack tried opening his mouth, but nothing came out, so he stood there speechless with tears still running down his cheeks.

It took a full minute for Zack to gain some composure, and all the while the two boys continued to stare at each other but were unable to speak—as if they were afraid to break the spell.

Roger watched in total fascination, feeling both stunned and moved. He was at first afraid to move a muscle and break the boys' connection, but finally found himself wiping his own eyes with his handkerchief. He had never experienced such a moving moment of emotional intensity in his entire career—maybe in his whole life, even considering the birth of his two adored children.

Finally, Zack spoke again. "Kyle, you're going to walk again. I know you will. Maybe you'll play football again and be a quarterback. If I am out of jail I'll come root for you at your games," he rambled on uncontrollably between sobs.

Kyle's dry lips awkwardly spread apart and, as if in slow motion, he formed the word "*Tha-anks.*" He then formed a small, but persistent smile, as large tears rolled down from his eyes and dampened the front of his hospital gown.

The nurse broke the spell several minutes later when she slipped back into the room and whispered in Roger's ear that the visiting time was winding down. She was worried that Kyle was too tired to continue at such a high emotional level.

Zack was almost relieved, because he didn't know what else to say. But part of him now felt safe in Kyle's room, like it was a place of hope for both of them. He almost envied the way people were caring for Kyle here, compared to the juvenile facility where nobody seemed to care much for anybody. Roger acted like he cared, but Zack guessed it was only because he got paid to act that way. He realized that his dad and Butch's visit was the only time he'd felt that somebody might actually like him and care for him besides his mother.

Zack quietly said goodbye to Kyle, somewhat reluctantly, and quickly touched his shoulder. "Maybe," he added, "I can come and see you again soon." He took several steps to the door and slipped out into the hallway. Feeling bewildered, he walked down the hall with Roger, realizing he could feel something besides numbness and pain. He was light-headed and wanted to shout something out loud, but he wasn't sure what would come out. He had connected with the notorious bully, Kyle Ritter, and to the father he had always hated. His whole body felt energized and, at the same time, his world felt like it was being turned upside down. He wanted to hug Kyle, or hug Roger, but it was much too awkward. He had never given anyone a hug except his mother, and once to Ramona. The last time he remembered hugging his mother had been at least five years ago.

Ramona. He had almost forgot about her in all that had happened over the last few weeks. He figured she had given up and gone back to New Jersey to live with her mother, now that her only friend and conspirator was in jail. He was pretty sure she would not have the ability to finish the bomb without his support. Not that she wasn't smart enough. She just wasn't the technical type of person who could do something like that. Zack wondered where she might have dumped the explosives they'd stored at her place. He hoped that she hadn't left them in her room where the landlord could find them after she moved out, and possibly call the FBI to track her down.

But who was this woman calling the school, threatening to blow it up? During interrogations with Baker, Zack learned about the phone calls. Baker had said the woman knew what she was doing and sounded experienced at this type of thing. That obviously wasn't Ramona. She couldn't even look a person in the eye when she talked to them, and she knew almost nothing about explosives—except the little that Zack had shown her and what she could read online on the bomb-making sites. It had to be somebody else. He remembered hearing Baker say that schools get bomb threats all the time, and so he figured it could be almost anyone who was pissed off at the school, even one of the teachers or another student. Regardless, Zack was afraid to tell Baker about Ramona . . . afraid they would arrest her anyway, because she was a Muslim, and put her in jail for a hundred years when they found out she was Palestinian.

Would he ever see Ramona again? Probably not, he decided, and he knew that might be for the best. Their lives seemed to be heading in different directions. Whatever might happen after this day, Zack knew his life had changed forever. He prayed he would never go back to being the angry, depressed, hateful Zack. That would be a fate much worse than death.

CHAPTER TWENTY-SEVEN
EVERYONE DANCES

Like most high schools across America, Martin Luther King High had a long tradition of holding homecoming dances. Originally, they held only one, in September during the football season. But during the mid '90s they added a winter homecoming in January, in the middle of the girls' and boys' basketball season.

At the faculty meeting on Thursday, December 1st, the teachers decided to make that January's winter homecoming dance a little different. They wanted to break with the old traditions and they hoped to make it more open to the entire student body, less elitist. When the teachers took a poll among themselves, they found that more than half of them had never gone to a homecoming dance or a prom while they were in high school. Surprisingly, the trend didn't seem to change much between the older and the younger faculty members. Anne pointed out that most teachers were good students and socially active during high school, but still maybe less than a third of them were attending these functions. At first, this figure seemed rather shocking, but the more they talked about which students attended dances and which did not, the total seemed more accurate. Every teacher, even Vern, agreed that this needed to change.

Penny—an adamant champion of every good cause and a newly elected member of the new Council of Elders—suggested they come up with some new guidelines for the dance that could be presented to the student body at large. She suggested that these ideas be written as a referendum, and the entire student body could vote on the proposals. The idea was to get the student body involved in the process, though no teachers were so naive as to believe all the students would participate equally, or even at all.

Anne and two other teachers, plus the first twenty-nine members from the Council of Elders and nine student-council members, met on the following Tuesday. They came up with twenty-five ideas from which the school body at large could choose. Each student would vote for the five which were most important to him or her. They also included five questions asking for input about the homecoming dance in general.

Two weeks later, the referendum was completed and handed out in homeroom. The feedback was much as the teachers had expected, but seeing it on paper was still an eye-opener. As had been the case with the teachers, less than one-third of the students said they would go to a conventional homecoming dance. Over half of the students thought the dances were very clique-ish, and that they wouldn't fit in. Four out of five of the boys and three out of five girls said they did not know how to dance. And a quarter of the kids said they couldn't afford to go even if they wanted to. About half of the students said they thought the idea of having homecoming queens and kings was snobbish and artificial, while many of the girls thought there was too much pressure already to be beautiful; voting for a homecoming queen just added fuel to that fire.

With only three weeks between reviewing the referendum information and the dance, Anne and her groups had their hands full. They all worked hard and took the students' desires to heart. They came up with a new name for the dance: "The Winter Solstice Ball." There would be no court or other distinctions that would make some students feel superior or inferior to each other. They made sure every student in the school knew about the dance and everyone was encouraged to come. Most of these discussions happened in the morning homeroom classes, where the teachers were invited to share their own experiences. They let the students know that most of their peers didn't know how to dance, either, so they were all in the same boat and there would be free dance lessons at the beginning.

The night of the dance arrived. That Friday afternoon, the senior class had decorated the gym with white crepe paper and blue snowflakes hung from the ceiling. Since there would be no royalty, the podium was built just large enough for the four-piece student band, The Renegades. Alan stood with Anne in the far corner of the gym by the exit door. Even though he was principal, he was trying to be as inconspicuous as possible.

"Well," said Anne, "It looks like we have a full house. I'll bet well over two-thirds of the kids are here."

"I think asking all the guys to wear a sport jacket with slacks or jeans makes most of them feel a little more relaxed," added Alan. "I hear that the thrift stores had a run on used sport jackets this week."

Alan chuckled as he watched the boys line up across from the girls for the start of the dance lessons. He was sure many of them had never danced a step, and they looked totally petrified. Some actually looked stunned to find themselves on a dance floor.

"I feel for those boys . . . glad I don't have to be out there," said Alan. "I have three left feet, myself, and never did learn how to dance."

"What do you mean?" asked Anne. "Maybe that's one of the reasons you're still a single man. You don't know how to have enough fun! Sometimes you're just a stick in the mud, Alan. This is your big chance!" she said, grabbing Alan's hand and dragging him out on the floor.

"You need to be a good example for your students," she laughed as they held hands. "If they can do it, you can do it, and this is a slow song. Look at Jed and Tess—they look like they have been dancing together for years." She leaned into Alan's ear. "That's interesting. Look how close they're dancing and Jed a confirmed bachelor since his breakup with Molly four years ago. Hmmm.

"So come on, you have lucked out!" Anne continued, "The kids decided they wanted some good old rock 'n' roll for this dance, your favorite, Alan. You also happen to be lucky enough to have a great dance partner."

"But—I don't dance," stammered Alan.

"Doesn't matter," said Anne.

A chorus of whistles and cheers went out from the hundreds of students in the middle of the gym as Anne and Alan joined the lesson. Alan hadn't had time to resist and, now that he was out on the floor, it was too late. There was nowhere to hide, so he gave a meager wave, and put his hand around Anne's waist, and started to shuffle his feet.

When the band moved into a faster song, Anne laughed and said, "Just shake it, Alan! Move your buns in time with your feet—now you're getting it. Just keep moving in the same steps. Look at our two dance instructors, Brad and Penny. They're just doing their own thing. Relax."

An hour later the lessons were over, and sweat was dripping from Alan's brow. He headed to the side of the gym to look for a vacant chair. He put his hand to his face, surprised to feel that his old smile had returned after many months of being -AWOL. Anne hadn't let go of his left arm, and the two of them sat against the gym's east wall, watching the dancing, arm in arm.

Karen Lynn walked up holding hands with Lindsey Scott. Alan thought the two tall girls looked striking together. *Wow—who would have ever thought. It's a brave new world.*

"You're a very good dancer, Mr. Carter," said Lindsey. "I'm impressed."

"Thanks," said Alan. "You must be buttering me up for something, but I actually did have fun. I can hardly believe I did that."

Anne added, "Sad but true!" with a bright smile. "Mr. Carter had forgotten how to have fun, but we are teaching him all over again, right from the beginning."

The girls both looked serious for a moment, and Karen Lynn said, "I can relate to Mr. Carter. I haven't had much fun this year, working so hard at school and basketball practice. But ever since I sprained my ankle and Lindsey pulled her hamstring, we haven't been able to practice all week, and I think we both have been having more fun than we've had in years. Speaking for myself, I rather like it, but don't fret. We will both be back for the playoffs in two weeks." The girls giggled as they said goodbye to Alan and Anne and moved across the gym, still holding hands.

"Very interesting," said Alan.

"Yes, indeed," said Anne with a thoughtful smile. "It's a good thing; it's nice to see those girls not so serious and tired looking. Well, Mr. Carter, are you ready to start dancing again?"

"Mmmm . . . I guess," said Alan, with a half-smile. He dropped his hand down to hers and gently gave it a squeeze, and then led her out on to the floor.

CHAPTER TWENTY-EIGHT
BEING HEARD AND GETTING OPTIONS

Alan had been right: as the teacher now in charge of counseling, Betty Bailey had become a very busy woman. She had hired two new counselors and was retraining three existing teachers for part-time positions. She was fifty-nine years of age, and it was no longer so easy to be on the run twelve hours a day. But that was okay, because she had never been happier. She had always believed that, given enough good counselors, she could make high school a more functional place. She had often dreamed that someday she could build a first-rate staff to be there for the students when they needed them. And now, after all these years, it seemed her dream was coming true.

Michele had never talked with a counselor of any type before. She sat in the attendance office, playing with her purse strap, crossing and uncrossing her legs a half-dozen times. She stood up and sat down several times in the ten minutes she waited outside the counseling office door. She tried to pull her skirt down lower, but it wouldn't budge below her mid-thigh. She was glad she had borrowed a big, light-blue sweater from Karen Lynn to cover her revealing tank top, so that she didn't look like a complete slut.

Shit, she kept thinking. *How did I get in this mess? Why me? I didn't ask for this. How could something like this happen to me?*

Suddenly the office door opened and out walked a tall, long-haired, blonde girl with a denim skirt as short as Michele's. She vaguely recognized the girl from seeing her around school. She did not know the girl's name and they both smiled briefly. The girl said, "Thank you very much, Mrs. Pool," and quickly walked out the door into the hallway.

Mrs. Pool motioned to Michele, "Come on in, Michele, I have your request on my desk." Michele walked in and sat down in a light-colored wooden chair in front of a matching desk, facing Mrs. Pool.

Genie Pool was a large-framed woman with bright, fresh skin and shoulder-length, brown hair. She looked to be in her late thirties, but chronologically she was forty-nine. Her youngest son had gone off to college two months earlier and she was glad to have gotten the job and returned to work. Twenty years before, she had been a school counselor at a Catholic high school, and then worked for the County Juvenile Department for three years until she had her first child. She had just been hired by Betty and Alan as one of the new school counselors and had finished her training three days earlier.

Genie and Michele chatted through several minutes of formalities to get acquainted, until Genie said, "Okay, Michele, so what's going on?"

"Well . . . it's like this: Plain and simple—my life is totally screwed up right now. I mean, it's a mess, Mrs. Pool. It's really embarrassing. I have either screwed or given a blow, um . . . oral sex, to half the boys in school and I still don't even have a steady boyfriend. No one has asked me to the prom, no one! Shit, I can't believe I am not going to the senior prom after all I have done for those bastards. You can't imagine how I feel. My life is over at seventeen. I am going to graduate from high school, but I am a fricking failure. Mrs. Pool, I have become the school slut and I guess I am not even very good at that because I am not appreciated! I just wanted the boys to like me, but they don't," she added in tears. "They just want me to drop my drawers and spread my legs, or give them a blow job, and then they're done with me.

"Shit, Mrs. Pool, would you believe my friend Melissa got asked to the prom by three boys? And she is a fricking virgin? But anyway . . . I thought about killing myself but that would be too messy, and I don't like blood. So here I am, and I need help badly! Oh, yeah . . . I almost forgot. I think I may be pregnant. I am not sure how it all works but I think, maybe, that I haven't gotten my period in like two months."

Genie took a deep breath and thought, *Wow. My first client of the day thought he might be gay and was afraid to come to school because he was tired of being made fun of. My second client has gonorrhea and her father has thrown her out of the house. And this is my third client. What the hell have I gotten myself into? And what did these kids do before they had us?*

"Well, Michele," Genie took another deep breath, "Let's take one step at a time. First of all, I wasn't asked to my senior prom, either, and I hadn't had sex with anyone. I just did their homework for them. I have always been big-boned and overweight. I was never thin like you. Boys never wanted me for my body, so I gave them my mind. I was a 'mind whore,' I guess you could say. But at prom time they didn't want any part of me because I was too large and wasn't cute enough. It wasn't fun. So I kind of know how you feel. I used to cry myself to sleep at night hoping I could be like you, skinny and cute. You know it's funny how it all works out with a little patience. Now I have been married twenty years and have been relatively happy and my life is good.

"But Michele," Genie continued, leaning forward, "you have got a lot more going on than not going to the prom. Having sex with multiple partners is like playing Russian roulette. I don't know how many partners you really have had, but you're scaring me, young lady. We need to have you properly tested for HIV as well as for pregnancy."

Michele explained, "I guess I have had just twelve partners in the last three years since I started having sex . . . maybe fourteen. I kind of lost count. I really haven't had hundreds—it just feels like it sometimes. It's not even exciting or fun anymore, and now I am scared shitless. I really don't want to be doing this anymore, but the boys just expect it and if I don't put out, they don't even want to talk to me."

"Michele . . . Michele. You could sleep with every boy in the school and that's not going to make them like you. In fact, it works just the opposite. They're not going to have any respect for you that way, and they will just use you and abuse you. I hate to put it so bluntly, but you're just a one-night-stand for any guy who wants to get laid."

"I know, Mrs. Pool. Karen Lynn tells me that all the time. I guess I am just a slut by nature. I've seen my mom do the same thing ever since my dad left. She works all day at Farrell's Candy Factory, then comes home and takes care of some bum she picked up at the bar the week before. The men, they just leave when they get tired of the same old menu of sex and her not-so-good cooking. Then they want me, and that's how it all started in the first place. At first that was kind of exciting, but now it's a nightmare. If I cut off my mom's newest boyfriend now, he would beat the crap out of both of us, and then he'd leave my mom. Then she would get more depressed and start drinking heavy again. There is no way out for me. It's hopeless. I need to kill myself," Michele continued tearfully, her mascara running down her face. "Do you have some tissue? I'm sorry I'm crying . . ."

"Here, Michele," Genie took another breath and handed her a tissue. She gazed at Michele honestly but empathically. "Wow, you *have* got a mess, girl—but you don't need to end up like your mom. You're a lot wiser than that and you're such a pretty girl with a bubbly personality. Please don't freak out, but I am going to have your mom's boyfriend busted, big time—and your mom is just going to have to deal with it. He will be in the slammer by tomorrow afternoon and we will make sure he doesn't get bail. This county is very, very tough on the rape of minors, even if you were consensual. We will also get your mom some help but her latest man is going to jail, and he is not coming out for a long, long time.

"After that, I want you to come and see me every week, on Mondays at three. We're going to start you on a new support program and I am going to be the head of your support team. We will see about getting Karen Lynn in on it, too.

"Okay, now let's hear more. You think you're pregnant. What's going on, or not going on?"

"No period yet this month, and I don't think I had one last month," Michele answered, putting her head in her hands as if wanting to crawl into the floor and hide.

"You don't *think*, Michele?"

"I guess I don't keep track very well. I signed up for that sex education class, but then it got cancelled. Then all of us kids got a letter from the school board telling us to go to church more often and not to screw anymore. So, I started giving more head to keep the two guys I was seeing happy, but you know how it is, Mrs. Pool . . . some guys just have to have it all."

"Yeah, okay," said Genie. "I know this is tough on you but first things first: Number one, you can start calling me Genie, because we're going to get to know each other very well, I expect, over the next few months. Take heart, Michele," Genie leaned over taking Michele's hands in hers, "Every day hundreds of American teenagers miss periods and they're not necessarily pregnant, so you're not the lone ranger. But you're right—cutting out sex education has been a disaster.

"Okay, now. At 4.30 today, you and I are going to the health clinic over on Devonshire. We will call your mom as soon as school ends. If you are pregnant, we will have to deal with that. I am not a big fan of abortion because I believe it leaves lifelong scars on the woman and deprives someone of having a chance of adopting the baby. But I also believe it must be your choice, so we will cross that bridge if we get to it.

"For the rest of this hour, let's get down to business and figure out how I can help you get your life back on track. It's not going to be easy, girl, but you can do it and I will be here to help."

Michele sat back in her chair and took in a deep breath. The last lone tear slid down her cheek. Life would go on; this wasn't the end of the world, as she had been imagining all week. A "White Knight" in a dress by the name of Mrs. Pool had arrived—there was help available that hadn't seemed possible an hour ago. She didn't need to kill herself after all.

"Hi, Mark," said Betty. "Sit down over here on the other side of my desk . . . no, it's not a problem to just drop in. I am glad to see you."

Mark Woods was student-body president at MLK. Betty knew him fairly well, as she had served as the student council's faculty advisor for several years. His father was Manny Woods, a well-known trial attorney in town. Mark was a tall, lean, olive-skinned young man who usually brimmed with confidence, at least on the surface. But today Mark looked tired and worried.

"I see what you have written on your fact sheet, Mark. Your parents are getting divorced and you're stuck right in the middle. You're an only child and both your dad and mom want you to live with them. So they're not getting along very well? Your dad moved in with his secretary and she is only twenty-six and he wants you to move in with them? So, Mark, how do you feel about all this?"

"I am totally confused, Mrs. Bailey," Mark blurted out. "I . . . I am having a terrible day, or maybe just a terrible life. I am not so sure . . . I am depressed and pissed off, and I have been that way for months. I keep having romantic dreams about my dad's gorgeous girlfriend, and I feel guiltier than hell about that. I mean, she is not much older than me, and sometimes she seems to go out of her way to just hang out wherever I am, and she kind of flirts. Sometimes when my dad's not there she goes skinny dipping in the hot tub and asks me to come in, too. I did last week, and she sat next to me and put her hand on my thigh when she talked to me, and my penis got so hard I was afraid I was going to come in the tub. She told me that sometimes it's good to have an older woman teach us about the birds and bees. Maybe she just wants to be friends, but I don't think so. It's really hard—I just want to touch and kiss her and I know I shouldn't be thinking that way. But she is so pretty, and she touches me and now I am masturbating almost every day when I think about her. What if my mother or father knew? They would die. It would be terrible for both of them for different reasons.

"I feel terrible for my mom already," he continued, his voice starting to choke and his face covered in deep sweat. "Having your husband run off with a younger woman is a real downer. Boy, if she knew I was after his girlfriend, too, then she would really flip out! I don't know what she would do . . . it would kill her. I am much closer to my mom, but I still love them both and I don't want to hurt either one of them. I mean this is really bothering me, Mrs. Bailey. I normally don't sleep well, and I am sometimes a worrier, but now I am not sleeping at all and I worry all the time," he said as he hunkered over his chair and looked at Betty with his big, brown, pleading eyes.

"Mark," said Betty, "you obviously have a lot more going on than just having a bad day. You have some very heavy-duty stuff happening in your life, and you need to understand this is not your stuff—you have not created it. It's perfectly natural to be attracted to slightly older women; most boys are. Like you said, she is a lot closer to your age than your father's age and she is probably feeling that, too. However, she is out of line coming on to you like she does, and she obviously has her own issues. I think she is dead serious about seducing you.

"That being said, it's not right or good for you to lust after your dad's girlfriend. As tempting as that can be, it can only cause everyone involved more misery. We need a strategy that will work for you and, to be honest, I think this issue is over my head. We need to set up a two-hour session with Mr. Bartow, our new part-time, cognitive counselor who specializes in students from divorced families. I think he is quite good. I think this is a crisis issue so we're going to start you out twice a week to get you over this rough spot. In this situation, I think talking to a younger man like Mr. Bartow might really be helpful; he is just thirty-two. Let me give his voicemail a call and we will set up a time."

"Thanks, Mrs. Bailey. I really appreciate this. I feel like you're saving my life. I haven't known who to talk to. You just can't imagine how much pain this has caused me. I was thinking about running away and going up to my cousin's in Oregon."

"I get it, I really do, Mark. I can imagine what you are going through. Unfortunately, none of us escape this life without this kind of pain at some point; that's just the way life is. I would like to tell you it's different, but it isn't. The good news is that you will make it through with just a little internal scarring to show for it. By this time next year, you will be away at college, and you will probably meet some girl who is your own age."

"That sounds good, Mrs. Bailey, it really does. Thank you very, very much."

"Hi," said Vern. "It's Dustin, isn't it?"

"Yes, sir, it is," said Dustin, as he sat down in the cushioned office chair by Vern's desk.

"Excuse the mess," Vern said, sitting back in his swivel chair. "We're in the middle of turning this old custodian storage area into a new office. I've just become a counselor again and I haven't done this in almost fifteen years, so bear with me and we'll get through it together.

"So, Dustin, from what I've heard, you are having a rough time this year. Very bad situation with Zack and Kyle, and I understand you were directly involved. In order to return to school after your original suspension, you had to agree to school probation for the remainder of the year—and you are suspended from the football team for the rest of the year as well." Vern paused, perusing Dustin's file for another few moments, "And it also looks like you're required to get counseling, and we're to figure out six months of community service for you too. Correct?"

"Uh . . . yes, sir."

"Any ideas on what's going on?"

"Not really, sir." Dustin stammered. "I mean, all this terrible stuff has happened, but I'm not sure what I'm feeling or what to do. I just feel kind of shut down and depressed . . ..

"Okay, Dustin. Instead of me asking you a bunch of questions, you just tell me what's going on in your mind right now."

"Well, it's been a rough year," acknowledged Dustin, while sitting straight up in his chair. "I still feel terrible about what we did to Zack and now look at Kyle. I think about the incident all the time. Um . . . we had been doing meds and rum in the bathroom, and we had cut the period before. We just got totally wacked out. I have given up drugs and drinking for over a month now, and I have been going to the teen AA and Alateen meetings after school. Anyway, they say I have to. I hope it's going to help."

"What is going on, Dustin? It looks like more than just drugs and booze. It seems like you have been on the edge for the last two years, with one suspension for fighting and three teacher referrals for screwing around in class." Vern continued to thumb through Dustin's rather extensive school file, "And you only have about an eighth-grade average. Not good—you're a lot smarter than that. These drugs are bad stuff and you guys really screwed up, big time, but let's try to get to the bottom of this. Do you know why you are so angry at everybody?"

"I don't know," was all Dustin could think to reply with a straight face and no sign of emotion.

Vern stood up and, without asking, handed Dustin a cup of water from a cooler he had brought from home. "Look, Dustin, I can't help you if we can't talk honestly. It's time we started moving ahead. I know it's an old cliché, but we can't change the past, we can only change the future. It's up to you, Dustin. I think you're a good person. We just need to get you headed in the right direction. But I think there is more going on here, and you're going to have to decide how much you're going to share."

"I understand that, sir. I guess I feel like a failure. Something is wrong with me, and I guess that's why I am here. I feel depressed, though I am not sure exactly what that means. It's like I don't have any energy. My mother is depressed some of the time, and once I swiped a dozen of her Prozac pills and took them for a week, but they did not seem to help much. In fact, I just felt worse, much worse."

"Dustin, have you been to a doctor or anything like that?" asked Vern. "As you know, taking other people's meds is very dangerous, especially anti-depressants. For some people, they can make you much more depressed."

"Yes, sir. My doctor says I have something wrong with me—that I have ADD, and that maybe I am dyslexic. It's the way my brain works—that's why I have such a hard time in some of my school classes like algebra and Spanish. But I am good in history and I like my business and Ag class, so I am not totally dumb. The doctor wanted to put me on some pills, but my mom said no. She said she did not want me doped up like her, and she thought I would just sell them to other kids, just like some of the other kids do."

"Yes, that can be a problem, Dustin. It sounds like you have been tested for what some people call, I believe mistakenly, Attention Deficit Disorder. I think a lot of your peers in school have it, to one degree or another. I've got it, too, though I have never been officially diagnosed for it. They didn't have labels for it in my day, but I know I've got it . . . always have, always will. I have known it since I started teaching—except I also have the H in my acronym, which stands for Hyperactive. That's why you don't see me sitting down too often, why I am always on the run. I just can't stand to sit still, and my mind is always going a mile a minute."

"You, Mr. Duncan? But you're the Athletic Director and you have ADD? Or hyper-ADD? How can you do that? Does Mr. Carter know? Won't he fire you if he finds out?"

"Fire me? No, of course he wouldn't fire me. Dustin, I am sure he knows I have ADHD. That may be why he hired me, because I get things done. Now Dustin, if you were in a wagon train out west, who would you want as your scout: somebody with ADD, or somebody who is interested in every little detail? We call the very detailed people "compulsive"; they often make good researchers and corporate lawyers, engineers and accountants, but not always good scouts, sales managers, athletic directors, movie stars, farmers, entrepreneurs, real estate agents, or even trial lawyers.

"You want the ADD or ADHD guy on the wagon train, because he is going to be right there, checking everything out to see if there are any Indians over the next hill, where the next water hole is, and so forth. He is going to know everything going on around him, so he can see the big picture. That's what ADD people do best. There are not many wagon masters or frontier scouts today, but these folks are the entrepreneurs, high-end managers, real estate people, social workers, artists, sales people, and politicians. They say the young President Bush had ADD long before he became President, but he listened to the wrong people. The big secret of being ADD is that usually you're a people person and a quick thinker, but you've got to slow down and look at all your options—don't make quick decisions unless you have to, and then use your intuition judiciously. That's why God gave it to you.

"Anyway, that's why I am Athletic Director, because I am supposed to be seeing the big picture, not just concentrating on one sport," said Vern, as he stood up and started pacing back and forth around the office. "Though it's very obvious, I have been missing the big picture lately. But that's another story that we don't need to go into right now.

"Dustin, as part of your retribution, I want you to report to Brad Smith tomorrow right after school. He has a new program called 'Empathetic Listening.' Basically, the group members share their stories and learn how to listen and hopefully understand each other better. It's a good class and I think it could help you a lot. Also, you're going to referee some of the intramural games after school. I think you will be very good at it and it will help get your mind off some of the other stuff going on in your life. It will count toward your required community service hours, too."

"Sure, it sounds good to me," said Dustin excitedly, his attention fully on Vern. "It's got to be better than getting kicked out of school, and I might like being a ref."

Vern nodded. "Dustin, I would like you to come back Wednesday at the same time and we can talk some more about what went on with Kyle and Zack. Even though it's a hell of a mess and a tough situation, maybe we can come up with some ways to make at least partial amends."

"Yes, sir, and thank you. It's been helpful talking to you," said Dustin hopefully. "And thanks for letting me referee some of the intramural games. I think it will be fun."

Sixty-one years old and I am still learning new tricks, thought Vern after Dustin left. It felt good for him to be working directly with kids again. It was also nice to have some supportive resources available to turn the kids on to. There wasn't much available back when he worked as a counselor in the '80s, and that really burnt out counselors fast.

Maybe Alan had been right all along. It was *time for some changes.*

Vern realized that he had built a very successful sports program, but that it had gotten out of balance. He had forgotten his real purpose along the way—helping kids, all the kids. He thought this was the best he had felt in a very long time.

CHAPTER TWENTY-NINE
A "WIN-WIN" TEAM

Butch sold his three-year-old, blue Chevy Suburban to an up-and-coming, smartly dressed couple with a nine-year-old daughter. They explained to Butch and Sam that they had just proudly purchased a new 4,000 square-foot home in Queens Heights and thought the Suburban would look perfect in their driveway. Butch had to hold his tongue. He wanted to give the couple a brief lecture on how unimportant "looking good" is, at least in the big picture, and tell them what he had just learned about the pitfalls of the ego. But he was also trying to learn to be nonjudgmental. So instead, he handed them the keys as they handed him a cashier's check and wished them well as they drove off.

By the time Butch paid off the finance company, he had only 900 dollars left. But that was enough for him and Sam to go down to Milligan's Used Cars on Fifth Street and buy a 1989 brown Chevy convertible. It wasn't pretty—the paint was faded and the tan, cloth top had a small rip in the left corner—but it had only 94,000 miles on its small, original, V8 engine. Sam said it would last them a long time if they took care of it, and it would get decent gas mileage to boot.

Sam had helped Butch get part-time work at the shelter. Butch received free room and board and a small salary of 400 dollars a month. He slept on a single army cot in the back storage room, which he shared with Sam and another employee. His feet hung over the end of the cot and his beefy arms hung to the floor. He had to fit all his clothes in a tiny locker, but Butch wouldn't have traded it for his king-size bed in his big, lonely master bedroom with the walk-in closet and the Jacuzzi tub in his private bath.

Sam had given Butch some of his own working hours, since the shelter did not have money in the budget for another staff person. The director, Buck Lewis, liked having a large man around who knew how to give directions and keep order, especially at night.

Sam liked Butch very much, even though they seemed quite different on the surface. Sam appreciated loyalty and loyalty was coming out of Butch's ears. He could also see Butch's sensitivity, a trait that Butch had always been ashamed of and had tried to hide since he was a kid. Sam felt like he had found his first adult friend in many years, and it felt very good.

Butch felt the same way about Sam and considered him a wise sage. For the first time in his entire adult life he listened to someone else's opinions, and felt he had an honest friend that he could trust.

Sam knew a number of poor, elderly people who lived by themselves in the neighborhoods surrounding the shelter. Living on small, fixed incomes left them without the resources or energy to keep their older homes in good repair, inside or out. In response to their needs, Sam and Butch started "S & B Repairs," a handyman service they built in between visits to Kyle.

They went to the hospital to see Kyle every morning. Every afternoon they would head out in the convertible with the trunk and backseat filled with tools and supplies they had conjured up from garage sales, donations, and thrift stores. They would perform repairs, paint, or even clean a home, and then chat with their elderly clients who were eager to have visitors. For the people who could pay, they charged six dollars an hour for their services. That would cover parts, gas, and repairs on their car. If they felt the people couldn't pay, they accepted donations, baked goods, crafts, or whatever else people wanted to give them. Soon they swore they were two of the best paid men in Arcadia, California, and they always had extra baked goods to take back to the shelter to share with the other men. Despite their ongoing worries about Zack and Kyle, both Sam and Butch felt like life was going their way. They were both content and peaceful—if not outright happy—much of the time.

CHAPTER THIRTY
TRANSFORMING THE PECKING ORDER

Juan sat with Claire, Dustin, and Karen Lynn in the cafeteria. "Well, Saturday was one hell of a day," Juan said, "I have never had an April Fool's Day like that before. Visiting Kyle and Zack in the same day was more than a full day."

Dustin glanced over at Juan with a pensive look. "I have only been to Kyle's house once before—he always seemed to be embarrassed about his dad . . . I guess he's kind of crazy or something. Their house isn't much, but his mom seemed nice and her chocolate-chip cookies were good."

"Yeah, that seems to be the word around school, but I heard his dad disappeared off the face of the earth after Kyle was paralyzed," responded Juan. His wary eyes scanned the milling students around them. "But his dad taking off is likely the best thing that could have happened for Kyle."

"Yeah, I agree," said Dustin.

"Maybe we should have called them first," Karen Lynn responded. "They were so surprised to see us all together visiting them. Seeing Kyle openly cry was amazing, and he was so open and honest; I couldn't believe it was him."

"Yeah," replied Juan, "he was *really* surprised to see me; I am not exactly his pal."

"I thought he was going to completely flip out when he saw us all together," Karen Lynn laughed. "It's probably the last thing in the world he figured could possibly happen."

"Yeah . . . me, too," replied Juan. "If you told me a month ago I would have been there with you three hombres visiting Kyle Ritter, I would have thought you were crazy. But it's all Miss Brigg's fault. I should have never signed up for that reconciliation class, but I needed the credits and so here we are all together."

"I love that class," Claire replied. "I think it's wonderful. There are a couple other kids I know who have mended past differences after getting in that class—and my friend, Becky, took the initiative to make up with her dad who she had not spoken to in years. But you know, with Kyle, after the shock wore off, he really seemed glad to see us. I think he needed to know that most of us have moved past what he did to Zack and that we care about him and want him to be whole again."

"Yeah, I was amazed he kept trying to talk about Zack, like they were buds or something," Dustin interrupted. "What's that all about?"

The kids looked at each other in bewilderment and no one said anything for a few moments.

"He is a changed person," Juan finally said. "He is not a bad hombre anymore . . . you can see it in his eyes. He and Zack have done their own reconciliation without us or any of our teachers. And it's good to see Kyle moving his arms, and I can kind of understood him when he talks. You can tell he is getting better at it."

"I think Zack is a changed person, too" chimed in Claire. "You can see it in his eyes; they're so soft now, not full of that raw hate that he used to carry around. And now he looks you directly in the eye when he talks to you, like he really cares and wants to talk to you."

"Well, Zack was sure glad to see us. I don't think he believed we, or anybody, would go down to Juvie just to see him," Dustin interjected. "I could tell it was a big thing to him and I was really surprised when he started crying as we left. I got tears in my eyes, too, but I kept trying to suck them back in."

"Me, too," Karen Lynn agreed. "Zack really is cute and he can be sweet if given the chance. It's just too bad we didn't take the time to notice that before. What was wrong with us? I was so engrossed in basketball that I had forgotten how to be a human being. None of us—but you, Juan—befriended him. How come, Juan? Why did you do that?"

"I don't know . . . just fate, I guess. Me and Poncho just walked in when he was in the middle of it with Kyle, and I felt something snap inside. But it wasn't just anger—it was like a hurt that I felt so bad for him that drove me to act. I really don't get it, but then I started liking the little peep. At first it was like having a puppy, but then I could tell he was smart and kind of interesting and needed a friend—*any* friend—really bad. I have always had plenty of friends in the Barrio. I never thought how it would be to not have any friends, not even one. So then I make him a friend and now I've got you dudes as peeps, too . . . it's so weird."

"Yes," Claire agreed, "I noticed him a number of times and walked past him just before the shooting. I wanted to say something kind to him, but I was too embarrassed. What a dork I am—I can't believe I was too worried what my friends would think. I am still so ashamed that I did that. I have learned so much in my Emotional Intelligence class about how I have treated people and I so want to be different. I hope he understood when I explained that to him."

"Yeah, he understood," Juan chuckled, "especially when we were leaving and you gave him that kiss on his cheek. His cheeks turned bright red and his face lit up and he looked like a little Santa Claus."

They all laughed for a moment, but then Dustin's face darkened. "Well, I may never forgive myself for my part. I was as bad as Kyle—I was all fucked up and couldn't think for myself. I didn't want to do it . . . I'm still trying to deal with it every day. It's like I don't know if it will ever be all right."

"Yeah, but," reminded Claire, "Zack may never have come out of the funky place he was in if that didn't happen. He was in a really bad place before the bathroom incident ever went down with you and Kyle. He looks and acts so much better now. He truly is a different person. It's like he is a grown-up all of a sudden and he actually smiles. I am a believer most things happen for a reason, and Zack needed something drastic to survive—he really did. So from acting in your own pain you provided that for him. But now it's time, Dustin, for you to let go and concentrate on getting your life in order, because you're a cool guy and you can do it!"

"That's an interesting way to look at it," Dustin replied. "It sure feels good when you say it like that; it's like this big, gigantic rock lifts off my shoulders."

"Trust the process, Dustin . . . trust the process," Karen Lynn advised kindly.

"Alan, it's line three," said Ruth. "A Mr. Murray Potter from Vanguard Publishing . . ."

Alan immediately reached for the phone. "Yes, Mr. Potter, this is Alan. I very much appreciate you taking the time to call me."

"Alan . . .thanks for taking my call. Did you receive the book proposal and consultant information I sent?"

"Yes," Alan replied excitedly. "I received your proposal to publish my book as well as your offer to hire me on as a consultant. It all came in yesterday's mail. Thank you, I am very impressed and flattered. I have heard of your company before—in fact, I have read numerous books published by your firm."

"Great. Did you have time to review the salary information?"

"Yes, sir, I read that in your proposal. It sounds like a most interesting offer and an excellent salary—that's more than triple what I am making now . . . . But why me, Mr. Potter? There are plenty of well-known authors who can write on educational reform, and who have much more experience than I do, as well as long-standing reputations."

"Well, Mr. Carter, your article, "The Pecking Order," was published in *O Magazine* this month and that carries a lot of weight, plus it is a very solid article. Our staff chose you from eight other authors mainly because you have a very good reputation in your school district. I was able to talk to your school board president—Lancaster, is it?— and he seemed to think you were the best thing that ever happened to the State of California educational system."

"Yes, I'm aware of your call with Bob. And it's true, I have received a lot of publicity in the last month or so, but I am not really an author or a public personality. Next week I will be doing an interview for OPB and I am very nervous about it! This all seems like a dream, or sometimes a nightmare. But I am just the latest small-time media fad. There are many other educators with much longer track records than mine."

"Mr. Carter, it's true that fads can change, but for right now that is what sells books."

"Well, Mr. Potter, I am very, very flattered, but I don't want to waste your time. The truth is that I am relatively happy where I am—and I do feel a strong obligation to finish what I have started. What would be the point of my writings if we didn't have the opportunity to see how this all works in the classroom and in the community. As much as I appreciate it, I am afraid I must decline your very generous offer."

"Are you sure, Mr. Carter?"

"For right now I am one hundred percent certain, but I will certainly keep your offer in mind when I finish my book. It's not often I am offered a quarter-million dollars up front to write one book that I have already half finished."

"Well, if you do reconsider, I hope you will keep me in mind."

"Yes, sir, if I change my mind I will give you the first opportunity. Thank you very much for calling."

Alan sat back in his chair and pondered his quick decision-making ability. But it was an easy decision. So what's 250,000 dollars, one way or the other? Because how often in one's life does a person get a chance to make a real difference? Alan knew this was his chance and it was worth much more than money. But it did sound like an interesting job: the chief writer for a series of three books on educational reform, with the most respected publishing firm in that genre.

He'd written the article two years before, but hadn't had any luck getting it published back then.

The Pecking Order
By Alan Carter, Principal
Martin Luther King High School

Seldom as humans are we in socially, politically, mentally, or economically balanced situations. What I am calling "the pecking order" influences our lives in all the above attributes—and in the way we dress, the cars we drive. the spouses we choose, how many children we have, the houses we live in, the way we vote, the friends we choose, the wars we fight, the professions we decide on, and where, how, and why we finally die.

It's often one of life's great superficial gifts to be at the top of a pecking order. On the other hand, it can seem like a great tragedy to those who feel that they are at the bottom. The impact that pecking orders have had on both individuals and societies throughout history may well be beyond calculation. Whether you're at the top, the bottom, or somewhere in between, the personal implications are enormous.

So what is "the pecking order"? The term originally had to do with poultry and the dominance of one bird over another. Every flock has its dominant birds, and they controlled the others by pecking them into submission.

For us humans, the pecking order is similar to an invisible caste system that an individual or a group falls into. It creates a real or imagined hierarchy with inherent aspects of dominance and subservience. It can be based on social, financial, educational, emotional, athletic, military, religious, sexual, or physical aspects. It may be job-related, ethnically determined, relationally determined, or an inherited status. It often extends what is perceived as "power" for some, while "limiting power" for others.

The pecking order is related to the Darwinian concept of "survival of the fittest." Some might argue that it is an essential quality of physical evolution. Both humans and many animals attempt to control one another through the pecking order, so they can get what they need, want, or feel they deserve. It has been used by most societies to keep order and protect the status quo. More importantly, for individuals, it's a way of having security of their position and knowing where they fit in. For those vying to be at the top, it often becomes a way to try to feel important and, ultimately, okay about oneself.

The reasons most of us find our place in pecking orders are vast. Family origins, genetic makeup (looks, personality, drive, etc.), race, intelligence, gender, sex drive, family dynamics, place of birth, and athletic ability all play a part. Whether gene-driven or through divine intervention, plain luck often seems to determine what attributes one has -- or one lacks.

But the number-one reason has to do with self-esteem or, more importantly, the lack *of self-esteem, self-worth, or dignity. The consequences of being in any type of pecking order are enormous, both to our culture and the individual. The obvious loss of self-value to an individual or group usually occurs when they feel they are on the lower end of the order. One of the most common examples is simply being born a woman or a minority. The "MeToo" movement is a recent revolution highlighting the inequality that has gone on for women for thousands of years.*

In our young people's culture, the pecking order comes into play via a high school cheerleader or varsity athlete. The cheerleader is often looked upon as more beautiful or vivacious than the average girl and, therefore falls into a higher social order. The athlete is set apart by way of the letterman jacket and the privileges they receive for being talented in a certain area, especially within the more popular and competitive arena of spectator sports. Usually the rest of the students in school fall into the pecking order from there on down.

Ultimately everyone is affected, even those who seem to be at the top. The cheerleader is under pressure to keep her (or his) position as the "best" and "most beautiful"—her beauty, physique, and personality may well become her master. Anxiety, anorexia, depression, overachieving, nervous breakdowns, and a false sense of superiority are all too common in this arena. As she ages, life becomes a race to remain looking young and attractive.

Those in the middle to bottom of the order are often under the false pretense that they're not good enough, that there's something wrong with them. Poor self-worth, isolation, depression, anger, addiction, overachievement, underachievement, negative drama, poor health, obesity, listlessness, gang or cult membership, and codependency are among the sad and toxic experiences for these individuals.

Many of our highest and lowest achievers fall into this second group. Some will just give up and become victims of their culture. Others will use personal achievements as a way to try and feel better about themselves. In the Western world, much of our economic infrastructure and national stardom has been built around the need to succeed by proving to ourselves, families, and the rest of the world that we're okay or that we're better than "they" are. How many politicians do you think fall into this group?

The long and the short of it is that few of us find meaningful balance in our daily lives.

Most folks, by the time they are out of high school, do not give much conscious thought to where they land in the pecking order. Many times we don't even know we're in one. But make no mistake—our subconscious is constantly evaluating our situation to determine how we fit in at our job, academically, with friends, family, social groups, politically, or according to what we see and hear in the media. Most importantly we're concerned with how we fit our own mind's expectations regarding the grand scheme of life.

Our society has formed an entire economic culture around how we want to look and feel; whether we play or watch the right sport; drink the best beer; have the latest electronic gadget; drive the coolest car; have the biggest house; the most stylish haircut; the sexiest clothing (or lack thereof); the thinnest body; whether we take the right drug; or smoke the best cigarette. Corporate America realizes that our outlook on life and our self-esteem has been deeply engrained from how we have coped with the social-economic orders we live and grew up in. The advertising industry has learned to exploit our perceived desires by continually telling us that if we only had their product, we would look or feel like someone higher up in the pecking order—such as an attractive model, movie or pop star, wealthy or healthy individual, or sports figure. Then, and only then, will we be truly "okay."

No matter what kind of pecking order one is in, or where they are at in the order, it is often stressful and anxiety-inducing. It takes a tremendous amount of energy by individuals, groups, our culture, and our nation just to maintain the status quo.

How we deal with the negative consequences of being in a pecking order could well be the largest and most important challenge our society faces in the new millennium. Fortunately, some have become too aware, educated, emotionally intelligent, or sophisticated to live by the survival-of-the-fittest credo any longer. But many others have not. The push-pull to have the most and to be the best has become enormous and has created a great divide among individuals, cultures, and nations. The ability of social media to show the differences between us has become huge. Has our country now become too divided? Will we ever be able to work together to make great social and economic changes?

Here in the United States, we have had a certain amount of political and economic freedom for generations, but now I believe many want and need something more. I think we want freedom to truly be ourselves, without the stress-inducing limitations of being continually judged, manipulated, or financially placed behind the eight ball. We want to be more than just another consumer domino that must continually buy more to keep the economy strong. We live in an economic culture that has the ability to provide the healthy food we all want, abundant living wages, and good physical and mental healthcare to every individual and family -- if we could only agree to do so. The question becomes, then, who is going to lead us: the greedy or the wise? Right now it's obvious to many that we have not picked the wise.

There simply may be too many of us on the planet now to make the survival-of-the-fittest mentality work any longer. The limitations this philosophy places on educated and aware individuals or societies is becoming too great. From the shootings in our schools to one's own private depression or addictions . . . all are affected, every one of us. Will we stand up and deal with the epidemic of mental illness -- or will it simply pull us under?

As a culture, we have made the choice to allow most of us to reproduce, become educated, vote, find our own religion, and choose our own mates. Our laws say we are all equal. Instead of being just equal under the law, maybe we must be equal in our own eyes and in the eyes of each other -- different but equal, and not just by race, politics, religion, or gender but simply by being another valued and unique human being. Could this be the next step in our evolution? Or a spiritual transformation, perhaps?

The kids in our schools who are shooting at fellow students are quite often aiming at those higher up on the pecking order. Yes, they are creating personal tragedies, but may be giving us a major cultural wake-up call. They are the most desperate ones. And now, with easy access to weapons of mass destruction (automatic weapons and bombs), they have found a way to fight back. Most of us struggled on through school, repressing our frustrations and disappointments, without getting physically violent. But damage is done to every one of us, and life-

long scars negatively affect many of our lives. By electing an angry, damaged, rich man to lead us, are we screaming out for help?

How we as individuals and as a culture respond to this issue may ultimately decide all our fates. It's a huge issue that most of us would rather not talk about. It's been much too personal and painful. It can shatter our illusions of self-identity and our perceived invincibility. Since we don't openly talk about these issues, we often begin to believe that we are strange . . . different . . . that there is something wrong with us. Our self-identity and value are damaged. Often we build up personality defenses and paranoia that separate us from one another, not realizing that, yes, we are all different, but if we're reasonably mentally healthy, most of us have the same desires, needs, and fears. We all want to be "okay" and to be seen, treated and respected as fundamentally "okay," by others – NOT as less than others.

In the larger social perspective, the answer to these problems on paper may be relatively simple—but in reality, they are difficult and divisive. Finding the cultural will to look at the issues and deal with them may be very difficult to achieve. But first we must stop listening to the most damaged among us—the angry, the most fearful, the power-hungry, the people who would give up our democracy in a minute for a dictatorship if they, or the person of their choice, were dictator.

Let's pretend we could teach and practice what we believe to be most important. Let's say we have the courage to start with ourselves, and our families, and then take it into our schools:

- *What would happen if we make acceptance, kindness, and the art of being non-judgmental the most important subject we teach each and every day?*
- *Could you imagine every kid in the country from kindergarten up spending two hours a day learning and practicing acceptance, tolerance, communication skills, and conflict resolution?*
- *Couldn't we all learn to finish each text or email with a kind, encouraging word?*
- *Couldn't each politician devote several hours each week to learning from a politician from another party?*
- *Couldn't we destroy our personal weapons designed for the sole purpose of killing each other?*
- *Could we not ensure that every living, breathing, soul in this country has access to the best mental and physical care?*

Couldn't most of us agree on doing that much? As a nation, what if we brought these choices to our relationships at home and around the world?

Would we continue to have these national tragedies in our schools?

If we could practice and teach what most of us really believe, yes—then we truly could change the world. But if we don't do anything positive, this could be the end of man's greatest experiment.

Alan closed the magazine and sat back in his chair. Yes, he was an idealist, maybe even a Pollyanna, and that was okay. He had a practical, realistic, persistent side, too, and that allowed him to get things done. His ex-wife always told him that was because he is half-Capricorn and half-Sagittarius, and an "earth sign"—whatever that meant. He knew the rest of the year was going to be tough. It was just four months into the new curriculum and things were going fairly well. He stood up and said to himself, "Yes, life is very, very interesting."

CHAPTER THIRTY-ONE
NEWSWORTHY—"A WELL-EARNED B+"

THE GLOBE
Changes Made and Changes Ahead at Martin Luther King High School
by Ned Bannister, Feature Writer

This is the final report of the eight-article series we offered this past winter about "Growing Up in Modern America."

Although we featured Martin Luther King High School as our lead educational facility, incorporated changes at various other schools are happening all over the state and the nation. Sparked by Zack Diamond's shooting of Kyle Ritter and Josh Smith last September, MLK has gone full steam ahead in an attempt to change the preexisting teen culture that existed before the shooting. Instead of just keeping guns out of the school, they are trying to zero in on many of the underlying issues that create the anger and stress teens have to deal with in this modern age. With the help of what MLK calls "The Council of Elders"—a group chosen by their peers consisting of PTA volunteers, teachers, parents, and students—the school has made significant changes that might otherwise have taken many years, if ever, to accomplish.

1. **Elective-Classes, Counseling, and Support:** The biggest change seems to be in the student culture itself, including the interactions among students, and with the faculty as well. "Bullying," as it has been coined, has become so frowned upon by these young

people that it seems to have all but disappeared from Martin Luther King High School. Most importantly, students are learning how to interact with each other in an open, honest way, with the goal of ensuring that no one feels left out because they do not fit in or are considered an outcast. We at *The Globe* see this as a huge step in reducing school violence and preventing school shootings. It's exciting to see the students themselves initiating many of these interactions. And if students have a grievance with each other, their parents, or with any staff member, they may request and receive a three-hour intervention session with selected volunteers from the school's Council of Elders. We must say that there is a maturity level here at MLK similar to what the students at Parkland demonstrated after their shooting tragedy; and it's what this country needs.

According to our polls of students, teachers, and parents, the Jigsaw, Self-esteem, Emotional Intelligence, Honest Communication, Empathetic Listening and Reconciliation elective classes definitely seem to be a success. There has been surprisingly little pushback that we know of, with only two official complaints from parents recorded by the school. Both cases were investigated and were found to be personal objections from parents due to their own belief system, having nothing to do with unfavorable incidents at the school. Due to the favorable response, multiple high schools throughout the district will begin offering these type of elective classes as early as this coming fall.

Also, any MLK student who suffers with any type of mental health issues—or personal- or school-related issues—now has a place to go to receive immediate, qualified help at no cost to them. The additional support of five counselors and the new, volunteer Mental Health Crisis Line is providing a positive effect throughout the student body. Interviewing twenty-four MLK students at random, we found that twenty-one of the students felt their life and school experience had been dramatically improved with the addition of the new counseling system and crisis line.

For all of us here at *The Globe*, the bottom line is to provide students with an environment in which they can find happiness, contentment, enthusiasm, and peace of mind – all of which can turbo-charge learning. Yet our nation seems to be going in the opposite direction, as a mental health epidemic continues to sweep the countryside. So, if these types of programs instituted at MLK can help our young people, then it would make more sense to invest in greater mental health treatments, rather than spending billions on weapons and defense systems.

2. **Competitive Sports and Intramural Sports:** MLK's competitive sports programs have not faltered since the induction of the revised curriculum. The girls' basketball team finished third in the State finals this year, and the boys' basketball team finished second in their league as well. The remaining teams and individuals seem to be holding their own or are slightly improved.

But the most exciting part may be watching the hundreds of students participating in the new, after-school intramural programs. At last count, 326 students are currently participating.

3. **Test Scores and Academics:** MLK performed very well on their standardized testing last month. The majority of the student body tested at average, or above average, except in history and social studies in which they received the highest scores in the entire district. Since the enactment of the new curriculum, it's obvious that academics have not suffered at MLK.

4. **Safety Issues and Gun-Control:** With the help of protesting local teens, parents, and teachers from across the state, California has recently passed the strictest gun-control measures in the nation, with Oregon and Washington State now following suit. The newly enacted West Coast Consortium for Safe Living Statute boycotts stores and online businesses that sell automatic weapons and ammunition. Walmart, the country's largest retailer, has recently ceased its sales of guns and ammunition of all types, as have many other retail sporting-goods chains.

In all three states it is now illegal to sell or buy any type of assault weapon, semi-automatic rifle, or handgun. It is also illegal to sell or own clips of ammunition holding over twenty rounds. In turn, bump stocks are now illegal to own or sell. And going in the opposite direction from the Texas model—with the exception of law enforcement personnel—it is now illegal to have any type of weapon within a hundred yards of any public or private school.

The Globe published MLK's "Council of Elders: A Proposal for Change from the Students at Martin Luther King High School" in our previous "Article No. 2" of this series. The attention it has received from nationally syndicated writer and PBS newsman, William Brown, has been nothing less than astonishing. Also,

Democratic Senator Carol Smith from Vermont, has introduced a bill to form "Council of Elders" non-profit groups across the nation, and to provide funding for such groups for the next several years. This is certainly another accolade for the young people and staff at MLK.

IN CLOSING, WE HERE AT *THE GLOBE* ARE GIVING MLK HIGH SCHOOL, THE LOS ANGELES COUNTY SCHOOL DISTRICT, AND THE STATE OF CALIFORNIA A WELL-EARNED B+ FOR ITS EFFORTS IN THE FIELD OF EDUCATIONAL REFORM.

CHAPTER THIRTY-TWO
COACHED FOR SUCCESS

Kyle sat in his wheelchair on the covered, front porch of his family's newly painted, yellow-frame house. His mother had dressed him in gray sweatpants, a white T-shirt, and white tennis shoes. He stared straight ahead, his mind deep in thought. His mother was busy in the kitchen doing up the morning dishes. She had told him it was 9:25 a.m., so he knew he did not have long to wait. Butch and Sam were always on time; they knew enough to plan their road trips around rush-hour traffic.

It was very quiet at the house without Kyle's father around. No one was fighting, bullying, or yelling. His mother had taken down the heavy, old, green drapes in the living room and put up some sheer-white curtains. She had also painted a light-beige enamel over the cheap, dark-brown paneling, and some of their neighbors had gotten together to paint the outside of their house. The difference had amazed Kyle. It was so much lighter and brighter, and not quite so depressing.

Things were tight financially, though, since his father had completely disappeared and taken what little cash they did have. But his mother seemed more relaxed. She wasn't exactly happy, but at least she wasn't angry or depressed. She was actually carrying on conversations with him, even if they were somewhat one-sided, but it was something she had never done before. Even more surprising was that she was losing weight—at least forty-five pounds, he figured—maybe due to the fact that she quit drinking beer nonstop. She was no Britney Spears, but she wasn't as unhealthy or overweight anymore. She used to put away at least a six-pack every night, sometimes two; now she nursed one can at suppertime and that was about it. Drinking had been the one thing that she and his father did together.

Ever since Kyle got out of the hospital, he would wake before dawn and just think about the fact that he was partially paralyzed from his neck to his toes. Usually at that hour he was groggy and he would have a hard time focusing. He would often become very depressed and sometimes wished he were dead. By 7:00 a.m., he had usually attempted to meditate for an hour or so, and when his mom came in to feed him and give him his antidepressant, his mind was usually feeling more hopeful. By 9:00 a.m. he would start to feel alive and think that maybe he was going to make it. And by 9:25, he was alert and anxious, watching for Butch and Sam's car.

Butch and Sam were Kyle's saving grace. They had become his guardian angels. Every morning, at 9:30 sharp, they arrived to pick him up. They'd put his collapsible wheelchair in the trunk of the old Chevy convertible and then go cruise around downtown for a half-hour. Sam would drive, and Kyle would sit in the passenger seat, strapped in with the extra belts that Butch had installed especially for him. Butch would tell jokes and Sam would be the straight man. He wondered where Butch got all the new jokes from. He seemed to have a couple of new ones every day. Kyle wondered if he got them from the Internet, but did Butch even know how to use a computer? He was too embarrassed to ask.

Kyle still couldn't talk very well. His mouth got tired quickly and the words came out slowly and slightly slurred, although Butch and Sam seemed to understand him just fine. The good news was that most days he seemed to do a little better and that gave him hope. Mostly he just listened to them banter back and forth, so very glad to have the company of the two men.

At 10:00 a.m. they would pull in front of Casey's Gym, an older red-brick building that was starting to show its age. Jim Casey was Butch's old high school friend, a tall, angular, blonde man who reminded Kyle of the Vikings that he had read about back in middle school. Jim gave them the royal treatment when they rolled Kyle through the doorway. He would put his arm around Kyle and hug him while he was still in his wheelchair. Jim offered constant encouragement the whole time he was there. Everyone else at the gym would greet him, too, and ask how he was doing. He felt like a minor celebrity.

The gym was built in the late '40s, with a clientele made up of mostly men born in that same era. Many of them were strong and muscular, some with ballooning stomachs from too much beer and pretzels. They were all different sizes and temperaments, but the one constant they shared was that every one of them treated Kyle kindly, even if sometimes they seemed rude to each other.

The workout was tough. For two hours Butch pushed him, and pushed him hard. Football practice was a piece of cake compared to this. The grind of trying to open and close your fingers or toes ten times in ten minutes sometimes overwhelmed Kyle, but the coach was relentless. Kyle was going to walk again inside two years, or else. Kyle wasn't sure what the "else" was and he didn't want to find out.

Kyle still couldn't believe how helpful Zack's father, Sam, had become. *What a weird twist of fate,* he often thought. He had taught Kyle how to meditate and to believe in a Higher Power, something Kyle couldn't have imagined in a million years in his previous life. He and his mother had started going to the Trinity Catholic Church just down the street on Sunday mornings. He could read, if ever so slowly, and had taken the teachings of the Pope to heart, believing he was one of the true hopes of the world. Now those habits of faith were helping to keep him sane while he spent so much of his day in his wheelchair. Life certainly was strange and knowing this helped keep Kyle going. He never knew what interesting phenomena was in store around the corner.

Zack was scared; being numb had sometimes had its advantages. It was very dark in his room and he could hear his roommate snoring softly in his bunk. The temperature was too warm and his whole body felt sweaty and clammy. He ran the palm of his hand over his newly shaved head. He couldn't sleep, and he had lain on his mattress, fully clothed in jeans and a blue-denim work shirt, for over three hours.

Two male deputies that he did not recognize had come to his cell earlier that morning and told him it was time for him to leave. The older one politely told him he was sorry, but that they needed to put handcuffs on him until he got to his new location. He had his blue duffle bags packed. Dr. Speiglman and his dad both told him that he would be moved to a more permanent location that week. But in truth, he had not mentally prepared himself to leave the place that had been his home for the last several months. In the last weeks he had become almost comfortable there.

They took him in the back of a patrol car from the County Juvenile Facility in downtown to the Jefferson Center for Boys, about seven miles north of town. Except for the twelve-foot, barbed wire fence, it looked more like a large Spanish-style apartment complex. The deputies escorted him into a large reception room where six unhappy-looking boys of all different sizes and nationalities—but with identical, newly shaved crew cuts—sat in metal chairs in the back of the room. He took the last empty chair and sat quietly, not looking to either side.

Half an hour later a tall, bearded man came out of an office attached to the reception room and introduced himself as Dr. Davis, the superintendent of the facility. He wasted no time and started pacing back and forth for almost an hour while talking to them. He told Zack and the other boys how lucky they were to be sent to a model rehabilitation and correctional center, and not a place of punitive retribution. He went on to explain that during their time there, the boys would learn to take responsibility for the actions that brought them to this place. He also explained that, at the same time, they would be learning a trade to take with them to the outside world, so they would have a better chance of not ending up back there or someplace much worse.

He said each boy would take a battery of tests and numerous hands-on projects designed to find their true vocational interests and talents. Each boy would then spend eight weeks on computer games simulated around their field of interest. They would spend two hours a day doing this, three hours on general curriculum, two on researching and writing papers on topics of their choice, and two additional hours on physical exercise, six days a week. It was a rigorous schedule designed to help them get disciplined, find a meaningful career, and get them into physical shape.

Davis went on to explain, just as importantly, that they would learn about taking responsibility for their actions. Five nights a week, after supper, they had group therapy that often centered on simulated role-playing of more positive ways to deal with their problems while understanding the needs of others. They also learned about and practiced the role of honest, direct communication. The secret, he told them, was to get out of the "I'm a victim, poor me" mentality, which Zack remembered was the exact same thing Dr. Speiglman kept harping on him about. Dr. Speiglman kept telling him every session that it's not what happened to him that was important, but what he did with what happened to him that counted. Zack had started to realize that, up until recently, he had played the victim role his whole life and it had become a vicious circle. Now he was gaining the tools to create a new life, and even though he knew he had some physical handicaps, he'd become aware that he had some big plusses, too. For the first time in his life, that gave him hope.

By now it was mid-morning and the world seemed like a different place. Only three days ago, in a session with Dr. Speiglman, Zack had finally realized that he had shot and almost ended the lives of Kyle and Josh. For the first time he thought about what dying meant, that death was real and permanent, at least at this stage of existence. He also realized how lucky they had all been during the shooting, as if a guardian angel had been looking out for them all the time. Maybe it was just good luck that he was a bad shot and that Juan had stepped in when he did, but he didn't think so. There was something more.

Last week, during a visit with his dad, more old walls had come tumbling down. Butch had visited him three days before and had praised his father to the ninth degree. Butch said he thought his father was an Avatar or something like that, and that he had saved Butch's life. Zack wasn't sure what an Avatar is, but he figured it must be good . . . kind of like an angel, though he couldn't imagine having an angel for a father. Butch told him about his dad's reasons for leaving Zack and his mom years before, and it all was starting to make some sense to Zack.

Zack was given a day-pass to go with his father to the beach and they walked along the sand for an hour, until Zack was too tired to walk any farther. Then his father took out a blanket from his knapsack and they sat on the beach and ate the boxed lunch his father had brought. They talked for over three hours. It had opened up a whole new world for Zack.

His dad explained to Zack that every person had their own unusual talents, and he thought Zack was a special boy with unusual insights and had an ability to see things that most people might miss.

"You're more compulsive than impulsive, more left-brain than right. You like detail work, like me. There are lots of ways to use your talents and many occupations. Heck, you can be in high-tech—a computer programmer or software designer, a science teacher or a scientist, even a minister, or an accountant," his dad had said. Surprisingly, all these occupations excited Zack, and his heart swelled with a hope that he could never remember having felt before. He always thought he was too much of a dork and a loser to do anything worthwhile, but suddenly the possibilities seemed endless. For once in his life he felt more like Yoda instead of Jabba the Hutt.

He asked his father how his life could ascend from a big zero and hopelessness, to having all these exciting possibilities, after all the horrible things that had happened in the last year.

"Zack," his father told him, "it's the way the universe seems to work. What often seem like terrible disasters can bring endless possibilities along with them. When I lost you and your mother I was broke, broken, afraid, and totally lost—I just wanted to die. I ended up at the mission looking for something to eat and a place to sleep after wandering the streets for weeks.

"That first night at the shelter I was so filled with anxiety that I couldn't sleep. I wandered into the dining room and saw a bookshelf with a large, blue book on it called *A Course in Miracles.* I was actually looking for a Bible, but I was desperate and restless, so I started reading this book and then never put it down until dawn. Every night since, I have read parts of it, and it has become a way of life for me. Some people use the Bible, some the Koran, others turn to Buddhist material. If it comes from love it is all true. For me, the *Course* rang true, though I still read the Bible occasionally.

"Zack, it taught me about real, absolute forgiveness, and staying in a place of love and trust instead of fear and anger. It does take practice, but since then my life has turned around and flourished beyond my wildest expectations. Even though I have few worldly goods, I have found a spiritual practice and a peace of mind that I never knew existed. I also found that I have an inner knowing—which I'll call my *"intuition"*—to guide me whenever I need it. I try to get quiet and stay out of my head. Then I turn on my auto-pilot and go about my day. That way, much of the time I seem to stay more focused and it makes my life so much easier.

"I don't want to sound like a preacher," he continued, "but there are laws of the universe that come from many religions and many teachers. If you can understand and practice those laws, life can be much more rewarding. I try and keep it simple, but I am part Buddhist, Christian, Jew, Muslim, Hindu, and Sikh. I'm drawn toward any religious tradition that practices staying present and love. I avoid sects of these religions that practice fear and hatred. I know that does not sound simple, but it's simply love without fear or judgment that is the deep basis of all these practices—regardless of what some angry preachers might say. That is what I strive to live by each and every day, and that is what, most of the time, gives me peace.

"Zack," his father told him, "if you don't judge people, you will find more inner peace, and you won't be judged by anyone who really matters. That will set you free in more ways than you can imagine. Try it for just one day. When you think about judging someone or something, just stop and try your best to think a loving thought about the subject instead. You will be amazed how peaceful you will feel. My biggest disappointment in life was my loss of you . . . but deep inside I never lost faith that we would come back together at the right time and for the good of both of us."

Zack wasn't sure how he felt about everything his father told him—some of it sounded kind of mushy, but he listened politely. He realized that he already did have a strong intuition, and that he could use it to his advantage instead of ignoring it and acting out of anger or fear, as he had done so often in the past.

As Zack nestled into his new bunk on his first night at the Jefferson Center for Boys, nothing seemed the same as the day before . . . or two days before that, or even two months ago. It was all very confusing and the only things that were clear was that he was very glad he hadn't killed anyone, and he was glad he was alive. Sometimes he felt frightened by these new feelings, because feelings had always caused him pain. But most importantly, he now felt he had something to lose, and he realized he was somebody . . . somebody talented and important in his own weird kind of way.

On a scale of one to ten, life had gone from a two to an eight almost overnight. It was scary but wonderful. And tomorrow Zack was going back to MLK for the afternoon, and it could be the biggest and scariest day of his life.

CHAPTER THIRTY-THREE
TO SEEK REVENGE … OR HOPE

Ramona was exhausted—her stomach ached and her head pulsated, matching her heart. She had never been very mechanical or technical. She had never put together an erector set let alone two twister-pipe bombs. Fortunately, Zack had gotten most of the explosives and the plans set before he flipped out. They had talked dozens of times about how they were going to use the bombs, but now she had to do it by herself. Zack had said the bombs were designed to be incredibly powerful yet were able to fit in a backpack. He had done months of research to find and make the exact bombs they wanted. But now he was in jail and it was up to her, and she had been up most of the night trying to figure out the last of the details.

She was as ready as she would ever be. The bomb had taken her many months to construct instead of just the six weeks she had initially anticipated, but she thought it actually might work. She wished there was some way to try it out, to test it. She didn't want to go to all this trouble if it didn't go off. What a fool she would make of herself standing there with a bag of explosives powerful enough to blow a hole in the side of the gymnasium, and have nothing happen. It would be just like the rest of her life: fucked up. She would be a fool in jail instead of an infamous martyr.

She sat on her bed and took off her plastic gloves. Zack always told her to use gloves whenever she handled the bomb, or even the backpack they had bought to carry it. He said that if, for some reason, it did not go off, the authorities would have a harder time tracing the bomb back to them. He always said that dying did not scare him but going to jail did. *And look where he ended up*, she thought.

She stared at the blue backpack on the floor next to the explosives. It was the same color as her own, but much bigger. Her stomach churned, and she thought she might throw up. She went over the plan in her mind again, as she had done a hundred times before. Her greatest fear was that someone would recognize her, or ask what she was doing back in school after so many years away, before she ever got to the front doors of the gymnasium. Getting through the gym side doors, she knew, was the secret. They were not set up with monitors and she could just rush in.

Part of her wanted to give this all up and get on a bus for Oregon. Her mother had sent her a ticket four weeks earlier, and it was good for ninety days. Her mom had been out of rehab for fourteen months now. Maybe she would make it this time, but she had thought that before. Her mom had apologized in her letters a hundred times over the last two years. She said she had been saving every dime from two jobs and had found a plastic surgeon for Ramona—one that would take monthly payments. Plus, her mom said she now had health insurance from a state government program that helped everyone to afford it, and she had already registered Ramona on her plan. Her mom also promised there would be no more crazy men in her life. Ramona touched her scars with her fingertips; the bones felt lopsided and distorted and wet with tears, and she did not trust her mother.

By the time Ramona walked three blocks she was tired and hot. She had on her tightest jeans, black gloves, and a short, black coat from the Salvation Army. Her large, blue backpack weighed on her back as she trudged on. She had put her long, black hair in pigtails, and wore some small, cheap, oval, plastic earrings. She had put on light-red lipstick and tons of makeup. She wanted to cover her scars and try to make herself look younger than her twenty-two years.

Ramona crossed the street and walked on to the school parking lot. The lot was completely empty of people. Everyone was heading toward the school. She hid behind a red Chevy pickup truck with tires almost as tall as she was, and watched hundreds of kids filing into the new gymnasium for an assembly. She had found out from a girl walking home from school one day by herself about the assembly on this date and time, but the girl did not seem to know what it was about. Ramona's plan was to set the detonator for five minutes and then walk into the assembly. Even if they stopped her there'd be too little time to search her and disarm the bomb. She didn't care if she died and, in fact, she looked forward to it.

She saw a light-blue van pull up in front of the new gymnasium. A tall man with a gray suit stepped down from the passenger's seat, walked behind the van, and opened the back doors. He proceeded to roll out a boy in a wheelchair. Ramona was stunned as she recognized the boy from his picture in the paper: it was the monster, Kyle Ritter. She knew he had not died but she couldn't believe they were letting him back in school. They had kicked her out just for fighting those crazy bitches who always taunted her, but now they were letting this bastard back in after what he had done to Zack?

Kyle's presence was attracting attention and a crowd of students gathered around him on the sidewalk.

Ramona's heart was beating a mile a minute. What a great opportunity to get revenge for Zack! She didn't know what prison he was in, but if she could blow up the gymnasium with Kyle in it, she was sure he would hear about it. She knew she had to be patient, so she pressed herself as flat as she could against the side of the big truck and watched through the side windows.

Within several minutes a white sedan pulled up behind the van where Kyle was still sitting in his wheelchair. The crowd he had attracted was treating him as a returning hero and Ramona was getting angrier by the minute.

She couldn't believe her eyes when the passenger door of the sedan opened and out stepped Zack, dressed in brown slacks and a tan button-down shirt. He looked a little dazed and frightened as he stepped out of the car. He had lost a lot of weight, had his hair cut short, and was barely recognizable, but she knew it was him.

Ramona watched Zack walk over to Kyle, and the two of them locked hands with smiles on their faces. Her stomach recoiled, and she thought she might throw up again. Rage rushed through her mind like a brushfire in hell. She bent down, opened the cover of her backpack and lightly ran her shaking fingertips over the red detonator cap.

CHAPTER THIRTY-FOUR
JOY FOR ALL

The assembly was designed to honor togetherness and the power of unity. Zack and Kyle were to be the honorees and keynote speakers. Banners were up all over the school. There was a festive atmosphere, combined with a great uneasiness among both the teachers and students. A lot of water had gone under the bridge in the past months, and everyone had been touched by the shooting tragedy to one degree or another.

Zack was granted a special day-pass to attend the assembly, with Lieutenant Baker acting as his sponsor. Baker had picked up Zack in his unmarked Ford sedan and they rode in silence for the first ten minutes. Baker wasn't sure how the day was going to go or what to say. He was at a loss for words, a rare moment for him.

Finally, Baker broke the ice and said, "Big day, aye?"

"Yes," said Zack. "I believe it is actually the biggest day of my life."

"You look good . . . nice set of clothes, looks like you lost some weight. So how are you feeling about all this?"

"The last months have been amazing for me, Mr. Baker. I don't feel anything like that person who sat on the school steps and then gunned down Kyle and Josh. I am still figuring out who I really am—with the help of Dr. Speiglman—but I think I am getting there. But this is really scary—going back to school with Kyle and facing everybody," he continued. "I don't know what to expect."

"Well, just remember, Zack, I am in your corner and I am your friend," said Baker. "I'm not going to let anyone bother you . . . so don't worry about that."

"Thanks," said Zack. "I appreciate that. It's pretty amazing that a police officer would tell me that, but I will take all the support I can get. I guess I am nervous wondering how the students are going to react towards me. Are they going to boo me and cheer Kyle, or vice versa? Maybe they will boo both of us. That, I think, would be better, because then I wouldn't be alone, and Kyle wouldn't be alone. One thing I know for sure is that I never want to feel alone again. Up until recently, I've always been a loner, so that's hard for me to admit."

"I bet it is hard, kid. I am not sure I have ever even admitted that myself," reflected Baker, "but I think maybe it's time I look at that in myself as well.

"We're just about there, Zack. I'll drop you off in front and I am going to park the car. I am not worried about you running away. A few of my men are around just for my piece of mind, but I don't expect any trouble and I'll be here if you need anything. Good luck."

Baker pulled the sedan next to the curb where Kyle was still sitting in his wheelchair. Baker could see three of his men in plain clothes milling around the entrance to the auditorium and he breathed a little lighter.

He had been amazed by the changes in Zack when he picked him up. He was like a different kid, so mature and polite. He'd lost some weight and looked relatively trim. Baker had visited him a couple times at Jefferson, and each time he had seen a positive change, but today it was different—Zack had become so much more adult. *Let's just hope these kids accept him and don't harass him or give him a hard time,* he thought. *It would be such a blow to the progress he's made if they booed him or even ignored him, after all he's been through.*

When he stepped out of the car, Zack thanked Lieutenant Baker, then immediately saw Kyle sitting in his wheelchair on the sidewalk. He looked back at Baker and the lieutenant waved him over towards Kyle. Zack's first instinct was to panic, but instead he took a deep breath and walked right up to Kyle who was looking straight at him. Both boys simultaneously put up their arms and grabbed each other's forearms with Kyle practically lifting himself up out of his chair.

"This is our big day, *compadre*!" said Kyle, with a giant smile. "Hey, I have been learning Spanish from Juan, but I only know about four words so far," he laughed.

"Well, *mon ami*," said Zack with a grin that lit up his whole face, "I have been studying French over the Internet and I know about nineteen words, so we're almost even. And yeah, this is a big day. We'll see what's in store for us when we get inside. I have never been hit with a tomato before, so that may be a first!"

"Yeah," said Kyle, his smile slipping away. "I start school again on Monday. I don't have a clue how I am going to be treated now that everyone knows what I did to you. I am scared shitless."

"Kyle, I am the guy who shot you and I am scared, too, but we're in this together. If things get too rowdy, Baker will get us out of here."

"Hey, Kyle!" came a voice from behind them. Both boys turned around to see Dustin, who had just walked out from the gym.

"Hey, Dustin," said Kyle, as they slapped hands.

"Good to see you, bro. I am glad you're coming back. Sorry I haven't been over after school the last couple weeks. Coach keeps me busy lately refereeing twenty-four/seven. We have a lot of catching up to do."

Dustin turned his attention to Zack and shook his hand. "Good to see you, too, Zack. I know I have apologized half-a-dozen times, but I still owe you the biggest apology in the world, man. All I can tell you for sure is that I am truly sorry—a lot of us around here have been doing a lot of growing up, especially me. I think we're a different school now, and we have all grown up a lot. We owe a lot of it to you. But brother, I can't again tell you how sorry I am for my part."

"Thanks, Dustin," said Zack, his voice starting to choke. "This whole experience has changed my life more dramatically than you can imagine. Things are better, much better . . . but thanks for another apology. It means a lot."

"Are you boys ready?" asked Alan, as he walked up and shook each boy's hand.

"Yes, sir," the boys answered. "We're ready."

Alan stepped back and studied them for a moment. "Yes, I think you really are. Let's go in."

Zack got behind Kyle and pushed his wheelchair into the packed auditorium. The gym went into complete silence as they crossed the floor. A lone sneeze from high up in the bleachers echoed across the gym, but it was the only sound heard.

Zack saw his dad and Butch walk up, both grinning broadly. The men hugged Zack and Kyle. "Good luck," said Sam. Butch was so caught up in emotions he couldn't utter a word. Both boys waved back to the men as they continued out to the middle of the gym to stand next to Alan and Anne.

Alan adjusted the microphones to the right height for the boys, and said, "This is your show, boys. This seems to be the age of teens who have grown wise beyond their years. I am not going to say another word." Alan and Anne smiled and shook their hands, then walked to the side of the gym to take their seats, leaving the boys to themselves. There was a deafening silence for a few moments as the two boys stood alone in the center of the gym.

Both boys' stomachs were doing flip-flops. Kyle saw his mom standing next to Dr. Hyde and Mary Beth, his nurse, who waved. He struggled and moved his right hand up maybe six inches and gave a slow wave back. *Man, everybody is here,* he thought.

"What do you think, bro?" he finally muttered under his breath to Zack. "I hope they don't expect us to do a song and dance, 'cause I'm a little out of practice."

Zack looked around nervously and answered with a half-laugh, "Do you think they will love us or hate us?"

"Don't know," muttered Kyle, "but maybe they're waiting for us to say something. I wrote down a little something but now I don't know where to start."

"Me, too," answered Zack. "I wrote a few lines, but I don't think I can do it now."

Then a lone clapping sound started from the middle row on the left side of the bleachers. Both boys looked up and saw Karen Lynn standing while clapping, and then her friends Michele, Claire, and Lindsey stood up and joined in.

Then they saw Josh rise, along with Dustin and Jeff, and they started to clap, too. Several seconds later a couple more students stood up and joined in. Way in the back, Juan Pacheco and Poncho and then a dozen students in the middle suddenly stood up, and were on their feet, clapping as well. Within minutes—one by one, then two by two, then three by three—the entire student body was on their feet giving them a standing ovation while chanting their names. The crowd went on and on and they wouldn't -- or couldn't -- stop!

Kyle and Zack had tears streaming down their faces as they locked hands together and held them high in the air. The cheers and whistles grew louder, and tears could be seen running down many of the students' faces as they clapped and stomped their feet in unison.

Anne, in tears as well, started to speak to Alan and Lieutenant Baker, but she could not finish. She just watched the scene and waved at Dr. Speiglman, who was standing across the way in front of the exit door. Behind him she saw Jerry Cutter, Zack's attorney, and Karen Kendrick from *The Globe,* both standing up and clapping wildly.

Lieutenant Baker shook his head and quickly wiped his eyes with his handkerchief. He looked over with a shy smile at Penny Briton standing next to him, and she returned his smile. He mumbled, "Who would have ever believed this? I think I am going to retire right now while this is all fresh in my mind, because it can't get any better than this."

Alan stood mesmerized with his hands in his pockets, forgetting to even clap, a smile larger than a cantaloupe on his face. He thought to himself, *YES! This makes my whole darn life worthwhile.* Then he took his right hand out of his pocket and put it in Anne's left hand and held it very tight. "You know," he said, "things are never going to be the same around here again."

She looked him in the eye and answered, "Yes, you're right about that, Alan . . . and in more ways than one."

Alan stared at her green eyes for several moments before looking back at the boys. The entire student body continued to chant: *"ZACK – KYLE – ZACK – KYLE!"*

Brad Smith canvassed the school parking lot, looking for vandals and kids cutting school, like he did every school day starting at 11:30. Today he was especially alert with the assembly going on. *What a time this would be for a bomb scare,* he thought, though there had not been one in over three weeks.

He walked through the rows of cars and looked over at a large, red pickup with giant wheels that was much higher than the rest of the surrounding vehicles. *That thing would run right over you in an accident,* thought Brad. *I can't believe they let these kids drive them on the road.* As if being guided, he made his way through the maze of vehicles to the truck, slowly shaking his head. When he got there, he noticed a dark-blue backpack on the pavement next to the giant front tire.

He stood looking at it for almost a full minute, his mind running through the endless possibilities of what could be inside. Then he approached cautiously, as if it were a snake. He gingerly picked up the pack, which weighed at least sixty pounds, heavier than a pack would weigh crammed full of books. It was zipped tight and he hesitated for a moment before opening it, unsure what he might find.

"Oh, my God," was all he could think to say. *"Oh, my God!"*

The 10:30 p.m. train for Eugene, Oregon, was right on time. There were eleven stops along the way and the conductor had said the trip would take twenty-two hours. Ramona put her pillow behind her head and wrapped the train blanket around her legs and lap. She thought, once again, about why she had not been able to walk into the gym and detonate the bomb. Zack had been kind to her and, as angry as she was, she could not kill him. Was it just that simple? Maybe not. She was exhausted, but took out the most recent letter from her mom and read it through one more time. As a small flicker of hope arose in her heart, she curled up and was sound asleep before the train left the station.

Alan and Anne walked across the school parking lot together three weeks after the assembly. "This has been quite an unusual year," said Alan, as they stood next to Anne's green Honda CRV.

"Yes it has, Mr. Carter . . . very interesting, indeed. It's felt like twenty years wrapped into one. I guess we may never know who the person is who left the bomb," she answered.

"No, I don't think so," replied Alan. "They were very careful not to leave any fingerprints. But whoever it is decided not to detonate it, and that's the good news. Maybe they were just trying to give us a warning, or a wakeup call . . . I just don't know."

"Well, they got my attention," Anne added. "Baker said even though the bomb was crudely assembled, and may or may not have worked, it was still very powerful. If it had gone off in the crowded auditorium, it could have killed and wounded dozens of people."

"We haven't had a call in three weeks since we found the bomb, and that is a very good sign," added Alan. "Let's pray that is the end of it."

"You know," said Anne, with a smile creeping across her face, "being vice principal has actually become fun again these last months.

I feel alive—like we're finally making a real difference—and I haven't felt that way in a long, long time."

"It's working, Anne; it's actually working. It's been slow going, but I think we are starting to break the survival-of-the-fittest cycle, at least on this campus," replied Alan. "If we can permanently change the culture here at MLK, then we can really help these kids. We can create an example for other schools to emulate."

"You're totally right, Alan, and we're going to get it all done. We have made such great progress these last months, and I don't think it's been slow at all. To me, it's been like a time warp."

Alan smiled, and both fell silent for a moment.

"Well, Mr. Carter, I think we decided last night that I will see you at my place for dinner at seven. Is that correct?" asked Anne, opening her car door. But before he could answer she turned and gave Alan a quick but passionate kiss on the lips. She giggled lightly, glancing around to see if any students were watching.

"So," said Anne, "I'm afraid we have become a popular topic of gossip around school since you gave me the engagement ring."

Alan grinned sheepishly, looking unusually happy, but managed to say, "Oh, yes, Anne . . . I have noticed. But after the fourth of June it won't matter. I've heard the rumor that you've invited the whole staff, the students, plus another hundred guests."

"Yup, that is correct . . . that is absolutely correct. Why else do you think I reserved the new gymnasium?"

Made in the USA
Las Vegas, NV
11 August 2022

53076082R00152